SOPHOMORE

(obviously)

Books By Michael Gerber

Barry Trotter and the Unauthorized Parody
Barry Trotter and the Unnecessary Sequel
Barry Trotter and the Dead Horse
The Chronicles of Blarnia: That Lyin' Bitch in the Wardrobe
Freshman

Books Michael Gerber SAYS He HAD Nothing to Do With

My Side of the Story, by Charles Manson
Making Money Through Natural Disasters
I, Breakdancer
The Tapeworm Diet
Are You There, God? It's Me, Hitler

SOPHOMORE

Another Novel of Ivy League Angst

By Michael Gerber

CU
CK
OO

For information address the author, c/o McIntosh and Otis,
353 Lexington Ave., NY, NY 10016.
First edition, for whatever that's worth
Printed in the United States of America
Attention type geeks: this book has been carelessly set in 11-point Garamond. The display face is the excellent Brubeck's Cube.
Cover photo © Tyler Olson/Olsonstock
Reinforced binding. DO NOT EAT.
Library of Congress Cataloguing-in-Publication Data probably lost under some filing cabinet somewhere.
ISBN 1-890470-03-1
Check out stuttsuniversity.com

To ENIV, in the hope
that there will always be room
on his tour bus.

In 1888, Mark Twain wrote the following to Timothy Dwight, then President of Yale University:

> "[Being a humorist] is a useful trade, a worthy calling; that with all its lightness and frivolity it has one serious purpose, one aim, one specialty, and it is constant to it—the deriding of shams, the exposure of pretentious falsities, the laughing of stupid superstitions out of existence; and that whoso is by instinct engaged in this sort of warfare is the natural enemy of royalties, nobilities, privileges and all kindred swindles, and the natural friend of human rights and human liberties."

President Dwight's response was not recorded.

In 1959, while a grad student at Stanford, author Ken Kesey was given mind-altering drugs (among them LSD) as part of a series of secret experiments run by the Central Intelligence Agency. Thirty-five years later, he told *The Paris Review* what happened next:

> "...I began to see that the books I thought were the true accounting books—my grades, how I'd done in other schools, how I'd performed at jobs, whether I had paid off my car or not—were not at all the true books. There were other books that were being kept, real books. In those books is the real accounting of your life..."

I think we can be *pretty* sure that this wasn't what the CIA intended.

1

The Eye in the Sky

(Friday, August 28 @ 3:42 pm)

Arcing lazily through the air, the Frisbee smacked against the window. "Ooo-oo!" a chiseled and shirtless boy teased as it wobbleplummeted to the ground. "Sarah's in troub-le!"

Beauty-boy was righter than he knew: Of all the windows on campus to hit, this one was the worst. It belonged to Stutts University's Professor of Clandestine Affairs, Glenbard North, a man who had destroyed more students than there were blades of grass on the freshly resodded Old Quad below.

Ignorant, the offending girl smiled and waved when the spectre-like North appeared. She might as well have been buttering up a shark. "Sorry!" she said cheerfully. "Is it broken?"

North didn't answer; instead, he took a digital camera from his pocket and snapped a picture. First his minions would identify her, then North would invalidate her parking permit. Let's see what a week on the grimy, crime-y streets of Great Littleton would do to Daddy's BMW.

Glowering down at the idyllic scene below, the spy-turned-prof tried to uncrick his neck. He'd been at his desk for hours, reading student dossiers. Each new year brought new threats, and North, the all-seeing eye, was Stutts' only defense. Stutts University was surrounded by enemies, outsiders longing to pervert its mission, plunder its treasures, and plunge it into impotence and anarchy. North didn't blame them; that's exactly what he would've done. He who controlled Stutts, controlled the future—the world's rich and powerful sent their children here, to the world's finest university, and Ma Stutts had just four short years to turn them from gibbering vats of hormone into the Leaders of Tomorrow. This meant not only teaching them the right ideas, but also protecting them from dangerous ones. Protecting them was North's job.

Forty years—was it any wonder he felt tired? North rubbed his eyes; still only on the "F"s. Either his agents were better than they used to be, or students were getting into more trouble. North glumly guessed the latter.[1]

1 For every student who came to Stutts ready to learn about the world in all its complexity, ten showed up begging to be told *exactly* what to believe. You could get mamby-pamby relativist bullshit at any school—what was all that tuition for, if not the keys, the answers, the truth? Glenbard North was happy to oblige. His class "Dirty Tricks and Double Crosses" was one of

Replacing his glasses, North scanned the mass of students milling about inscrutably three stories below. He didn't like what he saw. "More foreigners and cripples this year," North grumbled to himself. Their presence at Stutts offended him; it was improper, sentimental, decadent—exactly what he was fighting against. North's motto was "a place for everyone, and everyone in his place."

The student body was on full display today, the day of the Bazaar, when all the organizations on campus sat behind card tables and jockeyed for new members. The Madri-gals singing group belted it out next to a mime troupe trapped inside a Winnebago-sized invisible box; StuttsBellydancers plied their sinuous hobby, making *The Stutts Journal of Resume Padding* seem even more boring than it already was. And there, in a far corner, was *The Cuckoo*, Stutts' student humor magazine, shouting themselves hoarse and flinging back issues at anybody who made eye-contact…but we'll get to them later.

Stuttsies took this kind of thing very seriously. The newspaper, the political parties, the singing groups, even *The Cuckoo*—each tribe was convinced it alone knew the proper path to success at Stutts and beyond, and that every other tribe was filled with charlatans, enemies or fools. Even the campus frat, the vomit-flecked and boorish Comma Comma Apostrophe, considered itself to be the apex of the social pyramid.

The Old Quad looked as beautiful as ever. After a summer without students, it was a lush expanse of green dotted with large trees; paths of picturesque stumble-causing gray-blue slate divided the lawn at pleasing and useful intervals. By this time of day, shadows were starting to appear; the Old Quad was surrounded on all sides by buildings of four and five stories, each in stately High Colonic style (half Colonial, half High Gothic). Though copied by every college for a century, this architecture was quintessentially Stutts.

The Old Quad was the heart of the university, and never more so than on a late summer afternoon, when the slanting sunlight made the leaves shine and glow. Even the undergrads looked reasonably presentable; they were still dressing to impress, not yet through all the outfits Mom had cleaned and ironed in one final "only-because-you're-leaving" spasm of caretaking.

Stutts' biggest and provided him with a steady stream of acolytes.

Secrecy, proximity to power, a certain tweediness—North was bound to become a Stutts icon. He liked his Pantheon status a great deal, not only for vanity's sake but for its usefulness: the final exam for "DT&DC" was to assemble an eyes-only dossier on someone of North's choosing. Hence, the professor's files contained enough adultery, dirty deals, and perversion to bring anyone to their knees. North was, to those in the know, the most powerful man on campus.

The sight was a melancholy one for North, because he knew the Fall was coming. Soon, the sons and daughters of America's most prosperous suburbs would become indistinguishable from Great Littleton's homeless. Soon, the grass would be dotted with burnt patches and the trees festooned with underwear. Soon, dignified statues would be wearing t-shirts advertising improv troupes, and bedsheets bearing cryptic and unsettling messages would slouch crookedly from every fifth window.

Thoroughly depressed, North went back to his desk and resumed reading his secret files.

"FOX, HART CALVIN
Ht: 5' 9"Wt: 125 Hair: Brn Eyes: Brn
Tattoos/Marks: appendectomy, eyes in wrong sockets, moles on back spell out "OKRA SANDWICH" (if you connect them right)
Allergies: shrimp, talc
College: Dacron Year: Sophomore
G.P.A: 3.7 (2.3 w/o inflation) Major: Study of Things
Hometown: Sandy Dunes, MI HS: Farnworth (public) (B-)
Informants: JS, KQ, DB, AL, EN, MM, NS, VT

Parents: Max and Janelle; married 20 years (poor/poor/shaky+). Father is an "entrepreneur" currently on the lam from Interpol. Mother runs a boarding house in East Sandy Dunes. Career: Fox came to Stutts as the result of a deal with BURLINGTON DARLING III V '69. Mr. Darling, now Governor of Michigan, originally arranged for his son BURLINGTON III VI (a/k/a "TRIP," a family nickname for each multiple of three) to be admitted instead of Hart, in exchange for a new chemistry building. Mr. Darling wanted FOX to tutor his son and keep him out of trouble, in exchange for a miniscule stipend. FOX refused, insisting that he be enrolled at Stutts along with Trip. Governor Darling agreed reluctantly, but spared no opportunity to make FOX's life at Stutts difficult, especially after becoming Governor. This harassment ranged from vulgar late-night phone calls to funding several assassination attempts.

Once on campus, FOX immediately fell in with members of The Cuckoo, a shadowy student organization that–among several murky purposes–publishes a humor magazine. FOX quickly rose inside The Cuckoo, owing to some writing ability and an utter lack of competition. As an editor, FOX was instrumental in outwitting The Daily Spectacle student newspaper, The Cuckoo's campus rival. For decades, The Spec had destroyed all The Cuckoo's issues immediately after publication, explaining that they "contained offensive material." With no issues to refer to, the University had no choice but to stand aside.

FOX spent second semester rusticated, following his involvement in "THE DAY OF STINK," where the Victorian-era campus mail system was used to deliver a foul-smelling gas. Though it looked as though FOX would be expelled after his first year (for nonpayment of tuition), The Cuckoo was able to sell enough copies of a collection of FOX's humor columns to pay FOX's bills, as well as provide for all future Stutts-related expenses.

FOX is now co-editor-in-chief of the magazine and is determined to make it a force on campus, his star rising along with it. Plans for the year include publishing at least six issues, issuing numerous flyers and several pranks. A FOX-edited issue (see "Summer Fun Number" attached) was mailed to every Stutts undergraduate at their summer address in late July.

Analysis of the contents suggest deep antisocial tendencies among the staff, possibly the result of difficult potty-training. The Cuckoo appeals to the very worst elements of Stutts student body, and their subscriber list should be considered a rough guide to the most destabilizing individuals on campus. The magazine traditionally disrupts the Freshman Assembly, a speech given in Truax Hall forty-eight hours after students arrive on campus and the official start of the academic year.
ANALYSIS: Both singly and with his companions on The Cuckoo, FOX is a serious threat to the orderly functioning of the university; he should be a primary target for neutralization. Like Lenin and Stalin, FOX is a person of some talent but vastly greater ambition who resents anyone more fortunate than he. The longer FOX remains outside of the dominant power structure, the greater the likelihood of his being seduced by countercultural/alternative systems of belief. Sources characterize FOX as extremely determined to rise, and this, in addition to his modest middle-class background, suggests that buying him off may be cheap as well as successful. FOX confuses money with morality and has applied for a term-time job (as a waiter at University functions) simply to reduce the amount he siphons from The Cuckoo's sales of his book. He is sensitive about his

> poor vision; this may be exploitable. FOX is also extremely sensitive to being disliked, especially after becoming infamous several times during his freshman year. (See "MAD PISSER," DAY OF STINK.) He is currently dating [redacted]. This racial difference may be used to drive them apart and disrupt FOX's activities.
>
> See Also: CUCKOO MAGAZINE; ARMBRUSTER, PETER; RODRIGUEZ, REED; POKORNY, ELLEN; [redacted]."

"What the hell?" North growled. He held the page up to the light, but couldn't read the name or the sentence. Who was blacking out his files?[2]

He skimmed the dossier across the room angrily; the humor magazine tucked inside fell out mid-flight. After he cooled off, North got up and put the dossier away. As he bent over to pick up the magazine, some extra blood rushed to his brain and North made a connection: hadn't *The Cuckoo* been mentioned in one of this week's Daily Briefings? Maybe—things were so hard to remember these days.

The same grad student who typed up the dossiers also collated all the reports from North's agents all over campus, fashioning them into a single comprehensive report on the threats facing the University. North searched his office—he was, as always, drowning in paper (he refused to computerize, living in fear of hackers). This clutter was intentional; he loved his job as Stutts secret protector, and a slight amount of disorganization was just another way he could be immersed in it.

North had come from the Central Intelligence Agency—well, "come" wasn't exactly right. One day, he was sitting at his desk at the CIA in Langley, when somebody—he never found out who—hit him on the head with something heavy. The next thing North knew, President Kennedy was dead, and he was laying half-naked in the common room of Cummerbund College, Stutts' nicest dormitory. In one pocket, he had a piece of heavily redacted ID (his high school ID, with everything but the school's name,

[2] The answer would've shocked North to the core: the trusted grad student who prepared all his dossiers was a member of Stutts' thriving, underground vampire community—as was Hart's girlfriend Tabitha Twombly. Though the vampires had nothing to hide (they satisfied their dietary choice peacefully, and were generally considered no more threatening than your average raw-fooder) they realized that keeping Glenbard North ignorant was essential.

As diligent as Stutts' vampires were, this would've been impossible without North's own arrogant complicity. As with Queen Victoria and lesbians, or J. Edgar Hoover and the Mafia, North refused to believe that the world contained such creatures. Any informant unwise enough to mention vampires, much less assert they existed at Stutts, was flown to an undisclosed location and dropped in the middle of a bullfight.

Glenbard North, blacked out); in the other, a forged employment contract for an assistant professorship in Political Science. His memory had been wiped; he had no idea who he was, what he had done in the lost time, or what he was supposed to do now. Confused, vaguely guilty, and with a splitting headache, North decided to make the best of it.

Slowly, through means legal and otherwise, North began to amass power. He began collecting a group of acolytes, using them as his eyes and ears on campus. Within five years, he had created his secret-filled filing cabinets. This infernal index had grown exponentially ever since; every secret allowed North to blackmail another person into collecting dirt. Now it occupied an entire wall of the professor's office. They had to reinforce the floor below.

As North dug through a stack of paper near the window, a student on the Quad caught his eye, someone wearing a giant bird costume. Idiot, North thought. People like me sacrifice everything to protect non-entities like you. North saw History as a long train of men like himself, lonely, proud men who served without complaint and never had sex, so that others could dress up in bird costumes. People like bird-kid had always relied on people like North. Yet did they ever thank him? Of course not. God, how he hated them.

North found the Daily Briefing he was looking for.

> CUCKOO DETERMINED TO EXPAND OPERATIONS
> The Cuckoo, a student humor magazine, seems poised for a breakout this year. After decades of being held in check by their traditional rival, the Daily Spectacle student newspaper, The Cuckoo is now publishing regularly. Last April a spoof of the Daily Money, a national financial newspaper generated significant revenue for The Cuckoo. This windfall, plus growing popularity on campus, and a motivated staff, represents a "perfect storm" which may upset Stutts' delicate balance. The Cuckoo's antisocial tendencies are widely recognized, and its recent success forms an excellent platform for launching a wide range of disruptive activities. The magazine, which trades on nihilistic caricature and reflexive disrespect for authority, is reason enough to be concerned. But The Cuckoo's fervent desire and demonstrated ability to disrupt the University through pranks makes it a target of the highest priority. Our recommendation: Neutralize with extreme prejudice.

Looking out the window, North wondered if *The Cuckoo* had a table set out among the organizations below. "Where are my binoculars? They were right here."

Nothing in North's office was right anywhere—it was cluttered with mementoes and bric-a-bric, souvenirs from all the ops that he had done, or thought he remembered. North made do with the first thing at hand—a miniature Mauser rifle, covered with signatures. He squinted through the sniper's scope and began scanning the crowd. North found *The Cuckoo*'s table. "Should've guessed," he spat. "Bird-kid."

Putting the gun down, skimmed the rest of the daily briefing. President Whitbread was still trying to force him out, the fool...North got an idea. He picked up the phone and dialed the number of The Mugwumps, a super-secret student society, and one of the few groups he could trust.

Elegant, North thought as the phone rang. I could get rid of both *The Cuckoo* and Whitbread in one stroke—the students don't call me "Puppetmaster" for nothing.[3]

"Joe's Apizza," a Mugwump answered.

North knew the game; in fact, he was the one who had suggested it. "This is Glenbard North. May I speak to Balthazar?"

On the slate diagonal three floors below, Hart took off his bird-head. "I'm freaking dying in this," he said, streaming with sweat.

"Suck it up," Peter Armbruster said. Peter, Hart's roommate and co-editor, sat behind the table, collecting signatures and talking to cute girls. "Put the head back on. You're ruining the illusion."

"How come the only people you talk to are chicks?" Hart said.

"I can't help it if they're interested in my staff," Peter said.

"Ha, ha. I'm almost out of issues," Hart said. He'd been handing out extras of the "Summer Fun Number," which had a cartoon of an interning student trying to get a tan from an open photocopier. "How we doing?"

"Pretty good," Peter said, flipping through the clipboard. "A thousand subscribers, about twenty interested in joining. We've gotten more people than anybody except the frat-rats over there."

Hart looked over at the Comma Comma Apostrophe table, which was so busted and skeevy it had to be held up by hand. Luckily, CCA never lacked for lackeys, and two boys wearing red cloche hats were holding each end. Behind the table, Hart's high school nemesis Trip Darling lounged, trading beers for french kisses.

"I'm almost thirsty enough to tongue Trip," Hart admitted.

3 Actually, they called him that because North insisted on it.

"Yeah, right," Peter said. "Those guys tried to kill you."

"It was nothing personal, Ellen told me." (Ellen Pokorny, a senior and *The Cuckoo*'s former editor-in-chief, was a member of The Mugwumps and thus privy to all sorts of campus scuttlebutt.[4]) "Look," Hart said, "there's Reed."

Reed Rodriguez, *The Cuckoo*'s other senior, was browsing the Bazaar. He had no intention of joining anything, but like Peter, he was unattached and this was an excellent time to survey the field.

At any one time, only five thousand undergraduates were fortunate enough to attend Stutts University. Yet that relatively small student body somehow supported nearly eight thousand campus clubs. Fans of "The Simpsons" could belong to a comedy-lovers' club, a sitcom club, a cartoon club, and a club for the *concept* of TV. One club begat others, as members struggled for control and split into warring factions. Some groups—the Liza Minnelli Appreciation Society, for example—hardly had enough members to buy a pizza, but biggies like the Indifference Party at the Political Union, easily cracked a hundred.

The University did its best to monitor this viscous, pulsing mass of social interaction, to make sure that no group was incredibly objectionable, but this was impossible. It took a TV news crew from Great Littleton to expose Stutts Students for Denying the Holocaust. That single, wrong-headed junior cost the University millions in donations.

But while the University did what it could to keep people in their rooms studying and staying out of trouble, the student urge to form and join was irrepressible. To a Stuttsie, nothing counted unless it made it onto your resume. Compulsive joining had gotten them into Stutts, so they continued the pattern, hoping that a c.v. bristling with extracurriculars would magically launch them into the law school or consulting gig of their dreams.

Of course, *The Cuckoo* attracted a different breed. The only thing it could launch you into was trouble with the University and, occasionally—if you were talented enough—fleeting notoriety on campus. Notoriety meant a lot; it was an article of faith among Stuttsies that acclaim in the undergraduate world unfailingly led to world domination. In addition to being flattering to the students, this was proven just often enough to keep it the secret religion of every Stutts student.

4 The Mugwumps were a very secret society of Stutts seniors—and by "very secret," I mean something that every Stutts student knew loads about and was dying to get into. Last May, Ellen had been asked to join. Naturally, she had accepted: coming from humble beginnings, joining the 'Wumps might well change Ellen's life. Every person who'd ever walked on the Moon—or lived in the White House—had been a Mugwump. Everybody on *The Cuckoo* was proud of Ellen's being "pinched" (slang for being asked to join, from the distinctive twisting pinch that was delivered), but Peter's feelings were more complicated. Not only had

The Cuckoo had produced stars over its history, but not for a while—the *Spec* had been sabotaging, stealing or otherwise preventing any issues of *The Cuckoo* from being read on campus. (In fact, Hart and Peter's first knowledge of the magazine came at a huge, *Spec*-sponsored bonfire their freshman year.) Naturally, this state of affairs prevented *The Cuckoo* from getting the best talent, and it had languished until Ellen and Reed had decided to make it their project back when they were freshmen. Those two had kept it alive, holding weekly meetings, curating the office's collection of pop culture tchotkes, and "publishing" unread issues until Hart and Peter showed up last year. Through a combination of luck, hard work, and Machievellian cunning, *The Cuckoo* had broken through the *Spec*'s blockade.

Reed ambled over slowly, to ward off the heat. (Great Littleton was scorching until the end of September, when it started to sleet. The sleet continued until May, when it became scorching again.) Reed's t-shirt—and even the waistband of his chinos—was already dappled with perspiration. "Hey, guys, how's it going?"

"Well," Peter said. "Twenty interested. Many of them girls!"

"Right on," Reed said. "How are you, Hart?"

"Hot," Hart said. "Will you take a turn in the suit?"

"No way," Reed said, "I'm a senior." Stutts seniors were notoriously aloof, partly because they needed to find a job, partly because they had to do a big paper to graduate (Reed's was on pirates) and partly because they demanded a victory lap. "I sweated in that thing for three years straight."

"Come on," Hart pleaded. "Peter can't"—Peter was in a wheelchair—"and Ellen's too short. I haven't even unpacked yet."

"I'll do it if you pay for my fridge," Reed said.

"Done," Hart said. Saying goodbye to Peter, they picked their way through the crowd towards the English building. Once in the basement bathroom, they made the switch.

As Reed put on the brightly colored cuckoo's head, he gave a yell of disgust. "You sweat even more than I do!"

"And," Hart said, now just in street clothes, "I have no intention of paying for your fridge." Reed took off after Hart, but Hart got away easily.

Hart's dorm—or "residential college", to use the Stutts term—was named Dacron, after the synthetic fiber which had generated the fortune which

he and Ellen become quite close over the summer (he was one of the few people who could understand her research), the Mugwumps were his bete noire. Peter's family had been going to Stutts for centuries, and too many relatives he disliked had been Wumpsmen.

funded it. Dacron was the newest, the ugliest, and universally acknowledged as the least cool college at Stutts. This year was going to be grimmer still; Dacron was being renovated, so its students were set up in temporary housing.

Peter and Hart had been moved into a truly decrepit structure the University had been planning to tear down for decades. While the structure did get you out of the sleet, it wasn't good for much else. Hart minded it less than most. First, it was Stutts, and the one lesson he had learned over the summer back home in Michigan was that anyplace on campus was good enough for him. Hart had fought hard to keep from being expelled all last year, and as with so many other things, the thing you have to fight for is the thing you come to love. Second, they had a room on the first floor, because of Peter's disability, so in case of fire or collapse, they'd have a fighting chance of survival. And third, he'd probably spend more time over at Tabitha's place anyway. Girls' rooms always smelled so much better.

After a cool/suddenly-hot/now-icy/*fuck!*-really-hot shower, Hart put on some new, non-gross clothes. He had two hours before *The Cuckoo* meeting—what should he do? He wanted to read the collection of Quinn Bostick humor columns from *The New York Times* that his mom had given him as a bon voyage present, but since he'd just arrived yesterday, there was literally no place to sit. Reluctantly, he decided he'd have to unpack.

Hart would let Peter decorate the common room—his roommate would have many, many ideas about how it should look and what should go where. If there was one thing that Peter had a crap-ton of, it was ideas. So Hart hung the Stutts banner over the (non-working) fireplace, and walked into his bedroom.

This was a mistake. He hadn't gotten any sleep the night before; he'd gone straight from the train station to Tabitha's. Predictably, they had spent the entire night doing the deed, accompanied by her new Gilbert and Sullivan CDs. Then all morning, Hart had hauled boxes and trunks from the basement of Dacron two blocks away. So as soon as he saw his bed, the 19-year-old was done for.

Hart unpacked exactly one thing—his pillow—then collapsed into a coma-like, deeply satisfying nap.

2

The Creeps to Avoid

Thursday, August 27 @ 6:17 pm

Rested and refreshed, and not weighed down by the dining hall's nightly outrage (they weren't open yet), Hart actually whistled as he walked across campus. Several people shot him looks—non-intoxicated, non-ironic happiness was viewed with suspicion, as if the bearer was trying to show everybody else up.

Hart didn't care. He was back at school—AWESOME! This year, since he didn't have to take Trip Darling's classes on top of his own, he might even pull a 4.0. But it was Hart's plans for *The Cuckoo* that had him really stoked.

This year, he'd finally be recognized on campus for good things. The *Daily Money* parody last year won them all some acclaim, but Hart's real accomplishment—selling fifty thousand copies of his book of humor columns—had taken place over the summer. Nobody at school really knew about it.

The issue they'd mailed out a month ago was a step in the right direction. It built name-recognition, which was totally key after decades of suppression by their pompous, lame-brained rival, *The Daily Spectacle* student newspaper. The issue had obviously reached its mark: somebody had shown up at the Bazaar with the cover illustration on a t-shirt. *The Spec* had even singled them out in the Freshman issue as "joining these dopes is social suicide... *The* creeps to avoid—Stutts' lowest element."

An element? Hart liked the sound of that! All summer, Hart had been writing material, and was a much better writer than he had been. There was enough good stuff among the dross to fill two or three magazines. And that was just him; Hart figured if he and Peter worked hard (which they would), and the two seniors Reed and Ellen kicked in a few things here and there, six issues wasn't an unrealistic goal. That was on top of the bigger projects, of course.

Hart had come up with an idea last week that he thought was spectacular. Every year, *Daily Money* did a ranking of the top 100 colleges in the world, based on the percentage of the world's wealth held by its graduates. Naturally, Stutts was always first, Keasbey always second, that wasn't the point. The point was that every high school kid in America read it. Hart's idea was to parody that magazine. In addition to pissing off Trip's dad (the owner of *Daily Money*) a spoof would spread like wildfire in the high schools. High school kids would subscribe. The parody wouldn't even be that difficult to produce—Peter was a whiz with desktop publishing, he'd match the fonts in a snap. They could stage all the photos around campus, and enlist a friend or two at other schools if necessary. They might even be able to get it out before Christmas.

Excited by what was possible, Hart drifted into a reverie. The parody would get written about in all sorts of magazines and newspapers; they'd do appearances on TV and live chats on the internet...All sorts of famous and powerful people would read it and think, "Who is this Hart Fox? Let's bring him in!" The trip down to New York would be fun, especially since they'd have plenty of profits to spend on dinners and hotels; they'd make a weekend of it, and Hart and Tab would stay someplace nice, and eat an expensive dinner after Hart—recognized as *The Cuckoo*'s obvious star—would be offered a great internship. Or maybe even a real job!

I'll hold out for Quinn Bostwick, Hart thought. Bostwick was a *Cuckoo* alum who had just made the leap from a twice-weekly humor column on the Op-Ed page of *The New York Times* to a nightly half-hour television show. Bostwick was hot, incredibly hot, and Hart just *knew* that were the two of them to meet, they would recognize each other as fellow geniuses, fellow seekers. Sure, Hart might be a little raw, and "QB" might have to show him the ropes for a while, but Bostwick would see right off that Hart was his successor, maybe more—*maybe his better*. Hart determined right then and there, as he crossed Locust Street, that he would be gracious to the older man, and always defer to his comedic judgment—except when it was obviously wrong. Then QB would want him to speak up, for the sake of the show. To somebody like Bostwick, quality, not ego, was obviously the most important thing.

The college ranking spoof—and all the things that would inevitably follow—grew in Hart's head as he walked. Eventually they reached such proportions Hart had to stop and pogo-jump for thirty seconds, just to calm down. Everybody walking past Harriman Library looked at him, but Hart didn't care.

"Is that you, Hart?" a familiar voice said from behind.

Hart turned mid-jump, stumbling. It was Mr. President, one of Hart's roommates from freshman year. "Hey, Mr. President," Hart said. "How's it going?"

His parents named him Travis, but the fella oozed so much charm everybody was sure he'd be President of the United States someday. Last year, all the freshmen elected him President of their class—they wanted to get in on the ground floor. "I hate that nickname," Mr. President said sheepishly. "It makes people think I'm stuck-up." Mr. President was genuinely self-deprecating, a rarity at Stutts, and everybody loved it. This air of humility was another reason he would be President—he just couldn't avoid it. "Did you have a nice summer?"

"Yeah," Hart lied. The last three months had been boring, lonely, frequently annoying, and utterly useless from a career standpoint. "How about you? Did you do anything?"

"I worked for the Strong campaign," Mr. President said, without a shred of self-congratulation. This was remarkable, since the smart money was on Sterling Strong to become President in November. He was the perfect candidate: in addition to being a Stutts grad (most candidates were), he was youthful, vigorous, and had starred in the last three James Bond movies.

"Think your boy'll win?" Hart asked.

"It's going to be tough. The economy picked up over the summer—"

Really? It had? Hart was clueless.

"—but there's always hope."

The boys laughed. Personal ambition made you do funny things, like hoping for another Great Depression, just so you could get a cool job at the White House. "What did you do?"

"Oh, nothing," Hart said. "Wrote a lot." Hart was not going to tell Mr. President that he'd spent June, July, and the first two weeks of August as crustacean wrangler for a cheesy mall aquarium. "In fact, I'm going to a *Cuckoo* meeting right now, so..."

"No problem," Mr. President said. "Nice running into you." As he walked away he shouted, "I liked the summer issue!"

"Thanks!" Hart shouted back.

Mr. President was perfectly nice, and deserved every lucky break he could get, but shit, why did everybody always have a cooler life than he did? Well, that was about to change forever. He'd kick ass on the magazine so hard and so thoroughly this year that life would have no choice but to fall into line. *The Cuckoo* would raise him up—it had to.

He weaved his way across New Quad toward *The Cuckoo* office in the basement of Lytton Hall. Normally deserted (and rightfully so) the depressing concrete NewQuad was mobbed with students trying to bargain back belongings appropriated over the summer by Great Littleton's robust and unapologetic homeless population. Every spring, the students carefully stored their belongings in supposedly secure rooms in the basements of the residential colleges. Then every summer, these rooms were broken into and pilfered. It was just like the tomb-robbers in Egypt's Valley of the Kings, except with espresso machines and Bose radios instead of priceless relics. Every fall, the students would return to campus, only to see an ex-Christmas present sticking out of some post-apocalyptic looking lean-to. The students would buy back whatever they could, giving the homeless economy a much-needed infusion of cash. Thus, the cycle of life continued.

"But this is *my* toaster oven!" a girl in expensive clogs yelled. "My mom bought it for me over Parents' Weekend!"

"Thank her for me," a scraggly fellow said. "Look, since it has sentimental value, I'll knock off 10%."

This made the girl turn colors. When she got her breath back, she screamed, "I'm calling a cop!" She stomped away. "You're going to jail!"

"Bring it on!" he yelled. "Jail has air-conditioning." He smiled at Hart, to share the feeling of checkmate. Hart didn't approve, but he liked to be liked—so he smiled back, selling out his principles to avoid conflict.

To distract himself, Hart posed a question that would be repeated hundreds of times this year: Could he turn this into a *Cuckoo* article? Homeless jokes were chancy, people got offended. A spoof of the *Sharper Image* catalog might work, or maybe a board game?...Pondering, Hart ducked into gloomy Lytton Hall. The building smelled exactly the same as it had last May; it would take a hundred summers to air out all the fear-charged exam-stink that had seeped into these walls.

Hart could breathe deeper once he'd descended the stairs—the university buried the humor magazine underground, like nuclear waste. He heard laughter and swearing, and smiled, for real this time. (He also smelled pizza.)

Hand on the knob, Hart took a moment, bracing himself for abuse. One, he was fifteen minutes late. Two, he had sent them all regular emails over the summer, detailing the continuing success of his book. At *The Cuckoo*, if you failed, your fellow editors were the first to offer support, but success—that was chum in the water.

"You're late!" Peter said, looking up from a toy volcano he was trying to fix. The office was a riot of charming and useless artifacts, accrued over years by staffers. In one corner there sat an ancient Mac, decorated with glitter-pen and stickers. Posters covered the walls, some with nasty comments scrawled inside crude speech balloons. A whiteboard sat behind the head of the table, covered with last Spring's jokes and observations. In the middle of the room was a wooden table, around which the other three editors sat.

"Let me guess," Ellen said, chewing. "Spielberg called."

"That was last week," Hart said, playing along. Repartee was a big part of being on *The Cuckoo*.

"I vote groupies," Ellen's fellow senior Reed Rodriguez offered. More of a free-spirit than Ellen, the dark-haired History student was no less stalwart when it came to *The Cuckoo*. Reed got a faraway look in his eye. "You were captured and ravished by a horde of voracious groupies."

"It was librarians," Hart said, shuddering with mock-horror. "They were insatiable!"

"Better not let your lady hear you say that," Peter said. *The Cuckoo*'s resident cynic, Peter had broken his back in a high school football game; not only did this put him in a wheelchair, it channeled all that physical vitality right up into his massive, pulsing brain. Peter handled everything artistic for *The Cuckoo*, in-between a stream of outrageous inventions.

"Better not let Tab hear you call her 'my lady,'" Hart retorted.

"I ain't scared, I'll wear a chain metal scarf," Peter said. Everybody on *The Cuckoo* knew that Tabitha was a vampire, and was cool with it. "Where is Little Miss Nosferatu?"

"Still too light out," Hart said, sitting down. "And garlic doesn't agree with her."

"So the old wives' tales are true," Ellen mused.

"Some of them." Hart started to eat. In college, as in the wild, eating was done as quickly as possible. Hart employed the old New Yorker's trick—folding the pieces—to cram the maximum acreage of pizza into his mouth. Not that the pizza was very good; this bounty was the fruit of a food-for-ads trade with Ubriaco's, a dark, best-when drunk Italian joint favored by cockroaches and the chronically broke. But "free" always trumped "good."

"Fine. More for us, then." Peter tore a piece of garlic bread from the loaf and tossed it. It hit Hart squarely in the left eye.

"Aw, look," Peter said, "he's crying!"

"I can't help it," Hart said, blinking through stinging garlic salt. "I'm just so happy to see you all."

In classic *Cuckoo* fashion, Hart was telling the truth with a joke. All summer, sweating through a shitty job and annoying family, Hart had consoled himself with thoughts of his friends on the magazine. The stress of Stutts encouraged its students to form surrogate families—by year two, Great Littleton was home, not wherever you came from. Hart's especially hard first year made the bond even tighter for him; getting rusticated (Stutts lingo for being kicked off-campus) and then nearly murdered shows who you can depend on. For Hart, that was *The Cuckoo*, and nobody else. Hart reached into his messenger bag and pulled out four t-shirts. "I've brought presents. I hope they're the right size."

The rest of the staff unfurled the shirts. The front had a picture of an old man holding up Hart's book, pointing to it. He wore a flannel cowboy shirt and a goofy smile.

"Is this the guy who kept writing you?" Ellen asked. "Your 'Number One Fan'?"

Hart nodded.

"Should we put them on?" Peter asked. "I don't wanna sully such a sacred object."

"My mom printed up five hundred—without my knowledge or approval, obviously."

"*Obviously*," Peter said. Mrs. Fox was convinced that the old man's letters were the start of something big for her son. She started leaving out the Thursday *New York Times*, the pages pointedly opened to Quinn Bostwick's humorous Op-Ed. "Quinn Bostwick is a Stuttsie, isn't he?"

"Yeah," Hart would grumble, embarrassed at what his mom was suggesting. Quinn Bostwick won Pulitzers the way cautious people got colonoscopies—once every year after age 40.

"And he was editor of *The Cuckoo*, too, wasn't he?"

"Yes—God, Mom! Would you please stop wearing that shirt?" Mrs. Fox had a different colored one for each day of the week.

Back in the basement office, Reed read the shirt's back. "'I fell out of my chair laughing!'"

"Did he really write that?" Ellen asked, as she slipped her head through.

"Yep," Hart said. "I've got the letter in my wallet."

Peter looked at Reed and Ellen, then turned to Hart. "Tell me you're just kidding."

"He says he's my number one fan," Hart said, ignoring Peter, "but I think of him as *our* number one fan...After all, you guys published the book. Without that, we wouldn't have sold one copy, much less 51,132."

"He knows the exact number," Peter mumbled to Reed and Ellen.

"Shut up, Pete," Ellen said. By Stutts standards, Hart's outburst was genuine humility. To remain friends with any Stuttsie over the long haul, one had to be prepared to cut him/her a certain kind of slack. Self-love poisoning got everybody sooner or later.

"We're the wind beneath your wings," Reed said.

"Not me," Peter said. "I'm the wind inside your shorts."

"I thought we should all have a shirt, to inspire us," Hart said.

"Is Mom coming to Parents' Weekend?" Ellen asked. "And will she be wearing her shirt?"

"Not if I can help it," Hart said, then changed the subject back to the shirts. "Look at it—this shirt says to me, 'What we do is important. We can really touch people."

"You can really touch yourself," Peter quipped.

"Is he still emailing you every week?" Reed asked.

"Not for a month. But he wrote me another letter," Hart said, producing a slightly battered envelope from his back pocket. "I swung by the P.O. on the way over, that's why I was late. By the way Reed, a homeless dude has your boogie-board."

"Well, let's hear it," Ellen said, slurping a little iced espresso.

Hart handed the letter to Reed. "I'd feel weird reading it myself," he said. "Feel free to skip the more embarrassing parts."

"What's left?" Peter needled.

Surrounded by pictures of Hart's "number one fan," Reed began to read.

> "July 31
> Dear Mr. Fox,
> My name is Kimberley DiFazio. I'm Ben Malaluga's granddaughter. I'm writing to thank you—I don't know how Grandpa Ben found your book, but it gave him much pleasure during the last several months of his life.
>
> For weeks, we watched Ben sitting in his rocker, reading your book and just crowing, sometimes literally falling over he was laughing so hard. Finally, I asked, 'Grandpa, let me see that book you're reading.' Instead of giving it to me, he bit my hand and ran under the porch, where he stayed for the next three days.
>
> This wasn't like him.
>
> Still, we didn't get worried until we discovered he was stockpiling more copies of your book, "in case anything happens." He'd cashed out his whole pension, and was using his Social Security, too. We only found out when somebody came by saying he'd sold them my car! The final total came to just over 51,000 copies, all in boxes under the porch. He'd built a sort of fort down there.
>
> It turns out that Grandpa Ben was in the final stages of a massive, inoperable brain tumor. The doctors told us that patients with his condition frequently fixate on something, reading it over and over and laughing—usually it's something like a bus schedule or the phone book. According to the doctors, Grandpa's compulsive behavior (the buying and reading), the falling out of his chair, even the laughing itself, are all part of the syndrome and have nothing to do with—"

Reed stopped, unsure of whether to continue. Peter's head was down on the table; he was shaking with silent laughter. Hart, on the other hand, looked like he was going to hurl.

"I think we get the picture," Ellen said.

Reed's cell phone rang. "That's the other pizzas." The delivery guy had only brought two; their agreement was for four. Since cold pizza kept, the editors had every intention of living on it until the dining halls opened.

Peter sat up in his wheelchair, eyes red, cheeks sucked in, trying desperately not to laugh. "I'll get it," he croaked, and just made it to the door before busting out. They heard him laughing all the way down the hall.

Hart looked at the doomed weirdo smiling from the t-shirts. "Great," he said glumly. "My number one fan is insane. Sorry—*was* insane. Now he's dead." Nothing in Hart's life was ever simple and fun. Sooner or later, everything got complicated and unfun. It was just a question of when.

"A laugh's a laugh, I say," Reed declared, trying to put the best face on it.

"And sales are sales," Ellen said. "That's why we made the book nonreturnable. This guy's insanity will pay for your Stutts education—"

Reed interrupted. "—which you're wasting on something equally insane, *The Cuckoo*."

Hart laughed in spite of himself. "You can take off the t-shirts if you want," Hart said.

"Fuck you, I'm wearing mine," Reed said.

"Proudly," Ellen said. "This makes it better."

"I guess I got a little full of myself," Hart said. "Sorry."

They shrugged. Hart could've kissed them—they always made him feel normal. Like one of the group, not trapped outside it, trying desperately to figure out the rules.

Peter returned. "Sorry—I had to wait for the delivery guy to finish taking a bet."[5]

After everybody had started in on the new grub, Hart wiped his mouth and said, "I've got an idea, wanna hear about it?"

"Hart, we're *not* giving people brain tumors," Peter joked.

"I think we ought to do a parody of the *Daily Money* college ranking

5 Ubriaco's was a notorious den of vice and had been for decades; people boasted about using fake IDs made with crayons. It was owned by the cousin of Stutts' top campus cop, Oscar Renalli, so every "bust" was known about weeks in advance. The cops would swoop in, round up a bunch of freshmen too drunk to run away, and walk them home. The only person who had ever gone to jail as a result was one kid back in the Seventies, who insisted on it. Something about "experiencing every aspect of Life." Freak.

issue," Hart said.

"I know you hate the publisher," Reed said, "but didn't we do them already?"

"Yeah," Ellen said. "I'd be afraid that we'd be repeating ourselves."

"Nah, nah, nah," Hart said excitedly. "It's a special issue—totally different than the regular newspaper."

"Think we could make money on it?" Peter asked.

"Pete, every freakin' high school kid in the U.S. reads it, along with their parents," Hart said. "Not only would we sell a bunch, we'd sell subscriptions on top of that. Money would be falling out of our asses."

"Tempting," Reed said. "Any idea how we'd write it? Have you looked it over?"

"A little." Hart was trying to play it cool. "I have last year's edition in a box somewhere in my room. I'll bring it to the next meeting."

"When were you thinking it would come out?" Peter said.

"Christmas," Hart said. "The real one comes out in February."

"Jeez," Peter said. "That's close. We'd really have to bust ass on the design. And when I say 'we,' I mean 'me.'"

"Come on, Pete," Hart said. "I know you could do it. It would kick ass. At least look at it."

"Sure," Peter said.

"So," Ellen said, as they finished the second pizza, "how does everybody think the summer issue went down?"

"I found one in the English Department toilet," Reed said.

"Nice!" Ellen said. "A captive audience."

"Somebody actually brought it all the way from home, just to browse it in the crapper?" Hart asked.

"Apparently," Reed said.

"Think of how popular we'd be with a little publicity," Peter said.

"That's what the Freshman Assembly prank is for," Ellen said.

"Yeah, but it can't just be bingo again," Peter said. They usually handed bingo cards with President Whitbread's favorite words and phrases on them, stuff like "diversity" and "liberal arts education" and "tuition increase." "This year, it's really got to stand out."

"And when you say 'stand out,'" Hart said, "you mean 'traumatize people.'"

"You got it," Peter said.

Reed was bouncing a tennis ball off the wall. "Well, I'll help, whatever you decide to do," he said. "It's Hart's call."

"Hey, I'm *co*-editor!" Peter said.

"...in charge of Art," Ellen said, taking another drink from her iced espresso. "Pranks are considered Editorial, and that's Hart's side." She turned to Reed. "Please quit throwing that effing ball, you're making me twitchy. Also, every time you hit John Travolta, I die a little."

"Peter, no offense, but I don't want to do anything to tick people off. I spent most of last year as 'the Mad Pisser,' remember?" Hart said. "This year, I want people to like *The Cuckoo*."

"Not me," Peter said. "Hate all the way. Hate and fear." He dropped a pepperoni into his mouth and chewed. "I'm kidding. But you can't do a prank without pissing people off."

"Yeah, but you can't make people laugh if they're mad," Hart said, feeling like his grand plan was already slipping away. "And that's what *The Cuckoo* is for."

"Not entirely," Peter said. "Making people laugh is the lowest form of comedy."

"You stole that from Michael O'Donoghue," Hart said. "Let's vote."

"You can't vote on something like that," Peter said. "It's an aesthetic."

"We can vote on the direction of the Board," Ellen said. "All in favor of this year's first priority being popularity rather than fearless satire, raise your hand."

She raised her hand, and Hart raised both of his. "One's for Tab."

"You don't know how she would vote," Peter said. "She thinks most Stuttsies are tools. She might love the idea of fearless satire."

"You mean, abuse," Ellen said.

"Yeah, abuse," Reed said. "Pete and I are in favor of wanton abuse."

The Board was deadlocked. Ellen, wily and wise, had a solution. She picked up a game-piece taped to the top of the pizza box.[6] "I'm gonna flip this. New building, we play nice. Burned up building, we take no prisoners."

She flipped it. The new building showed.

"So we play nice," Hart said, thinking it was settled.

Peter disagreed. "I demand a re-vote," Peter said, "with the full Board."

"You are so goddamn stubborn!" Hart said, and was about to lash out further when he stopped himself. All the things he wanted —no, *needed*—to do this year required Peter. Peter was his designer. Luckily Hart was a born peacemaker, and after a deep breath, came up with a compromise. "Why don't we do this, Pete: you do whatever prank for the Freshman Assembly you want—"

6 Ubriaco's was celebrating the anniversary of its re-opening; twenty-five years ago, it had burned down under mysterious circumstances. The cops (a young Oscar Renalli) fingered "student radicals," but the rumor was insurance fraud.

"Anything?" Peter asked, eyes suddenly alight.

"That's what I said," Hart said, already regretting it. "Then, everything we do after that point is designed to make us the funniest humor magazine on Earth."

"Seems fair," Reed said.

"And it might work together nicely, from the publicity standpoint," Peter said. "Deal." Hart and Peter shook on it.

"I can't eat another bite," Ellen said. "It's customary to end a staff dinner with toasts. Does anybody have one?"

"I've got one for you seniors," Hart said. "May your year be untouched by the real world."

There was nervous laughter all around.

Peter turned to Ellen. "Can I have a taste of your iced espresso?"

Hart was suprised when Ellen slid her drink over; she was usually a bit of a germophobe.

Peter drank, then made a face. "Can't understand why anybody likes this stuff," he said. "Too bitter."

"That's funny," Hart said. "I've heard people say the same thing about you."

As food began to fly, Reed raised his glass. "Guys! Guys, please: this toast's very serious." He cleared his throat. "Here's to Ellen finally losing her virginity."

Peter, clearing his mouth of the espresso, coughed into his coke.

Ellen laughed loudly. "Oh, Reed, if you only knew," she said, laughing. "I've got a real one. Here's to a memorable year, and here's to Ben Malaluga, without whom Hart would be back home working at McDonald's."

"Hear, hear!" the table said in unison. For better or worse, Hart's sophomore year had begun.

3

Satan Comes to Stutts

Sunday, August 29th, 5:22 pm

For four months, Stutts University dozed like a sphinx in the sun. The combustible mixture of youthful ambition, sexual tension, and undiagnosed mental illness that powered the campus was on hiatus, scattered to the world's better neighborhoods. Nobody stayed around by choice: Great Littleton's heat and humidity made you feel like a poached egg. If the light was right, you could actually see the sidewalks steam.

Summer always seemed out-of-place at Stutts; bright sunshine made the buildings look fake. Which, of course, they were—as impressive as it was, none of the High Colonic dated back further than 1910. Like many things, Stutts was most beautiful when you didn't look too closely.

Since time immemorial[7] *The Cuckoo* had tickled the campus back to life with a prank at the Freshman Assembly. Of course, they always denied having anything to do with it, traditionally blaming *The Daily Spectacle*. As long as there wasn't any serious repercussions, everybody kept a sense of humor about it.

Everyone, that is, but P. Preston Whitbread, Stutts' current President. Whitbread followed the Two Commandments of University Presidents, which went like this:

1) Thou shalt have no gods before fundraising.
2) When in doubt, see #1.

To Whitbread, the Assembly was the first step in the decades-long, deadly serious process of money-extraction, not a venue for sophomoric joking. You couldn't expect the students to understand, most of them couldn't even balance a checkbook. All Whitbread could do was fine them. The Cuckonians paid up, gladly; they had nothing against Whitbread, he was simply a symbol, a stand-in for all the forces of authority everywhere.

Whitbread was not so sanguine—there was another, more personal reason for President Whitbread's antipathy. Way back when he was a freshman, *The Cuckoo* had disrupted the Assembly by dropping a bunch of chickens from the ceiling. The resulting mayhem had left him violently phobic; even a buffalo wing gave him the willies. And his phobia was getting worse: over

7 1954.

the summer, a hen-shaped Quickie Chickie delivery van had scared him so badly he'd driven into a mailbox.

It was not a good situation, but it didn't really keep President Whitbread from doing his job. Nobody knew about it except his wife and his shrink. And the pills helped. But wouldn't you know it—this morning, President Whitbread had forgotten to take his meds.

Hart and Tabitha kneeled in front of a window in the musty, dusty cupola atop Truax Assembly Hall. Slim, red-haired, and buoyantly pretty, Tabitha was looking down at the courtyard below with a pair of binoculars.

"Look, there's President Whitbread," she said.

"Is that his wife?" Hart said. "She looks like a dump truck."

"Unkind!" Tabitha said. "I'm glad she didn't hear you say that."

Imagining this triggered Hart's anxiety, which was never far from the surface. They had broken into the cupola, and Hart was worried somebody was going to get mad.

"Wafting through a keyhole isn't a hanging offense," Tabitha said. (One of her vampiric talents was an ability to turn into a fine mist. Of course, being Tabitha, it was pink.) "What we're *about* to do, however…"

"I hate pranks," Hart said with feeling, elbows on the peeling sill. "They make me goddamned nervous."

"So why did you agree?" Tabitha said, adjusting the binoculars. "You could've told Peter 'no.' It'd be good for him."

"I need him happy, so he'll design the issues and the parody," Hart said.

"And that's worth making yourself miserable?"

Hart didn't respond to such an obviously nonsensical question. Of course it was worth it! *Anything* was worth it. "I figured, give him one big prank at the beginning of the year and he might get it out of his system."

Now it was Tabitha's turn not to respond to nonsense. Peter had spent the last 48 hours planning his "masterpiece," drawing diagrams, gathering materials, in general working like he was possessed by an evil spirit. And maybe he was—they'd just have to do the prank and hope for the best. Pranks tempted Fate in a way that Hart did not appreciate. This whole thing was like a painful medical procedure; he couldn't wait for it to be over.

Tabitha scanned the crowd of freshmen shuffling into the assembly hall below them. "Every crop looks the same." She would know: Tabitha had been a Stutts student since 1867.

"Gimme," Hart said, reaching for the glasses. "I think I see somebody I went to high school with." It was a false alarm. "No way I looked that young last year," Hart said, lowering the binoculars. "Look! That one is actually a fetus."

Tab snorted. "Lucky for you I like younger men."

Tabitha was Hart's first real girlfriend, and he worshipped and objectified her as only a first-timer can. Previously catholic in his tastes, Hart was now violently prejudiced towards women of her height (medium), complexion (milky, with an easy blush), hair color (red, which she wore neck-length, and when it got long, piled on her head or under scarves until she couldn't stand it). Before Tabitha, preppy girls had seemed stuck-up. After, Hart got hard just looking at the Brooks Brothers catalog. To Hart, Tabitha was perfect. This made him feel a little powerless, so he liked to tease her.

"Younger men? You have no choice." Hart turned to look at Tabitha through the binoculars. "Though I must say: for a 157-year-old, you have a spectacular rack."

"You're an ass!" As a vampire, Tabitha was invisible to mirrors (and binoculars), but no lady appreciates that kind of talk. "With increased vision comes increased responsibility. Hand 'em over."

Hart did so. "*You* don't seem to be worried."

"College drags like hell after the first century," she said. "You gotta shake things up every once in a while. Variety is the spice of life."

"How about riots?"

Suddenly, Hart had an excellent idea. A man of action, he tried a frontal attack.

Tabitha parried his grabby hand expertly. "Down, boy. We can visit[8] after the prank," she said. "God, it's stifling up here."

Hart liked it when Tabitha got sweaty. It made him think of other times when she was sweaty. "Which is exactly why we should take off all our clothes."

Tabitha ran a fingertip along the ground. It came up black.

Hart shrugged. "What's a little Ebola in the name of love?" His determination in these matters was adamantine. "We'll put down that banner. It looks…fairly clean."

"What banner?" They were surrounded by a jumble of musical instruments and silly props; the whimsical Stutts Marching Experience used the cupola for storage.

Hart pointed and read aloud. "'Beat Keasbey. Or Not. We Don't Care.'"

"Inspiring," Tabitha said blandly. She resumed watching the students

8 "Visiting" was Tabitha's demure euphemism for everything from light necking to things that made the Marquis de Sade nauseous.

below. Hart and Tabitha were in charge of recon. So far, everything had gone perfectly. Friday night, Peter had planned; Saturday morning, items were purchased and/or created; Saturday afternoon, they had been installed, with Hart and Reed posing as summer custodial help. Sunday morning had been spent testing circuits and fixing last-minute stuff, and now Sunday evening, everything was in position and ready to go. Nothing was being left to chance.

His advances rebuffed, Hart descended back into anxiety. Stomach acid simmering, he thought of all the state and federal laws they were about to break. "I hope people don't end up hating us."

"Or dead," Tabitha said blithely.

Hart coughed—in his horror, he had swallowed a gnat. "How? You don't really think there's—"

"It's happened before," Tabitha said. "Back in the eighteen-whatevers some idiots pumped Freshman Commons full of ether. Five boys bought it."

Hart suddenly saw his future. Expulsion. Jail. Buggery. "Oh, God!"

"Relax," Tabitha said, chuckling. An excess of perspective gave her a weird sense of humor. "No big loss, trust me—I dated a few of them."

Hart's cel phone chirped. He put it on speakerphone but heard only gibberish. "Pete, I can't understand you. Turn off the scrambler."

"—was using the scrambler. Isn't it the best?"

"What's the point if you can't understand someone?" Tabitha said. She wasn't impressed by technology for its own sake, having lived through "oodles and oodles" of it.

"Luddite," Peter said. "How's it looking? Don't answer, Mr. Magoo."[9]

Tabitha scanned the sea of semiformal seeping into the doors below. "Just a few stragglers left," she said.

"Great!" Peter said brightly. The aristocratic anarchist was always happiest when he was about to cause trouble. "I'm switching off now so they can't trace the signal. Remember, when you hear my whistle, check to see there are no campus cops, so I can get away."

"What about Reed and Ellen?" Hart asked. Those two were already hiding in the rafters above the crowd. "How will they get out?"

"Oh, they'll blend in with the crowd—or 'the screaming throng,' as I

9 Hart had been born with his right eyeball in the left socket and vice-versa; as a result, his vision wasn't too good, and he lived in a world vastly colored by his mental state. When he was happy, a splash of color seen out of the corner of his eye would be a yo-yo, or a leprechaun. When he was depressed, or anxious, there were shark fins among the waves, and king cobras in every shadow.

like to call it. If we do this right, everybody will much, *much* too freaked out to notice." Hearing Tabitha squeal, Peter paused. "Hart, promise me you're going to stay focused, okay?"

"I wasn't doing anything," Hart said, whipping his hand from under Tabitha's shirt. "Whatever gave you the idea that—"

"Spare me," Peter said. As an engineer, he was constantly frustrated by the fact that people were seldom as reliable as a five-dollar calculator. "I'm signing off."

"Pete, what if—"

Peter cut Hart off. "Stop worrying, Hart. Everything's going to be fine. See you at Der Rathskeller."[10]

President Whitbread had precisely one speech, "The Challenge of Diversity." He had downloaded it off a website catering to college presidents. Occasionally, he rearranged it a little—"A Diversity of Challenge"—just to see if anyone was paying attention. They weren't. They were drunk.

President Whitbread would've been, too, but his wife was a stickler for appearances, especially other people's. Rigid, proud, unyielding, Estelle Whitbread was the kind of woman who belonged on the prow of a ship.

Mrs. Whitbread thought her husband should write a new speech. "It can't be good for your brain to say the same words over and over," she said.

"You said that last year," President Whitbread retorted.

"Don't be cute, Preston. I know what I know." This was Mrs. Whitbread's standard line when defending her rather unique ideas of medicine. Still, they obviously worked for her; in the words of her Fifth Avenue doctor, she was "built like a cinderblock lavatory."

"Never marry young," President Whitbread told his son Patterson, a dimwitted Sand College junior. "Never. Marry. Young. Repeat it, so I know you're listening."

"Never marry Mom."

Whitbread sighed; his son was a moron. "Close enough."[11]

But back to the speech: President Whitbread's oratory was as unchanging as the tides, and like the tides it produced a feeling of being carried away

10 "Der Rat" was the traditional campus spot for celebrations of the more elegant sort. Of course, elegance was far from guaranteed after a few "buckets," large silver pails filled with a secret mixture of champagnes.

11 Whitbread needn't have worried. There was no danger of his son marrying anyone. Patterson was known all over campus as "Carpetbomber," after his penchant of letting off juicy ones during sex.

against one's will, followed by sensations of envelopment and suffocation. Yet—not knowing any better—the freshmen actually looked forward to the Assembly. Not only was it an opportunity to bask in the glorious Stutts-ness of it all, they were also ready for a rest. The fevered anticipation of arrival, constant physical exertion of moving in, and the endless stream of new people had many first-years teetering on the brink of complete psychological collapse. *The Cuckoo* was about to push them all over the edge.

Peter crouched in his basement command center like a spider in its web. Cackling softly, he removed the folding keyboard from the armrest of his wheelchair, then slipped the visor over his head. Eyes nestled in the soft rubber eyepieces, Peter could see all around the auditorium, thanks to a the fisheye periscope Reed had drilled out of the mouth of a gilded cherub on the stage's proscenium. He watched the freshmen take their seats. When President Whitbread appeared onstage, the crowd quieted.

Whitbread's detractors said he was nothing but an empty suit, but even they had to admit that it was a *nice* suit. He resembled a Founding Father, or a mature bowtie model. He was trim (Whitbread smoked, mainly to spite his wife), impeccably tailored and slightly Botoxed; he was gray, but only in the most distinguished places. He often wore suspenders. Most of all, Whitbread sported the healthy glow, inner and outer, one can only get from prolonged exposure to money.

Arranging his papers, putting on his reading glasses, the President took a moment to bask in the awe coming off the tipsy-yet-still-impressed students. This was the only part of the evening that was even remotely enjoyable to him, and Whitbread wanted to make it last. Experience told him that his gravitas would seep away, drip by drip, until these callow and cologne-drenched undergrads became rich alumni, and the tables were completely turned.

Whitbread waited so long that the University's Provost crept over. "Everything all right?" the Provost whispered, hoping the answer was "no."

"I'm fine, Patrick!" It was so *obvious* that Provost Rivington wanted his job. Well, let him try: thanks to an arrangement with a certain CIA-connected member of the faculty, President Whitbread was in possession of several grainy photos showing one Patrick Manolo Rivington engaging in koalalingus.[12]

12 Though the photos were obviously faked (North could never get the heads right; Rivington's head was cartoonishly big) the Provost was still vulnerable. Rivington had set himself up as a paragon of virtue—he was currently riding the bestseller lists with a slim book of inspiration,

Whitbread waited for the Provost to return to his seat. Then, with a slight nod to the dignitaries in the front row—donors, Trustees, prima donna faculty—the doomed man began to speak.

"Incoming class, on behalf of the entire Stutts family, I would like to welcome you to our community of scholars."

The students applauded themselves lustily. This came naturally and would continue, in some sense, for the rest of their lives.

"They call Stutts 'the Queen of Colleges,' but that hardly tells the story. Five thousand years of excellence. Five thousand years of innovation. Five thousand years of leaders. And now—you." Far below, Peter gave a rueful laugh; his periscope had caught a "leader" picking his nose.

"When you look at the world around you, you see what Stutts hath wrought. It is like a glorious tapestry. But unlike a tapestry, it cannot be ripped or torn, or burnt up in a fire. Whatever happens outside this community of scholars, our tapestry of excellence endures.

"But there is a question to be asked: Will you do your part? Will you help weave the next panel? Or will you refuse? Might you even pick at the tapestry when you think no one is looking? That is for each of you to decide. But as our school song says, 'Time is fleeting, ever bleating,' so"—he pulled a starter's pistol from his pocket, raised and fired it— "let the educating begin!"

After everybody's hearts settled back into their chests, Whitbread continued. "Perhaps what I'm talking about isn't a tapestry at all, but a journey. Let us split the difference. Let us say that a Stutts education is a journey, carrying a tapestry. This journey will not be easy; the tapestry—by which I mean the accumulated accomplishments of the students that have come before you—is weighty indeed. That is, the accomplishments are impressive and difficult to equal. But you must carry it—*i.e.*, go to school here—and never let it trail upon the ground—*e.g.*, by running afoul of any of the regulations in the Student Handbook. Nor, obviously, can you drop the tapestry into the mire—*c.f.*, fail to graduate. *Q.E.D.*"

"Things El Jefe Taught Me"—and the merest hint of impropriety with a marsupial would be devastating. "El Jefe" was the Provost's maternal grandfather, Jesus Maria Manolo, ex-Maximum Leader of Umídor. Awaiting extradition for war crimes, General Manolo was living in California, faking various illnesses and making large political donations. The Provost's book was a part of a wide-ranging attempt at rehabilitating El Jefe's reputation; the Provost had just forwarded a petition to the United Nations with signatures from over 100,000 Umídoreans asking that the General "be allowed to return and resume his rightful place at the head of our nation." What the Provost didn't know was that the signatures came from people who his grandfather had "disappeared." El Jefe had a weird sense of humor.

Several freshmen had raised their hands, hoping to correct the President's Latin. This was just like a certain type of Stutts student, and yet another reason why Whitbread didn't much like them. President Whitbread was not himself very bright. Though he attended Stutts, Whitbread never actually graduated, receiving an honorary degree after several years of being President. Sure, other schools laughed at Stutts for having a President without a college education. Then Stutts bought them, razed them, and sowed their quads with salt.[13]

"On this travesty-laden journey..."

"Tapestry!" a few students yelled. The descent from awe to insolence had already begun.

"...you will learn that Stutts has always stood for two things: diversity, and the pursuit of knowledge for its own sake. Knowledge about freshwater dredging, for example. Truly one of the engines of American prosperity." Whitbread nodded to a sludge baron in the first row who had just donated $25 million for a fleet of new golf carts for the campus police.

"Stutts has always been a remarkably diverse place. Some of our founders were landed clergymen, others were devout landowners. Some of them came from Connecticut, others hailed from Rhode Island. Others still, from Northern Rhode Island. Think of the diversity: Pilgrims *and* Puritans! It must've been quite a place.

"They were diverse in their beliefs, too. Some held to the doctrine of predestination, believing that God has chosen the elect before birth—and naturally those lucky few should rule this world, too. Others turned things on their head, believing that wealth and temporal power were sure markers of whom God loved best.

"People were tortured, banished, even killed over such chasms of doctrine. And that is why ever since, we here at Stutts do not presume to say which things are right. That is for others to decide. We simply provide the tools for inquiry, and let everyone else suffer the consequences.

"It was that belief in the healing power of suffering, and willingness to punish others for what you believe in, that brought my ancestors here to Great Littleton. The first Whitbread in America was Banishment Coordinator for the Great Littleton Colony. This was an important job. In that first brutal winter, more than half of the settlers were banished, driven into the

13 In addition to being a useful pretext for intercollegiate conquest, Whitbread's scholastic futility came in handy for a certain type of student—Trip Darling, for example. Whenever Trip's parents complained about his grades, Trip would trot out President Whitbread's post-collegiate success as proof that "grades don't matter." The "if you have enough money" part was unspoken but understood.

forest for inappropriate deportment. But though this remorseless culling kept the colony small, it was a marker of health. In a vigorous marketplace of ideas, there is no place for soft-heartedness—some ideas prevail, and some freeze to death in the snow."

Five floors below Peter flipped open his cell phone. "Stage one, please," he said evenly, signaling the team in the rafters. Trying not to giggle, Reed and Ellen switched on several pairs of laser pointers fastened together with masking tape and began waving them around. Suddenly, four sets of red eyes, invisible from the bright stage but all too obvious to the audience sitting in the dark, danced demonically around the room. A high-strung freshman gave a yelp.

"Settle down, settle down…Please do not goose each other until after the speech," Whitbread said, then continued. "But while unfettered debate rests at the very heart of any University, there is no need for intemperate behavior. I say to you now: as long as I am President, this institution will not be bullied into any course of action, no matter how reasonable, by any group of people who value politics over propriety." Whitbread removed a doorknob from his pocket and held it up. "You may see wood and glass, but I see our shared heritage!"[14]

There was whistling and stomping from the front row. "However," Whitbread continued, after the tumult had died down— "in a gesture of goodwill, we will *lower* each one three inches."

The demonic eyes were losing effect, so Peter kicked things up a notch. "Stage two, please." Reed pushed a button and a clutch of flies swarmed out of an unused heating vent. Great Littleton was well known for its flies, and these monsters were as big as cigar butts. They didn't fly so much as drop like gobs of hairy, winged spit.

Down below, President Whitbread remained ignorant. "Look around you—it is easy to feel that you are all very different. Some of you grew up on the east coast; others on the west. Some attended prestigious private schools; others rich public ones. Some of you want to be doctors; others, lawyers, maybe even executives."

A group in the back had met the flies. President Whitbread misinterpreted this hubbub as enthusiasm.

"In the midst of all this bewildering diversity," he continued, "there

14 This part of the speech was new, and merits a little explanation. The campus Wymyn's Cyntyr had been fighting for years to have Stutts replace its current doorknobs with slightly smaller ones, more comfortable to female hands. This measure had been strongly opposed by a clutch of reactionary alums, some of whom were sitting in the front row.

is something that can bind you together: a common enemy. The founders of Stutts found theirs in the indigenous peoples of this land. Without it, perhaps we would not be sitting here today. You see," the President said, "during that first terrible winter, the Native Americans took in settlers as fast as my ancestor could kick them out. This was a diabolical move: soon, the Great Littleton Colony was surrounded, powerless in the face of their neighbors' kindness.

"But, scrawny as they were, miserable as they were, the few unbanished Englishmen banded together, never doubting that God was on their side. It was the colonists' love for each other that saw them through. And by 'love for each other,' I of course mean 'resistance to smallpox.' That kind of love is a powerful thing."

The flies buzzed and swooped, sowing general disgust. The Satanic eyes still dancing, Peter gleefully perceived dread taking root in the audience.

"So I ask you, as I ask each incoming class: what will be your common enemy? Who will be your Indians, crouching behind their Machiavellian charity? Think before you answer, for it is a harder question than you know. Earlier classes had it easier. They could say, 'Why mess with success? We'll take the Native Americans!' Or, 'Immigrants!' Or 'Hitler.' The choice facing today's Stutts student is not so clear-cut. We know all too well that America has no monopoly on virtue, and that other cultures have much to teach us. The wise man strives to understand a culture before destroying it. I am sure that the chiefsof those great tribes, now so nobly memoralized in a complex of casinos less than 30 minutes by car from campus"—another nod to the front row—"are looking down from their Great Canoe or Wigwam or whatever, nodding and smiling when I say: we killed our enemies not wisely, but too well."

There was a loud yelp as a fly flew up someone's skirt. President Whitbread paused. Oh shit, he realized, it's a prank, an entirely new, even worse one. Why didn't those *Cuckoo* idiots just do "bingo" again? Why did they have to make things difficult?

Speed was his only defense, so he started talking faster. "If you were to ask me, 'President Whitbread, who would you pick?' I would say, 'I hope the common enemy of this class will be ignorance.' Ignorance is a worthy adversary. No one can criticize you, and you run a very low risk of landing in jail."

Buzzing and biting, the flies had reached the dignitaries in the front row. Whitbread heard a loud curse. He peered out into the audience, shading his eyes. "Hold fast, my friends. It's just a prank."

"No, it ain't!" A oilman stood up, swatting his expensive cowboy hat to and fro. "It's a goddamn plague a' locusts!"

"We must protect the donors," Rivington hissed, suddenly at Whitbread's elbow, Iago-like.

"I know! Sit back down!" As the donors were enveloped by the biting insects, Whitbread knew he had to regain control, and fast. He skipped forward blindly, picking a page at random and speaking rapid-fire. "Yet it is not grades that count nor progress on a mythical path towards a chimerical goal! It is where that goal leads that's important! Will you be a success, or a failure! A credit to yourself your family and your school! Or end up in a pauper's grave!" Someone in the back couldn't take it anymore, screamed, and bolted out of the exit.

Sensing his moment, Peter moved to Stage Three. He typed a few strokes into the keyboard, accessing Truax's public address system. "Get out," Peter whispered urgently into the mic. "Get out!"

Unsettled by the eyes, unnerved by the flies, the crowd reacted to the voices seeping from the speakers with genuine panic. Several more students screamed, while others dropped to their knees in prayer. The students were cowering in their seats; some boys had even pulled their blazers over their heads in a pitiful attempt to hide.

Sounds of weeping from the audience confirmed that the fragile psyches of the freshmen were starting to break. Whitbread wasn't looking that great himself—he had definitely lost his cool. But he was determined to finish the speech, belting it out as if he could shout himself back into control. "It is not what you learn that is important, but learning how to learn. Also, learning how learning how to learn. And learning how learning how learning how to learn! And—"

The release of a small crate of garden snakes elicted a galvanic reaction. This was followed by a few frogs, then some of Tabitha's pet rats, trained to form pentagrams and the number "666."

Above, Reed and Ellen appraised them like fireworks. "I like the snakes. Simple, classic."

Ellen disagreed. "Tabitha's an artist," she said. "Do you have any idea how long it takes to train a rat?"

Below them, chaos bloomed. "Ladies and gentlemen!" President Whitbread didn't look well. He was gripping the lectern, and a thick sweat had broken out across his brow. "This is just the work of a few malcontents. Someday, you'll look back on this and laugh! *Ladies! Gentlemen!*"

Provost Rivington stood up again. "Preston—"

Whitbread turned and chucked the doorknob at him. "Stay back, bastard!" His mouth flecked with spit, Whitbread whipped around to the donors and shouted a desperate excuse: "Food poisoning! From the dining halls!" As plausible as this was, it came too late. The bigwigs were cramming their ample haunches through the exits.

"Aaron! Joe-Bob! Giuseppe!" Whitbread babbled. "Come b—*OH GOD!*"

Glowing red blood oozed down the walls of the auditorium. Around the exits, fistfights broke out, and everywhere there appeared the unmistakable odor of fright-pee.

Watching contentedly, Peter suddenly remembered a last-minute addition, the coup de grace. The sophomore turned his microphone up to maximum volume. "Buk-buk-buk-b'KOK!" he crowed. "Buk-buk-buk-buk-buk..."

At the first cluck, President Whitbread jerked as if shot. Drained of color, every muscle was clenched, and his face was a mask of shock. With the force of Peter's final, industrial-strength cock-a-doodle, alektorophobia shattered Whitbread's mind.

Gibbering nonsensically, Whitbread began stripping off his clothes; Rivington and the others on the stage tried to corral the President as he darted this way and that. The unhinged executive, seeing not colleagues but razor-beaked roosters, exited stage left. The rest of the administration followed.

With a bird's eye view, Reed said to Ellen, "Wow, that really worked. Kudos to your Mugwump pal."

"Being in the group does have its advantages," she said.

As this was happening, Oscar Renalli, head of the campus police, was standing on Locust Street, having a conversation with a very angry student. "This is University Parking only."

"But I just bought this parking pass," the girl said, pointing to it in the BMW's window. "It's good for the whole year."

"Look, I believe you," Renalli said, not believing her, "but the computer says the number's invalid. So I gotta give you a ticket."

"$250?" the student said, looking at the orange slip of paper. "How the fuck am I supposed to—"

Renalli raised a hand. "Please, miss, no profanities," he said. "You can appeal it."

"Where am I supposed to park in the meantime?" she shouted. "I can't leave it on the street. My car'll be up on blocks in two hours." She was right—Great Littleton was the car theft capitol of the Northeast.

"Should'a thought of that before," Chief Renalli said wearily, getting into his new golf cart.

"But I did! That's why I bought a—" Seeing that Renalli wasn't listening, the girl became enraged. She made a lips-shut growl as she kicked the cart's tire. *"Mm!"* Then she gave two more kicks. *"Mm! Mm!"*

"Hey!" Renalli said. "That's University property!"

He and the girl stared at each other. Finally, she stuck her tongue out at him, got into her doomed car and huffily drove away.

Renalli looked at the tire—there was no damage, thank goodness. The cart was brand new; he'd just picked it up from the customizers; the job took quite a chunk out of the department's budget, but if you want a cool ride, you gotta pay for it. Professor North would probably tell him that flaming skulls "weren't appropriate" but that old geezer could blow it out his…

"Oscar!" Provost Rivington ran up to the cart, panting but jubilant. "Oscar, get over to Truax! There's been some sort of riot!"

"What do you want me to do about it?" Renalli turned the key, and the cart was bathed in pre-recorded engine noise, the unmufflered rumble of a V-12.

"You're—could you turn that down?" Rivington shouted.

After a quick mental scan of the University chain-of-command, Renalli complied.

"Just reestablish order," Rivington said. "Arrest some people, fire your gun into the air. That thing's got a bullhorn, right?"

Renalli grabbed the mic and spoke into it. "HELL YES," he said.

Rivington jumped. Deafened, he continued. "Rioting's a crime—look for clues to see who's behind it."

Renalli listened, breathing into the mic. "ALL RIGHT," Renalli said. "I'LL CHECK IT OUT." Riots could be lucrative. People dropped wallets in riots.

"Thanks!" The Provost took off again. As Chief Renalli executed a leisurely three-point-turn, snarling traffic in both directions, Rivington turned back and yelled, "The Lord works in mysterious ways!"

Halfway through the prank, Hart and Tabitha had become distracted—they had put down the banner, and were investigating some placards the Stutts Marching Experience had made for a long-forgotten Kama Sutra-themed halftime show.

"This position is called, 'Water Buffalo Grinds Millet," Hart said. Coming up with something Tabitha wasn't totally bored with (after more than a century of sex) was a challenge. "Looks tough," Hart said.

"Did it," Tabitha said. "Me and Dwight Eisenhower. Or was it Marcel Duchamp?"

"Okay, how about this one?" Hart flipped the cards one after the other. "'Elephant Ascending Lotus.'"

"Done it—" Tabitha said, "—done it—done it—ooo, rugburn, still have the mark—refused to do it—tried to do it, tore my ACL—"

"Yikes," Hart said. "Ever notice how it's the woman who has to bend like a pretzel?"

"Damn patriarchy," Tabitha said. "First, the doorknobs, and now this."

"Let's make it ladies' choice," Hart said. "Consider it reparations."

"Your mother would be proud of you," Tabitha said. "I'm really looking forward to meeting her on Parents' Weekend."

Hart sighed. "And there goes the boner..."

Tabitha cocked an ear. "What was that?"

"I didn't hear anything." There wasn't much blood near Hart's ears.

Tabitha heard it again: Peter's whistle. "Oh shit! Where did you put your phone?"

"Over there," Hart said. "Maybe it fell behind those boxes."

Tabitha scurried over to a bunch of boxes containing props and uniforms and began digging around. "We're never going to hear the end of this!" With every whistle, the couple got more frantic. Tabitha waved at Hart. "Go over to the window to look for cops."

Hart crouched in the lee of the window, cupping his groin.

"For God's sake, Hart, who cares if somebody sees your johnson!"

Hart reached for the binoculars with his free hand—and deftly knocked them out the window. "Tab, I—"

"Found it!" Tabitha flipped the phone open. "Can I whistle back?"

" I—" Hart was unwilling to trust his vision, which was notoriously faulty.

"Is the coast clear?" she barked. "Do you see any cops?"

"Uh—" Hart squinted. Was that a cop? No, it was a statue...Was that thing a dumpster or a cop cart?

"HART!"

Hart took a wild guess. "Yeah, sure. He can go."

When Chief Constable Renalli pulled up to Truax, he found himself surrounded by freshmen claiming they'd just seen Satan.

They were more elated than fearful; the appearance of Beelzebub himself was yet another way Stutts totally ruled. "Do you think he bothers with state schools? *Please.*" The smart money was betting that Old Scratch would torment them again in four years, at graduation. "We're the 'Class of Satan', dude!" T-shirts were already in the works.

Ranelli wasn't so sure. It smelled like a prank to him. First, the whatchacallit did one every year, and second, his right knee was aching. The other campus cops teased him, but that knee was practically money when it came to ferreting out student mischief. Of course, the media went wild the one time he'd been wrong: two graduations ago, he'd tackled Nelson Mandela, convinced it was a notorious student prankster. Everybody screamed "police brutality," but nobody mentioned how Mr. Nonviolent had let his bodyguards get in a few discreet kidney shots. Liberals were so hypocritical.

Renalli walked around the perimeter of the building, then went inside. After pocketing four wallets, two necklaces, and a valuable-looking ring, Renalli hitched up his belt, and ambled around to the back.

Since this was going to be *The Cuckoo*'s only ass-kicking prank of the year, Peter savored the mayhem for as long as possible. Then, working quickly but carefully, he packed all his gear into his backpack and attached it to the back of his wheelchair. Picking his way through a sea of flattened folding chairs (this was where Buildings & Grounds stored all the junk for graduation), Peter got to the basement door. He opened it a crack; the alley looked empty. He turned on his phone, and whistled. Nothing.

So he tried again. And again.

Goddamn Hart and his libido, Peter thought. I oughta just go for it…Then there was the sound of someone fumbling the phone, and Tabitha whistled back. The coast was clear.

Except it wasn't. Just as Peter rolled through the door, Chief Constable Renalli rounded the corner.

Renalli nearly whooped with joy—for once, he'd caught a student red-handed! That meant they could *punish* him, no matter what confusing, snobby answers he gave! The Truax basement was a restricted area, just like the steam tunnels, and being in a restricted area was an automatic trip to the Chamber.

As Peter motored away, Renalli considered making the cuff right there. The cop's heart said "yes," but his bad knee said "no." For the umpteenth time, Renalli wished he had a boomerang with a taser attachment. Then he remembered the digital camera Professor North had just given him. It was for blackmail purposes only, but Renalli decided to make an exception.

"Smile, punk." There would be no denying it this year: Peter's wheelchair had a novelty license plate: "*Cuckoo.*"

4

Ignorance Was Bliss

Wednesday, September 1 @ 3:43 pm

As with any other gazillion-dollar operation, the right hand of Stutts seldom knew what its left hand was doing. So even though Peter had been caught dead to rights, Chief Constable Renalli's photo had to trickle its way through the bowels of the University, stopping at this department and that, before it could solidify into a crisis. Only at that point could it be excreted all over our heroes. For several days after the prank, the members of *The Cuckoo* lived in blissful ignorance, unaware of what was about to hit the fan.

Everything was groovy during "Shopping Period," the week in which Stutts students browsed possible classes for the semester. Homework was minimal, discipline nonexistent. Life was perfect…for the moment. The prank had made the Cuckonians campus celebrities, as least to the upperclassmen—they, unlike many freshmen, knew to attribute the hijinks to the humor magazine and not Beelzebub. Sure, the *Spec* sounded its usual sour, self-important notes, but nobody read the Op-Ed page.

"Gwen Talbot and Miles Monaghan are irritating enough in person," Peter said as he and Hart strolled across campus on their way to a prospective class. "Their editorials are stupidity in its purest form. Like a crystal."

Hart put on a TV pitchman's voice. "Want some idiocy, but you can't find a member of the *Spec* E-Board? Now, you can take the idiocy with you!" The boys laughed. Dissing the *Spec* was something they could always agree on.

Stutts was at full power. Every patch of grass—even the ones marked with red insecticide flags—had a student lolling on it, soaking up the sun. People crouched on the flagstones, bits of chalk in hand, scrawling advertisements for groups. On this corner, the pitch of The Meistersingers handed out flyers for their inaugural concert; on that corner, someone from one of Stutts' million mime troupes silently bellowed Fall Rush. A girl sitting on the low wall next to Harriman Library waved at Hart and Peter as they passed. "Good job!" she yelled. "My little sister wet her pants!"

"Glad to hear it!" Hart hollered back, while Peter bowed as best he could, given his seated posture. Hart may not have enjoyed doing the prank, but he did like the notoriety. This shot of confidence made him even more excited about his plans for the magazine. Hart had spent the morning talking to gruff-voiced newsstand distributors all over the country, telling them about his idea, then asking —"just theoretically, you understand"—how many copies they'd be willing to stock. All the estimates added up to more than 250,000 copies.

"...and that's just the initial run," Hart babbled as they walked. "Who knows how many they'll want if it starts to sell!"

Peter didn't say anything.

"Did you hear what I said?" Hart asked. "250,000 copies!"

"I heard you," Peter replied.

"Then what part of '250,000-freakin'-copies' do you not understand?"

"I think it's great—for what it's worth."

Hart was a little put off. "What it's worth is maybe a million bucks into our pocket!" Hart said, trying to defibrillate the conversation. "Pete, this could make us."

Peter shot him a glance. "Do you mean 'you,' or *The Cuckoo*?"

"Both!" Hart said. Why was Peter being a dick?

"Look," Peter said, "I'm all for doing the project, but how are we going to pay for it? We don't have enough money in the bank to pay both your tuition and print up 250,000 copies."

"That's why I have a term-time job."

"At what, fifteen bucks an hour?" Peter said. "And what if it's successful, how many more will we have to print then? A million?"

"But if they're selling, y'see, we'll automatically have enough money to pay for them."

Peter was getting a little exasperated. "You obviously didn't read that link I sent you," he said hotly. "We'll still have 90 days between when Joe Schmoe buys the mag and we get paid for it. Do you want to ask our printer for a loan? 'Cause I don't," Peter said. "I like my kneecaps." Peter was convinced their printer was Mob-owned.

Hart had a trump card, which he decided to pull out. "I didn't want to tell you this, because I don't know all the details," Hart said, "but have you heard of the World Domination Fund?"

Peter paused. "I think so...but refresh me."

"The World Domination Fund is a fund of money set up way back. It's kept by the University to help its undergrads dominate the world. It funds projects and stuff—all you have to do is apply for it. But since nobody knows about it, nobody applies."

"Interesting," Peter said.

"No doubt!"

"No way there'd be enough," Peter said. "I mean, we'd need a mint."

"They probably have a mint. It's Stutts."

"Every so often," Peter said, "I realize why I go here. May I ask how you discovered this? One of Ellen's Stutts history lessons?" (Their fellow Cuckonian was always spilling some arcane fact about the school; collecting them was her hobby.)

"I was in the Library this morning, reading back issues of the *Spec*."

"God! *Why?*" Peter asked. "Cyanide's quicker."

"Did you know Quinn Bostwick's first movie was funded by the WDF?"

"You're obsessed with that guy. Hey," Peter asked, "how was 'Tanya and Vanya'?"

At Stutts, as at every college, noteworthy classes had nicknames: Rocks for Jocks, Tropes for Dopes, PoMo for Homos, the list was endless. "Tanya and Vanya" was a husband and wife—she a radical Communist, he a rabid Fascist—who team-taught a survey of 20th Century history, analyzing everything from their opposing viewpoints. Students loved it: the professors became so enraged at each other, they often forgot to assign homework. What little *did* get assigned was absurdly freeform, borne of apoplectic splutterings like, "Write 5-7 pages on why my husband should be the first one up against the wall!"[15]

"It was fucking absurd," Hart said. "I felt like I was watching *Who's Afraid of Virginia Woolf II: The Final Chapter*. How was Professor 'the Peen'?"

"As crazy as advertised," Peter said. Professor 'the Peen' was a once-respected biologist who had been struck by lightning while golfing. Ever since, he had been gripped by a single obsession: all activity on this planet took place solely to service the sexual organs. "The mouth exists merely to deliver water and essential nutrients to 'the Peen.' Clothes warm 'the Peen,' and, if sufficiently colorful, attract it a suitable mate." It was mind-numbingly repetitive; and to some, highly offensive.

"Some women presented him with a petition," Peter said, "asking Professor 'the Peen' to say 'the 'Gine,' 52% of the time, to reflect the world's population."

"Seems fair to me," Hart said.

"Not to Professor 'the Peen,'" Peter said. "He went berserk. Some dudes

15 "Tanya" was so nicknamed because she had been the first poor-little-rich-girl kidnapped by the Symbionese Liberation Army back in 1973. Then her father had lost everything in the Oil Shock, and "Tanya" was dumped at the bus station, with not so much as a "thanks for playing" and a version of the home game. Unlike Patty Hearst, Tanya never recanted her Marxist beliefs. Her husband "Vanya" was the nickname of her husband, a one-time Red-Diaper baby from Brooklyn, who lucked into an IPO in the mid-Eighties and never looked back.

was filming it. Apparently it's like an annual event—they ask, he explodes. There's an archive of past freak-outs on YouTube."

Hart chuckled. "You going to take the class?"

"Heck, no!" Peter said, as they arrived at Lytton Hall. "I get enough nuttiness from you, Quinn Jr."

"Don't call me that," Hart said, embarrassed. The boys rode the orange-walled elevator to the sixth floor.

"Why does it always smell funny in this building?" Hart said to their fellow riders. He turned to a fuscia-haired Asian girl standing next to him. "Does it smell funny to you?"

She pulled the earbuds out of her ears. "What?"

"Nothing," Hart said, feeling stupid. The doors opened and they walked out.

"Why are we here?" Peter said. "I've heard this guy's a tool."

"Unquestionably. But he's also famous," Hart said. "If you hang around famous people, sometimes it rubs off. Maybe he can help me find an agent."

"What a shame," Peter teased. "Selling out so early…"

"Shut up, blowhole. It's not my fault the world doesn't come up to your standards," Hart said. "Some of us *want* to be successful. If I'm more ambitious than I used to be, it's your fault." That was true; it was mainly thanks to the sales of his book that Hart, a Study of Things major, was considering doing a concentration in Orthographical Sequencing (which sounded so much more academic than "writing"). There was a rumor that any undergrad who got a book published could apply his or her sales for extra-credit.

When Hart and Peter arrived in the small, wood-paneled seminar room—the kind Stutts reserved for hardcore academic action—Professor Lemonade hadn't shown up. Yes, that was the teacher's name; he'd chosen it while in this very classroom as an undergrad, five years ago. Looking for a memorable, one-name moniker, senior Joshua Barrigan of Lemonade College had an epiphany: "Everybody likes lemonade," and 1,000,000 copies later, that much was undisputable. For in this very classroom, pretending to take copious notes, Lemonade had started writing a memoir, *The Scintillating Story of Me.*

Filled with vivid descriptions of pet death, anime addiction, and unfulfilling internships, *Me* became the *Mein Kampf* of the junior-lit set. Literary but not difficult, disaffected but still a good quote, Lemonade had become somewhat rich, and gossip-magazine famous. (He even had a sex tape.)

Though Hart's heart belonged to Quinn Bostwick, he was willing to go the Lemonade route if necessary. His own *roman a flunkie* was taking shape in his mind, based on his tour of duty with the crustaceans. And Hart wasn't alone: every student in the room (except for Peter, who was just being Hart's wingman) had a similar manuscript ready to dump on Lemonade.

As the seconds mounted without a professor, the atmosphere in the room began to get sticky. In situations like this, whenever they were unsure what to do, Stuttsies started picking at each other, making they were first in line for whatever treat came next. Since none of them had read each other's work yet, everybody was reduced to criticizing the size and formatting of each other's manuscripts.

"You ought to put it in a serif," a girl two chairs away from Peter said to the boy next to her. "It's a lot easier to read."

"I prefer the clean compression of a sans," the boy replied. "It keeps the manuscript from becoming"—he paused to let the venom collect—"overweight."

Next to them, another couple sparred. "Any reason why you stapled instead of using brads?" a boy said. "There's a sort of naïf charm to it, I suppose…"

"I picked it up from my dad," the girl replied matter-of-factly, then pushed the nuclear button. "He's a famous screenwriter. Dad's agent says he'll sell anything I give him, so I'm taking this class."

Peter's major ("The DaVinci Program," a brand new multidisciplinary course) had its fair share of assholes, but this was ridiculous. Finally, he could take no more, and leaned over to Hart. "I'll wait for you downstairs," he said, and headed towards the door. When Peter got there, he bumped into a lanky, unshaven man in a jacket so tattered and filthy that it was more fungus than tweed.

"Excuse me," Peter mumbled. "I'm in the wrong room." He rolled away quickly, afraid that the jacket would extend an amoeba-like pseudopod and slurp him into the Mother Colony.

Lemonade's class was blessedly short; for various reasons, the celebrity lecturer was angling to be fired, and hoped a display of disinterest and disdain would end the seminar before it had begun. Unfortunately, that's not how Stutts students worked. They smelled a "gut"—an easy class—and by the time Lemonade had shambled out the door, Hart had penciled the seminar into his schedule.

Now he and Peter were walking back to their dorm, with a stop at the post office. "Say we got the money from the World Domination Fund to do the parody," Peter said as they crossed the heat-shimmered expanse of green tarmac that was New Quad, "there's still issues and stuff to pay for."

"Piece of cake," Hart said. "We invite people to speak at Dacron. College Conversations are the easiest money around. Master Wilkinson'll pay us $500 in advertising for every celebrity we bring to campus."

"Right," Peter nodded. "Got anybody in mind?"

"No," Hart lied.

"C'mon, don't play hard to get," Peter said. "How about Quinn Bostwick? He's hugely hot right now."

"Oh, he'd never come," Hart said, not daring to dream.

"Of course he would, niblick," Peter said. "It's Stutts, we're students, he's an old Cuckonian. I'll bet you fifty bucks he comes."

"If you feel that strongly," Hart said, trying to conceal his berserk joy at the mere possibility, "I guess I could write him a letter."

"You guess you could...Tell him you're his 'number one fan.'"

"Very funny," Hart said. "Listen, if he comes, we gotta make sure that issue of the magazine is great. People on campus have to love it."

"If he comes," Peter said cynically, "everybody will. Stuttsies are sheep."

Delicious air-conditioning hit them like a fuzzy wall. The campus post office—invariably shortened to "the P.O."—was a relic of an earlier age, a Gilded Age retreat created by the University, a place for Stutts students to clip and mail bond coupons without being hassled by poor people.

Nowdays, though, the P.O. was as faded and sad as an old movie house. The bar[16] had long since been ripped out, along with all the leather couches and Waterford chandeliers, but you could still see faintly lighter squares on the wall, where the oil paintings of famous alums had hung. The campus was littered with places like these, where Stutts' WASPariffic past had been sincerely but clumsily retooled to fit more democratic times—as if the only thing keeping the college from being an egalitarian paradise was a bit too much Tiffany and marble. Hart found this sweet, like a society matron with a fetish for ditch-diggers.

Hart and Peter saw Ellen at the other end of the row of mailboxes, sketching a wall for her "Stories of Old Stutts" class. Ellen saw them and waved.

"Five dollars she starts off with a Stutts fact," Peter said.

"You're betting-crazy today," Hart said.

"Hey guys!" Ellen said. "Did you know they had a masseuse on duty here until the 50s?" he said.

"I win," Peter said.

16 During the 1870s, when the P.O. was being planned, a few Stutts students—scions of prominent local families—had been discovered sleeping off a drunk in a notorious local honky-tonk. The administration immediately incorporated a bar into the P.O., to provide Stutts students with a place to quench their thirst without mingling with the masses.

"No, you don't," Hart said. "She started with 'Hey guys!'"

"Come on!" Peter said, aggrieved. "I'm continuing under protest."

"What's up?" Ellen said.

"Nothing," Peter said. "Hart just owes me five bucks, that's all."

"Blow me," Hart said.

"We'll talk about this later," Peter said, then turned to Ellen. "Taking a break from your senior project?" Peter said. Every Stutts student had to produce some massive thing to graduate; what, exactly, depended on the major. With the help of her advisor, famed scientist Ernst Yttrium, Ellen was attempting to create nanobots. With luck, her microscopic, solar-powered manservants might well change the world (or at least fight off the germs she loathed).

"Oh, yeah," Ellen said. "I had a terrible morning. My 'bots were being total brats. First they insisted I say 'please.' Then, whatever I asked them to do, they'd do the opposite. Finally they wouldn't answer unless I guessed their 'secret names.'"

"That's something, though—right?" Hart asked. What people like Ellen and Peter did—the activities of the entire Science tribe—was completely opaque to him.

Ellen picked something out of her hair. "They threw cream of wheat at me; I need to go home and take a shower." As she left, Ellen dispensed a final fact. "They used to have showers here, you know. There was a whole other wing, modeled on the Baths of Caracalla..."

"It's cute," Hart said after she was gone, "Ellen still doesn't believe she got in."

"Even sitting in the Mugwumps' Pyramid," Peter said acidly. Peter came from a long line of Mugwumps, and his familiarity had bred contempt.

"Did you and Ellen ever get together, over the summer?" Hart asked. "I saw you share that espresso. She never lets anybody drink from her glass."

"No comment," Peter said.

"Beneath that lab coat beats the heart of a woman," Hart cracked.

"And lots of 'bots," Peter said blandly.

Hart kept pushing. "Do it for humanity, Pete. You're the only one who understands her research. If she doesn't get laid, I'm afraid she'll turn evil. Only you can prevent Dr. Doom."

"I don't 'do' Mugwumps," Peter said.

"She's only half-Wump. The other half is *Cuckoo*."

Unlike Peter, Hart saw the Mugwumps' appeal; no one elitist enough to attend Stutts could be totally immune. But Peter was so elitist he was in danger of ripping the Time/Space continuum; he resented even the suggestion that some outside group, no matter how impressive, would dare to restrict his behavior. Peter thought Hart was too susceptible to the Mugwumps' allure—it was all part of Hart's "wanting to be liked" go-getterishness, which Peter was beginning to hate. Still, Peter admitted that the Mugwumps were powerful—he saw their hand in every front page. He truly believed (for example) that the Euro was a Mugwump conspiracy. "Maybe she gets a 'friends-and-family discount on the exchange rate?" Hart joked. "She could make you rich…"

"I'm already rich," Peter said.

"Good point." Hart wondered if Peter really believed all the conspiracy theories he spouted, or whether the Mugwumps were just a convenient stand-in for his father, with whom he didn't get along. So Hart changed the subject. "Hey, Pete," he said, "wanna shop 'History as Psychodrama' with me tomorrow?"

"Nah, I gotta start designing the poster for our organizational meeting."

"Shit, I totally forgot that was Thursday."

Peter looked at his watch. "Twenty-five hours and counting." *The Cuckoo* was merciless; things might lighten up once the annual influx of new staffers came in, but until they were trained, everything fell on the shoulders of Peter and Hart.

Hart sighed. "I don't know how Reed and Ellen did it—imagine it being just you and me, for two-and-a-half years…"

"Two words: murder/suicide." Peter reached into his mailbox, a little cube with a filigreed door of onyx and jet, a relic of the P.O.'s past. He pulled out a letter; it looked official.

"Christ, Peter, stop winning scholarships," Hart said when he saw it. "Leave some money for people who need it." Hart opened his box, and found the very same letter. He flipped the letter over. There was no return address.

"What the fuck?" Hart tore it open, and a picture fell to the ground. Hart picked it up and looked at it. It was Peter's wheelchair from the back, with a date and time stamp. Then Hart read the letter:

> "Hart Fox DC '09
> Box 5468 Stutts Station
> Great Littleton, US Autonomous Region[17]

17 Through a quirk of international relations, Great Littleton had been presented as a gift to Queen Victoria. She had, very sensibly, refused it—but as the entire gambit was designed to help the states of Connecticut, Massachusetts and Rhode Island, each of which had refused the troublesome and squalid city, the Queen's snubbing left Great Littleton in a cartographic/political gray area, which persists to this day. "US Autonomous Region" was everybody's best guess.

Via campus mail
Dear Mr. Fox:

The actions of *The Cuckoo* student magazine at last week's Freshman Assembly were in violation of the University Code of Conduct. Though the total of violated rules reaches well into the hundreds, I call your attention to these few, each one of which carries significant punishments:

6a. *"Endangering the lives of students, faculty, or administrators."*
13r. *"A misuse, or unauthorized use, of University facilities."*
21b. *"Conduct deleterious to the dignity of the University."*

This letter is a formal request for you, and the other editors of *The Cuckoo* student magazine, to appear at a disciplinary hearing tomorrow at 9:00 am at The Chamber. The Chamber is located at 36 The Avenue of Our Glorious Insect Overlords. Failure to appear will result in immediate expulsion.

Though legal representation is not required, it can be permitted with prior approval from the Disciplinary Committee. I have included a photo taken of you by Chief Constable Oscar Renalli, directly after the riot that you and the others so irresponsibly caused. If you would like to dispute this evidence, you may do so at the hearing.

Sincerely,
Glenbard North
Acting Chief Justice, Displinary Cmte.

P.S.—Your parents are receiving a copy of this letter, which is also being placed in your permanent file."

Hart's stomach dropped to the floor. "My mom and dad are gonna *shit.*"

"That's the last thing you should be worried about," Peter said. He whipped his wheelchair around and took off full-blast towards the doors.

"Hey! Wait up!" Hart chased after him. "Where are we going?"

"To the bank!"

"Why?" Hart said, a few steps behind (in both senses).

"Your book money's still in *The Cuckoo*'s bank account," Peter said, barreling onto the sidewalk and almost crashing into a mime. "We gotta take it out before the University freezes the account." Peter singlemindedly launched himself into traffic, holding up a palm. Nobody stopped—they never did—but somehow he made it through. Seeing no alternative, Hart followed.

"They can't do that!" Hart said, dodging a grad student in a beat-up

Karmann-Ghia. "How do they expect me to pay tuition? What if we need to hire a lawyer?"

"Exactly," Peter barked. "Grab on to the back. I'm going turbo."

◦ ◦ ◦

Thanks to Peter's consummate skill (and rampant violation of traffic laws), they got to the bank seconds before it closed. Hart took the certified check over toTabitha's. They hid it inside her "If you don't have anything nice to say, come sit next to me" sampler-pillow.

But it wasn't the thought of sleeping on a six-figure check that kept Hart up all night, nor was it Tabitha's obsessive re-playing of "The Mikado." It was this: if *The Cuckoo* was put on probation tomorrow, the World Domination Fund would be off-limits to them, and all his grand plans would come crashing down. They would—*he* would—be back to square one. Laying there on Tabitha's futon, with his girlfriend snoring demurely beside him, Hart couldn't think of anything worse.

Lucky him!

5

Stutts Justice

Thursday, September 2, 8:37 AM

You won't find "the Chamber" listed on any campus map, not even under its proper name, The Steve and Trudy Hathorne '66 Memorial Courtroom. Yet if one place could be considered the soul of Stutts, that place where the past, present and future of the institution all hung out together, the Chamber was it. For as long as Stutts enrolled students, some percentage would cry out for punishment; the Chamber was where the hammer was brought down.

At first light, Hart had walked from Tabitha's crypt in the cemetery to his and Peter's room in Dacron temporary housing. For an hour, he sat in the dining hall trying to eat. Everything tasted like ass.

It was surreal; Hart saw all the people coming in, happy, acting like it was just another day. The usual earlybirds read the newspaper in their usual seats. Somebody dropped a glass. A guy in Stutts Sailing sweats bellowed, "We're out of Froot Loops!" A woman swore as her bread got caught in the back of the conveyor-belt toaster. Students with bulging backpacks trundled past, starting the long walk to the science buildings. Sipping a bitter-tasting orange juice, Hart realized Stutts would go on, regardless of what happened to him. This pissed him off, so he took an apple and left.

Listening to Peter snore was only marginally better. He tried to write—a "Chamber Diary" would be just the thing for the next issue—but couldn't. There may not be a next issue, he mused glumly. They couldn't really close down *The Cuckoo*, could they? Tabitha's opinion had been that they could, and she listed several depressing historical precedents.

"But those were all dangerous," Hart had said to Tabitha, hours before. "*Student Bombmaking Quarterly*? I would've shut that down, too! *The Cuckoo*'s just a humor magazine."

"Which caused a riot," Tabitha said.

"A little one! Whose side are you on?"

"Don't get me wrong, Hart I like the occasional disturbance, it keeps me from getting bored. But the University doesn't."

"What about my plans?" Hart said, thoroughly miserable. "This was going to be my year."

"It's the University's year, goofy," Tabitha said. "It's always their year. Now go to sleep."

"Impossible," Hart grumbled, and it had been.

Sitting in his common room hours later, Hart closed his eyes, but found he couldn't sleep there either. Finally it was time to get ready; Hart took a shower and got dressed. His button-down was clean, but it was as wrinkled as an old lady's bottom.

"Nice shirt," Peter said, adjusting his tie in front of their Putz Ice beer mirror, a memento of happier times.

"Don't fuck with me today, Pete, I can't take it," Hart said. "Christ! I can never do this! Do you really think we need to wear ties?"

"Absolutely," Peter said.

This made Hart even more nervous; Peter didn't observe social customs, and reserved his most withering comments to people who did. To see him so anxious about making a good impression was straight-out terrifying. "Here, let me do it," he said. "I'm sick of watching you screw up."

Peter set to work. Hart swallowed to give him more room. "Did any of your relatives get hauled before the Chamber?" Hart asked. He was trying to keep the silence from filling up with dread.

"Only the ones that got expelled."

"You had relatives that got expelled?" Hart exclaimed. Expulsion from Stutts was almost unheard of. "What the hell did they do?"

"My great-great-uncle Jonathan tried to blow up the old Freshman Commons," Peter said. "He got pissed off when Stutts declared its neutrality during the Civil War."

Hart was genuinely impressed. "Your relatives are cool."

"Only the dead ones," Peter said. "Ol' Jon-o lit the fuse, then had a change of heart, so he whizzed on it. The papers called it 'The Micturation Affair.'" Peter pulled away, finished with Hart's tie.

Hart checked the knot; it looked good. "Thanks. What's Freshman Commons?"

"Where everybody used to eat," Peter said, rolling into the hall. "They knocked it down when they built Stutts Field. That's where the Chamber is, five stories under the 50-yard line…I don't know about you, but I need some caffeine."

"None for me," Hart said. "My stomach hurts already."

They swung by the dining hall, but the coffee seemed to worsen Peter's mood, not improve it. "Burnt mud, as usual." As the prank's creator, as well as its mission control, Peter suspected he would get the worst of it. And frankly, the idea of the Chamber gave him the creeps: a little brick tomb hacked out of the stony New England soil, centuries old…he'd read too much H.P. Lovecraft as a kid to like the idea of that. As he and Hart walked in the incongruous sunshine Peter said, "My grandfather told me the Chamber was where they used to torture students suspected of being Quakers."

"Maybe the ghosts leaked out and cursed Stutts Field," Hart said, trying to cheer Peter up so his own mood would improve. "It explains the football team."

"Nah. They just suck," Peter said. "I read in the *Spec* yesterday that our quarterback is blind in one eye."

The light changed and they walked across the street. One entered the Chamber via an old subway station[18] that had long ago been converted to University offices; now it housed the Romance Languages department. Peter and Hart lingered outside the doors, waiting for Reed and Ellen.

Hart was relieved to find that certain parts of him were less miserable than others. "Is it me," he whispered to Peter, "or are all these grad students fantastically hot?" Some of them were coiffed and stylish, others looked like they'd just rolled out of bed, but every one seemed to exude the same killer Euro-sexy vibe.

To take their minds off of the ordeal to come, the boys started guessing the nationality of all the hotties that walked in. "French." "Italian, definitely Italian." "Spanish!"

Hormones worked where humor hadn't. "If we get out of this, I am *totally* taking a language," Peter said, showing his first spark of the morning.

Something was poking Hart's shoe. He looked down and saw a rat, one of Tabitha's pets. There was a slip of paper under the pink ribbon around its neck.

"Tab sent us a note," he said.

"I predict there are little hearts over the 'i's," Peter said.

"Naturally," Hart said. Tabitha was so girly, especially for a member of the undead. Hart reached down and slipped the note free, then skritched the rat on the head like he'd seen Tabitha do. Hart read aloud: "'Whatever happens, keep this in mind: all of my most famous boyfriends got kicked out.'"

18 During one of the town's brief spasms of prosperity, a wildly rich alumnus had constructed a private subway line connecting his Great Littleton mansion to New York City, where his wife liked to shop. After the alum died, he bequeathed the mansion and its private subway to Stutts. The mansion was torn down almost immediately (even in 1915 space was scarce in downtown Great Littleton), but the subway was kept. In fact, by 1923, the University had expanded it to include stops at several women's colleges. Peter's family manufactured the train cars, which were comfortable and elegantly appointed; there was even a speakeasy. Out of sight of God and their parents, males and females mingled, and the obvious occurred with ever-increasing frequency.

"Kicked out? Shit, could she be more discouraging?" Peter said.

"She was just trying to be funny," Hart said. "When you've lived as long as she has, your sense of humor gets weird. Did she tell you about the prank that killed a bunch of people?"

"I don't need to hear that story right now, okay?"

"Don't get sharp with me, Pete. *You're* the reason we're here."

"No, I'm not," Peter said. "It was Ellen's fucking Wumps-friend. How was I supposed to know that Whitty would freak out?"

"So it's the Mugwumps' fault? As usual? How fucking convenient!" Hart hissed. "Pete, because of you, my whole year, my whole plan—" Hart was about to tear into Pete, but then felt a tapping on the top of his newly shined loafer. The rat-messenger wanted a tip, so Hart tore a little piece off his unfinished apple and handed it over.

"You shouldn't feed that," a gruff, accented voice said. "It's vermin."

Ernst Yttrium, Ellen's advisor and one of Stutts' Pantheon of academic gods, was out for a morning stroll.

"It's okay, Professor Yttrium, we know him," Peter said.

"That is what they all say. Don't come crying to me when you get with the bubonic plague," the professor snorted. "I hoped that you had more sense, Armbruster," Yttrium said, and walked away. He was followed by a stream of groceries that seemed to be carrying themselves.

Hart pointed at the groceries. "I guess Ellen worked the kinks out of her nano-bots."

Peter grunted, glum again; he'd hoped to work with Yttrium his senior year. Stutts really was full of wonders, Peter thought, and the possibility of having to leave it, however remote, darkened his mood even further. It wasn't our fault Whitbread was a psycho, he thought. "If I'm going to get kicked out, I want it to be over something important, like Uncle Jonathan."

"Look on the bright side—getting expelled would really piss off your parents."

"They'd just send me to Keasbey. Same school, different address."

Normally, these were fighting words. As it was, Hart didn't even respond.

Looking uncannily like adults, Reed and Ellen came into view. Ellen was waving a piece of paper excitedly.

After the Crash, the rest of the country looked on such upper-class frolicking with less favor, and it was clear that the heyday of what Stutts students called "the Pipeline" was over. The womens' college stations were the first to go; this made New York the sole focus of Stutts' students revelry, and within five years, that city was fed up as well. In 1937, Mayor Fiorello LaGuardia grinned at the newsreels as he poured in the ceremonial first shovelful of concrete.

"Good morning, Neville Chamberlain," Hart said. (Study of Things was great for giving your wisecracks a high-culture sheen.)

Reed, a History major, got the reference. "You're in a good mood for someone about to be on probation."

"If we're lucky," Peter said. "I wouldn't be surprised if I got expelled."

"Me either," Reed said. "Ellen and I ran the magazine for years without a problem, and in one week, you get me hauled in front of the Chamber."

"Blow it out your ass," Peter growled. "You wanted to do the prank just as much as I did."

"Stop that, you two!" Ellen said, in a tone of voice usually reserved for bickering children (or nanobots). "We're going to get off."

"Probation, you mean?" Peter asked.

"Not even that. Just a reprimand, probably," Ellen said. "We won't miss an issue."

Hart's heart leaped. "What about the college-ranking parody?"

"We could still do it. The WDF doesn't say anything about reprimands," Ellen said, supremely confident. "I've got the hook up. I talked to somebody in my group"—"Mugwumps" was understood—"who was called to the Chamber two years ago."

"Oh, great," Peter said in a cutting tone of voice. "Let's trust the same people who got us here in the first place."

Hart jumped in, to forestall a fight—and keep his own flicker of hope alive. "Hey Ellen, we saw Professor Yttrium with a bunch of your little dudes."

Ellen gave Hart's attempt a polite smile, then turned to Peter. "You'd like Don Quixote.[19] He stole the Keasbey Beaver last year." (A bronze rendering of Keasbey's mascot sat on that school's main quadrangle; stealing it had been a goal of Stutts students for 150 years. Last year, it had disappeared right before the first Stutts-Keasbey basketball game.)

"Stole it?" Peter said. "It must weigh a ton."

"*Two* tons," Ellen said. "He miniaturized it somehow, won't tell me how. Just stuck it in his pocket and walked off. We've been sending it to alums all over the world, who pose it in famous locations. Then we send the picture back to the *Keasbey Daily Khronicle*. It drives them crazy."

"But I saw the statue over the summer," Reed said. He was considering law school at Keasbey; for any Stuttsie, career trumped school spirit.

"It's fake," Ellen said. "Totally plastic. You can tell if you lick it." Ellen's mania for experiment made her do some strange things. "Anyway, Don Q

19 Not his real name, but his club name. All Wumpspeople had very special, super-secret club names, given to them upon admittance. Ellen's was "Madame Curie."

says if we follow this script, everything will be all right. Shall we go in?"

Without a word, the group walked out of the sun and sea breeze into the dusty darkness of the lobby. Ahead of them was the circuitous walk down to the Chamber, and their ultimate fate.

◦ ◦ ◦

To calm everybody's nerves, Reed picked up a brochure in the lobby, and read it to them as they descended the stairs. "What Studio 54 was to disco-era Manhattan, the Chamber was to Great Littleton in the late 1600s," he read. "One judge became so famous that his distinctive 'I sentence you to bu-u-urn!' became Colonial America's first catch-phrase."

"I don't think I believe that," Hart said.

Reed kept reading. "The facility ran 24/7, like a steelmill during wartime. Not only did the University rent it out to local groups wanting to interrogate their enemies in a private, professional atmosphere, there was the college's own witch problem to keep under control."

"Witch problem?" Hart said. "Don't they mean vampires?"

"Just let him read, Hart," Ellen said. "We can have question-and-answer time later."

"Back in those days," Reed continued, "anyone possessing knowledge that was the least bit unusual—geometry, French, personal hygiene—was suspected of trafficking with the Devil. This tended to keep the lid on Stutts' students level of academic attainment; if drink and natural torpor weren't enough to discourage studying, being burned at the stake certainly was."

"I like whoever wrote this brochure," Ellen said. "It's saucy."

"Agreed," Reed said, then read on. "Witch-mania pervaded Stutts for decades longer than in the rest of New England. This was partly due to the university's knee-jerk love of tradition, and partly because the witch-hunters had tenure. It wasn't until the Presidency of Incense Mather, the proto-hippie black sheep son of Cotton, that students and junior faculty stopped being tortured and burned. Townies had to wait somewhat longer."[20]

"Whew," Hart said, pausing for a second and looking backwards. "Not only do you get punished, you have to walk back up all those stairs."

"I feel sorry for Peter," Ellen said, as they finished the last flight down. "Sitting there all by himself." The Chamber was built centuries before the Americans With Disabilities Act, so Peter was alone in a conference room many stories above. He would participate via closed-circuit TV.

"I'm not," Hart said. "I think he's a little claustrophobic."

20 1954.

"Then he'd hate this joint," Reed whispered.

The Chamber itself was a small, semicircular room of salt-fired brick, this type of masonry being believed by the Puritans to ward off evil. Fifty feet under the street, it smelled heavily of earth and mildew and the sweat of the accused. The walls were black, except for the one directly behind the judges; that one was dark red, the red of blood—or movie theater seats, depending on if you were the accused or the audience. The viewers sat, clutching bags of popcorn, in the small gallery along the curved back wall.[21] Opposite them, on the flat side of the semicircle, sat the judges, under portraits of august, piggish-looking predecessors.

Hart saw Master Wilkinson, the Master of Dacron College, looking vaguely pissed-off and in need of caffeine. Next to Wilkinson sat a scrawny, balding man with a prominent adam's-apple. "Is that the Mayor?"

"No, an observer from Amnesty International," Reed said mordantly.

Ellen looked up from the notes Don Q had given her. "He's the alternate judge, in case one is sick," then continued her brush-up.

"Interesting," Hart said. He did find it slightly fascinating, sitting there in the dock, thinking how many famous/infamous sets of buttcheeks had preceded his. Tabitha was right; a trip to the Chamber was on many a notable resume. According to his bestselling memoir, even Quinn Bostwick had passed through.[22]

As the staff of *The Cuckoo* waited quietly for the trio of judges to arrive, Hart looked at the monitor. Peter looked small and anxious. Reed was meditating. Ellen was rereading her crib sheet, and rehearsing her responses in a rapid mumble. I wish this would hurry up and get over, Hart thought, fingering a rusty, ancient-looking manacle. Was Ellen right? Or was Tabitha? The waiting was killing him.

Finally, the judges trooped in, decked out in Puritan-era garb: powdered wigs, black gowns, hats with buckles. First came Chief Constable Renalli, then a professor Hart had seen around campus but never met, and a third man riding a Segway. Much younger than the other two, Hart recognized

21 The Chamber was once *the* place to be seen (and perhaps spattered with blood). The school's original Charter gave all townspeople the right to attend trials in the Chamber. In fact, campus legend holds that the Puritans first learned about popcorn when some native Americans brought it to munch as they watched the crazy white people kill each other. Nowdays, with television and video games, the lust for actual blood was considerably less. About five townies showed up per calendar year, and at least three of these had gotten lost looking for a bathroom.

22 He and some buddies had built a wooden structure that made it look like the Statue of Liberty was sticking out of the Turbid River. This was fine until the President's sailboat crashed into it.

him as the famous, pugnacious owner of an internet company.

The professor rapped with his gavel. "I call this session of the Chamber to order," he said. "Professor Glenbard North, presiding in place of President Rivington; Chief Constable Oscar J. Renalli, Sergeant-at-Arms, and McTrent Molloy, '00, Associate-for-a-Day."

Hart leaned over and whispered to Reed. "That guy was on *Daily Money*'s 100 Most Annoying list."

Reed made an impressed face.

The judges were in a good mood. It was rare for any case these days to be serious enough for the Chamber; most infractions were small enough to be handled by the Master of each College. So the Chamber was a special occasion, and if you could avoid getting hung up on the whole "justice" thing, it was fun to pass judgment on your fellow man. McTrent Molloy obviously thought so; he'd purchased his day on the bench via a silent auction in the Stutts alumni magazine. Unfortunately for *The Cuckoo*, he was determined to get his money's worth.

Even worse for *The Cuckoo*, Professor North felt the same way, only more so. He'd given President Rivington a rather coveted pair of tickets to a Broadway musical in exchange for the chance to preside, and make sure these kids didn't get off. This morning's hearing was the last step in his elegant plan to neutralize several enemies of the University at one throw.

North smiled to himself. I win again, he thought. He would expel these kids, then have an early lunch, and then maybe a nap.

North cleared his throat, then spoke. "Staffe of *The Cuckoo*e, thou hast beene accused by people of good character and reputation of having consort with the Devill, submitting to him in body, mind, and spirit, and summoning him to Great Littleton, so that he might turn the Godly and righteous students of Stutts..."

Someone made a noise of disbelief. Hart thought it was the Mayor.

The judge paused, looking over his reading glasses. "I know it's hokey. This part is strictly traditional. We'll get to the charges in a minute."

"Uh, those are the charges," Renalli interjected.

Professor North looked over at the pudgy cop, surprised. "Really? There are two more pages..."

"This is the group that disrupted the Freshman Assembly," Renalli said. "Didn't you read my report?"

"Oscar, I don't have time to read...I'm a professor. If I read everything that crossed my desk..." He turned to the students. "Who will speak for the defendants?"

Hart was about to stand, but Ellen beat him to it. "I will, your honor."

Fine, Hart thought. Better you than me.

The young alum looked up from his Blackberry. "Turn around, give us a good look." Molloy craned, taking her all in. (He was facing multiple sexual harassment suits.)

"You can't be serious," Ellen said, stunned. This type of thing didn't happen at Stutts.

"Like you're not working it," Molloy said. "I notice you decided not to wear a bra."

"I am *so*," Ellen said.

North stepped in—there could be no irregularities. "Mister Molloy—"

Molloy cracked open an energy drink. "I move that the punishment be, the girl takes off her shirt."

"Mister Molloy, *please!*" Professor North said. "I don't know what the standards of behavior are in your workplace, but I ask that you treat these proceedings with a little more respect!"

"T'cha, right," Molloy mumbled. "How much do you want for this whole joint?"

Professor North let that go, but made a mental note to leak some embarrassing information about this clod—something that would slice his share-price by half. That would take e-Moneybags down a peg or two. North turned back to Ellen. "Young lady, I apologize for my colleague. What's your name?"

"Ellen Pokorny, your honor."

"Ms. Pokorny, on behalf of yourself and the others accused, how do you plead?"

"Guilty of witchcraft in the first degree, your honor."

Hart and Reed turned to Ellen, appalled. Upstairs, Peter exclaimed: "What the —?" The last word was beeped out; Peter was on five-second delay.

"Trust me, okay?" She turned back to the bench. "I am sorry, your honor. My colleagues are still slightly possessed by Satan."

"Uh…okay," Professor North said. This trial was already too religious for his comfort. "Do you wish to inform the court of any extenuating circumstances that may lighten your punishment?"

"No, your honor."

"This is insane," Reed said. "Your honor…"

"Begone, Satan!" Ellen shouted. "Get OUT of this boy's body!" She whacked Reed on the back of the head. Then, in a normal tone of voice, she told the judges. "Apologies."

"I've got a taser, if that would help," Renalli said, offering it.

North soldiered on. "Okay, is there any additional evidence that you'd like to—"

Ellen's voice was calm. "No, your honor."

Hart was too amazed to say or do anything. Reed broke ranks again. "Your honor, I'd like to—AGHH!"

Ellen had stomped on his foot, hard. "Your honor, to express our deep repentance for our actions, and in the interest of time, I'd like to suggest that a proper punishment for us be *peine fort et dure*."

Molloy stopped talking on his cell phone. "I hope that's Latin for 'take my top off'."

Reed was fighting through the pain. "Don't listen to her, she's crazy. She's—" His forceful words were ended by a punch in the stomach.

Post-punch, Ellen said, "It's a method of torture—Hart, don't you dare—" (Hart had opened his mouth) "—a method of torture in which the victim is placed between two boards, and slowly crushed by piling heavy stones on top."

Behind the defendants, the Mayor stood up. "That sounds illegal," he said.

Ellen turned around to address him. "I assure you it's not. It's in the town charter."

"Oh," the Mayor said, sitting down. "I hate this place," he said quietly to no one in particular. "It makes absolutely no sense."

At that moment, Hart totally agreed. Creepy-ass New England, he thought, really wishing he'd gone to school back home. Or that Tabitha was here to create a distraction and give them a chance to run for it.[23]

"Ellen, what are you doing?" Peter howled.

"Miss Whatever-Your-Name-Is," Molloy asked, "in this method of torture, is the person naked?"

"Can be," Ellen said, hoping to swing his vote.

"Then I think it's a great idea," Molloy said, then returned to text-messaging.

"Well, I don't care what you think," North said. "These are Stutts University students, not some people who've just wandered in off the street."

"Boo!" someone called from the gallery, who had wandered in off the street.

"Look, old fart"—Molloy was 28—"I left Vegas early to make it here this morning, so I'd like to see some tits, or gore, or both. I'm the customer."

Professor North's expression grew very bland, always a bad sign. He was

23 Tabitha had wanted to come. But since the University had no photographic evidence that Tabitha was involved, and *The Cuckoo*'s internal records hadn't been updated since 1954, the rest of the staff had decided to spare her the considerable difficulty of going out in the daytime.

trying to remember who he knew in industrial espionage. North's memory wasn't what it used to be, but he could always look through his files and plan something. That would be fun.

Renalli spoke. "Professor North, I received a communication from Interim President Rivington about this case this morning."

"Really?" North asked. "What did Pat have to say? Besides thanking me for the new job?"

"Huh?" Renalli was confused.

"Forget it," North said.

"He gave me this." Renalli showed President Rivington's communiqué, which was on a roll of parchment.

North said, "Parchment, huh? Somebody's high on himself."

Renalli unrolled it. "I, Patrick Manolo Rivington, Speaker of the Faculty Senate, Supreme Commander of the Campus Constabulary, Editor-in-Chief of the University Press, Honorary Fire-Chief of—"

North sighed. "We can skip all the titles."[24]

Renalli jumped down three inches. "—bring you greetings. Each of us have certain flaws which are given to us by our Creator, and while Stutts students are unquestionably less flawed in comparison to other individuals of same age, they too can sometimes act in accordance with the baser parts of our natures. They are a higher type of human, but human nevertheless. As this is a function of nature and not wholly of choice, it seems unjust—"

Professor North whimpered, "Skip to the important part, I beg you."

"...I hereby grant this group, the staff of *The Cuckoo*, a satirical student magazine, utter and complete clemency..."

Hart couldn't believe his ears—they were saved! His plans were saved! He wouldn't be infamous, he wouldn't have to start all over. Quinn Bostwick could come, Hart could still intern at his show—he could still get to the top of the heap!

"Are you kidding me?" North said. He tried to look impassive, but the shock and annoyance was too powerful. "Gimme that!" he barked, swiping the parchment from Renalli.

"They are to be protected and held harmless from any punishments, public or private," North read incredulously, "as a result of activities undertaken on September 1 of this year at Truax Hall. I do this in a gesture of goodwill towards the Stutts community. I fervently hope that this act of generosity will

24 Since a bloody faculty revolt in 1763, the President of Stutts never referred to himself as that in internal documents. He was merely "first citizen," holding a collection of offices which, in theory, could be revoked at any time. In practice, however, he was the President.

inspire the love of my people, and augur a long and peaceful reign."

Professor North was quiet for a second, processing this new information. "Well, it's highly irregular, but..." Rivington was a fool, but North couldn't change the decree. He'd just have to think of another way to neutralize these threats. Finally, he said, "All charges are dropped. You may go."

Hart let out his breath. He hadn't realized he'd been holding it. Peter gave a whoop. He was elated; Ellen, vindicated; Reed, bruised but happy.

Molloy, however, was hopping mad. "I didn't pay"—Hart's mouth fell open at the astronomical sum—"just to see these punks walk..."

That's it, North thought. Time to get a virus created, one that only targets his company's browser.

"...I want blood, or two chicks wrestling, or something!" He stood up, and pointed to Ellen. "C'mere, Skinny, lemme give you a spank—"

Chief Constable Renalli reached over and tasered the alum, who collapsed back into his seat.

"Thanks," Professor North said. "We'll get him lunch at Der Rathskeller. A bucket or two and he won't even remember it."

"I'm sorry I punched you," Ellen said to Reed. "Don Q said I should, if I needed to. Are you okay?"

"Yeah," Reed said. "Remind me to punch Don Q."

Suddenly, via the monitor, they heard the sounds of a scuffle upstairs. A stranger's face, not Peter's, now filled the screen.

"Who the hell is this guy?" Reed said.

Hart shrugged. None of the Cuckonians had ever seen him before. If he was a professor, he was a particularly unhousebroken one: The man wore a rumpled funeral suit, and his hair was a wild mane of scraggle. The eyes behind his heavy rectangular glasses looked like goldfish in a bowl.

The man was tapping on the camera lens, trying to get everyone's attention. "Excuse me...Is this thing on?...Hello?" The man looked down periodically—Peter was trying to pull him off the desk he'd had to stand on to get to camera level. The man was a shrimp, but feisty, and his conversation was paced with their battle.

"I am...this organization's...lawyer and I demand...that it be disbanded," he said, kicking at Peter below him. "Would you STOP?" he said to Peter. "I'm doing this for your own good."

"He's not our lawyer, your honor!" Hart yelled, feeling their victory slipping away. "We didn't have time to get one!"

"Reed Rodriguez's father has retained me to act on their behalf," the lawyer said.

"No, he hasn't!" Reed said. "You're high!"

"Hello, Guy," Professor North said. "So nice to see you above ground."

"And you, Glenbard," the lawyer responded, stamping on Peter's fingers.

The Cuckonians were in shock. Peter barked through the monitor, "Hart! Call Tab! She's got to take this joker out!"

Hart, Ellen, and Reed all tried their cell phones simultaneously.

"Shit!" Hart snapped; nobody could get a signal—they were too far underground.

Guy the lawyer took a piece of paper out of his jacket. Shaking it open with one hand, he pressed it against the camera. "These are Articles of Dissolution. You'll see that they're in—shit! Quit grabbing my crotch, kid!" The document disappeared. Peter had finally grabbed the lawyer, dragging him off the desk. "All right," the lawyer said, "now I'm pissed!"

Molloy was coming to; Professor North needed to wrap things up. "All right," he said happily, tickled that his plan would work out after all—in spywork, it always helped to be lucky. "By its own request, this student organization is hereby disbanded until further notice." North's gavel sounded like a gunshot to the temple.

The Cuckonians sprang to their feet.

"You can't do this!" Hart yelled. "It's not fair!"

Even Ellen was livid. "We demand an appeal!" she said.

"There are no appeals in the Chamber," North said brightly.

Scattered voices from the galley called out: "Boo!" "It's a fix!"

North banged the gavel again, then droned boilerplate. "You are required to vacate any and all University-provided spaces, return any University-provided equipment, and provide the keys to any and all storage facilities on University campus no later than September 15 of this year. Court is adjourned."

On the monitor, the staff watched the tiny no-good wriggle away from Peter. He threw his trenchcoat over Peter's head; this bought him enough time to skitter out of the room. Peter's tranquilizer dart (a recent addition to his chair) thunked harmlessly into the closing door. Peter's string of profanity was positively maritime.

North grimaced; swearing was so uncouth. "Jane, could you please..." Rivington's secretary Jane was acting as court recorder. She leaned over and turned the monitor off. "Thank you."

Reed was the first one running. "Go get 'em!" somebody shouted from the gallery. Reed was in decent shape, but by the time he reached the lobby above, Guy was gone. And so was *The Cuckoo*.

"What happened?" Molloy said, groggily. "Did I miss anything?" He smacked his lips. "My mouth tastes like batteries..."

6

Hart vs. the Anti-Funny Rays

Monday, September 13 @ 4:00pm

Thanks to the mysterious lawyer, *The Cuckoo* was defunct—not suppressed, not recharging, but done. Over. Extinct.

Hart spent the next week in a daze, reeling from all the fast-unfolding plans that had suddenly slammed to a halt. The Organizational Meeting had to be cancelled, the issue they were working on, scrapped. Even the college-ranking parody had to be forgotten.

But Hart didn't forget it. Because they would never be able to do it, the project loomed even larger in his mind. Doomed, it became perfect, not merely a chance at fame and fortune but a guarantee.

Stutts students were a dramatic species—it was either triumph or tragedy for them, nothing in between. In the weeks after his visit to the Chamber, Hart became convinced he'd live the life of a failure; and he was sure that when they looked back (whoever *they* were), the doomed college-ranking parody would be Hart's tipping-point, the fulcrum where his life slipped from a story of promise fulfilled to one of self-delusion, bitterness, and poor oral hygiene.

Slowly, shock turned to depression. Hart moved as little as possible, and ate less. Even thinking seemed to hurt. "Sorry I'm no fun to be with," he told Tabitha.

"That's all right, cutie," she said. "Catatonic is what I need right now." Wearing a paint-daubed polo shirt (it was difficult to tell where the paint ended and the Lily Pulitzer began) Tabitha was painting Hart into one of her nighttime landscapes.[25] Hart was a centaur.

"Can I scratch my nose?"

"I wish you wouldn't," Tabitha said. She changed brushes. "You know

25 As a vampire, Tabitha was more-or-less immortal ("So far, so good—I try not to push it"). This meant that she had to develop new interests and hobbies fairly constantly or be bored to suicide. Over the summer, thanks to Stutts Summer Session, she had developed a passion for landscape painting. However, since she could only tolerate sunlight in very, very small doses, the preppy vampiress had to paint them all in the dark, using night-goggles. (She used a lot of green.)

what I would do if I were you?"

People always love hearing this; Hart gritted his teeth. "What?"

"I'd write a column for the *Spec*."

"You're kidding, right?"

"Hart, as they said in that TV show you made me watch, '*The Cuckoo* is an ex-parrot.'"

Hart couldn't argue that point. "But they'd destroy everything I wrote in the editing," he said. "It's the *Spec*, for fuck's sake. They radiate powerful anti-funny rays."

"Are you sure?" she said. "Why not try? What could it hurt?"

Hart was in no mood to be pushed. "Okay, Tab," Hart snapped, scratching his nose defiantly, "if you think that's such a great idea, why don't you do it?"

"Maybe I will!" Tabitha snapped back, inaugurating their first no-sex night of the year.

Two hours later, laying there in the dark not having sex, Hart took a mental inventory of all of his friends. All of them were fighting with each other. Some on the staff blamed Peter for the demise of the magazine, which he vociferously denied. Others blamed Reed's dad, which Reed resented. Peter blamed the Mugwumps, which Ellen didn't like. Tabitha had let slip that she and Hart had been "visiting" when Peter had called them to see if the coast was clear, so everybody blamed the couple. On top of all this Hart, naturally, blamed himself; if he hadn't offered that fatal compromise, if he'd just put his foot down, none of this would've happened...

Hart woke up the next morning with a steely, sour thought in his head: Peter always told him that he cared too much about getting along with other people. From now on, Hart thought, I'm not going to worry about that. This is the "new" Hart. I'm out for me; Stutts is my one big chance— and if I don't take it, somebody else will.

The "new" Hart lasted exactly one hour—the length of a meeting with Miles Monaghan, Managing Editor of *The Daily Spectacle*.

"I knew you'd come crawling," Miles said with a smirk. "Don't feel bad; all the other campus publications fold sooner or later. It's great for us—we think of all you fly-by-nights as our farm team."

"Really." Hart's teeth were already on edge. He remembered how this tool had tried to stop *The Cuckoo*'s all-nude revue last year...and had ended up spending the night in jail. The memory soothed Hart.

"So," Miles said, leaning back and putting his scuffed topsiders up on his desk, "think you're ready for the big leagues?"

"Sure." Was this guy serious? Of course he was—this was the *Spec*, a magical land untouched by notions of competence or quality. The worse the paper got, the more pompous the people who ran it became. (All things considered, it was excellent training for the real world.)

Oh shit—Hart saw Peter outside, through the big bay window. He'd lied to his roommate, saying that he was going to the bookstore to pick up a packet for Tanya and Vanya. Peter was savage enough these days; for the sake of domestic tranquility, Hart needed to hide. He tried to scrunch down…

Miles noticed. "What's up? Something going on out there?"

Peter had walked on. "Nothing, just somebody I didn't want to deal with."

"Ah," Miles said. You had to watch these *Cuckoo* guys every second. They were always up to something. "We do have an opening for a columnist," he said. "Chondra Jefferson-Levy just got a book deal. Do you read Chondra's column?"

Hart side-stepped the issue. "She's in my writing seminar. Lemonade abuses her."

"Lemonade abuses everyone, so I'm told," Miles said. "It's only a matter of time before we take him down. He'll feel the power of public opinion. Anyway, Chondra wrote from a pago-vego-Afro-lesbo perspective—"

"Pago-whato-whato?"

"Pagan-vegan-black-lesbian," Miles said. "With a little neo-con in there, too. Which is only natural, given who her father is."

Hart didn't know who Chondra's father was, so he bluffed. "Of course."

"Between you and me, she couldn't write worth a damn," Miles continued, "but she serviced *a ton* of demographics. What demo would you service? Have you thought about that?"

"Uh…" Hart was at a loss. "…the funny one?"

"I was hoping you wouldn't say that," Miles said. "Funny makes advertisers nervous, and we can't have that, not right before we sell it."

Hart was shocked. "You're selling the paper?"

"President Rivington's put together a deal that was just too sweet to pass up," Miles said. He looked at his watch. "Which reminds me, in five minutes, there's a meeting for all of us with stock options. so let's keep this short. If we accept you—and I'm not saying we will—you'll spend the first six months working under my assistant, getting what we call 'seasoned.'" Miles paused. "Anything wrong?"

"Nope," Hart lied. If he worked for the *Spec*, he'd definitely have to improve his poker-face.

"You'll like my assistant," Miles said. "She's just a freshman, but sharp.

Her mom is Chairman of Coca-Cola. You'll probably work with her more than me; by the time you're seasoned, I'll be less involved with the day-to-day stuff. As the EIC, Gwen appears on TV a lot, but second semester she'll be busy interviewing for jobs, so I'll be filling in for her. Isn't that great?"

"Yeah," Hart said listlessly.

"I know, right?" Miles said, cheering himself on. "Anyway, you've made the right choice. You've started too late to make it to the top, but one thing you'll learn here is, playing by the rules works. I'm living proof."

That's not all you're living proof of, Hart thought. He considered setting Miles' cardigan on fire. "Do you think I could get fast-tracked since I've run another publication?"

"Oh, no!" Miles said, smiling. "That's exactly why you couldn't! We can't reward people for being on the competition. Don't worry, you'll have your hands full: you'll have to learn house style, and that takes a solid year," Miles said. "Then, for a year after that, everything you write will be rewritten. By the time you're a senior, your stuff'll make into the regular editing process. If you work hard, that is, and not get leapfrogged by some frosh star. There are 'naturals' every so often. I was one, it just came easy to me...For the first month, you'll be on night duty, 8 pm to 8 am..."

Hart zoned out. It sounded like Miles was describing where wicked writers go when they die.

"...and that's it," Miles said. "Simple, really. Well, for some. Others just never fit in. Do you have some samples for me to read?"

Hart tried to hand them over, but he couldn't. Then some words leaped out of his mouth. "I don't think this is a good fit, Miles."

"Oh," Miles said. "Well." He was a little annoyed that he wouldn't have the pleasure of tormenting an ex-*Cuckoo* editor. "You know, if you weren't serious you shouldn't have wasted my time."

"I was serious," Hart said, "but I'd forgotten that you were an asshole."

Miles was speechless. Nobody had called him that since high school. By the time he got his composure, Hart was already out of his office and halfway through the reporters' bullpen.

"You'll be sorry you said that, shitheel!" Miles yelled from his doorway. "Just for that I think I'll accept your girlfriend's column proposal."

"What the fuck do I care?" Hart said, and walked out the door.

"Oh, you'll care!" Miles said. "It's a sex column! Tell me, Hart—do you *really* cry when you come?"

7

Advice From A Hobbit

Tuesday, September 14, 6:19 pm

Speaking of tears: Hart was willing to do whatever it took to keep Tabitha from writing a sex advice column for the *Spec*, up to and including turning on the waterworks. That night, in Tab's crypt, they had it out.

"Hart, I have a right to do whatever I please," Tabitha said.

"Yeah, but I'm a public figure," Hart said.

"Just barely."

"What is that supposed to mean?" Hart said, stung. "I'm the editor of *The Cuckoo*."

"Oh, for the next 26 hours or so," Tabitha countered. "Then you'll slip back into obscurity and I can write the column."

To Hart, that was the exact opposite of what he wanted. "I didn't come to Stutts to slip into obscurity."

"So it's good enough for the rest of us—for me—but you're special?"

"That's not what I mean," Hart said, then tried another tack. "Look, anybody's boyfriend would be freaked out by this."

"You're not anybody's boyfriend, you're *my* boyfriend, and I would hope you'd support me in doing whatever I like."

"Everybody will look at me," Hart said. "They'll guesstimate the size of my johnson."

"So let 'em," Tabitha said. "I promise to exaggerate. Hart, most people are too busy thinking about themselves to pay the least bit of attention to you. If people think at all, it'll be, 'He's having sex with that tera-foxy *Spec* sex columnist."

"*Tera*-foxy?" Hart said.

"Foxy x 10^{12}."

"Cute. Tab, I want my sex life to stay private."

"It doesn't have to be about our sex life," Tabitha countered. "I've got oodles of material. I had sex for a 100 years before I met you."

Hart stopped playing with a rat. "Thanks for reminding me."

Tabitha saw how upset Hart was about it all. She, unlike every other Stutts student, recognized that not everything came down to getting famous. "All right," she sighed. "If it really bothers you, I won't do it."

"Thank you," Hart said. "Thank you thank you thank you."

"You're welcome. But you owe me," Tabitha said.

"Name your favor."

"*Favors*," Tabitha corrected. "First, I want to go to the basketball game."

Hart groaned; the gym always smelled awful. But a deal was a deal.

◦ ◦ ◦

When they got there, Hart realized just what a bullet he'd dodged—Tabitha had brought copies of what was going to be her first column, and the rest of the staff was in stitches.

The Cuckoo needed the levity—it was the last night before they were kicked out of the offices in Lytton Hall, and they had hours and hours of office clean-up ahead of them. "I can't believe the University would actually charge us one hundred freaking bucks an hour to clean out the office," Peter had griped, but it was the truth.

Naturally, the group had decided to put it off until the very last minute...which was why they were packed into the humid rafters of Horst Gymnasium, watching Stutts lose to St. Sinusitus in basketball.

"'Love Letters,' eh?" Reed said. "Nice title, Tabitha. It's restrained."

"The whole thing is restrained," Ellen said. "I would've never imagined I could read a whole column about blow-job technique without gagging."

"So you liked the cucumber thing?" Tabitha asked. "The *Spec* wanted me to be graphic, but I didn't think that was appropriate."

"I still think it should be 'Tales of Hart's Wang,'" Peter said.

Hart gave him a shove. "Shut up and watch the game."

"This only looks like a game," Peter said. "In reality it's something much worse."

"A crime against humanity?" Reed offered. "A degradation of the human spirit?"

"Stop it, you guys. Don Quixote is nice," Ellen said. Her fellow Mugwump was Stutts' captain. He was 5'10" and played center. "Come on, Don!" she shouted. Don, unused to cheers, missed a layup.

"I didn't realize that 'Don Quixote' was Gilbert from Dacron," Hart said.

Ellen calmly took a paper bag out of her backpack, then placed it over her head. This was standard operating procedure whenever a Mugwump secret—in this case, a member's identity—was revealed in public. "I can neither confirm nor deny," she said monotonically through the bag.

The horn sounded for halftime. "47-5," Peter said; the numbers were sour in his mouth. "Is that legal?"

"Enact Federal 'slaughter rule,'" Reed said, pulling out his pocket notebook.

"Ah, the Book o' Jokes," Hart said. "Good to see it again."

"Not a joke book anymore." Once used for jokes, the pad now held more serious stuff. Reed's reaction to *The Cuckoo*'s hosing was a determination to get into Stutts Law School and right the wrongs of the world.

"They didn't even hit the friggin' rim," Peter said. "Not once. Do you realize how difficult that is?" Stutts' broad-based, wide-spectrum ineptitude in sports took a toll on Peter. Once-athletic, still competitive, watching his classmates flounder turned him into a mass of thwarted impulses; Peter visibly twitched every time a Stutts player did something dumb—like the time in this first half, when one had gone up for a dunk and knocked himself unconscious on the backboard.

"I miss the old days," Ellen said, munching some of Peter's popcorn. "The gym stank, but at least we won." Faced with year after year of highly intelligent but vastly uncoordinated players, the Stutts basketball coach had a novel stratagem: heavy meals before games. "Reed, remember 'Spaghetti Night' freshman year?"

"How could I forget?" Reed said. "The 'Chopped Liver Game' was worse."[26]

Titanically disgusting (and semi-legal at best), the coach's strategy was a success, keeping Stutts in games with much more talented teams. Two years ago, during Reed and Ellen's sophomore year, Stutts had booted, yacked and hurled its way into the NCAA tournament. Their first-round win, christened "The Pea Soup Game" by a horrified national press, represented the school's first victory against a ranked opponent since 1717.

The coach tried the same thing in the second round, taking the team to a local chili joint an hour before tip-off. Then Stutts suffered a bad break: the game had to be postponed because of some loose ceiling tile; in the intervening three hours, the Stutts team digested themselves into a loss.

"I'm convinced that second-round game was fixed," Peter said.

"Peter Paranoia strikes again," Ellen said.

Peter was undeterred. "It was the networks. People wouldn't watch a game filled with projectile vomiting. Advertisers would demand their money back."

"I wish they still did it," Reed said. Though small schools all across the country had seized on it as a way to even the odds, a group of Stutts alums had cried foul. "In my day," the alumni thundered, "we beat teams fair and

26 This was a disaster of scheduling. The entire first row had been occupied by students from a local school for the blind. When the evacuation reached its peak, all the service dogs-bolted from their owners and began licking it up. The crowd was disgusted, and the team almost disbanded...but it was the lead story on SportsCenter.

square"—neglecting to mention that, in their day, 6'2" was tall and everybody made their own sneakers. They had pressured the athletic department to end its practice of selecting recruits for stomach capacity and a hairtrigger gag reflex, in favor of the old, fruitless search for kids who thought like Einstein and played like Jordan.

The Stutts team trotted back onto the court. They began to warm up, mainly by bumping into each other and falling down. Don launched an airball.

"Look!" Peter said, his voice rising into a screech. "They *still* can't do it!"

A few players, seniors leftover from the old days, were visibly battling psychosomatic reflux. Whenever they lost this battle, a student rushed out with a broad, flat mop and scrubbed the court.

"I don't think I can take another half of this," Hart said. "As my last act as Editor in Chief, I move we adjourn and go clean out the office. Those in favor..."

Nobody said anything.

"All right," Hart said. "I guess I'll go over there and do it myself." Hart grabbed his backpack (he planned to take a few souvenirs) and walked down the row to the exit.

Glumly, and with great weariness, the rest of the staff got up and followed him out.

Things were better once they had started. There was a lot of reminiscing, and Ellen spewed many *Cuckoo* factoids, a few of which were actually interesting. The old banter returned, if only for an evening. "...I'm not anti-Polish. All I'm saying is, you are not honoring a national cuisine by letting the Dining Halls at it," Hart said as he archived the hard-drive of *The Cuckoo*'s ancient Mac. "I love a good, juicy kielbasa."

"No comment," Peter said.

"You're coming with me, big boy," Ellen said, rolling up the poster of John Travolta. She turned to the group. "Okay, I'm done. We can set a fire now."

"How many back issues should we keep?" Reed said from behind a pile of boxes. "Five per?" Hart offered.

"And one for the archives," Tab said, thumping the side of a cardboard box.

"Ooh, I hope you're not planning on storing that in your crypt," Ellen said. "That cemetery is too damp. They might mold."

"Mold? In *chateau moi?*" Tabitha replied with mock-indignation. "I hope everybody doesn't mind, but I've convinced Chauncey to keep it for us in the storeroom of his shop, in exchange for first dibs on whatever we decide to throw out."[27]

"Fine," Hart said, "as long as I don't have to haul it over there."

"You will, my sweet," Tabitha said. Hamlet-like, she held up a small, plastic, slightly crosseyed bust of JFK. There was a scorch-mark on its face where some prior Cuckonian had tried to burn (or smoke?) it; she tossed the bust into a trashbucket, then asked, "Who owns the furniture?"

"The university," Reed said.

"Good!" Hart plunged an x-acto knife into a chair cushion. He was still plenty angry when he let himself be. Mid-vandalism, Hart heard the sounds of ping-pong from the hall outside. He immediately felt a pang; would he ever be able to hear that hollow *pok-pok* and not think of *The Cuckoo*? The din was constant, and though they had never been able to find out who was playing, the back-and-forth punctuated by roars of outrage and triumph had been the magazine's soundtrack. Goodbye, phantom ping-pongers. Goodbye, water fountain that tastes like acetone. Goodbye, crumbling acoustic tile that dropped on your head. Throat tight, Hart climbed on a table and started pulling all the pens and pencils that had been flipped into said tile. There were hundreds, and some of the pens were leaky. "This sucks," he said. "Remind me to kick that lawyer in the sack."

"Who the hell is he?" Peter asked. "Does anybody know? Reed, is he really a pal of your dad's?"

"He changes the subject every time I bring it up," Reed said.

"Does he still think his phone is tapped?" Ellen asked with a smile. There was a small crash. Everybody looked; Ellen was covered with plaster dust. "Poster was load-bearing," she coughed. "Hey, guys—c'mere!"

Somebody, far in the past, had dug a hole in the wall, and patched it with plaster. The poster (Dylan by Milton Glaser) had been placed over it when it was wet. The plaster had dried to the back, so that when Ellen took the poster down, some plaster came down with it, and the hole was exposed.

"I didn't know Andy Dufresne was on *The Cuckoo*," Peter said.

With the staff gathered round, Ellen stuck her hand into the hole and began extracting what was wedged inside. The first thing she pulled out was an issue of *Ramparts* from 1968 with some Stutts students on the cover. Reed looked at it with a sinking feeling. "I think that's my Dad," Reed said glumly.

The next item was a folded piece of notebook paper. Ellen handed it to Hart, who read it aloud. "'Dudes of the future, this is a time-capsule. Enjoy the Vonnegut.'"

27 Tabitha's friend Chauncey owned a resale shop on the main drag called The House of Old; last year, *The Cuckoo* had made quite a chunk of money selling bric-a-brac Hart and Tabitha had stolen from Harriman Library.

"The huh?" Peter asked.

"Maybe there's an interview with Kurt Vonnegut in the magazine," Tabitha offered.

Ellen pulled out the final object, a bottle about the size of a mason jar. It was made of brown glass, and had an eyedropper cap. There was a label on it, but the spidery ink had faded over the years to become illegible.

"Can I have the bottle?" Tabitha asked. "Maybe Chauncey can sell it."

"No!" Peter said. He shook it. "There's something in it. I want to find out what it is."

Hart couldn't resist being a peacemaker. "Pete and I will try to figure out what it is, and if it's not worth saving, we'll pour it out and you can give Chauncey the bottle."

Reed dumped an armload of yellowed back issues into the trash can, then shook the plastic can, testing its weight. "How the hell are we going to move these things?" The University had left several jumbo contractor-style garbage cans by the office door, and the staff was tossing stuff into them left and right. There were literally hundreds of pounds of crap in the office, stuff accumulated over decades.

Hart looked around; all five of them had been working for an hour, and the place still looked like the lair of a pop-culture obsessed serial killer. Snowshovels—that's what they needed; would they have those at 24 Hours of Crap? "Hey, who's going to take Mrs. Morganthau?" Hart asked. Originally *The Cuckoo*'s bookkeeper, this became the name of the magazine's finicky Macintosh.

"Reed is," Ellen said. "I don't want that hard drive anywhere near me. Has he shown you the picture of a woman putting her—"

"Strictly scientific interest," Reed said blandly. "Ellen, you're such a prude. How did you ever manage to jill-off in front of 12 strangers?"

"Jill-off?" Hart asked.

Ellen rolled her eyes. "I'm not explaining it."

Tabitha said, "Think about it for a second."

Ellen, exasperated, wiped her sweaty brow with a grime-coated hand. "We don't masturbate, we just tell our life stories. *With* our clothes on."

"I found out a secret, I found out a secret," Reed sang, pleased with himself.

"But that's boring," Peter said. "You dumped all your friends to do that?"

"For somebody who's dumped all her friends, I'm doing a pretty good impression of spending the fucking evening cleaning out our office," Ellen said.

"Here we go again," Hart mumbled to Tabitha, tossing a broken pink flamingo into the trash. But just as the squabble really blossomed, there was a knock at the door.

"Come in!" several people yelled at once.

"Hello, folks! Having fun?" Guy the lawyer walked in, wearing a big smile and an even bigger novelty sombrero. He was clutching a bottle of champagne by the neck. "I assume Mr. Rodriguez has explained everything. I just came to offer my congratulations."

Reed bellowed like a bull, then charged. Guy dropped the bottle of champagne and took off running. Luckily for Guy, Peter was parked between Reed and the door, and by the time Reed had negotiated the piles of junk *and* gotten past Peter, the smallish lawyer had a healthy head start.

"Don't kill me!" Guy yelled over his shoulder. "I can explain!"

"Wait up, Reed." Hart took off with Reed; it was fun to be working together on a common goal—even if it was chasing a near-stranger, so they could beat him to death. Tabitha turned into a pink mist, then wafted along next to the boys effortlessly.

"You destroyed our magazine!" Hart yelled.

"I didn't destroy—whoop!" The sombrero flew off Guy's head, and Hart gave it a good stomp as he passed.

"Bullshit!" Reed roared. "I sacrificed a 4.0 for that fucker!"

"It's still alive! I swear it!" Guy dug into a pocket and retrieved his cell phone. He tossed it blindly over his shoulder. "Call your father! He'll explain everything!"

Reed and Hart skidded to a stop in front of a T-junction. On a level straightaway, they would've caught the short-legged lawyer immediately, but subterranean Stutts was a warren of sloping, twisting passages. Students called it "the Catacombs."[28] Every prefrosh had heard at least one story of someone who'd lost their way and never been found again.

Hart tried not to think about that. "We gotta keep him talking," he told Reed. "Otherwise we'll never find him."

Reed paused for a second, not knowing what to say. Then he yelled, "You're a friend of Dad's?"

"Yes! Exactly!"

28 The constant hunt for office space had forced every College and department to colonize some space underground, only to abandon these spaces after aboveground space came available. Then clubs like *The Cuckoo* would be moved in; they would occupy it for awhile, then become defunct. After a century of this, nobody really knew how many rooms were in The Catacombs or what was in them. And there were rumored to be whole complexes, underground vastnesses, that the University had declared off-limits. Most students obeyed. Others…

"My father's friends are *dicks!"* Reed yelled back.

While they were standing there, Peter and Ellen caught up. Reed motioned for them to be quiet; they all started to creep silently towards the voice. "Dad wasn't even on *The Cuckoo*."

"Yes, he was—for about a minute." Guy's voice echoed strangely down here. "I was his editor. Loved your summer issue, by the way!"

Hart's confusion began to cool his anger. Suddenly things seemed too complicated to hunt the little lawyer down and shake him until his eyes rolled out. They turned another corner. "Where are we, Pete?"

Peter's wheelchair had GPS. "Two blocks north of Lytton, heading north-northwest."

"Have you ever considered doing a blog?" the lawyer shouted. His voice seemed to be getting farther away.

"Yes!" Peter answered.

"We've been a little precoccupied," Hart yelled, "thanks to you!"

"Stop! Stop! Go back!" they heard the lawyer say. "You made a wrong turn!"

Ellen spoke for all of them: "He *wants* us to find him?"

"Follow the chalk marks!" the lawyer's voice said.

Following the chalk marks on the walls, they walked through gloomy, half-lit hallways and into dank steam tunnels, squeezed through rust-stuck fire-doors and past piles of obsolete equipment. They scuttled through cobwebbed corridors and rooms half-sized high. They startled two girls doing their laundry, and found the guys playing ping-pong. The game was a recording; they were really watching Spanish telenovelas, and crying.

"We didn't want people to think we were dorks," one explained.

The journey continued. The Cuckonians inhaled asbestos. They banged their heads on heating ducts. They hugged the walls to avoid scalding pipes, and burned themselves anyway. It was a drag. And ll the while, they could hear Guy, lingering just out of sight.

It was humid down there, and hard to breathe. Everybody started to pant. Reed, not paying attention, took in a gulp of Tabitha.

"Sorry," Reed sputtered. "Sorry, Hart, I just inhaled your girlfriend."

Tabitha materialized. "Oh, poo," she said. "My hair is going all frizzy."

"Ever been in this part of the 'combs, Tab?" Hart asked.

"Nope," she said. They looked around. The brickwork was different—definitely older than in the basement of Lytton for example. More carefully wrought; artistic, not institutional. The ceiling was an intricate herringbone of shiny green brick which reflected the old-fashioned, clear-bulbed electric lights flickering at regular intervals along the walls.

"I'm over here," Guy's voice called. "Go to the end of the room, take a left, and walk about fifty feet."

Reed started forward.

Ellen grabbed his arm. "What if it's a trap? You still have to finish your Senior Paper."

"I couldn't find my way back anyway," Reed said.

"We could use Peter's GPS," Ellen said. "Forget this guy, he's bad news. Let's just find an exit and—"

Reed freed his arm and began walking again.

"Reed," Ellen said, "don't get hurt over some bullshit college thing." She turned to Peter and Hart. "No offense, guys."

Reed continued walking. Everybody else had no choice but to follow.

"Screw this, I'm dematerializing," Tabitha said.

They turned a corner and stopped. "I think I see him," Hart said, squinting into the gloom.

"Forgive me if I don't trust your eyes, Hart," Peter said, flipping on his chair's powerful floodlamp.

The wee litigant waved. "I thought you'd never get here," he said.

Reed took off again, like a dog after a squirrel. If Guy had set a trap—dug a spike-bottomed pit, say, or rigged darts to shoot out of the walls, Indiana Jones-style—Reed would've been done for. Luckily, Guy had other plans.

The lawyer was leaning next to an ornate bas-relief of a bird, cool as could be. "Did any of you happen to pick up my sombrero?" he asked. "I got it from a senoriña down in Tiju—ulp!"

"You bastard!" Reed grabbed Guy by the collar and lifted him up. Guy's short legs dangled like a child's as Reed shoved him hard against the wall.

"Careful, Reed," Peter said. "He's a *Cuckoo* alum—sell him a subscription first." Everybody but Reed and Guy laughed.

"If you hadn't stuck your nose in," Reed said, "*The Cuckoo* would still be in business," Reed growled. "Do you realize how hard we worked to keep that thing going? *Do you?*" He gave Guy's collar an extra crank of malice. With his free hand, he pointed at Ellen. "She worked so hard she's never gotten laid!"

Ellen looked sheepish and scratched the back of her neck. "Uh, Reed..."

Peter, of all people, was the voice of reason. "Reed, let him go. The magazine's gone. Abusing him won't bring it back."

"The magazine is not gone," Guy gasped.

The staff scoffed as one.

"I can't prove it to you unless you put me down."

Reed released his grip, and Guy slid to the floor.

"You're just as much of a hot-head as your father was." The Capote-esque litigator turned around and started jumping, trying to reach something in the bas-relief. The sculpture was of a bird, singing, with wings outstretched. The students watched him try and fail many times, until the wee lawyer said, "Don't just stand there gawping, grab its head!"

Hart grabbed the bird's head.

"Now twist," Guy said.

It didn't budge.

"Okay, that's it, it's weirdo-spanking time," Reed said, grabbing Guy again.

Guy wriggled free. "Try the other way."

Hart did so—and the wall swung open.

"Ladies and gentlemen of *The Cuckoo*, welcome to your new office," Guy said. "Well, actually, your old one."

As soon as they had fixed a burned-out fuse (Peter stuck a penny in), the splendor of the room became apparent. Upon walking through the door, one was standing at the end of a long room, dominated by a mahogany table. The table was covered with initials, hundreds of them, and even the occasional caricature.

Hart tapped a line-drawing with his finger—"Don't tell me that's Mark Twain."

"Certainly is," Guy said. "Probably posed for it in the very chair you're occupying. I knew he came down here more than once. This was the secret office of *The Cuckoo* from 1763 to whenever they moved into the building in…1919, is that right, Ellen?"

"Sounds right." Ellen the Stutts buff was in heaven, peering at all the photos that crammed one of the long walls. They were year-end snaps of staffs, joke portraits, and framed newspaper clippings detailing the magazine's exploits.

Hart sat in the throne at the head of the table. The chair was just his size; he liked it. A set of initials caught his eye: Q.B.—Quinn Bostick. He traced them with a tickly digit.

"Look at this!" Peter said. In the panel behind Hart, an ornately carved bird was emerging from an egg; both bird and egg were heavily gilded, except for the bird's beak, where the gold had been worn away.

"Look in its mouth," Guy said.

"A spigot," Peter said. "For beer?"

Guy nodded.

Reed was crouched down, investigating the bound volumes arrayed under the pictures. Tabitha was doing the same thing with the volumes on the other side, looking up friends. "Who are those people?" she asked, pointing at the painting on the wall in front of her. In dark browns, golds and ochres, a row of people stood there gaily, staring out of the canvas at posterity. By their dress, the painting could be dated to around the First World War. Some in the lineup wore suits, others were casual, but all of the figures exuded the same mix of intelligence and bemusement.

"Is there a switch on that wall?" Guy asked.

"Yeah." Tabitha stood up and flipped it.

The canvas started to scroll from right to left. The figures started becoming more and more old-fashioned. "I thought so," Guy said. "This is a group portrait of all the magazine's members from its beginnings to 1919."

Hart spoke for the group: "Wow."

"Check out the ceiling!" Peter said, and everybody did so. Tiny pricks of light were arrayed to show the Great Littleton sky at night. In the middle of the array hung a large, golden moon which illuminated the room.

"It's moving," Guy said. "Slowly, slowly, the sky is heading towards dawn."

"So, wait," Ellen asked, "you're saying that the ceiling is what the sky looks like right now?"

"Precisely," Guy said. "The students found that they were spending so much time down here, they were losing track of time. Very elegant solution, don't you think?"

"How did you find this place, Guy?" Tabitha asked. She and Hart had spent considerable time rummaging around in the Catacombs beneath Harriman Library last year.

"Research, lots of research," Guy said. "It was a bear—took me years. The old *Cuckoo* always kept their location secret. You should do the same."

"I wish you had showed us this before you put the magazine out-of-business," Hart said.

"Out-of business?" Guy scoffed. "Hardly. It's only out-of-business in the eyes of the University."

Peter said, "Guy, dude—*The Cuckoo* is a Stutts student publication. If Stutts says it's dead, it's dead."

"Preposterous," Guy said. "Peter, for you of all people to believe that…"

"I'm sick of mysteries," Peter said. "Reed, you can twist his nipples now."

Hart stepped in front of Reed, who was significantly larger than he was; Hart would have to pull rank. "Reed, I'm the editor-in-chief," Hart said. "I'll handle it." Then Hart faced Guy. "Mister—"

"Free. Guy B. Free."

Hart let that go. "We're all totally sad, we've had a hard couple of hours,

Ellen is covered with plaster dust... *The Cuckoo* is dead, you helped the University kill it, end of story."

"That's exactly the attitude that forced me to do what I did," Guy said. "*The Cuckoo* doesn't need the say-so of those tightasses in the Chamber to live. All it needs is a group of people who demand that it live!"

"You're crazy," Hart said.

"The University admitted you," Guy said, "it didn't *buy* you. Have some balls! Do what you want. Do you still have a staff? Yes. Do you still have an audience? Yes. Then put out another issue—only this time, as free men and women!"

"The University would go berserk," Hart said.

Guy shrugged.

"Easy for you to say, you've already graduated," Reed said. "Anyway, they'd impound all our issues."

"Yeah," Peter chimed in. "It'd be just like the old days with the *Spec*, except they'd kick us out, too."

"Ever heard of the First Amendment? Do you realize how much publicity you'd get if the University expelled you?" Guy said. "You all should be begging for that, praying for it," Guy said. His face was lit with a queer joy.

Tabitha noticed it. "I think he's bonkers," she whispered to Hart.

Guy didn't hear. "*The Cuckoo* isn't dead, people—it's been born-again! Your story isn't over, it's just beginning!"

The staff wasn't sure they believed Guy, but the more he talked, the more they wanted to. And they naturally deferred to anyone over forty. So they let him ramble and rant—especially after they found a bottle of primo claret hidden in the paneling.

"I live down here—all this is my home," Guy explained, sloshing his wineglass. (The more he drank, the more he gestured, and the spillage kept him from becoming too drunk.) Guy rubbed the wine into the table, turning the initials a darker shade. "I have the biggest apartment in Great Littleton."

"Isn't it dangerous?" Hart said, remembering the University's ever-sterner warnings about investigating the steam tunnels.

Guy snorted. "That's exactly how I feel about the surface," he said. "I've never been mugged down here, and if anyone tried, I'd simply run away. I know these tunnels better than anybody."

Ellen was charmed. She sensed Guy was a goldmine of weird Stuttsiana. "Are we still in the Catacombs?"

"'Pends on what you call 'Catacombs,'" Guy said. "If you're asking whether you're in the part the University recognizes, no, you're not. They don't recognize miles and miles of tunnels. They used to, but at some point some administrator decided that it was too expensive to maintain—or maybe it was the insurance—so they sealed off whole sections and let 'em go to pot. Or would've, if we had let them. How do you like the wine?"

"It's great," Hart said amiably; alcohol was alcohol. Ellen thought it didn't really compare to what she drank Tuesdays and Sundays at the Mugwumps Pyramid, but was too polite to say so.

Guy threw back the last drops that lingered in his glass. "Passable," he said. "Anyway, it's the best thing that could've happened. The University leaves us alone, and that's just the way we like it."

"We?" Reed asked.

"The people who live down here."

"Grad students, right?" Tabitha asked. Her cemetery was full of grad students on microscopic stipends, looking for someplace dry to sleep.

"A handful," Guy said. "Mostly they're bohemians. Do you still call them that?"

"We call them 'hippies," Peter said helpfully.

"The name changes. These are people who don't 'fit' aboveground—and don't want to," Guy said. "I can introduce you around. They call me 'the Mayor.'" Guy looked around, taking in their surroundings like it was the first time he'd seen them. "I've been looking for this room for years," he said. "It's a nice feeling...You'll understand, once you're older—the goals become smaller. You wake up one morning not *wanting* to conquer the world any more. It's too much trouble, you like your life the way it is...you just want to find that hidden room," Guy poured himself a bit more of the ruby liquid. "Or get that slightly better job, or buy that slightly nicer house. My goals aren't bad ones—they're not important, but they don't hurt anybody, either.

"Anyway, I finally found it over the summer. Yet more evidence that the time was right to set our plan in motion."

"*Our* plan?" Peter asked.

"Reed's father's and mine," Guy said.

"So my dad destroyed the magazine," Reed said. "I apologize everybody. He's totally getting shafted this Christmas."

"Not destroying it, Reed, *remaking* it!"

"We liked it the way it was," Hart said. "People were starting to read."

"Yeah," Ellen said. "We do it so people can enjoy it—"

"Some of us do," Peter interjected. He sensed a kindred anarchy in Guy—but still resented the intrusion. "Regardless, we didn't ask for your help."

"I know, I know, but it was the only way," Guy said, eyes swimming behind his thick glasses. "You may not believe me when I say this—Stuttsies never do—but there's a limit to what you can accomplish within the rules."

The claret had lessened Hart's inhibitions. "Bullshit," he said.

"A polite *Cuckoo* isn't worth much, Hart. No matter how many readers you have, no matter how much money you make, no matter whether you get into the right clubs—"

"Polite? Have you read our magazine?" Hart said. "Our sex jokes are so dirty, even I don't understand them."

"I'm not talking about sex jokes," Guy said. "To be polite is to value inoffensiveness over honesty. To trade your integrity for popularity."

Peter beamed. "The old weirdo agrees with me."

"No, I don't," Guy said. "You want to fritter away the magazine's integrity with pointless anarchy."

Peter was crestfallen. "No offense," he mumbled to Reed, "but your dad hangs out with assholes."

Tabitha had been listening intently—it was so rare to meet a new kind of person at Stutts. "So what do you think the magazine should be, Guy?"

"Fearless! Intelligent! Unafraid to judge!" Guy said. "Then, based on those judgments, you must attack whatever is pompous or hypocritical or false, or inhuman or hateful or wrong."

"And that will make us popular," Hart asked.

Guy laughed. "Oh, god no," he said.

"But not do a ton of pranks, either?" Peter asked.

"Never frivolous ones, no," Guy said. "Ones that make people *think*."

"This is ridiculous," Ellen said. "We're taking advice from a hobbit with a law degree." She turned to Guy. "Thanks for the office, we'll move our stuff in right away. But really: leave *The Cuckoo* to us, okay?"

"No! I won't—what you're doing is too important!"

"Yep, definitely bonkers," Tab whispered to Hart.

"*The Cuckoo* should be jester to Stutts' king!" Guy said. "To express those truths can only be said through a joke."

"I didn't join *The Cuckoo* to change the world," Reed blurted. "In fact, I joined it specifically *not* to change the world. That's the problem with everybody here."

"Well, I'm sorry to have to tell you this, Reed," Guy said. "But *The Cuckoo*'s *got* to have some purpose past its own perpetuation. Being jester to the king is the only role it can have and not dissolve into irrelevance, or disintegrate into anarchy.

"You've made it strong again. I've been waiting a long time for it to happen, but most people who pass through here…" Guy paused, then said, "As long as you were aboveground, the temptation of playing by the rules would eventually overwhelm you. It was already starting to happen: you caused a riot at the Freshman Assembly, but because things worked out in his favor, President Rivington was all set to let you off scot-free."

"And this is bad how?" Peter asked.

"You'd think you were rebels," Guy said, "but you'd really be housepets. You'd get famous on campus for your outrageous pranks. Meanwhile, Hart would be pursuing his dreams of glory—no offense, Hart, the EIC's always like that—and more and more people would join, to bask in the group's reflected glory. Soon, your staff would be filled with people who thought *The Cuckoo* could get them somewhere." Guy clearly had a lot of time to sit and think. "Oh, sure, they'd *pretend* to be rebellious, while playing the same old Stutts game as viciously and stupidly as ever. By pardoning you, Rivington was destroying you, and believe me, he knew it."

Nobody on staff quite knew what to say to that, so Guy continued.

"After your riot, I called Reed's dad. He and I talked about it. We thought the magazine won't lose its edge no matter how popular it gets, if it's underground," Guy said. "You want freaks and outlaws, not brownnosers. *The Cuckoo* needs to be a cult, a sacrifice, not a career path."

"This totally sounds like my dad," Reed said.

"Even if you are right, Guy," Hart said, "it's kind of dickish to do it without asking us."

"I apologize," Guy said. "But there are things at work here too big for a student to see. I didn't see them either, when I was an undergrad—nor did Reed's dad. We thought we were changing things. Now a bunch of years later, we realize that all our protests are just another opportunity for Stutts to fundraise," Guy said bitterly. "It's an unpleasant feeling, especially when you're too old to start over. We wanted to save you that.

"You've got money, and now you've got a secret office owned by no one. You're untouchable. You can do all the things we wanted to do…" Guy said. He turned to Hart. "Quinn Bostwick wanted to take *The Cuckoo* underground, but his staff rebelled."

"You know Quinn Bostwick?" Hart asked.

"'Course I do," Guy said, "He was two years younger. You kind of look like him—but I'll tell you: you better get wild if you want to run in his league."

Ellen, the one of them with the most to lose, made a final attempt. "But why can't we co-exist with the University?"

"The king is the king, and the jester is the jester," Guy said. "Rivington's a selfish, stupid man, and he's not the worst of them. He might use

The Cuckoo—but as soon as you weren't useful anymore, he'd get rid of you. There'd be no magazine by the time Peter and Hart graduated, if they graduated…Face it: your future is underground."

Nobody knew what to say to that, until Tabitha spoke.

"Guy, I've met a lot of Stuttsies," she said, "and frankly, most of them are pretty boring. Just when I think I'm ready to move along, I meet a real freak who convinces me that maybe this place is worthwhile."

"Thanks, I think," Guy said. He looked at his watch. "Oh, golly. I have a University function to endure. Would anyone like to walk with me to the Cummerbund College Senior Fellows' room?"

"Reed and I are working that," Hart said. "Can everybody else finish packing up the office?"

"Oh, sure," Peter said, "now I see why you got that work-study job."

"You have my permission to throw everything away," Hart said.

"But not Mrs. Morgenthau!" Reed said. "I want that picture of a woman putting—"

Ellen cut him off. "Spare us," she said.

8

Past, Present, and Future

Tuesday, September 14th, 7:57 pm

Hart wasn't sure he agreed with Guy, and even less sure he wanted to bet his whole Stutts career on the little lawyer's theory of the jester versus the king. He was frankly pretty glad when they parted ways, he and Reed going into the kitchen, and Guy upstairs to the Senior Fellows' Room.

"This is a good venue," Reed said, as they changed into their horrific polyester togs (cornflower blue with red piping). "You can watch from above." The room had a gallery at one end, specifically designed for the waitstaff to monitor the meal.

"I see what you mean," Hart said, after they had served the drinks. He and Reed could watch the entire event from above and behind the table—anticipating every diner's wish, but entirely out-of-sight, so that no one important would be reminded of their grubby presence.

Filled with wood and brass and leather, Cummerbund College Senior Fellows' room was a common locale for alumni functions. It made alums feel special—and wealthy, which made them give more money.

The ones that had it, that is. Contrary to outside opinion, not every Stutts graduate was well off. Increasingly, more and more of them were not, for two reasons: first, the university was admitting more kids who were smart, but poor; and second, a lot of graduates went into high-prestige, low-salary jobs like teaching or community organizing. So Hart shouldn't have been surprised to see roughly half of the room below filled with people wearing their one nice jacket. (Or, in one case, a favorite poncho from the old days.)

Although everybody was roughly the same age, there were definitely two distinct tribes on display. There were the suit-and-tie folks, which grouped themselves to the right of President Rivington, and there were the others, who sat to Rivington's left. No single aesthetic held together the causal side, except an almost visible shimmer of hostility towards the suit set.

"Man, some of them look *broke*," Hart said, feeling something inside him tremble. "Which one's your dad? Which side, hippie or richie?"

Reed laughed. "Hippie. Blue shirt, no tie, balding, just to the left of Rivington…"

"Got it," Hart said. "Boy, he really looks like you. Same 'powerful frame.'"[29]

"You should've seen him when he had hair," Reed said. "We were like Russian dolls, one small, one large."

Hart laughed. He was shocked at how obvious the schism was between the two sides; it was like an eighth-grade dance, with boys on the one wall, girls on the other. Still, as different as the sides were, they came together in affection for Stutts. This gave Hart what his mom called "a warm fuzzy," and remembering the phrase almost ruined the feeling, but not quite.

Reed looked at his watch. "Refill time," he said, and the boys quietly walked downstairs. They got pitchers of ice water from the kitchen, and performed their duty without incident.

As the boys circulated, Interim President Rivington clinked on a glass. "Ladies and gentlemen," he said, "we meet here tonight to commemorate the thirtieth anniversary of a great event in Stutts history, The Great Meditate-In."

"Whichever side of the debate you were on," Rivington said, "radical or legacy, protestor or shock troop, we should all remember that the system worked: our friends to my left were able to protest, and our beloved University was able to continue functioning, as if there had been no protest at all. Both sides won."

Guy coughed loudly into his napkin: "Bullshit." There was a burst of laughter from his side of the room.

Rivington had always hated the lawyer, precisely because he did stuff like that. "Did you have anything you wanted to say, Guy?"

"Only that Reggie might look at it a little differently," Guy said. "As some of us remember, Reggie Williams died from the mace."

"Not our fault," Chief Constable Renalli said. "That kid was allergic to *everything*."

"Like getting hit in the head with a baton," Reed's father shot back.

Rivington stepped in, hoping to keep the evening on track. "It doesn't surprise me that passions still run high; it was quite a time in all of our lives."

"Fascist," mumbled the man with a scraggly goatee on Guy's left.

Rivington ignored him. "Thanks to the fine people at Harriman, we have a montage of photographs taken from that week. Could somebody get the lights?"

To the strains of Crosby, Stills, Nash and Young's "Four Dead in Ohio," Rivington clicked through slide after slide. Each photo illuminated some aspect of the thirty-year-old controversy. There was Mr. Rodriguez standing

29 This was a running joke between them. Hart had once opened Reed's high-school yearbook and read all the mentions of Reed in it. He'd especially liked a photo of Reed playing hockey—"badly," Reed admitted—that had noted Reed's "powerful frame."

at a podium, gesturing passionately. Then, one of Guy, holding a sign that read, "Stutts Students Express Their Total Solidarity With the Oppressed Peoples of Umidor."

"Guy, I may not agree with your politics," Professor North interjected (he was sitting to the right of President Rivington), "but you can squeeze more onto a sign than any other person I know."

Guy grumbled something, but the montage continued, showing the mammoth meditate-in that Mr. Rodriguez had led on Old Quad. "I like the time-lapse effect," Rivington said as he clicked. "The grass is growing around you"—click, click, click—"you guys are getting thinner"—click, click—"we're laughing at you"—a shot of a youthful Renalli pouring a cup of beer over the completely passive goatee-man's head—"and finally, the cavalry arrives."

"Nazis!" a woman in a kaftan and comfortable shoes said loudly.

"Oo-RAH," Renalli bellowed. Breaking up the meditate-in was as close as he ever got to the military (he had other priorities). Still, he considered it a definite highlight of his life. The campus cops had deputized the entire Stutts football team to go in, wearing full pads, and bust up the demonstration—after a photo in *Flag* magazine showed that the meditating protestors were spelling out "FUCK STUTTS" when viewed from above. "We wiped you out, Che!" Renalli gloated, using his dismissive nickname for Reed's dad.

The left side of the table rose to the bait. "You did not!" Mr. Rodriguez pointed out angrily. "We left because somebody was stealing our stuff!"[30]

"People, people," Rivington yelled, trying to calm everybody down. "This is a happy occasion. We have to remember what happened: this was a victory for both sides." He turned to Mr. Rodriguez. "Che—sorry, *David*, you can't pretend that you weren't allowed to protest."

"Big deal," a frizzy-haired dude to the left of the kaftan woman muttered. "The Meistersingers sponsored a Umidorean death squad!" The Meistersingers were Stutts oldest, most prestigious singing group.[31]

30 Prior to the protest, Mr. Rodriguez had gathered all the protestors' valuables and put them in a safe-deposit box in a local bank. After the protest had become an embarrassment to Stutts, a then-youthful Professor North had taken it upon himself to call in a few favors from that bank. Within an hour, the contents of that safe-deposit box had been delivered to him, and he had passed it to some trusted acolytes for fencing. The news that "there are some guys outside the library selling all your shit" dispersed the meditate-in within moments.

31 *A capella* singing groups infested Stutts with a ferocity topped only by mime troupes and black mold. The mime troupes were more popular, as the bar of talent was even lower. More than once, Hart had wished that students in the 1800s had taken up something less obtrusive and more useful, like needlepoint. Or hara-kiri.

"I resent that," the man sitting to the right of Renalli said angrily. "We performed at their headquarters for El Jefe's birthday. They were really nice." Then he added, "They could teach some of the people here a thing or two about patriotism."

"Please—folks—we're all alumni here," President Rivington said.

"...even though some of us give more money than others," the ex-Meistersinger yelled at the frizzy-haired man, who responded with a middle digit.

"Corporate whore-drone!"

"Oh, nice one. Shaved your legs lately?"

"I'm a *dude*, idiot!" Things teetered on the edge of outright fisticuffs. Hart and Reed appeared at the foot of the room, holding plates with salads on them. President Rivington signaled furiously for them to enter—free food would calm the savage breast.

"Ah, the food is here," Rivington said. "We can continue reminiscing after we eat. Now, speaking of The Meistersingers, Bob here has been gracious enough to hire them for the evening, to serenade us with a few songs."

A group of well-scrubbed students, all in tuxedoes, trooped into the room. In the decades since the meditate-in The Meistersingers had gotten even more reactionary; they'd dedicated their last CD to "that American aristrocracy, the Military-Industrial Complex." This year's "pitch" (the de facto leader) was also high up in the Party of Contempt, the place in the Political Union where Stutts students playacted Hitlerian.

Mr. Rodriguez leaned over to Guy, who had tucked into his salad. "Did you try to get The Magic Dragons?" he asked, naming the campus' liberal counterpart to The Meistersingers.

"I called them forty times, but nobody called me back."

Mr. Rodriguez sighed. "I blame pot," he sighed.

"We've written a special song for the occasion," the pitch said, eliciting a groan from the left side of the room. "We hope you enjoy it."

"Guy, let's jet," Mr. Rodriguez said. "I'll introduce you to Reed some other time."

The group began to sing, full-voice. "A-one, and a-two...*Deutschland, Deutschland über alles...*"

The room erupted; the right whistling and cheering, the left indignant and furious. Rolls flew, even pieces of salad were launched, yet The Meistersingers sang on, plowing through their new show-stopper.

The left side, led by Mr. Rodriguez, stalked towards the door.

"Still can't take a joke," Renalli said, as Reed's dad walked by.

"Still a piece of shit," goatee-man said. "Politics isn't the Stutts-Keasbey game, meathead."

"Don't expect a donation from me this year," Mr. Rodriguez said to President Rivington.

"Wait—"

The Meistersinger grabbed Rivington's sleeve and said, "Let him go—I'll double mine."

"Why are you making such a big fuss?" Professor North asked Mr. Rodriguez. "They're just kids..."

"No," Reed's dad said. "You're just kids. All of you." He left.

Guy was right behind. "Pat," he told the President, "I just want you to know that what happened tonight was totally insulting." He left, too.

"Thirty years later, and they're still running away," Renalli said. Then called after, "Call me when you grow a pair, Guy!"

"Call me when you make some money, loser," the kaftan woman said, by-accident/on-purpose grazing the cop's head with her expensive handbag. Renalli unbuttoned the holster of his taser.

"Do it," the woman taunted. "I need a topic for my next documentary."

Renalli backed down, and she left, laughing at him.

Hart and Reed watched the whole fracas unfold from their perch in the gallery. "This is fucking crazy," Hart whispered. "Do people ever really graduate?"

Reed shrugged. "I'd love to kick that old Meistersinger's ass."

Hart was torn—if they got involved, wouldn't they be perpetuating this asinine feud? In the end, weren't they all Stuttsies? Then he looked at Reed; his friend was mad, and had every right to be. Hell, Hart thought, I'm mad, too. North and Renalli, those guys were assholes. "I know what we're going to do," Hart said.

"Hold that old guy down while I punch him?" Reed asked.

"Reed," Hart said, "violence never solves anything, especially if you get caught. Here's my plan. Got any pennies?"

Reed dug in his pocket. "Yeah. Why? We're going to buy them off?"

"We serve them dinner, then dessert, just like normal," Hart said. "Then come the buckets they ordered from The Rat, right?"

"They're chilling in the fridge downstairs. Hurry up and get to the part where they suck it," Reed said.

"Down in the kitchen, we'll pour a bunch of dish soap into them. Those things are so alcoholic, they'll never taste it."

"So we give 'em the squirts," Reed said.

"But not before we jam pennies into all the bathroom doors we can find."

Reed laughed, then said, "Wait a sec—won't they trace it back to us?

Won't we get fired?"

"Fuck this stupid job," Hart said. "Who wants to hang around people like these?"

Reed was surprised, and delighted—Hart was usually the peacemaker to an annoying degree. "You sound like Pete," he said.

"Bite your tongue," Hart said.

"No, I think it's good," Reed said. "You gotta be able to kick ass occasionally, now that we're underground rebels."

"We're just settling a score for your dad."

Reed wrapped his big arm around Hart and gave him a squeeze.

"Quit it," Hart said, feeling that something was changing and not sure he liked it. "We gotta go serve the fish."

Down below, The Meistersingers gave it their all. Halfway through the third encore of "The Horst Wessel Song" (with new, Stutts-specific lyrics), the alum held up his hand.

"That's enough, boys," the old Meistersinger said. "Great job. We really enjoyed it... Well, *some* of us, anyway." Grinning lupinely, he dug out his wallet, then extracted a half-inch of bills. "Go get drunk on me."

"Wow! Thanks!" The pitch took the money. The group filed out, chattering and jubilant.

Hart and Reed appeared at the door, carrying two silver buckets. Each was filled to the rim with Der Rat's famous Black Velvet concoction. This being Stutts, the ingredients were a closely guarded secret. The boys put their buckets down on the table. Cakes of ice floated serenely in the brew (which had just a *touch* more of a head on it than usual). Reed and Hart untied the cloth aprons that hung around their waists, and laid them flat on the table; inside each one was a pouch containing twenty or so sterling silver straws.

An alumnus picked one up and admired it. "I haven't seen one of these in years."

"You should get back to Great Littleton more often," President Rivington said. "There's only one way to drink down a bucket."

"Does anyone need anything else?" Reed asked sweetly.

President Rivington said, "I think that will be all, boys. Excellent work."

"Hope you enjoy it," Hart said, and they disappeared.

"A toast to President Rivington," one alum suggested; this was lustily done.

"Pat," the old Meistersinger asked, "what's this I hear about increasing the University's profit margin? Can you share any details?"

Rivington looked at Professor North. "What do you think, Glenbard?"

he asked chummily. "Can we chance it? Is the room bugged?"

"Only by me," Professor North said. Everybody pretended he was joking.

"My vision is simple," President Rivington said. "Stutts is a *business*. Just like any other business, we need to reduce our costs and maximize our profits. Outsourcing, offloading—the private sector shows us how to do it. Can we move some departments to, say, India? Can we go totally virtual, and rent out the campus? Or get the city to pay us *not* to do it?"

"Sound idea!"

"Bra-*vo*, man!"

Everyone's enthusiasm encouraged Rivington. "The second half of the equation is increasing our revenue. I plan to pursue every possible avenue. No amount of money is too small. Can we put advertisements behind the professors, for example?"

"Or make them wear it, like NASCAR drivers," an alum offered.

"See how simple it is, once you make the paradigm shift?" Rivington said. "It's time to stop thinking of Stutts as an ivory tower, away from the rough-and-tumble of capitalism. I say, let's enter the 21st Century, and make some *real* money!" Over the cheers, Rivington continued, really warming to his topic. "Who needs the SAT? Why are we keeping those people in business? We're going to make our own test, and charge people for the privilege of taking it."

"Should've been done years ago," an alum said, chewing.

"Stutts is synonomous with the best in eductation," Rivington said, "so we're going to marketize that by endorsing 'feeder' schools. Everybody from your local Montessori to the snootiest prep school will pay through the nose for our seal of approval. Why? Because we'll suggest—never directly, of course—that students from approved schools will have a better chance of getting in."

"What have we been doing all these years?" another alum said. "When I think of all the money we haven't made..."

"Don't," Rivington said. "Instead, think about our new line of educational toys. The deal's almost done. Chinese company. Slave wages. Pure profit."

"Get a customer young, and you've got 'em for life," the first alum said.

"My administration will be about three things: Brand loyalty. Vertical integration. And profit," Rivington said.

"To profit," somebody murmured. "To profit," the rest of the room responded.

Then the dish soap hit.

9

Everybody Loves Lemonade

Thursday, September 23rd, 3:14 pm

Hart thought about the alumni dinner a lot in the days and weeks that followed. It was like *The Cuckoo* versus the *Spec* forever, sensible individuals disappearing into a tribe and letting it drag everyone down to their lowest level. Was that what being an adult was about? Choosing sides, then settling scores? And if it was, could Hart transfer to another reality?

Reed was calling their childish trick "the first act of the new underground *Cuckoo*." Hart wasn't ready to go there quite yet, but remembering what he and Reed had done (not to mention reading about it later in the *Spec*) gave Hart a savage, I-am-a-sword-of-Justice sort of pleasure. He knew it had been petty, knew that he was better than that—but what if the world wasn't?

Hart mulled things over as he walked through the afternoon sun to his seminar with Professor Lemonade. I understand where Peter's coming from, he thought, but I'm not as bad as him. There are still some things I believe in.

Or were there? Hart had always taken it as a given that adults were much wiser and more intelligent than himself, and that they ran the world in a compassionate, sensible way. After what he saw at the dinner, he suddenly wasn't so sure. Alumni could be childish, sure—but this was a fund-raising dinner, not a football game. Even worse, President Rivington didn't lift a finger to stop it, neither did Professor North; they practically instigated all the hostilities. Didn't they see how stupid and petty it was? Of course, you could say that he and Reed had sunk to their level, but that wasn't quite fair. We *had* to do it, Hart thought, as an errant football narrowly missed his head and landed in an ivy-covered moat. Those guys needed to be taught a lesson.

Hart grabbed the football and tossed it back. "Thanks, dude."

Hart walked on, a chill wind at his back; it stirred the leaves strewn about the slate footpath. Kicking a spiky sycamore pod, Hart wondered if the people running Stutts were any smarter—or better—than he was. Maybe they *weren't*. Maybe all the things that they did were as impulsive, selfish and, let's be honest, essentially random as the things Hart himself did. That was a scary thought; Hart took the Lytton Hall steps two at a time, as if he could outrun this new doubt. He would be safe inside Lytton; all the classes held there would ward off any evil. Even if the people who ran Stutts acted like children, at least the classes were good. At least the education you got, all the stuff they painstakingly crammed into your head, at least that was useful. Undeniably good. At least it amounted to something.

Didn't it?

Hart's writing seminar with Lemonade, while light on actual instruction, was pretty damn entertaining if you could avoid being hit by the wreckage. Many Stutts professors had a reputation for being eccentric; as far as Hart could tell, that was a job requirement. Yet because he was young, and because he was used to being catered to, Lemonade took this to a whole new level. The swearing was the least of it. There was also the lashing-out, and the lack of preparation, and the body odor—all of which the students were paying an astronomical sum to endure. A single credit at Stutts cost more than a week at the Waldorf-Astoria.

Still, dear reader, one must save a scrap of sympathy, for those strange, lonely chalk-smeared men and women standing at the front of the class. A whole Stutts' seminar's worth of ambition was tough to face all at once, especially when you felt like a fraud and a failure, as people often do. God knows Lemonade did.

By the time Hart met him, Lemonade was a desperate man, battered by what he called "The Year of Four Revelations." Twelve months ago, just after his 24th birthday and halfway through his anxiously anticipated follow-up book (a sprawling, time-shifting, postmodern allegory blending a golem, experimental face transplants, and the fast food industry) Lemonade suddenly realized that he didn't have anything to say.

This was the first revelation.

Initially, he chalked it up to the Aderol, an addiction left over from his Stutts days. Then it got worse: he realized that he hadn't ever had much to say—*The Scintillating Story of Me* could've been about any coddled, media-addled, fame-hungry kid from the NPR-belt. That was why people loved the book so much; not only could it have been about them, the book was so blank it practically *was*. Lemonade's book wasn't as much a memoir as a 550 page Mad-Lib: "Growing up in rich lily-white suburb, phoning it in at school and caring about nothing but meaningless bit of pop-culture, I thought everybody's parents made sick amount of money a year."

This was the second revelation.

As Lemonade's mentions in the gossip columns dwindled, his agent was getting antsy. "How's the book going?"

"Not good. I think I'd rather be a lawyer."

"All the greats say that. Are you taking those pills I gave you?" his agent asked. "They're awesome." She was hoping Lemonade would get hooked. Recovery stories sold, and so did young death. It was a win/win. But try as he might, Lemonade couldn't have a single psychotic episode.

"Work with me," his agent said. "Take more. Mix them with alcohol. I'll call the ambulance, I promise I will!" Lemonade fired her and took solace in food.

Watching him pack away another expensive lunch, his editor suggested, "Have you considered an eating disorder? Male body anxiety is very hot right now. Metrosexuals would eat that up."

"Yeah, but they'd throw it up later!" Lemonade had said, ordering dessert. He gave it a shot, but unfortunately genetics had cursed him with a pitifully weak gag reflex, and the writer ballooned to nearly 300 pounds. His dance single went nowhere. The bipolar Ukrainian model he'd been dating dumped him and took their marmot with her.

It was time for the third revelation.

Sitting there in his underwear, eating cream puffs and sobbing, Lemonade came to the third revelation, which had two parts. Part one: His life was a mess, but it wasn't a salable mess. Part two: he was serious about that lawyer thing. Or maybe computer programming?

First, he had to get out of his book contract. So Lemonade laid in some supplies, unplugged the phone, and worked as he never had before, diligently destroying his prose. Confident that this was the worst work he had ever done, Lemonade turned the novel into his editor.

"I'm not just your editor, I'm a fan—this is one of the greatest days of my life," he burbled. "Me, too," Lemonade said, then almost sprinted out of the building. He didn't want to be around when his fan hit the shit.

Lemonade figured that being presented with a vile, bloated, incoherent, self-aggrandizing, and even ineptly paginated manuscript would send the editor into a *grand mal* and their contract into court. Lemonade would give some of the money back, be drummed out of the book biz, and live happily ever after.

Then a funny thing happened. The book wasn't just bad, it was legendarily bad. As its reputation for awfulness grew, so did Lemonade's reputation—he became an emblem of the writer's struggle. A fundamentally passive guy, soon he found himself schlepping around to all the TV shows, talking about writer's block, blood-sugar swings, and the terrible price of fame. Totally against his will, Lemonade became more celebrated than ever.

A Stutts professor who was doing a monograph on the semiotics of Oprah Winfrey heard about Lemonade's plight. Thinking he was being helpful, the prof called Lemonade and offered him a spot as a visiting lecturer: "Maybe a change of scenery will do you good." At first Lemonade was going to turn it down, thinking that the reflected glory of such a prestigious college could only push him further into the life he was desperate to escape.

Then he had the fourth revelation.

If he could be thoroughly inappropriate in such a public position—if he could just be outrageous enough, for a sufficient length of time—surely he would go too far. The place of no-forgiveness had to exist, even if you were famous. If Lemonade could just get there, would be scorned, ostracized—and left in peace.

The first semester last spring had gone depressingly well, with everyone looking the other way as he carried on an affair with two of his students at once. The rivals' climactic cat-fight was the talk of Finals and even made the front page of the *Spec*; but this scandal only increased Lemonade's profile.

"Look, you idiots," Lemonade shouted at a post-brawl air-clearing/panel discussion sponsored by the Wymyn's Cyntyr, "I'm not transgressive! I'm not commenting on society! I'm just an asshole! Leave me the fuck alone!" The next morning, he woke up to a student editorial praising his "plain-speaking in the best American tradition."

But a new year brought new opportunities. Crouched outside the seminar room, Lemonade was determined to make this semester different. Though he had tried his best to be sour, unhelpful, and nasty during Shopping Period, the class was full. Even worse, the first few weeks had gone dishearteningly smoothly.

"Time to take it up a notch," Lemonade said, splashing a bit of coffee on his jacket. He dressed in foul clothes, and tried not to shower, but still, there was something missing.

At a permissive place like Stutts, sex was obviously the wrong approach; this time he'd try drugs. And not anything hip or intellectual; just beer and rotgut, the cheaper the better. He wasn't going to actually be drunk—drunks could be charming, and the way his luck was running, Lemonade would probably be beloved, canonized as a campus character. He would fake it. Lemonade would be stone-cold sober, the better to hone his obnoxiousness to its utmost edge.

Lemonade finished his coffee and slung the half-full cup onto the floor (unfortunately, nobody saw him do it). Okay, he thought. Showtime.

He pulled the doorknob towards him vigorously, knowing full well it opened into the room. Lemonade tried it again, harder, and threw in a few muttered swearwords.

In the seminar room on the other side, some students began to snicker.

"He's totally wasted?" offered a girl sitting next to Hart. (She was from California so everything she said sounded like a question.)

"Good," said the turtlenecked boy across the table from her. "He won't notice when I slip this into his briefcase." He held up a manuscript.

"You'll have to get through me, first," said another student. One-by-one six manuscripts plopped onto the seminar table. Looking at the pile, Hart felt good about not imposing on the professor, then felt really stupid for not bringing something. What was seven, when there were six already? Ambition gave his ass a sharp bite.

Outside, Lemonade was making no progress. "Goddamn it!" he slurred from behind the door.

"Maybe he's brought enough for everybody," said a beefy boy in a backwards baseball cap.

"Don't worry," Hart said. "This room is so small we'll get a contact buzz off his breath."[32]

After a little more yanking and swearing, Hart finally got up and opened the door. Lemonade weaved in. "Thank you," he mumbled. Improvising, the writer "tripped" on a course packet and broke his nose. "Oh, fuck..."

It was a masterstroke; several students bolted out of the room, unable to handle the gushing blood. Lemonade blew a gout into his hand, and smeared it all over his face. "Guess what movie this is?" he yelled, trying to look catatonic.

"Silence of the Lambs," Hart offered. "When Lecter eats that guy's—"

"Nah! Come on!" Lemonade said. "It's *Carrie!*"

Nobody laughed but the professor. Lemonade's instincts told him it was time for a violent mood swing. His face darkened into a sour frown. "You guys suck." He took a silver flask out of his jacket pocket and took a mighty pull (of water, but the students didn't know that). "Who's got some tissues? I'll give you an 'A' for the semester, I'm serious," Lemonade said.

Five minutes and a pound of bloody Kleenex later, the class was underway. Lemonade was angrily expanding on his incredibly punitive and unfair

32 Since the introduction of deodorant in the mid-1800s, Stutts had cultivated an educational fetish, which could be summed up mathematically: quality of education = (professor / number of people in the class) x the inverse of physical distance from lectern. This meant that the smaller the class size, the better the education—with an emphasis on being able to touch the hem of the professor's garment, if at all possible. So a Stutts education tended to produce acolytes—and more often than anyone cared to admit, *really* messy love affairs.

attendance policy when there was a knock.

"FUCK! Now I'll never remember my place!" The instructor stood up, none too steadily, and ripped upon a door. "I DO NOT TOLERATE TARDI—"

A student mumbled quietly, "Closet."

Lemonade turned, eyes aflame. Hair askew, face a mask of dried blood, tissues hanging from each nostril, Lemonade looked positively demonic. "Don't you *ever* correct me, you little prick!" This was the role I was born to play, Lemonade thought as he opened the right door.

He gave it to the girl, both barrels, hoping that he could make her burst into tears before she even entered the classroom. When Lemonade finally ran out of breath, the student gave him a cheerful smile.

"That's all right, Professor Lemonade. I know you're under a lot of pressure," she chirped. "I read that interview you did in the June issue of *Dopers & Mopers.*"

"Yeah, don't worry," Turtleneck chimed in, as the girl squeezed past the gawping writer. "Don't let it get you down. Genius is always misunderstood."

Lemonade walked back to his chair, dazed. He'd given them his best shot, and they were still coming. It was only a matter of time before the autographs, Lemonade thought, hauling out his flask again.

The California girl sitting next to Hart said (pseudo-confidentially, loud enough for everyone to hear), "When I saw him cry last year on Oprah I knew he was my favorite writer ever?"

Lemonade glared over his flask, sizing the girl up. For a long moment he considered bolo-punching her, but then decided against it: There were no cameras. And he had to hold something in reserve—it was clearly going to be a long, long semester.

Lemonade decided it was time to flee, to cut his losses and end the seminar before California girl asked him to inscribe her breasts. He knew where *that* ended—an invitation back for next semester, with more money per.

"I gotta go," he lied. "I'm gonna puke." With a sway, he grabbed the door and strode through it.

It was a closet. Lemonade decided to wait them out; when they didn't leave immediately, he pretended to be noisily sick. He had to stay in there for an hour before the last student jammed his manuscript under the closet door and left.

° ° °

Hart stumbled out of Lytton Hall bewildered by Professor Lemonade's performance. *That* was a class? *That* was a professor? I know he's famous, Hart thought, but jeez. Lemonade certainly didn't play by the rules.

Lemonade, the alumni dinner…a lot of stuff was bouncing around Hart's head. If the adult world was fucked-up, and they rewarded you for telling it to go to hell, maybe being a rule-follower wasn't the way to get ahead. Maybe giving Teacher what she wanted, though it had gotten him to Stutts, didn't work in the long run. Maybe an underground *Cuckoo* was a quicker way to the top of the heap—and on his own terms, too. Every Stuttsie wanted to be successful, but you got extra credit for "doing it your way." You could rebel, but only if you were eventually recognized by whatever you had rebelled against. Hart didn't mind being a rebel if there was no risk in it. An underground *Cuckoo* might be able to have its cake (be popular), and eat it, too (but not seem to care). His mind was changing—but still there was resistance, inside. Authority had been good to him. Who was he, of all people, to question it?

Deep in thought, Hart didn't see the golf cart coming. "Outta the way dumb-ass!" Chief Constable Renalli yelled through his bullhorn.

Hart jumped away just in time, landing in the Harriman Library moat.

Another kid saw him standing there, knee-deep in ivy and plastic bags. The kid pointed at the cop careening off into the distance, his electronic horn blaring "Dixie."

"I feel a lot safer with him around, don't you?" the kid said.

10

Hippy-Trippy

Friday, October 1st, 12:03 pm

At Stutts, you learned to ignore TV crews, especially if they were just local ones. The Great Littleton station was always tromping around campus, taping "kooky kollege kids" segments; they trotted them out whenever the day's quota of bloody mayhem came up short.

Last week, they had spent an hour in Hart's college. Some freshman's parrot had learned to imitate Great Littleton's sporadic gunfire. "Pow! Po-pow-pow!" Really cute—unless it kept you up all night. Peter was threatening to cook it.

Today the TV crew was in Reed's college. Corset had a quirk in its founding documents: during mealtimes, several comely undergrads were required to cruise around the dining hall clad in nothing but underwear. (This was their workstudy job.) The students had to be gorgeous, and the undies had to be Featherbottom brand—for it was Featherbottom's founder who had originally put up the money for the College's construction.

"How's my hair?" the reporter asked, then launched into a retake. "Could you eat every meal next to a beautiful stranger—who was in her underwear? Well, thanks to a quirk of history, these Stutts students have to…or they don't graduate."

As the reporter said this, Reed had "wandered" into the background. He stared directly into the camera, then began opening and closing his eyes and mouth like some demented guppie.

The cameraman swore. "Bob, a kid's in the shot."

The reporter turned around. "MOVE, dumbass!"

"Sorry," Reed said, taking an e-x-t-r-a long time to get his apple juice.

Thanks to the constant skin, Corset students considered themselves to be the most sexually liberated on campus; in reality they were just bored.[33] Even so, trapped in repressed Dacron, Hart ate there whenever possible.

"How's this year's snowsuit calendar coming?" Hart asked after Reed

33 In an interesting quirk of human behavior, a profusion of scantily-clad colleagues had pushed the Corseteers towards a diametrically opposed kink: Corset's most beautiful specimens sported layers, and lots of them. The College system tended to do things like this, creating bizarre fetish-studded subcultures. There was no harm in it, as long as you were at Stutts. After graduation, however, Stuttsies usually needed a lot of therapy.

had returned. Every year, the students of Corset produced a snowsuit calendar and donated the proceeds to charity. Reed had gotten very involved with this year's edition, when it looked like *The Cuckoo* was gone for good.

"Awesome," Reed said. "The girls are totally hot."

"Really?" Hart asked hopefully. "Stutts student" and "totally hot" were almost perfect antonyms.

"Yeah, they're sweating like pigs," Reed said. "But that's somebody else's problem, now that we're back in business."

"Are we?" Hart said. "I'm sorry, I've never run an underground magazine before. What do we do?"

"Anything we want, I think," Reed said.

"So let's do an issue," Hart said. He felt like a cow that needed to be milked.

"We have to announce ourselves first," Reed said. "Everybody thinks we're dead."

"We're undead," Hart quipped.

"Guys!" Peter hollered from the other end of the dining hall.

Everyone turned; "Peter really needs to work on his shyness," Reed said.

"Tell me about it, I have to live with him," Hart said, as Peter rolled towards them.

A man and woman walked by in their undies, but Peter didn't even give them a glance. He grabbed the backpack from the back of his chair and took out the glass bottle and magazine they had found in the time-capsule. "Guys, I know what 'Vonnegut' is," he said.

"Really?" Hart said.

"Yeah!" Peter flipped through the magazine. "I was reading the magazine on the crapper, and came across this." He put the magazine down, and tapped on an article. "Read it."

> "*GOV'T RED-FACED OVER THEFT OF DESIGNER DOPE*
> GREAT LITTLETON—Only weeks after the campus was torn apart by 'The Great Meditate-In,' another controversy is pitting freaks against feds at the world's most prestigious university.
>
> Rumors have been circulating for years that the CIA has been using Stutts University students as guinea pigs in its continuing search to find truth serums, mind-control drugs, and other chemical aids to skullduggery. Though several Stuttsies have gone public with lurid stories, government officials have always denied any wrongdoing. Last year, in a speech to alumni, Stutts' President McGregor Paladin, characterized the tales as "the product of overwork and a few too many 'buckets' at Der Ratheskellar."
>
> Now, some student radicals (or merely rascals?) have forced officials to admit that there might be more to the story. Last week

two members of *The Cuckoo*, Stutts' student humor magazine, broke into the office of Professor Glenbard North. Reputedly the CIA's pipeline into Stutts, North is invariably fingered as the overseer for all the drug-testing.

According to a communication sent to *Ramparts*, the Stuttsies pilfered a 12-ounce bottle of a colorless, odorless substance code-named 'Vonnegut,' (in an ironic homage to the popular countercultural writer). "They were hoping it would turn us into zombie-assassins," the students wrote, "but it didn't. It just made us write jokes nobody else understood."

Professor North has demanded that the students, Guy Guillaume and David Rodriguez, be expelled. "This drug is completely harmless, but it is government property and must be returned. I assure everyone that it has no useful properties," he said to *Ramparts*. "It really has no effects whatsoever."

The students disagree. "In our experience—and we've both had multiple doses, unwilling and otherwise— 'Vonnegut' strips away social conditioning. Peer pressure, who you think everyone wants you to be, it's all gone with 'Vonnegut' in your system. It allows the user to access his/her true nature, and impels them to act in accordance with it. It's not a high exactly, and depending on how you're lived your life so far, can be no fun. 'Vonnegut' strips away the mask, and reveals the beauty, or ugliness, beneath.

"Turns out they found themselves a truth serum—good or bad, asshole or saint, 'Vonnegut' shows who you *really* are."

Hart didn't know what to say—it sounded scary. He shook the bottle. There was still plenty in it. "I wonder if it's still good?"

"Only one way to find out," Peter said, sticking out his tongue.

"Wait," Reed said. "That won't tell us anything. Much to our chagrin, we already know who you are. Bending under peer pressure ain't your problem."

"Unfair!" Peter said. "I demand tangerine trees and marmalade skies!"

"I say we give it to Hart," Reed said.

Hart didn't like the sound of that. What if he was different than he thought he was? What if he was *really* a jerk? Everybody would find out! "I nominate Reed!" he said defensively.

"Nah, Hart," Reed said, "I'm already fucked-up by the drug. My dad's chromosomes are probably little cinders. My vote is Tabitha."

"She's not human," Peter said. "No offense, Hart. All I mean is, it might not work on her, even if it is still good."

"I just thought of something," Hart said. "What if it's deteriorated or something? It could be poisonous."

"Good point. So who's expendable?" Peter mused aloud. "Somebody who we know, who's not all Vonnegutted-up already, and who we don't care whether it kills or not..."

There was a commotion behind them, at the entrance to the dining hall.

"Over there, Pukes!" Trip Darling yelled, his tuber-like head poking out from the curtains of his new litter. "Take me to the hottie in the peach panties!" The two boys carrying the vehicle maneuvered it into the corner and set it down.

"Um, Trip," one of the litter-carriers said, "technically we're not Pukes."

"That's right," the other said. "Technically, we're Gnomes."[34] To emphasize this point, the boy adjusted his red felt cloche hat. According to CCA tradition all Gnomes wore this hat at all times, even when asleep.

"Technically, you're both pieces of crap," he said. "Biff, get me a Coke! Beekman, get me a muffin!"

The two boys scuttled past. Reed pointed at Beekman. "How about him?" he said. "He's in my Calc class. Totally high-strung."

"Sounds like he needs to lose some social conditioning," Peter declared.

"Nice nips!" Trip brayed to the underwear model inching away in disgust. When she didn't respond to his pillow talk, Trip took his annoyance out on his minions. "Don't wait in line, fart-knocker!" he commanded. *"Cut!"*

Hart, Reed, and Peter had a simultaneous thought. Without a word, they sprang into action.

Beekman walked past, carrying Trip's muffin as carefully as a five-year-old ringbearer. "Hey, Beekman," Reed said. "Got a second?"

"Really not," Beekman said.

"Do you know when the Calc midterm is going to be?" Reed said. "Is it next week, or the week after?"

Beekman put down the muffin, and pulled out his PDA.

"Isn't that hat hot?" Hart asked.

Beekman glanced at Hart, whom he'd spent most of last year trying to kill. This made him nervous, and he dropped the PDA's stylus.

Peter, concealing the bottle's eyedropper cap in his hand, did the deed. As Beekman bent down, Peter took the eyedropper and jammed it into the

34 "Gnomes" were students admitted to Comma Comma Apostrophe strictly for the purpose of keeping the frat's GPA from entering the realm of imaginary numbers. CCA's Gnomes, Biff and Beekman, had been fast friends at Ponce, a Manhattan prep school known for its proud tradition of student fellatio. Unfortunately, Biff and Beekman received no fellation whatsoever during their four years of high school. Confused, resentful, and more than a little hurt, the pair was determined that college would be different. Last year, as freshmen, Biff had conceived yet another in a long series of horrible ideas: they would rush CCA. Surely membership would put them in line for some action! By the time the boys realized their mistake, they had been installed in squalid basement digs and were responsible for doing everyone's homework. Now they wanted out, but the Gnomery agreement was almost impossible to break. (Beekman had even tried a note from his mom.)

soft side of the muffin, squeezing the bulb dry. This left the muffin looking slightly mussed, with a small hole in the side, but so much of the food produced by the dining hall was already manhandled by the angry staff that no one would notice such a minor defect.

"It's next week," Beekman said, then closed his PDA.

"What is?" Reed had been watching Peter.

"The Calc midterm. You asked me when it was, remember?"

"Oh, yeah, right. Sorry," Reed said, more to his fellow Cuckonians for almost dropping the ball.

Hart handed Beekman a note. "This is for Trip."

"Okay," Beekman said, the word obscured by a profanity yelled by Trip. Beekman rolled his eyes, grabbed the muffin, and left.

All eyes were on Trip; would he accept it?

He didn't.

Back at the table, Hart's insides were tied in knots. Trip Darling was a maggot, a waste of space. Hart loathed Trip for all that he had been put through last year. Hart despised Trip for nearly stealing his spot at Stutts, for getting him fingered as "The Mad Pisser," for "The Day of Stink," and finally for him almost getting killed. Now, revenge was within his grasp, sweet, sweet revenge…But was it right, what they were doing? Did it cross the line? What if Trip died?

Hart decided he'd be okay with that. He looked at Reed. "Come with me," he said.

As the boys walked toward s Trip, they heard what the problem was. "I hate fucking blueberry. Go get me chocolate chip."

"They were out." Beekman said. "There were plenty of zucchini."

"You know why?" Trip said. "Because zucchini *sucks*, that's why." He examined the muffin. "This one looks daggy," Trip said. "Looks like you stuck your dick in it."

Biff laughed. "Oh, he got you there, Beekman!"

"Shut up, Biff. Beekman, go back and get me a zucchini one. And try to keep your wang out of it!"

"Hey, Trip," Hart said, as he and Reed walked by.

Not even looking, Trip flipped them off.

As they got to the glass doors, Hart said loud enough for Trip to hear, "So blueberry muffins can get you wicked high?"

"Yeah," Reed said. "But only if they're old. The berries have got to be fermented or something." They pretended to walk out, but stood just behind the doors, listening. They could see Trip, but he couldn't see them.

Trip thought for a second, then grabbed the muffin back from Beekman. "Gimme that." He did it so roughly that it started to crumble, so the meathead had to shovel the whole thing right into his mouth.

Back at the table, Peter pumped his fist. "Yes!" Then he gave a short burst from his chair's air-horn, something reserved for special occasions.

Everybody in the dining hall jumped.

"It must be Dork Day or something," Trip said, swallowing the last of the muffin. Then he grabbed the Coke from Biff. As Trip tipped the bottle back, Hart opened the dining hall door and stuck his head through.

"Trip, that muffin had drugs in it," he said.

"Bullshit," Trip said.

"No, really," Reed added. "It's a secret government drug from the 60s."

"It's called 'Vonnegut'," Hart said.

"What?"

"'Vonnegut,' dipthong. It makes you express your true nature," Hart said. "You don't have to be a frat-rat anymore. You can be whatever you really are. In fact, you don't have a choice. Vonnegut *makes* you."

"My true nature is kicking your ass, Fox," Trip said belligerently.

"It's 40,000 times more powerful than LSD," Reed lied. The placebo effect could only help.

Hart picked up Reed's lie and embroidered it, just to fuck with Trip. "The Vietcong sprayed it all over our soldiers. That's how people became hippies," Hart said. "We just turned you into a hippie, dude."

Trip took a menacing step towards them. Hart and Reed sprinted to the safety of the library, knowing how Trip felt about books.

Stymied, yet desperate for violence, Trip turned to Biff and Beekman. Biff saw the look in his eyes and ran. "Hit Beekman! He likes it!" Biff bounced off the TV crew, who had finished up and were sauntering towards the door.

Beekman wasn't so lucky; Trip grabbed him. Trip wasn't much bigger than Beekman, and he was incredibly out-of-shape, but his flabby fists packed enough mass that a punch would really hurt. Beekman, who had declared himself a pacifist in fourth grade (after a really regrettable incident involving the swings), closed his eyes and waited for the blow.

It never came. Trip suddenly had a weird thought: Why did he want to hit Beekman? Why would anyone ever want to hit anyone?

"C'mere, pal," Trip said, then gave Beekman a big hug. "Whew—you're a little ripe."

"You won't let us use the shower," Beekman grunted through Trip's hug.

Trip released him, then he saw the TV guys. "Dudes! Turn on your camera," he said. "I've got a very important announcement to make."

The reporter shrugged. "Freakshow for B-roll," he said.

Trip grabbed a water glass, then asked the underwear girl, "Could you hand me that knife?"

"I wouldn't do that," Beekman warned her, still frightened. She did it anyway.

Trip waited for the cameraman to finish getting the camera ready. "Let me know when we're rolling, brah." When he got the nod, Trip clinked the knife against the glass. "People, can I have your attention?" he yelled. "I just realized something: We are all *children of God.*"

The dining hall just stared at him.

"That's right. All of us, even you guys on the lacrosse team," Trip said. "Breathe through your noses, fellas. It's more comfortable that way…I guess all I'm saying is: try to be good to each other today. Peace." He shook the hands of the reporter and the cameraman. Trip hugged Beekman again, then cocked an ear. "I hear Mother Earth calling." With that, he was gone.

Biff, who had been watching the whole thing from behind a tall metal tray holder fifteen feet away, crept up next to Beekman.

"Well, *that* was some shitty footage," the reporter said. They shuffled out.

"Sorry!" Beekman called after them. "Usually he's really violent!" Then the boy looked out the dining hall window. "I see him," he said to Biff.

"Is he coming back?" Biff prepared to run.

"Nah." Beekman saw Trip sprint towards a girl collecting signatures for Greenpeace. Expecting the old Trip, she took off, terrified; Trip gave chase and they were soon out of sight. "What do you think that was about?"

"The muffin, maybe," Biff said. "Fermented blueberries are, like, 40,000 times more powerful than LSD."

"Oh, come on."

"No, really," Biff said. "I definitely heard that somewhere."

"Did you see his eyes?" Beekman said. "They were all…muppet-y." He paused. "Do you think the new Trip would let us out of the frat?"

The two boys desperately wanted out of Comma Comma Apostrophe, for several reasons. First, they were sick of doing everybody's homework. Second, they had to live in the unfinished basement of the frat house. Third, they were apparently eternal Pukes. And fourth, Trip had used Biff's teeth to open a beer. "Even if he did, the other guys would veto it," Biff said.

"No they wouldn't," Beekman said. "They don't know what 'veto' means."

"Maybe not, but they sure as hell know what 'chain you to the refrigerator' means," Biff said. "Help me pick up the litter."

"Blow me! 'No Trip' equals 'No litter-carrying,'" Beekman said. "Anyway, I think I have a hernia."

"Impossible," Biff carped. "They never descended in the first place."

"Screw you, dick," Beekman said.

"Loser."

"Douchebag."

"Douchehose."

Beekman thought for a second—was there anything else douche-related? He came up dry.

"At least I don't drive a frickin' cho-mo van," Beekman said.

"'Cho-mo'?" Biff asked.

"Child molester," Beekman explained.

"That would be '*chi*-mo,' dork."

"I refuse to be held responsible for the argot, you wad."

"My van's a frickin' chariot," Biff said. "It's a bone-wagon."

"Biff dude," Beekman said, "the only way that monstrosity would be a bone-wagon is if you stole a dinosaur."

"Are you kidding?" Biff laughed. "The shag in the back is four inches thick, Beekman! That's twice as big as your wang."

Beekman remained unimpressed. "It smells like cigs and strippers."

"It's not my fault Trip commandeered it," Biff said. "Anyway, how the hell would you know what a stripper smells like?"

Beekman sniffed, "Ponce senior prom. You were there."

Biff grew serious. "Beekman," he said with a stern look, "Caitlyn Rice and Caitlyn Murray sharing a wine cooler then taking their tops off is not the same thing as a professional stripper." Then he said, "Can we continue this discussion *while* we carry this piece of shit back to the house? I don't want all of Corset having sex in it."

"Trip had a burrito for lunch," Beekman said. "Anybody who went in there would come back out in a hurry."

Biff grabbed the poles and heaved up the front end. "Can't risk it."

Beekman reluctantly grabbed the back. As the boys went through the doors, he said, "Maybe Trip's got a split personality."

"Trip doesn't have a personality—all he's got is symptoms. Watch the door!" The door smacked the side of the litter, scraping off some of the gold.

"Shit, sorry," Beekman said. Slowly, they walked into the common room. There, sitting behind a card table, was Glenbard North. He was wearing a t-shirt that read, "Join the [redacted]". There was a large poster behind him that showed happy young people standing in front of famous locations all around the world. They all had black bars across their eyes to conceal their identities. North was recruiting for the CIA.

He wasn't doing this officially, just freelance. Nobody on campus knew it, but North had been cut loose by the Agency decades ago, after being blamed for the loss of the Vietnam War. However, anybody who found out this fact—administrators, faculty, ex-students from North's seminars—were all kept silent by the professor's secret-filled filing cabinets.

But silence is not the same as acceptance, and North's last dream before he died was to be reinstated at the Agency. He missed the camaraderie; he missed the respect; most of all, he missed the decal for the rear window of his car. You could get out of parking tickets.

North had sent in countless resumes, and written hundreds of letters explaining how Vietnam wasn't his fault. He'd called Langley so often they'd had to change the phone number. But North wasn't licked yet; he planned to keep the campus nice and quiet for the interim President, then in May ask for an introduction to Rivington's uncle. El Jefe's word was gold at the Agency. In the meantime, he'd show them he was a good soldier. According to "The CIA for Dummies," freelance recruiting like this could only help, and it maintained his "legend" on campus, even if he did look preposterous in a bright yellow t-shirt.

Biff saw Professor North and had an idea. "Stop!" he yelled.

Beekman couldn't handle the sudden stop, and the litter smacked Biff in the back of the head.

"Dude, c'mere," Biff whispered when he came to. "I have an idea."

Beekman's guts froze. He'd had years of experience with Biff's "ideas." Joining Comma Comma Apostrophe had been Biff's idea. "Oh, no way. Not today. My arms are killing me, and I wanna go home."

"Stop bitching, little girl," Biff said. "Do you wanna get out of the frat or not? We *need* to join the CIA," Biff said heatedly. "It's obvious."

North overheard him. "Boys, this isn't the CIA," he said, maintaining plausible deniability.

"Sure it isn't," Biff said, playing along. "We were just trying to throw people off the track...What is it?"

"The U.S. Department of International Literacy," North said blandly. "We teach people how to read."

"Ri-i-ght," Biff said, lips tight. "We read all the time. We love reading," Biff said, giving North an exaggerated wink.

Beekman recognized all the danger signs. "Uh, Biff...I don't think..."

Biff rounded on his friend, embarrassed. "Don't be a pussy! This is our chance—CCA would never mess with the CIA. They'd shoot 'em!"

"Who'd shoot who?" Beekman said. "I'm confused."

Biff turned to North. He was a man of action. "We wanna join, both of us. Me and my friend here. How soon can we carry a gu-, I mean, book?"

"I have no idea what you're talking about," Professor North said. He liked to make them work for it.

"I already know how to fire a book—my grandpa taught me." Biff said.

"I think you're mentally ill," North said. This was all part of the pitch.

"C'mon, Biff," Beekman said, grabbing his fellow Gnome's sleeve. "You heard the guy. Let's go."

"No!" Biff jerked his sleeve away. He hated to be wrong. "C'mon, what do we need to do to join?"

North began to reel them in. "I can't answer that, for reasons of national security."

Biff followed: he was being tested. Let the chess game begin. "You are Professor North, are you not?"

"I'm going to have to decline to answer, for reasons of national security."

"I submit that you totally are, because I saw you on TV."

"I'm sorry, as I said before, I am unable to answer for—"

"Right, right, '…national security.'" Biff said. "I get it. You're being spy-ey. I can be spy-ey, too," Biff said. "I sneak up on him all the time! Don't I, Beekman?"

"No," Beekman said.

"Don't be a dick! This guy could kill you like, six thousand different ways, and he wouldn't even have to use a book."

North got up. This pair would do—all he wanted was a couple of kids to do errands—but they were attracting too much attention.

Biff saw Professor North preparing to leave, and went all out. "I've got tons of skills. I climb ropes really fast. I can hold my breath underwater, as long as my nose doesn't get wet."

"That's nice," North said noncommittally.

"Really? You think so? Which part?

North sighed. "I'm really not at liberty…"

Biff cursed himself for being overeager. "No, right of course not. Stupid of me to ask." He needed to change the subject, keep things positive. "Listen, I know I'm sort of a slam-dunk, so I would appreciate it if you would take my friend here, too."

Beekman was digging in his ear. "What? No! I don't want to! I'm happy as a private citizen!"

"That's right," Biff chuckled chummily, "we're all private citizens here. Just a couple of private citizens, looking to spread literacy."

"Quit screwing around, Biff!" Beekman said, alarmed. "I'm just a college student."

"That's his thing—disguise. Isn't he great? " Biff asked, helping North fold up his chair and table. "So how about it? When can we get our first assignment?"

"Never," North said.

Biff was flummoxed for a moment, then recovered. "Oh, I get it. You really *are* good. Say we were walking by your office. When would we stop by if we wanted to—not talk to you, far from it—but say we wanted to be in your office at the same time you were there, when should we come by?"

"I'm sorry, I can't...

"Boy, this national security thing is a bitch. Now I understand why a hammer costs the Pentagon so much money," Biff said. "Okay, look: I'm going to step on my friend's foot, and if you don't tell me to stop, that's a yes, okay? How about tomorrow?"

Beekman had been distracted by an underwear model. "*Ow!* Biff!"

"It'll have to be the afternoon, is that okay?"

"*Shit!* Why the hell—"

"After lunch, obviously?

"SON OF A—STOP IT!"

"Three o'clock work for you? Don't run away, Beekman. I have to do this, for the sake of international literacy..." Beekman juked, Biff pursued. "Should we wear ties?"

Beekman grabbed his shorter friend. "Do that to me *once* more..."

"Beekman," Biff said, "the first thing you have to learn is to be in total control of your emotions. Look at me. I'm calm. Like a quiet pool of water.

"Hold still for a second." Beekman brushed Biff's shoulder.

"Was it a spider?" Biff did a tarentella of revulsion. "I swear to God, if I have to spend another year in the basement of that shithole..."

"It wasn't a spider, Quiet Pool. You had some muffin on you."

Biff looked over—the Professor was gone. "Wow," Biff said. "He's like a ghost..." Biff yelled at the distant figure, "It's going to be excellent working with you!"

"I don't know what you're talking about," North called back.

"We'll do great, you'll see!" Biff yelled louder. "We'll be the best recruits you ever got! I'm fulfilling a boyhood dream!"

"Stop talking to me! I don't know you! We never met!"

"Sure you do," Biff screamed. "I'm Biff and—" He suddenly snapped to the professor's gambit. "Incredible," he said to Beekman. "That's why they call him 'the Puppetmaster.'" Biff picked up his half of the litter. "How's your foot?"

"Shitty, thanks to you."

"I did it for reasons of national security," Biff said, as they resumed carrying the litter back to the frat house. "Would you quit limping, retard?"

11
The Bird is Back
Thursday, October 7th, 11:31 pm

It was only fitting that the undead *Cuckoo*'s first public activity be carried out by Tabitha's vampire friends. Last year, the Children of the Night, an all-vampire distribution service, had stuck 100,000 copies of *The Cuckoo*'s *Daily Money* parody inside newspaper boxes all over the country. They were quick, they worked cheap, and their fingerprints all led back to dead people—which made them perfect to slap posters all over Great Littleton announcing that "The Bird is Back!"

But the posters went further than that: they skewered campus figures, and commented on hot topics. One had a picture of the now-feral President Whitbread eating out of a dumpster, with the line: "Have you seen this man?" Hart especially liked a photomontage which put The Meistersingers at the Nuremberg rallies. Even Rivington came in for a whack over his latest bit of absurd penny-pinching.[35] Peter had mocked up a photo of a bibbed Rivington sitting in front of a table loaded with delicious-looking food, and Hart had supplied the line, "Where all the leftovers come from."

"Rivvy's gonna shit," Reed had predicted. But there was nothing Rivington could do. The bird was back, indeed.

Trying not to be seen, Hart and Tabitha crouched in the lee of a dumpster behind Strikeout's, handing piles to the Children's crack street team. "Remember: if you get caught, drop the posters, and mistify," Tabitha said to a guy with close-set eyes and an Afro. "We don't want any hassles, and we can always print more."

"Got it," the guy said.

Hart recognized him as the late-night sandwich dude at the local convenience store. "You make a mean Italian sub," Hart said. "What's your secret?"

The guy smiled. "Salad dressing."

Hart recognized a lot of local people, the backbone of the town's graveyard shift: office cleaners, hotel desk clerks, gas station attendants. There

35 "The dining halls," Rivington announced, "must be much more aggressive in repurposing leftovers. The insides of today's lasagna could be scraped out, for example, and reused as topping for tomorrow's spaghetti. Discarded fried chicken could be stripped, then ground into chicken salad. Not only will this provide student jobs, it is a financial necessity. We can and must do this, to keep pace in today's fierce global market."

were even a few students.

"Hey, is that lane fixed yet?" Hart asked, handing the last couple posters to a vampire named Gilly. Gilly worked at the bowling alley, and the Cuckonians had been known to get the urge at 3 am.

"Just yesterday," Gilly said, walking away. "Come roll."

"Wait!" Tabitha said. "Are those the last ones?"

Hart shook out the box. "Yep," he said.

"Gilly, let me have one. Snag!" (Tabitha often provided her own sound effects.) "Thanks. I'm totally putting this up in my room," Tab said, as Gilly ambled off.

"I wonder if it really works in black light?" Hart asked. Peter had come up with a final, non-timely poster, one that showed a gigantic, psychedelic bird looming over Stutts' gray spires. Underneath, in block letters legible for a block, the poster read: IT IS EVERYWHERE.

"Don't you think it's great, Hart? Won't it be great to wake up tomorrow and see the posters all over the place?"

"Yeah," Hart said. "I'd like some for my room, too, but 'we must maintain—

"'—plausible deniability'!" Hart and Tabitha chorused, quoting Guy. As annoying as he could be, the old freak was proving to be pretty useful, as far as clandestine operations were concerned. Tabitha opened her green toggle coat and slipped the folded poster inside.

"Is this the first appearance of the coggle toat?" (Hart had called it that one drunken night last winter, and so it had been, ever since.)

"Yes," Tabitha said. They walked out of the alley, and onto the sidewalk. A rat peeped out of the pocket; Tabitha pushed its head gently down with a finger, so as not to arouse comment. Even though it was past midnight, it was a Thursday, and so the sidewalk was crowded with all sorts of people getting an early start on their weekends, pursuing love, oblivion, or both.

"What a nice night," Tabitha said. "I like the fall. It's not too cold, just cold enough." After they'd gotten away from the crowds, Tabitha asked, "How are you feeling about this? The postering, the guerrilla stuff—I know outlaw isn't your style."

"I'm getting more okay with it," Hart said. "Partly because I think the way we were dissolved was bullshit, and partly because I think following the rules *might* be overrated. It's tough, though—I'm a recovering teacher's pet."

"It's gonna make you popular," Tabitha said. "You watch. Girls love a rebel."

"I think I have my hands full with you, thanks," Hart said, as they turned the corner to Tabitha's cemetery, where he was going to spend the night, "Hey, I have a question for you."

"Natural redhead," she said, then held up two fingers. "Brownie's honor."

"I mean, it's nothing important—it doesn't keep me up at night or anything—"

"For god's sake, Hart, ask it before I really get worried."

"Out of everybody at Stutts, why did you pick me?"

Tabitha gave a little laugh. "Are you asking why I fell in love with you?" Tabitha said. "Because if you are, I don't totally know the answer to that." The wind rustled the dry leaves that were collecting along the wrought-iron gate which ringed the cemetery.

"Partially," Hart said. "But I mean, you could have any guy you wanted—or girl, I guess—so why me?"

"Aww, you're sweet to say so," Tabitha said. "But I don't think that's true."

"Why a human, though?"

"Some girls have types, even girls like me," Tabitha said. "Some girls get goofy for artists or jocks. I like humans. It's not always convenient, but it could be worse—I could go for drummers. Though that *would* drive my parents nuts…Why did I pick you? Well, why did I?" As they walked arm-in-arm, Tabitha cast her mind back to when they'd met. "I thought you were cute, obviously. And funny, and modest—that's a big one. You can look for a long time here without finding somebody who's truly modest."

"With good reason," Hart kidded. "Seriously, I'm not that modest."

"Seriously," Tabitha said, "you are. It's good. It shows real self-confidence."

Tabitha mistified, then helped Hart over the locked gate. They walked along the gravel paths to Tabitha's place, a sizeable crypt in the middle of the cemetery. It was dark, but they both knew the way. "I think if there was one thing that attracted me to you, Hart," she said, "it was a feeling I had that your life would be interesting."

"You're right so far," Hart said, "Sometimes it's a little *too* interesting, frankly."

"That's why so many of them tend to get famous," Tabitha continued. "When I think about all the different people I've dated, that's the one thing that I've thought about all of them: 'you are going to have an interesting life, and I would like to see some of it.'"

"So do you think I'll be famous?" Hart asked, trying to keep his voice even. The intensity of his desire embarrassed him. He thought it might mean he was shallow.

"You've got a shot," Tabitha said. "Even if you don't, I think you'll be a good person. That's also important, regardless of what they teach here."

They arrived at Tab's place. As she unlocked the door, Hart said, "If you don't mind me saying so, that seems like a pretty unique criterion for picking a mate."

Tabitha shrugged. "It's as good as any," she said. "When you're immortal, you need all the diversion you can get."

"Well, prepare to be diverted then." Hart grabbed her right there.

12

College is For Making Memories

Friday, October 15th, 2:07 pm

Whether it was the need for a father figure, a shared mistrust of authority, or the sheer entertainment value of kookery, Peter quickly became Guy's biggest fan. First, he started calling in to "Wise Guy's," the pirate radio show that Guy broadcast from somewhere in the Catacombs. These short conversations led to longer ones over meals in Dacron—always painful for Hart, because Guy belched a lot and put mustard on everything. Finally, Peter started disappearing for long stretches. Hart's roomie would eventually emerge, smelling of mildew, his wheels tracking mud, flushed with excitement and talking fast. "Guy showed me his collection of moths" or "Guy had the smartest thing to say about women" or "We explored the University's old toffee factory."[36]

"You know what Guy told me today? He said that back in the thirties, *Cuckoo* staffers went all around the world, putting enemy bodies in all the Tombs of the Unknown Soldier! Isn't that cool?"

"Uh-huh," Hart said, not listening. He was writing the first *Cuckoo Communique*, a short blast of text that would be emailed to every student via an untraceable non-University account. "Listen to this:

> 'Ever since the Founding Fathers buggered Britain, Americans have loved rebels. However, like a virus losing potency over time, our rebels are getting more and more useless, less about changing the world and more about looking cool in a leather jacket. So what's the next step in useless, ephemeral rebellion?
>
> *Us!*

36 During the first flush of the Industrial Revolution, the University hit upon starting businesses as a way to generate income for the school. The first was a bullet factory (now University Health Services). Others included a toffee factory, a yarmulke weavery, and a rifle plant. After making guns for both sides during the Civil War, the university recognized government contracts as its biggest, fattest cash cow, a tradition continued by Not-A-Secret-Government-Lab Laboratory, among many other outfits scattered around the campus.

With this Communique, we officially declare *The Cuckoo* underground. Some might call this a cheap publicity stunt (it is), or a shameless attempt to get the staff laid (someone's got to do something), or just another immature stunt to get everyone's goat (we love you, really we do), but it's not…'

That's all I've got so far," Hart said.

"Seems too jokey to me," Peter said. "I wish you'd be meaner."

"Mean isn't funny, Pete. Mean is mean."

Peter tossed his coat onto the coattree. "What's the point of having the freedom to say anything, if you don't any anything?"

"I'm the editor," Hart said. "I handle the writing. You go do some really mean graphic design."

"Maybe they'll turn on the heat." Peter draped his wet scarf over the radiator in an act of faith, then rolled in front of the TV. He switched it on.

"Please don't," Hart said. "I can't write with that on."

"Sorry," Peter said. He picked up a copy of Keasbey's student humor magazine, *The Outrage*. "Anything worth swiping in this? Not that we'd ever."

"Never," Hart said distractedly.

"How's the letter to Quinn Bostwick coming?"

This was a sore spot. Hart had been working on it for weeks. Whenever he sat down to write it, he got overwhelmed by a sense of his own dorkitude. It was so much easier just to dream…"Still working on it," Hart said.

Peter sensed he shouldn't push Hart, so he changed the subject. "Isn't that interesting? What Guy said? Imagine all those good, patriotic people, praying over the body of their enemies. Now there's a prank that *means* something."

"I'm more interested in what your wheels are tracking on to the carpet."

"You're just being dense on purpose," Peter said.

"No, I'm not," Hart said, realizing he was. Guy was interesting—in a 'note to self: do not end up like this' kind of way—but there was just something about him that Hart didn't quite trust. Old and weird and living underground…how could anybody from Stutts end up there?

As annoying as Hart occasionally found him, Peter really was bursting with ideas. When he wasn't designing the magazine, Peter was thinking up pranks. Clearly there was something about a prank that was close to Peter's heart, perhaps the obnoxiousness or illegality of it, or maybe that it was physical, a joke made flesh.

Peter's profusion of schemes ranged from the sublime to the "life without parole." The problem was, you couldn't tell which was which without trying them. "...and the beauty part is, the chemicals for the explosives are all available over-the-counter!"

"I think I'm too anxious to be your friend, Pete." Hart and Peter sat on the Old Quad one bright October afternoon, feeling Great Littleton crisping towards winter.

"So get meds. The infirmary hands 'em out like Halloween candy. This one's for depression, and this one's for anxiety, and this one's if you can't work...You just bring your little plastic pumpkin, and they fill it up." Peter was browsing an issue of *Destructive Science*. "'War in Space'?" he read. "Could we do something with that?"

"I think Guy is poisoning your mind," Hart said.

"It was already poisoned," Peter said, his eye catching on an item. "Cool!"

"Do I wanna know?"

"Apparently there's some sort of radio frequency that makes people lose control of their bowels." Peter got a misty look. "Science is amazing."

Hart didn't respond, hoping Peter would lose interest. "Look over there. Is that Professor Lemonade?"

"He's not a professor. He's just a guy. I read it in the *Spec*," Peter said. (Lemonade had acted as his own Deep Throat, giving damaging information about himself to the *Spec*.) "What the hell is he doing?"

As part of his ever-racheting efforts to outrage someone, anyone, Lemonade was applying a blow-torch to the statue of Stutts' first President. He'd melted the nose and part of the right eye when Chief Constable Renalli pulled up in his golf cart.

Renalli turned off the cart's sack-jiggling pre-recorded engine noise. "You work here?"

Lemonade shut off the torch. "Yeah, but I'm only a visiting instructor. Wanna fire me?" he asked hopefully.

"Nah," Renalli said, laughing. "I know modern art when I see it...That looks like thirsty work." The cop reached into his cooler and pulled out a beer. When you drove on the grass as much as Renalli did, it was important to be on Buildings and Grounds' good side, so the cop liked to play Beer Claus whenever possible.

"No thanks," Lemonade said glumly, flipping down his mask and returning to work.

"Suit yourself," Renalli said, opening it and taking a swig. *"Ciao!"*

Hart watched Renalli drive away. "Why didn't he arrest him?" The head of the statue increasingly resembled soft serve ice-cream, or a Claes Oldenburg sculpture. "You can't just go around *melting* shit."

"Faculty can," Peter said blandly. "Guy told me that, according to the Stutts charter, faculty can kill anyone who—"

Hart cut off his friend. "I declare this conversation a no-Guy zone."

"Hey," Peter said, closing the magazine, "what would you think about Lemonade being *The Cuckoo*'s secret faculty advisor? He's pointlessly destructive yet apparently untouchable—just like we are."

"Pete, why the hell would we ever want a faculty advisor? Isn't that the whole point of being underground?"

"Guy says being underground is only Stage One," Peter said. "The real goal is to create an alternative to the status quo."

"And hanging out with Professor Violent-Mood-Swings will help us how?"

"It could help to have a friend on the faculty."

"He's just visiting faculty."

"Picky, picky."

Hart pulled at a cold blade of grass. It was true that Lemonade abused him comparatively less than others in his class; maybe he actually liked Hart. In that collection of Quinn Bostwick columns his mom had given him, there was one about Lemonade—maybe they knew each other? Even if they didn't, Lemonade would come in handy when it came time to hawk a book or screenplay or otherwise whore for the Man. Hart didn't want to be one of those people who spent their lives trying to sell out with no takers.

"Okay, if you want to," Hart said, getting up. "No harm in it, I guess." Actually, Hart could think of a lot of harms, but career concerns trumped everything else, and it didn't feel smart to put all his eggs in the Quinn Bostwick basket. "Let's go ask him."

As he drove away, Chief Constable Renalli thought about that guy with the blowtorch. What if he wasn't authorized to deface that statue? Renalli was a little jumpy when it came to student art. Last year, he'd arrested a couple for having sex on a memorial dedicated to the bocce team (they'd all died in a plane crash), then gotten an earful. How was he supposed to know it was their Senior Project? Stutts wasn't like it used to be; year after year, he was watching his beloved college turn to shit.

Finishing his beer, Renalli saw Trip Darling. The post-Vonnegut Trip had become must-see campus viewing. Stutts' meatiest of meatheads was now sporting a dashiki, Birkenstocks, and a wispy chinstrap beard. His brutally antisocial tendencies had been replaced by a fierce crunchiness; where he once chugged PBR, he now quaffed fair-trade yerba mate. Trip ranted about NAFTA and globalization with an ire once reserved for chicks who wouldn't swallow.

This hurt Chief Constable Renalli deeply. "Why did you do it, kid?" Renalli cried, pain welling up from deep inside. "Why did you switch sides? You had *everything!*"

Trip waved as Renalli whizzed by. "Peace, dude!" He turned back to his latest victim. "Time's a completely arbitrary construct," he hectored, crowding a delicate girl with glasses. "What time do you have?"

"3:45," the girl said.

"Oh yeah? Says who? Who gave *you* the right to say what time it is?"

"You asked me."

"What does '3:45' even mean? As a human being, I have a right to say its 3:46—or 8:46, or even 32:96!"

"So say it," the much-smaller girl asked. "Who's stopping you?"

"Don't you know?"

"No," she said, exasperated. "That's why I asked."

Trip paused, his brain whirring feebly. "'The man' is."

"But how is it different for me if I agree with you that it's 32 whatever-whatever? Doesn't that make you 'the man'?"

This question made Trip uncomfortable, so he ignored it. "I'm gathering signatures for a petition to abolish Time—it's 'time' to do something about it. How 'bout it, sister?"

Stuttsies didn't like to sign anything that might come back to haunt them later. "Normally I would—really—I'm late for class."

"That's exactly what I'm saying! Who knows?" Trip said. "If I'm successful, you'll always be on time!"

Christ, the girl thought, you couldn't walk anywhere on campus without getting accosted by some cause-addled idiot. "My parents don't want me to get mixed up in politics..."

"Oh, don't be such a pussy," Trip said, his new hippie outlook slipping a bit. "Who cares what their parents think? I certainly don't."[37]

"I don't know..." the girl said.

Trip nodded to a CCA brother, one of several that were lurking nearby. They were frankly puzzled by their leader's sudden wussification, and were simply trying to humor him until he came back to his senses and returned to chucking kegs off rooftops, stuff like that.

37 Trip was the forty-seventh man in his family to attend Stutts, and all 47 had been rugged individualists, succeeding *in spite of* their advantages.

"YOU!" Brother Steroids bellowed. "Sign the frickin' paper!"

The girl, quaking, did so.

"...and the e-mail list," Trip added. "Thanks!"

After being convinced of the utter worthlessness of their enterprise, Professor Lemonade had agreed to Hart and Peter's offer—then chased them away with his blow-torch. As a result, Hart and Peter were within Trip's vocal range. "D-U-U-D-E-S!" he yelled, waving his clipboard. "Come sign!"

Peter buzzed right over. He liked to check on Trip every so often anyway, just to see how the Vonnegut was changing him.

Hart, less enthusiastic, hung behind, signing as "I.P. Freely." Hart still hated Trip, believing that—drug or not—assholes didn't change their stink. But Peter had the mind of a scientist, and couldn't resist poking and prodding this new monster they had created.

"Are you going home for Thanksgiving?" Peter asked Trip blandly.

"Nah," Trip said. "My dad's set something up so I can go hang with the Dallay...Dolly...something. Anyway, he's like some holy dude. Whatever."

The Cuckonians walked away. "Amazing," Hart said when they'd gotten out of earshot. "Vonnegut changed him, but only partially. He's still a snobby, idiotic bully, only now he's a sort of eco-bully."

"There's no bully worse than an eco-bully," Peter said. "They hit where it really hurts—in the conscience."

"Spoken like somebody whose never been kneed in the balls," Hart said.

"Not physically, no," Peter said, pulling out that day's *Spec*. (He'd just installed a auto-pilot prototype on his wheelchair, and was testing it out.) "But psychologically—emotionally—every day of my life."

"You've been nipping at the Vonnegut yourself, haven't you?"

"No, it's just that girl he was bullying blew me off for a date last year." Peter said scanning the front page. "What do you think of Sterling Strong?" he asked. "Think he'll get elected?"

"Seems like a tool," Hart said. "I thought the gadgets in the last one were stupid."

"Well, looky, looky: the Chairman of the Federal Reserve is coming to campus tomorrow."

"...and you're thinking of a prank to destabilize the world economy," Hart said.

"My face always gives me away," Peter said. "It'll just be a hiccup, I promise."

"Pete, please don't—my money has to last me three more years," Hart said. "Rivington's sure to jack up tuition every year, and I have barely enough as it is."

Peter was unfazed. "I worry about you. You didn't used to be this obsessed with money."

"Shut up, rich boy. Didn't we have a deal?" Hart asked. "One prank."

"That was before," Peter said. "Come on, Hart—college is for making memories."

"But why do a prank? Why can't—" Hart tripped on an uneven piece of slate, a Stutts tradition.

"Why do a prank?" Peter said, as Hart picked up his scattered books. "You might well ask, 'Why breathe?' 'Why fall in love?'"

"'Why destroy the world's economy?'"

"Do you realize how much publicity we would get?" Peter said, half-serious. "Anyway, you worry too much. I'm sure the stock market will be fine. It's totally simple: first, somebody goes down to New York, and meets this Fisher dude…"

13
Better Dead than Head of the Fed
Thursday, October 28th, 5:43 pm

Every year around October 29th the *Daily Spectacle* student newspaper held its "Black Friday Banquet," to honor that individual who, during the previous year, had done the most to increase the paper's mammoth endowment.[38] (The dinner used to be held on a Friday evening, but sometime during the 1980s, *Spec* staffers shifted it to Thursday, to keep their weekends free.) This year, the guest of honor was Irving Fisher, the crotchety, choleric Chairman of the Federal Reserve.

Six weeks ago, the famously plain-speaking Dr. Fisher had testified in front of Congress. He was discussing the health of the economy, which had been shaky.

"This recent downturn has been entirely caused by the selfishness of the American consumer," he said. "'I want this!' 'Give me that!' 'Cheaper!' 'Better!' 'Non-cancerous!' 'No birth-defects!' Always take, take, take," Fisher thundered. "Now it's time for them to give," he said, in full evil-wizard mode. "Any citizen who does not own at least $10,000 of stock by this time next week should, in my opinion, be deported. These freeloaders are economic terrorists, weakening our country from the inside. I don't care what their birth certificate says, we should get rid of 'em. America is for people who pull their own weight."

Fisher's stern words worked like magic; billions of dollars were immediately intimidated into the market. Not only did this spike aid Fisher's patron in the White House (a Keasbey grad named Hamilton, who was sweating out a nip-and-tuck sprint for reelection), it allowed the *Spec* to purchase its very own tax-deductible news-yacht, "to gather news all the places limousines can't go."

On the night of Fisher's visit, said news-yacht was sitting calmly at an-

38 October 29th was always a day of celebration at the *Spec*, a day to remember the less fortunate, and to make fun of them. Legend had it that, a few days before the original Black Friday—October 29th, 1929, when the New York Stock Exchange suffered the biggest one-day plunge in its history and millions were ruined—the alums in charge of the *Spec*'s endowment got a tip. This allowed the paper to sell before the bottom fell out, then reinvest once prices were at their lowest. This little bit of insider trading was responsible for the paper's fantastic wealth today.

chor in the sanitary canal that snaked through the campus. Its passengers—the hyper-ambitious editorial board of the student tabloid—were markedly less calm: Dr. Fisher, noted for his punctuality, was late.

As the martinis turned to straight gin, the *Spec*'s managing editor tried to calm his editor-in-chief down. "Don't worry, Gwen," Miles said. "I'm sure he just got stuck in traffic."

"Easy for you to say," Gwen said tensely. "You're not graduating!" She crunched an ice-cube as she talked. "There's a little thing called 'getting a job,' Miles, and pissing off the Chairman of the Fed doesn't help!"

"What more could we do? We sent the limo," Miles said. "It's top-of-the-line."

"Get real, Miles. There isn't even a hot tub in it." Gwen specialized in the country-cousin putdown.

Miles swallowed his anger. "He's probably stretched out in the backseat, taking a nap." Fisher was 84, so that was a pretty astute guess. It was important the old man got his rest, and his prunes, and his rubdowns, and his scotch; the merest burp from Fisher sent money scurrying this way and that, like ducks after popcorn—him in a crappy mood meant no dinner for whole countries. "I predict he'll wake up refreshed and ready to dispense internships," Miles said optimistically.

Gwen didn't buy it; she was deep into freestyle worry. "Did catering order the prunes he likes? How about the scotch?"

"I'll go check," Miles said. "Gwen, I'm sure he's perfectly comfortable."

That part Miles had right—but Dr. Fisher wasn't in the *Spec*'s limo, he was in *The Cuckoo*'s rail car.

Peter's family had been building "luxury rail coaches" since the age of Carnegie and Vanderbilt. They kept a few down in Grand Central at all times, just in case a client of theirs was passing through. Once Peter had verified that the "S.S. Aga Khan" was free, *The Cuckoo*'s nefarious plan could begin.

A few minutes before the *Spec*'s limo pulled up in front of the Waldorf-Astoria, a scrubbed and dapper Reed had appeared at the front desk. "My name is Miles Monaghan," he told the concierge. "I'm from the Stutts University *Daily Spectacle*. Could you ring Dr. Fisher's room? Our car is here to take him to Great Littleton."

"One moment."

Fisher came down, looking even more cantankerous than his picture, then spent two minutes berating a hotel employee. Every second increased the possibility of being found out, so Reed finally stepped in, mumbling something about traffic being especially bad tonight.

"Tariffs?" Fisher barked. (His hearing wasn't too good.) The old man reluctantly broke off his tirade, and allowed Reed to steer him outside just in time: as Reed was helping the liver-spotted plutocrat into the back seat of a limo, he saw a *Spec* Senior Editor saunter into the lobby.

Once safely in the railroad car, Reed called Great Littleton.

"The big fish has been hooked," Reed said.

"Reel him in," Hart said. Whatever misgivings Hart had might've once had were gone; that day's edition of the *Spec* had contained a parody of *The Cuckoo* called The Poopoo, edited by none other than Miles Monaghan. "We'll call you at the dock."

Back with Fisher, Reed tried to keep the small talk to a minimum, which was difficult; Fisher was in a reminiscing mood, especially about *Spec* legend Harold Sproul, who was a Wumpsman the same year Fisher was. Reed knew little and cared even less about Sproul, the *Spec*, or the Mugwumps. Even more than that, he didn't want to get caught in a lie.

"Dr. Fisher," Reed said, truncating a story of binge drinking with Glen Miller, "we have an arrangement that we reserve for our most distinguished guests. I wonder if you'd be interested?"

"Certainly," Fisher hissed. (His bridgework wasn't of the best, and he sprayed.) Fisher had a well-known weakness for luxury.

"It's a private railroad car," Reed said. "We think it's a little more comfortable."

The switch was made without a hitch, and no one was happier than the old plutocrat. "You Specsters certainly know how to treat a guest," he said as Reed helped him figure out the intricacies of the wet bar.

"Glad you think so." Reed held up two crystal decanters. "Bourbon or scotch?"

"Mix 'em. In the old days, that was called a 'trainwreck'…Or was that bourbon and vodka?"

Within fifteen minutes of Reed's retiring to the servant's quarters, Fisher was tucked into a recliner, fast asleep in front of "The Nightly Business Report." This was lucky for him, because *The Cuckoo* had a long night in store. After meeting him at the train station, the staff whisked him off to Der Rathskeller, where they had booked a private room.

"I thought the evening was taking place at the *Spec* building," Fisher said.

Hart, already massively nervous, leapt in with an excuse. "Uh…the electricity went out last night," he said. "All the food was spoiled."

"The food's better here, anyway," Tabitha said. An appreciator of the female form, Fisher had insisted that she sit next to him.

"Glad to see some things have changed for the better," he said, ogling with abandon. "Gwen, will you excuse me?"

"I didn't like him the first time I knew him," Tabitha (known for the evening as 'Gwen Talbot') said when the old man had toddled off for the first of many bathroom breaks. "Everybody called him 'Creamcheese.'"

"Why?" Ellen asked. "Do I want to know?"

"I was lucky enough never to find out," Tabitha said.

"Creamcheese," Hart said. "I wish you hadn't told me that. I know I'm going to slip up."

"Five bucks if you call him that," Peter said to Reed.

"So when are the rest getting here?" Fisher said, after he'd returned. With an empty bladder and a slight buzz, he was ready to speechify.

"Rest?" Ellen said. She and Fisher had bonded immediately over their shared Wumpitude (even after she informed him that the special handshake wasn't in use anymore). "This is all of us."

"The five of you put out that whole paper every day?"

"Yep," Reed/Miles said.

Peter leaped in, before the flicker of confusion on Fisher's face kindled into suspicion. "We use a lot of computers," he said.

"Ah! I see. Improved efficiency," Fisher said, totally in the dark. Peter might've said, "We pray to Osiris," for all Fisher knew about it. Anyway, whatever suspicions the old man might've had were tamped down with a heavy Rathskeller dinner, then drowned by a squadron of buckets. In a back room no outsider had seen for a century, different champagne-based concoctions were mixed together in ornate silver buckets. Then chanting waiters brought them to the table, where the buckets, amid much exuberant and profane ritual, were slurped up through a single communal straw.

The old man acquitted himself marvelously: eight, nine, ten buckets were drained—accompanied by loud warbling, of course. Everything past a certain age at Stutts had its own song. Thanks to the tongue-loosening capabilities of alcohol, "buckets" had a multitude, each dirtier than the next.

Then came the limericks. At first Fisher was shy about swearing in front of the ladies, but as the buckets mounted, his inhibitions melted. Everyone noticed that he mispronounced "clitoris" but decided to let it go.

"This guy's got a liver of iron," Hart said to Reed as they stood unsteadily in front of Der Rat's exquisite marble urinals. "Look! I'm whizzing on the Keasbey mascot!" Way back when, some waggish craftsman had carved a bas-relief lobster into the back wall.

"That's the kind of craftsmanship you just don't see anymore," Reed kidded, zipping up. The subject changed back to Fisher as the boys wobbled out. "You'd drink too, if you were personally responsible for the Norwegian tungsten bubble. The economy cratered. People were selling their hair."

"That sucks," Hart said, with the understatement of the drunken-but-just-holding-it-together. "I just hope we get out of tonight without wrecking the world somehow."

Reed didn't answer, but gave a wicked smile.

"Wait—what?" Hart bumped into a coattree. "Excuse me," Hart said, then forgot his question.

As was the custom, Dr. Fisher was given a final, one-person bucket at the end of the evening, then presented with a silver straw as a keepsake. His name and the date was engraved upon it.

"Just a little something to remember us by," Peter said. The look in Peter's eye told Hart he should be worried.

"I'll treasure it," Fisher said, slipping the straw into his breast pocket.

"No! No!" Peter and Reed cried. "Use it!"

"That's not how we used to do it," Fisher said.

"Well, times change," Tabitha said, batting her eyes.

The old lech was meat. "Whatever you say, Gwen." Fisher finished the bucket with a long suck.

Looking at Peter and Reed, Hart knew exactly what had happened: The inside of the straw had been liberally coated with Vonnegut.

"Don't say anything," Peter whispered. "Wouldn't want him to have a bad trip." Hart sighed, and finished off the last bucket. What else could he do?

"All the sudden, I don't feel so good," Dr. Fisher said five minutes later, as they were putting on their jackets. He looked down glumly, then turned to Tabitha. "Didja ever feel like your whole life was a waste?"

"Oh, you're just having 'a Stutts moment,'" Tabitha said, unflipping and smoothing his lapel. "It's hard to be around young people. All their choices are still ahead of them, so you wonder if you made the right ones." She handed him his Cummerbund College scarf. "It's only natural."

Dr. Fisher paused. "Gwen, how'd you get to be so smart? You talk like an old person."

"Oh, Dr. Fisher, I bet you say that to all the girls," Tabitha said. He wasn't such a bad old guy, she thought to herself. If his life had just gone a little differently, if he'd just gotten a little push at the right time from the right person, maybe he would've turned out different. But he still smelled like creamcheese.

◦ ◦ ◦

On the way back to the train, Dr. Fisher had vomited so vigorously into the Harriman moat that he had lost his toupee. Hart lost "paper-scissors-rock" and had to retrieve the nasty object. But it didn't stay in *The Cuckoo*'s possession for long. After pouring Fisher onto the train, they stuck his toupee in an overnight pack addressed to Sterling Strong.

As Peter folded a note, Hart asked, "Your fingerprints are on that note."

"Yep," Peter said. "So's my signature."

Fear-chemicals smashed through the alcohol still in Hart's system. "Do we really want Strong to know it was us? That thing's daggy!"

"Too late, it's already sealed," Peter said brightly.

"I mean, if things break right, Strong might be the next President," Hart said. "Not really somebody you should fuck with."

"Oh well," Peter said, as the pack hit the bottom of the bin with a thud. "Too late now." Peter saw Hart's genuine alarm. "Relax," he said ineffectually. "I know what I'm doing."

"That's what I'm afraid of," Hart said.

"Start writing the letter," Peter said. "It will take your mind off things."

Peter was right; Hart was soon totally absorbed. Normally, Hart's sweet nature would prevent him from pounding the *Spec* too hard, but tonight was different. Maybe it was the alcohol, or the late hour, or the fact that *The Cuckoo* was probably already in deepest shit. Whatever the cause, Hart let the gloating flow.

> "Hello Careerist Hacks:
> As you might have noticed, Irving Fisher did not attend your banquet. He did, however, attend ours—unwittingly, of course.
>
> "Don't worry, we showed him a wonderful time—a better one, certainly, than you would've. As far as he knows, the *Spec* is full of lively, interesting people, not career-crazed sphincter-smackers. If we were you, we'd play along. He loves the *Spec*. There's no need to thank us—the evening was its own reward.
>
> "However, we might not be so kind to your next guest... Or the next...Or the next. We are outlawed; as far as the University is concerned, we don't exist, so there's nothing more they—or you—can do to us. You've tried for years to kill *The Cuckoo* and now, to quote Obi-Wan Kenobi, 'we have become more powerful than you could possibly imagine.'"

("What do you think of the shout-out?" Hart had asked as they wrote. "I'm digging the cosmic overtones," Peter said.)

> "If you do not wish us to systematically abduct, then perform outrages upon, every speaker you invite to campus, you must comply with this single demand: From now until the Sun explodes, you must print every issue of our magazine, and insert it inside the entire 8,000 copy run of the *Daily Spectacle*. Our print specifications are below; you will notice that they represent a significant step up from our past issues. Stop complaining—you can afford it.
>
> "If you hinder our circulation in any way, we will not be responsible for the consequences. If you agree to our terms, send an email to the (untraceable and disposable) address below.
>
> Have a nice day,
> *The Cuckoo.*"

"Game, set and match," Peter said, reading the final draft. "Now we can do a magazine whenever we want. "

"Pete, before this moment, I never really knew what it meant when people called somebody 'a diabolical genius.' If you ever try to take over the world, I wanna be on your team."

The same moment this bit of blackmail was being read aloud amongst mounting outrage in the *Spec*'s Sproul Conference Room, the televisions in the reporters' bullpen were breaking into that morning's programming. "We take you live to New York, where the Chairman of the Federal Reserve has called a surprise press conference. He plans to make, in his words, 'The most important announcement I will ever give...'"

The press corps gasped as the octogenian shuffled to the podium. Fisher usually dressed like a small-town banker, in dark three-piece suits, complete with a pocket watch. Now, he looked like a beach-bum, with stoner overtones. Fisher's bare, fuzz-covered man-tits hung nearly to the waist of his baggy shorts. His pale, flip-flopped feet looked like twin snails escaped from their wingtip shells. The decay of advanced age hung about him like the Reaper, and the pukka necklace only made it worse.

"Ladies and gentlemen of the press," Dr. Fisher said, "I'd like to thank you all for coming here on such short notice. I must be brief, because I have an afternoon flight to the Big Island.

"I have decided to resign effective immediately, and devote my remaining years to finding the perfect wave. I plan to donate my fortune to charity, and my only source of income will be a small endorsement deal with Mr. Zog's Sex Wax," Fisher said. "It *is* the best for your stick.

"I will now take questions."

There was a surreal patch of silence as the press corps processed the new reality. Then a woman asked tentatively, "What's Sex Wax?"

"It's for surfboards," Fisher said.

"Is this permanent?"

"Yes," Dr. Fisher said. "I need to stop living a lie. As all of you have surely noticed, I've taken off that ridiculous toupee."

The press corps genuflected in disbelief, just in case it was a test. "I honestly never noticed it." *"You?"* "Everyone just assumed you were Italian."

"Yeah, yeah, yeah," Fisher said, scratching his scraggle-covered chest. "You all knew it was fake. It looked like a wombat. Any other questions?"

"Uh...do you have any idea what caused you to go crazy like this?"

"Not that it's not great!" another reporter chimed in.

"A trip back to my alma mater, Stutts University and a long conversation with the spirit of the moon."

"What job will you do next? Academia, perhaps? Or consulting?"

"I'll just crash on the beach," Fisher said. "I've decided to donate all my money to the people of Norway."

"But *why?"* asked one newsman, the strain of anger in his voice. "Why are you throwing it all away?"

"I'd ask you the very same question," Fisher said.

Hart and Peter were watching the announcement at Great Littleton's most authentic English pub, the Cause and Effect. (It was so authentic, they had to slip Dennis the bartender £5 to watch an American TV channel.) Peter couldn't stop laughing, but Hart was alarmed.

"Ohhh, shit!" Hart moaned. "I knew we shouldn't have done this."

"What are you talking about? It's great!"

Hart pointed to the stock tickers at the bottom of the screen. As Dr. Fisher spoke, the tickers started to plummet. By the time he left the podium with a "hang loose" wrist waggle, the market had been shut down automatically, to keep the drop from triggering a massive, worldwide depression.

Peter was utterly unconcerned, slurping from his black-and-tan. "Ahh, don't worry about it."

"Don't worry about it?" Hart said, voice rising. "We just triggered a financial catastrophe! And my school money is in the market!" Hart buried his head in his hands. "I'll end up back home, working for McDonald's…If they're still in business."

Peter silently offered his mate one of the C&E's famously stale pretzel nuggets.

Hart waved it away. "Too nauseous."

Peter was annoyed with Hart. "It's a blip. Everybody will freak out, *Daily Money* will sell a shitload of newspapers," Peter said, "and within 48 hours Fisher will be replaced with an even stuffier stuffed-shirt. He'll say all the right things, and everything will be up 10% by the end of the week," Peter said. "You'll see. We just made a lot of people a lot of money." He dug in his wallet and slapped some bills on the bar. "Thanks for being such a buzz-kill."

Hart watched him wheel out, certain that Peter's predictions were crazy. But that's exactly what happened.

14

Grade Deflation

Friday, October 29th, 10:10 AM

As Irving Fisher was switching his religion from capitalism to the search for the perfect wave, Glenbard North was in his office having his own "Stutts moment." One of the grimmer entries in the campus lexicon, a "Stutts moment" was the uncomfortable feeling that the person inside didn't match what outsiders saw.

Though each of them thought they were the only one, Stutts was riddled with men and women suffering through this. On the outside, they appeared confident, happy, sure of right and wrong, the very picture of contented success. But inside boiled extreme dissatisfaction—shame and humiliation, even—about their lives, their looks, their spouses, their children. The details varied, but the story was always the same, because to get to Stutts, one had to be driven. Once there, whatever drove you to these heights did not turn off; it simply turned inward.[39] And then the "Stutts moments" began.

Professor North felt this way every time he pulled out the old scrapbooks. There, his pitiful career in espionage was suspended in yellowing newsprint: "Leader Escapes Assassination Attempt"; "Fraud Fails to Swing Election"; "Suspicious Fire Almost Destroys Campaign Headquarters"; "Coup Thwarted by Overfriendly Dog"; "Student Radicals Expose CIA Agent"; "Pranksters Moon Accused Spy." A *Cuckoo* from around the time of Watergate slipped to the floor. It was the "Spooks Among Us" issue, and North was on the cover.

He felt a familiar surge of victory as he picked it up; this student rag was no more. North had seen the posters, but those were clearly death-throes. It was too bad that the editors couldn't have been expelled, but crushing the magazine would do for now. Funding that *Spec* parody of *The Cuckoo* had been his symbolic victory dance.

North closed the scrapbook and slid it back into the bookshelf next to his voluminous files. The old spy was not one to reminisce—his sense of regret was much sharper than any remembered pleasures— but he had no

39 If what drove you to Stutts was your father's chauffeur, the Stutts moments were less frequent. That was why people like Rivington were always so frighteningly productive—you can get a lot done, if you aren't excessively concerned about making other people's lives a hell.

choice. The fact was, North was remembering less and less.

It had not always been so; there had a time when his memory had been impeccable, and he used it like a sniper uses his rifle. The bullets were the secrets, locked in file cabinets directly behind his desk. Memorizing them meant that you always held the whip hand, whether someone stole their file or not. He couldn't do that anymore—his mind didn't hold the facts.

"Age catches up with everyone," North said to himself, feeling every inch a lion in winter.

But it wasn't age, dear reader, which was causing facts to flee North head. It was the cumulative effects of all those chemicals—from LSD to BZ to "Vonnegut"—that he'd administered in the 60s. All of them were odorless and colorless; this made them useful in spycraft, but it also made mistakes inevitable. A drop on the skin here, a mist inhaled there—and thirty years later, North's brain was swiss cheese. His faculties grew more finicky by the hour.

There was some sort of ruckus outside. North paid no attention; his office door was marked "Electrical Closet." His acolytes knew that, and everybody else could go to hell. Along with his memory, his ability to make nice was also wearing thin.

As if on cue, his phone rang. Rivington, North thought, shooting the Caller ID a dirty look. What the hell did he want? You make a guy President, he should have enough common courtesy to leave you alone. "Hello, Pat."

"Glenbard! Thank God you're there," the President said in a shrill voice. "Are you watching the[40] goddamn CNN?"

North admitted that he wasn't.

"Well, turn it on!"

North went over to a shelf and turned on a small set usually reserved for Yankees games. "FED CHAIR STEPS DOWN TO SURF," the screen crawl said. North read it, and within fifteen seconds, knew the bones of what had happened.

"Glenbard? Are you still there?"

"Yes, Pat," he said. "How strange."

"That's all you have to say? After the greatest public-relations bungle in Stutts' history?"

North heard somebody calling his name in the hall outside, then pounding on doors. "Pat, simmer down," North said. He swiveled around

40 Because he grew up speaking so much Umidorean Spanish, President Rivington frequently inserted extra articles in front of things like "CNN." If you listened to him long enough, you didn't even notice it.

into "non-listening" position, his feet up on the filing cabinet.

"*Simmer down? Simmer down?"* the President's voice rose to a squeak. "The endowment's down seven percent in the last hour! Thirteen out of the fifteen members of the Body[41] have called me in the last hour to tell me to, and I quote, 'Shape the fuck up.'" Rivington was almost hyperventilating. "They swore at me, Glenbard. People like us don't swear! Not at each other!"

"Well, at least two of them are still on your side," North said. His eyes played over his Wall of Photos. It showed North shaking hands, having dinner, and going to nightclubs with the world's elite. Sadly, all the other people's heads had been razored out for security reasons, and North no longer remembered who was who. "Two is a start."

"No it isn't," Rivington said. "They would've called, too, but they had heart attacks on the golf course. *Both* of them."

"Oh, that's awful," North said. The banging and yelling outside kept getting louder. "So Fisher said that it was a trip to Stutts that caused it?"

"Yeah," Rivington said miserably. "Nothing good ever happens when we let the students meet adults...I wasn't doing anything wrong... I was just sitting here in my office talking to a management consultant."

North saw an opening. "Are you still thinking about bringing someone in to cut out the fat?" He was playing for time.

"Don't change the subject!" Rivington said. "You were supposed to keep things running smoothly! I would've never agreed to your plan if I'd known that—"

"Pat, stop yelling at me," North said. "It doesn't help, and I'm starting to get angry. Now: what would you like me to do?"

"We have to find out which students are responsible for this. And after we find out, we have to punish them," Rivington said. "Swiftly and publicly. And then maybe again, more harshly, in secret."

"You did the right thing coming to me," North said, grabbing a cheap-looking giveaway pen. "Let me write down what we know. Damn." The pen wouldn't write (it was actually a remote-control detonator/laser) so North took down the details with a miniature golf pencil. "On campus yesterday...Saw some students...Got it," North said. "Should be easy. Anybody who invited Fisher to campus wouldn't keep quiet about it."

"Let me know as soon as you find anything out," Rivington said.

"Can I destroy them? No kid gloves?"

41 The Stutts Body was the University's main governing body. It was comprised of tycoons, foreign dictators, superlawyers, and a celebrity or two. The Mayor of Great Littleton was also a member, but nobody paid any attention to him.

"Are you kidding?" Rivington said. "The more violently the better." The President hung up.

◦ ◦ ◦

It took North exactly fourteen seconds to find out who had invited Fisher to Great Littleton—in other words, exactly long enough for him to dig through his recycling bin, pull out yesterday's *Spec*, and browse the front page. There it was: "Fisher to Address *Spec*." The paper never missed an opportunity to congratulate itself.

North scanned down the staff box. He had to be careful about the *Spec*; they were too well-connected to bully willy-nilly. The outgoing editor, Gwen Talbot, was a Mugwump and thus untouchable. But her number two, Miles Monaghan, was unprotected. North dialed the paper and asked to speak to Monaghan.

"Miles, I don't know if we've met, but I'm Glenbard North."

"Wow, Professor North," Miles burbled. "It's an honor to talk to you. I took 'Trojan Horses' last year and…

"Thanks," North said, cutting Miles off. "I keep an eye on the university's information grid, and I"—North needed something alarming, but still plausible—"have reason to suspect the *Spec*'s system might've been hacked."

"Oh, that's awful!" Miles said. There was porn on his computer.

"Not if we catch it in time. Would you come over to my office this afternoon?" There was no need to rush—North wanted to let President Rivington stew a bit, just to show him who was driving.

"Sure, Professor North, just name the time," Miles said. "And thanks a lot for calling!"

Just after lunch, North met Miles outside the building, blindfolded him, and let him a needlessly circuitous way to his hidden office. He sat Miles down in a metal chair. When he tied Miles' arms and legs to the chair, Miles became alarmed.

"Hey! What—why do you have to do that? I…I think I better come back during office hours." North ripped off Miles' blindfold. "Ow! My eyes!

"Okay, champ—start talking as fast as you can," North barked. "What did you do to Dr. Fisher?"

Miles was a *Spec* man, and Specsters are nothing if not proud. Physical pain was nothing compared to having to admit they'd been outsmarted by *The Cuckoo*. But Professor North had been around Stutts students for long enough to know their weaknesses. He punched a few keys, then swiveled the screen of his computer around so Miles could see it.

"This, Mr. Monaghan, is your Stutts transcript. Examine it closely—

you will see that it is correct in every detail. All A's...Grade inflation is a terrible thing, don't you agree?" Miles didn't respond, so North continued. "Let's do our part, shall we?" North hit a key or two. "Let's change this one to a B. Or maybe a C?..."

"Hey! That's not fair!"

North paid no attention. "That one looks much too high as well," North cooed. "Another 'C,' perhaps. Or a 'D.' Yes. Much better."

"Stop it!" Miles said angrily. "I have to get into law school!"

"Not with all these 'D's," North purred sadistically. "Tell me what happened to Dr. Fisher, and I'd be happy to change them back."

Miles wasn't budging. "Listen, if you don't untie me right now, I'm going to call my dad. He's a lawyer."

"Ooh, I'm scared. Let's add a few 'F's, shall we?"

A bead of cold sweat rolled down the back of Miles neck.

North heard him give a whimper, and pressed two keys rapid-fire. "Two more A's to F's. Now, will you tell me what you did?"

"No!" Miles said. "I don't care what you do to my grades. They don't matter, anyway," he said, desperately trying to regain control of the situation. "I can always be a journalist!"

"A journalist, huh? What if we note here on your permanent record that you are a plagiarist...No, that won't work. How about 'arsonist'?"

"You bastard!" Miles said.

"Or do you prefer 'compulsive public masturbator'?" North said. "Bet that'll go down well at the *Times*."

Miles saw his whole career crumbling before his eyes. "Stop," he said, beginning to weep. "Please stop."

"You can make me stop," North said. "Tell me what the *Spec* did."

"We didn't do anything—"

"Who did? Spit it out!"

"I...can't," Miles said.

"I know what we'll call you," North said, as if it was just occurring to him. "'Koala molester.' I hope you never go to prison, Miles, because marsupophiles are the lowest—even pedophiles'll stick a shiv between their ribs..."

Crying, Miles broke. "Okay, okay!" he said. "It wasn't us, it was *The Cuckoo*!"

"But they're defunct," North said. "I did it myself."

"Somebody better tell them that," Miles sniffled. "Can I have a tissue?"

° ° °

After North heard the whole story, he dismissed Miles with a brainwashing lollipop. Then he called President Rivington. "I found out what happened to Irving Fisher," he said. "It was *The Cuckoo*. They stole him."

"*The Cuckoo*? You mean those jerks from the riot?" Rivington yelled into the speakerphone. "I pardon them, and this is the thanks I get?" Rivington paused to throw a mug of pens against the wall, then continued. "I don't care if they drove off Whitbread, we're just going to have to expel them this time."

Rivington's secretary Judy put a bulky interoffice mail envelope on his desk. "Judy, can't you see I'm on a phone call?" he said hotly.

"I think you'll want to see this," Judy said.

"Hold on, Glenbard." President Rivington said, untying the envelope.

"What's going on?" North asked.

As Rivington opened the envelope a cloud of stink wafted out. "Oh my god. Whatever's in here smells like the self-serv counter at Liquor Lovers." There were two items inside: a letter, and Fisher's distinctive wombat-like toupee. "North, I just received Fisher's toupee, and a letter."

"Who from?"

"*The Cuckoo*, obviously!" Rivington flipped it over, then uttered a surprised profanity. "It's from Sterling Strong. How's he mixed up in this?"

"I don't like where this is heading," North said. The actor/candidate, Strong combined several kinds of Stutts prestige and power. "Maybe he's RSVPing for reunions," North quipped bleakly. "Read me the letter."

"'Dear Puppy,'" Rivington read, "'just wanted to let you know that I'm keeping an eye on things in Great Littleton. This latest dip in the stock market has done wonders for my campaign, and I'm very confident that this time next month, there will be a Stutts alum in the White House again.'... "Lot of good that will do me," Rivington said. Strong was Hollywood liberal to the core.

"Keep reading," North commanded.

"'You should know that I'm aware exactly who at Stutts has been responsible for my good fortune. If you take any action against them, I'll consider it a personal slight. By the way, tell Professor North that the villain in my latest movie looks like him. Yours truly, Strong. P.S.—*The Cuckoo* guys overnighted this to me as proof. Since Fisher's always been a hero of yours, I thought you might like to keep it.'"

"Goddamn it!" Rivington balled up the letter and threw it across the room. It landed among the mug shards and pens. Then he threw the toupee, which skimmed out into Judy's office. "So what the fuck do we do now?"

"The only thing we can do," North said. "Rot *The Cuckoo* from the inside."

"We'll need somebody utterly stupid," Rivington said. "I mean, who joins a defunct magazine?"

"How about Whitbread's kid?" North said. "He's dumber than a pile of misprinted diplomas."

"'Carpetbomber'?" Rivington asked.

"Who?"

"Everybody calls him 'Carpetbomber,' I don't know why. Don't use him," Rivington said. "Use somebody with no connections to the President's office, some loser. I have to appear in control," Rivington said, an edge of desperation in his voice. "Other college Presidents are already starting to crank-call me!"

North suddenly recognized the voices that were calling his name in the hall. It was those niblicks he'd met in Corset yesterday.

"Don't worry, Patrick," he said. "I know just the students for the job."

15

Infiltrate and Destroy

Friday, October 29th, 2:34 pm

North let Biff and Beekman walk the halls for a little while, then wrote "Glenbard North in here" on a piece of typing paper, and stuck it to his door. Then he waited. He always liked to be on the phone, pretending to be talking to somebody important, when students came to see him. So he cradled the silent phone against his shoulder and played computer solitaire as he waited for Biff and Beekman to arrive.

It took the boys three more passes back and forth, before they spotted the sign. They really were masterpieces of ineptitude, North thought with satisfaction, though holding this phone was beginning to be a literal pain in his neck.

Finally, Biff burst into the room followed by a sheepish, hanging back Beekman. "Professor North! Thank God we found you!" Biff said. "We were beginning to think you might've been kidnapped."

"*You* were beginning to think," Beekman mumbled.

"You were, too!" Biff shot back, then asked North, "Professor, did you know your office door says 'Electrical Closet'? You should really get that fixed."

North put his finger over his lips.

"Would you like us to leave?" Beekman whispered hopefully.

North shook his head no. "President Rivington," he mouthed silently. North was a practiced mime. Keeping students waiting built mystique.

While North pretended to talk, Biff and Beekman whispered to each other.

"I've already done ten spy things today," Biff said.

"Like what?" Beekman said.

"Like putting salt in all the sugar bowls."

"That was *you*?" Beekman said, outraged. "I had to throw away a whole bowl of cereal."

"Well, now you know what kind of dude you're dealing with," Biff said. "I'm everywhere."

Beekman scowled.

Biff continued. "You didn't need the extra calories, trust me. Every time you take your shirt off, you look like a furry gnocchi."

Beekman was stung. "I don't think switching the salt and sugar is very spy-like," he said. "Not like stealing the 'L' from signs that say 'Public.'" (Beekman claimed to have invented this prank, along with scratching out parts of words on electric hand dryers in the men's room.) "Now that's sabotage."

"Yeah, right," Biff said. "You did that before we even went to college."

"I think that makes it more impressive." Beekman was right; it was impressive. For four blocks in every direction, all the pay phones around Ponce said "Pubic."

"I'm talking current," Biff said. He looked around at all the office bric-a-brac, memorabilia from North's career. "Lotta cool stuff in here." Biff started playing with North's toy Mauser.

"Excuse me, President Rivington." North cupped his hand over the receiver for extra verisimilitude. "Don't play with that."

"Sorry!" Biff said, and put the gun down with a clatter. As Professor North returned to his conversation, Biff pulled out a composition book. "I bet I've done lots more spy things since yesterday than you did."

Beekman craned his neck over. "What, did you write them down? That's not spy-ey. Anybody could read it."

Biff pulled away, shielding the notebook. "Get away, fag. These are my ideas. I'm going to chart my progress," Biff said. "And one day, it'll go in the museum."

"Of course," Beekman said.

"Fine, don't believe me. You can come Tuesdays, when it's free."

North pretended to finish up. "I'll get on it, Patrick, and report back to you as soon as possible. Goodbye." Professor North put down the phone. "Sorry, boys. What can I do for you?"

"Don't you remember meeting us?" Biff said. The thought that he might not make an indelible impression on an adult was inconceivable. "We want to join the CIA."

"You do, do you? Please stop playing with that," North said.

Biff whipped his hand away from the gun again. "Sorry."

"One doesn't just join the CIA," North said. "One is asked. Every candidate must prove his worthiness."

"I'm unworthy." Beekman got up to leave. "Good luck, Biff, I'll—"

"Sit down!" Biff said. "You can't leave! You're in too deep!"

These two would be perfect, North thought. Nobody would ever link him or Rivington to such colossal idiots. North put on a slightly sad smile. "I'm afraid your friend is right, son. It's already too late."

Beekman crumpled, slumping back into his chair. "Oh God!" he moaned, head in hands. "It's happening *again*."

"So what do we have to do to prove our worthiness, master?" (Biff had watched a lot of kung-fu movies.)

"Something very important. In fact, it's so big, the future of the University depends on it."

No Stuttsie could resist a come-on like that. "Great!" Biff said, then elbowed Beekman until he too muttered, "Great."

"First," Professor North said, "I need each of you to swear that what I'm about to tell you will never leave this room."

"You bet!" Biff said perkily.

"No!" Beekman yelled, seeing his opportunity. "I'll blog it!" The other two just looked at him until he caved. "Okay, *fine*."

The professor explained all that had happened that day so far, about the Fed Chairman, and the Stutts Body, and the *Spec* and *The Cuckoo*, repeating parts as requested by Biff.

"So what would you like us to do?" Biff said, taking out a pen and opening his notebook.

"Uh, not write anything down," Professor North said.

"Toldja," Beekman said triumphantly.

Biff slugged Beekman, not looking. Beekman retaliated; then Biff again, then Beekman, until finally North had to shout for them to stop.

"BOYS! Settle down. Save that for our enemies," North said. "What I'd like you to do is infiltrate *The Cuckoo* magazine, and rot it from the inside…Sabotage their operations, sow discord, hinder them in any way you can think of, until they collapse."

"Cool!" Biff got so excited, he grabbed a stress-ball off North's desk.

"Biff, please don't—" Before the words had left Professor North's mouth, Biff had given the ball a squeeze, which spurted a small cloud of yellowish-gray sleeping gas into Beekman's face. The boy coughed weakly, then collapsed onto the floor, sound asleep.

North sighed. "He'll be out for two hours, at least." No matter—Biff seemed the stupider of the pair. North moved to the front of his desk, and sat on it chummily. "It doesn't matter—you're the one I'm interested in, Biff," North said. "I can see you're the brains of the operation."

"Thanks," Biff said, blushing. "Beekman *tries*, you know? We've been friends ever since kindergarten."

"Well, you're good to look out for him," North said. "While he's asleep, we can begin your education in earnest." For the next two hours, Biff was educated in the lingo and history of spying. Professor North even told him—as much as the old man could remember—the stories behind some of the momentos scattered around the room. Some were simply gifts (an obsidian paperweight, a rectal thermometer made from a narwhal's tusk, a talking plastic trout) given to Professor North after unsuccessful operations. Others were examples of spycraft at its most fiendish—seemingly harmless objects which, when activated in some way, transformed themselves into weapons of ferocious destructiveness.

"This looks like an ordinary bouquet of roses, but once you put it into water, it becomes a powerful incendiary bomb. White phosphorus," North said. "I sent it to my ex-wife."

"Cool!" Biff said, utterly enchanted. Being here, one-on-one with the master spy...Biff knew he would never forget this moment. But just in case, when Professor North's back was turned, he slipped the toy Mauser into his pocket. Then, whenever Beekman didn't believe him that North and him had hung out and become buds, Biff would show him the gun.

North saw him take the momento—the kid did it with all the subtlety of a cow giving birth. "I admire the impulse," North said, "but put that back."

Biff was crestfallen for a moment, but his ADHD kept him from staying depressed for too long. He saw a video game hooked to a small TV on a shelf. "Wow," Biff said. "I didn't know people as old as you knew about video games."

Normally, any student unwise enough to mention North's age suffered the mysterious siphoning of an entire semester's worth of dining hall flex-cash. But North needed this kid, so he let it go. "That's no video game. That's an interrogation rig. The controllers deliver powerful electric shocks."

Biff held up a controller. He wasn't being shocked. He even pressed it against his tongue. "Nuh-hing," he said.

"Whoops!" Professor North said, amused. "No wonder my great-grandson never wrote me a thank-you note."

He walked over to the phone. "I have some work to do, so I'm afraid it's time for you to go. I'll call Buildings and Grounds for a wheelbarrow for your friend." But North wasn't taking any chances. "Until they arrive, please repeat your mission to me over and over until I tell you to stop."

"Infiltrate...infiltrate something, right?"

"*The Cuckoo*," North said. "Infiltrate and destroy *The Cuckoo*."

"Right," Biff said, then started in. "Infiltrate and destroy *The Cuckoo*. Infiltrate and destroy *The Cuckoo*. Infiltrate and destroy *The Cuckoo*..."

16
Parents' Weekend
Friday, November 5th, 1:09 pm

Unaware of the peril he now faced from Glenbard North and his minions, Hart braced himself for the more immediate danger on his horizon: Parents' Weekend.

As you have seen by now, dear reader, Stutts was like every other college, only more so. The same thing went for Parents' Weekend. The university, always giddy in front of a captive audience, capered and preened. It showed its best side, explaining away the bad publicity (Irving Fisher), and trumpeting the good (a possible Stutts IPO). The campus was spruced up relentlessly, and everyone was pitching in: members of the Stutts College Council started showing up at mealtimes, asking everybody to "hold off puking and stuff in public, just until after everybody's parents have left." They might as well have asked the drizzle to stop falling, for all the good it did, but to their credit, many students did their best to hurl more neatly.

Once the parents arrived, everybody was on edge. Stutts was ruled by two clans, the young and the old, and it was weird to have all these middle-people lurking around. No hangout was safe; you never knew when you'd overhear somebody spilling the gory details of their mortgage or prostate. The only fun was teasing your friends about how dorky their parents looked (and, of course, how much they looked like them).

For the dorkiest of parents, the university ran a series of lectures. Though they purported to give an overview of Stutts in all its multifaceted glory, they could be boiled down to this: (1)The "real cost" of a Stutts education isn't covered by tuition; (2)The lion's share comes out of the endowment; (3) But a terrible crisis is coming! (4)We don't know how much longer we can keep it up; (5) So you must give us more! More! MORE!

The students knew this Chicken Little routine well, and made fun of it. "The 'real cost'?" Hart slurred to Peter the morning his mom was set to arrive. "They know nothing of 'the real cost'!"

Hart looked tired and dinged-up—the pair had hit all the parties last night, and there had been many. Students had a powerful need to dance and drink all the demons out one last time before Mom and Dad came. "Every time I go to a party," Hart said, "I wake up with big-ass bruises in the weirdest places."

That made Peter laugh, and swallow a little toothpaste.

"How the hell am I going to survive this weekend?" Hart complained.

"Wha duh se wa 'o 'o?"

"I have no idea what you just said."

Peter spat out his toothpaste. "I said, 'What does she want to do?"

"She wants to sit in on a class, but all I've got on Fridays is Professor Lemonade," Hart said. "That's not as much a class as a floor show—you never know whether he'll be wearing pants."

"Don't worry, even Lemonade will be on his best behavior. Otherwise Rivington'll flay him," Peter said. "What else?"

"Dinner with Tab."

"Yipes!"

"No kidding," Hart said. "If I survive that, we're going to the football game on Saturday. Wanna come?"

"Sure. Not like I'll have anything to do." Though Peter's parents didn't live very far away, they never visited him. Peter was both bitter and relieved about this. "Then what?"

"After that, the weekend stretches out like a vast Arctic plain."

"Speaking of Arctic, it's really freakin' cold in here," Peter complained. He glanced out of the window before closing it. "Benjamin Franklin is passed out in the parking lot."

"I told you he'd never amount to anything," Hart said.

The campus was swarming with people dressed as famous Stutts alumni; Rivington's scheme was to have them ask parents for change. "You can say 'no' to Joe Homeless," he said, "but not to George Washington. 'Excuse me, madam—I need fifty cents to become the father of our country.' Who's going to stiff Helen Keller? 'I'm blind and inspiring, gimme a dollar.'"

The plan would've worked to perfection, except that they ran out of drama students and were forced to hire some of the authentically inebriated/insane types that roamed erratically around Stutts' campus. Ralph Waldo Emerson had already been in two fistfights, and last night, on his way to a party in Sand College, Hart had been accosted by a drunk and disorderly Gandhi. "Gimme a buck for a hamburger!"

Back in the bathroom, the boys shivered. Though the window was closed, a wicked draft still whistled through. "This building sucks," Peter said, rolling into the shower. "Even 'Dream Dorm' would be better."[42]

42 "Dream Dorm" was an ultra-luxurious, completely fake dormitory that Rivington had gotten School of Drama set designers to build inside a soon-to-be-demolished building. Every campus tour guide was required to make a stop with Mom and Dad.

"Just think, though: this time next year, Dacron will be totally renovated."

"Lipstick on a pig, Fox, lipstick on a pig."

Hart laughed; Peter was the only one he allowed to call him by his last name, annoying prep school habit that it was. He muscled the window. It was busted—the lacrosse dope across the hall had bent the shit out of the frame—so Hart jammed a towel into the gap. While doing this he leaned against the radiator and burned his bare calf.

"Ow! Shit!" Stutts spent a lot of time making its new buildings look old, and no time at all making its genuinely old buildings functional. "Fucking radiator!" Hart swore, splashing cold water on the burn. "I would like to go through one day here without injuring myself on this goddamn building!"

"It warned you," Peter shouted from the shower. "All those knocks meant 'stay away' in Morse code. You deserved it."

"Oh yeah?" Hart reached out with his other hand and flushed the toilet. Peter was suddenly drenched in hot water. He yelled; Hart sprinted out before his roommate could retaliate. Hart could expect a pintglass of icy water dumped on him the next time he showered. Knowing Peter, he probably would've gotten one anyway.

At Stutts, it was usual for significant class time to be wasted in useless chatter: the professor's inability to conceive, or their summer home's recent infestation with fire ants. Some students specialized in kicking off these digressions; Reed, for one, was legendary, and honed his skills like a Jedi master. But the faculty was instructed to run a tight ship that Friday, just in case any parents decided to sit in.

Believe it or not, the students welcomed this single day of rigor. If your parents thought Stutts was some sort of academic Devil's Island, they would squawk less when you came home with lower grades. Nearly every Stuttsie had gotten perfect marks in high school, so the slide from As to Bs to B-minuses to B-minus-minuses was a bit of a shock. Of course nobody spilled the beans about grade inflation. Everyone got B's; anything lower than that took real anti-effort. (Hart knew one kid with a straight-C average, and he was in a coma.)

To return to the original point, keeping alive the fiction of Stutts-as-academic hell encouraged parents to spend more money over the weekend. The restaurants were packed, and every dorm room sported at least one piece of "pity furniture."

Parents' Weekend was not cheap. Last year, Mrs. Fox couldn't come, because all the family's spare cash was being spent keeping Mr. Fox in the air and out of jail.[43] Now, with her husband finally in the hands of the authorities, there was a little more money on hand.

Mrs. Fox had reacted to her husband's incarceration with the usual berserk aplomb. As soon as she stepped off the train, Hart's mother announced that she and his father were now in an open relationship. "At least until he gets out of 'der slammer.'"

"WHAT?" Hart looked around, hoping that nobody he knew had overheard. Then he grabbed his mother by the arm and hurried her into a taxi. "When you say 'open,' you mean 'having-sex-with-other-people', right?"

"Not 'people,' Hart—friends."

"Oh, God." The nausea hit like a fist.

"And just one at a time," Mrs. Fox said, trying to soothe her son. "At least at first."

Hart prayed the driver didn't know much English. "But why?" he asked.

"Hart, are you aware that your father has turned into a woman?"

"Yeah." The footage of his father's Hyde-like transformation was the toast of the Internet during the first week of school.

"Well, *you* may not mind having two mommies, but I don't swing that way."

"Not yet," Hart griped, then added bitterly, "I knew I'd regret getting you a MySpace account."

"Could we at least wait an hour before the priggishness starts?" Mrs. Fox said. "I'm sorry you're upset, but look at it from my position. I put him through Honduran medical school, took in boarders to finance No-Preg, I've even bankrolled him while he was on the lam. All alone. Five years without sex of any kind—which, since you're half me, you know has been torture."

"Yeah, but I'm the *upper* half," Hart snipped. They spent the rest of the short cab ride in silence.

After dropping off Mrs. Fox's luggage at the hotel, she and Hart went to his writing seminar. Hart hadn't wanted to take the chance, but his mother insisted. "I saw Mr. Lemonade on *The View*," she said. "He seemed sweet."

43 Hart's father, a medical entrepreneur, had created a contraceptive liqueur called No-Preg which was sold—briefly—in Europe. Unfortunately, the massive amounts of synthetic estrogen contained in this beverage caused many male drinkers to lose their secondary sex characteristics. A thousand lawsuits bloomed. Mr. Fox was in a plane between Prague and Oslo when the news first broke; thinking quickly, he called the airline from the plane and bought a ticket from Oslo to Tokyo, then from Tokyo to Istanbul, and so on. He was forced to travel constantly in this way to avoid Interpol. Most of the time, his frequent-flyer miles were sufficient to keep him aloft, but whenever they weren't, Mrs. Fox had to dig into their savings. In September, after over a year on the run, Mr. Fox had pushed his luck, dashing off the plane at Frankfurt to buy a traveler's neck pillow. Unfortunately for Mr. Fox, Interpol had been waiting.

Mrs. Fox was immediately shown how very wrong she was. Lemonade burned the first three-fourths of the class in a frenzy of withering abuse. His first target was a bookish junior named Duncan.

"I want you out of this class!" Lemonade thundered. "In the name of all that is right and good, I want you to stop writing, burn all your notebooks, and swear you'll never pick up a pen again!"

Duncan refused—like all Stuttsies, he was convinced he was capital-G Gifted. Every week, Duncan brought in the same piece, ersatz-Lovecraft slightly reworked to fit the current assignment. This drove Lemonade crazy, but nobody else cared—they didn't do the reading. "Dunc, as much as I love the idea of C'thulu ravaging Fairfield County" (this week's assignment had been to write a short story in classic *New Yorker* style) "I think John Cheever would have some issues with your ripping off the plot of 'The Swimmer.'"

"It's an homage," Duncan said brazenly.

"Bullshit!" Lemonade hollered. "It's seven pages of the same thing happening over and over: C'thulu emerges from the swimming pool; C'thulu ruins the barbeque; C'thulu consumes a few WASPs, C'thulu sends the rest bolting into the underbrush, spilling their martinis and gibbering. Face it, kid, you've got nothing to say."

"Could it be a comment on materialism?" another student offered.

"Shut up, you!" Lemonade yelled, eyes blazing. "Don't you dare encourage him!"

"does he alwys yell???" Mrs. Fox wrote in the margin of Hart's notebook.

"except when he is passed out" Hart wrote back.

"Okay, Dunc," Lemonade said. "Since you wanna write this crap so badly, next week's assignment is to write a horror story. Any style, seven to ten, double-spaced."

The class opened their notebook, wrote down the assignment, then realized it was only half-assigned. They looked at Lemonade. "Why the frick is everybody looking at me?" the addled prof sputtered.

Hart raised his hand.

Mr. Fox had insisted on representing himself, with disastrous results. His entire defense was an unyielding insistence that No-Preg was perfectly safe. He attributed the drastic changes in the afflicted men to excessive cell phone usage. "Ladies and gentlemen," Mr. Fox had said in his opening statement, "I am so confident that this product is harmless that I will drink some in front of you, now. Let your vision of me, whole and unchanged, be the bulwark of my innocence!" Mr. Fox threw back a titanic gulp. Clutching his throat, he dropped to the floor, out of sight in the witness box. The gallery gasped as he fell, then began to murmur with concern when he did not reappear. After a few seconds, Mr. Fox stood up again. "See?" he said in a high, girlish voice. "Noth—HOLY SHIT!"

Hart wouldn't be seeing his father for 17 years, 12 with good behavior.

"Yeah, Hart?"

"Any specific topic?" Hart tried to help things along every once in a while, to stay on Lemonade's good side.

"Nah," Lemonade said. "Just make it scary." He noticed the older woman sitting next to Hart. "Hey, new kid. Are you a Lifetime Learner or something?"

Mrs. Fox blushed. She never did well around famous people. Hart saw her discomfort and leapt into the breach. "It's Parents' Weekend," he said. "This is my mom."

Lemonade had a brainstorm: If sex with students didn't scandalize anyone, maybe sex with parents would. He stared at Mrs. Fox for an extra second, then said, "Wanna meet after class? Unless you're on the rag—I don't go there."

After a moment to process the obscenity, Lemonade's students erupted. Hart had been dreading a moment like this ever since his mother had told him she was coming for Parents' Weekend. He should stand up and defend his mother's honor (as far as anybody in the class knew, she had some), punch Lemonade, walk out. But he couldn't—Lemonade was the magazine's advisor, and Hart wanted to get career help from him. Utterly paralyzed, Hart placed his head on the desk. This is a just dream, an awful, awful dream. I'll wake up any moment now.

"Listen up, fellas," Lemonade said, delighted to have hit a nerve. "She may not be much to look at, but nothing beats an educated cranny."

"Agghh!" The comment scorched Hart's ears; he put his hands over them and began humming "My Favorite Things."

"That comment was repugnant, reprehensible, uncalled for, and ageist!" said a student who was high up in the Party of the Moon, the feminists' outpost in the Stutts Political Union. "You're creating an environment hostile to women, and inappropriate for—"

Lemonade cut her off. "Yeah, yeah," he said, almost giggly. "Don't get your panties in a wad, Gloria Steinem. I know how to say 'thank you.'" Lemonade pressed both palms against his cheeks, to mimic a pair of vice-like thighs, then wiggled his tongue violently. Then he tipped his chair back, and began writhing and gasping in a despicable parody of female sexual ecstasy. "Oh, Mr. Lemonade, you're the best! Oh, daddy!"

Mrs. Fox took this in, an unimpressed look on her face. Then, she dug in her purse, pulling out the weapons-grade mace that Hart had given her for Mother's Day. Just as he brought his display to faux-orgasm, Lemonade got five squirts, right in the eyes.

"Aah! Ooh! Aah! Oo—IT BURNS! IT BURNS!" He hit the floor and began writhing around.

"Class dismissed," Mrs. Fox said blandly. Students stepped over the thrashing body of their professor.

"I hope it was good for you, too," she said to Lemonade, as she and Hart walked out.

◦ ◦ ◦

Hart had to go home and take a nap. While her son dreamed of being an orphan, Mrs. Fox strolled around the campus. Never having finished college herself, she felt like she was in fairyland. Great Littleton always looked its best on an autumn afternoon; the weaker sunlight tended to hide its flaws. Nobody knew that she was married to that sex-change freak from the internet. And several people came up to her, thanking her for putting Professor Lemonade in his place.

Hart met her in front of Sauron's, the Tolkien-themed restaurant where they were having dinner with Tabitha. It would be the first time the two women in Hart's life would meet, and he was nervous. Though he'd never admit it, he wanted his mother to like Tabitha.

As they waited for Tabitha (who wasn't due until dusk, for obvious reasons), Mrs. Fox asked out of the blue, "Hart, dear, I've been meaning to ask: does your girlfriend have pointy teeth? I just want to know what to expect."

Hart closed his eyes and exhaled. Then he said, "Mom, I know this is impossible, but please don't embarrass me."

"When have I *ever* embarrassed you?" Mrs. Fox asked. "This afternoon doesn't count, he provoked me."

"I'll try to remember that when I fail the class."

"Isn't that Albert Einstein?" Mrs. Fox said, glad for a change of topic.

"Einstein's dead, Mom," Hart said, "that's a bum."

"I wondered why he was drinking malt liquor." Mrs. Fox saw a toddler in the arms of a passing parent. "Hey, cutie!" she said to the child. "Are you enjoying your trip to college with all the big boys and girls?"

"Good evening, Hart." The kid's voice sounded like David Niven's.

"Hi, Ragnar," Hart said, "I'm-sorry-she's-my-Mom" written all over his face. "Have you started the take-home for History?" After they had gotten out of earshot, Hart hissed, "Mom, Ragnar's a sophomore. He's a prodigy."

"Oh, dear," Mrs. Fox blushed, then grew defensive. "Well, how was I supposed to know?"

"Just do me a favor—" Before Hart could finish that sentence with something heartfelt and profane, he saw Tabitha flouncing up the street. "Tab!" He waved with both arms, like a drowning man. She waved back.

"That's your girlfriend?" Mrs. Fox asked.

"Yeah, do you have a problem with it?"

"Absolutely not—I just thought—she's so pretty."

Hart didn't know whether to be flattered or insulted. His mom had a gift for that.

Introductions were made and outfits complimented, then they went inside and found a table. Tabitha pulled a small, green-and-black square out of her purse. "Mrs. Fox, I brought this for you. It's called, 'Night on Great Littleton Common.'"

"Tabitha paints," Hart said, amazed at his girlfriend's consummate mom-charming ability.

"Thank you, Tabitha," Mrs. Fox said. "I'm sorry I didn't make anything for you—except Hart, of course."

"Sweet but a little gross, that's my mother." Hart blushed under the two women's affection. "Tabitha's got a million hobbies," he said.

"Anything to fill the decades," Tabitha said lightly.

Mrs. Fox look turned from happy to confused to concerned. To keep the conversation on track, Hart apologized again for forgetting to make reservations. "This was the only place in town that could seat us before eleven," he said, as a bored-looking waitress slopped ice-water into their cups at a 75% success rate. "And now we know why," Hart whispered after she left.

"Now, Hart," Mrs. Fox said. "I've had jobs like that. Her feet probably hurt, her outfit itches, and she's pissed she has to work on a Friday night."

"I waited tables at this very restaurant for about two weeks, back in the Forties."

"Really?" Mrs. Fox asked.

"Yep. Back then, it had an Ayn Rand theme," Tabitha said, wiping up the puddle in front of her. "Tolkien freaks can't tip any worse than the Objectivists did."

That Tabitha was a fellow ex-waitress won Mrs. Fox over immediately. "Tabitha, don't take this the wrong way, but after all the things Hart told me about you, I wondered if you'd be down-to-earth."

"That comes from sleeping in it," Tabitha shot back.

Everyone laughed nervously. The always-direct Mrs. Fox decided to leap right in. "I went on the web and found out that 'vampire' is Stutts slang for a 'goth,' is that right?"

"That's what the Admissions Office would like you to believe," Tabitha said. "It's not a big deal—strictly dietary. I'm like a vegan, except for blood."

Hart watched his mother intently; it was nice to see *her* squirm for a change. "I see," Mrs. Fox said. "Back in my day, it wasn't so different. Everybody called themselves 'Marxists.' College is a time for experimentation."

"Tabitha isn't experimenting, Mom," Hart said. "It's what she is."

"Of course, Hart," Mrs. Fox said, patting his hand. "Tab, will you be able to find anything on the menu?"

"I already swung by the hospital for take-out," Tabitha said, "but I might get an uncooked steak and lick it. Would you excuse me?" Tabitha glided off to the ladies room.

"So, what do you think?" Hart asked.

"She's lovely," Mrs. Fox said. "Eating disorders are terrible things. I saw an Oprah—"

"Mom, Tab doesn't have an eating disorder. She really is a vampire. She has rats."

"Is that like crabs?"

"I'm serious."

Mrs. Fox sighed. Then she said, "It's hard to watch a child become an adult. You teach them as best you can, try not to pass along your own faults, but sooner or later, you realize that they're going to make their own mistakes."

"Look, if you don't like her, tough."

"I do like her, Hart. I like her very much. It's just—I think she might be a little too experienced for you."

Hart's temper flared. "That's hysterical coming from Mrs. Orgies-begin-at home."

"I just don't want her to freak out and bite you, that's all." Mrs. Fox said. "Look at it from my side. I knew you'd meet all sorts of people at school, I just wasn't prepared for them to be…"

"You can say it, mother," Hart said. "Undead. My son's girlfriend is *nosferatu*."

"Nos-fer-what? I was going to say, 'crazy.'" Mrs. Fox said. "When I was at college, everybody was alive."

"How do you know?" Hart parried. "Maybe you didn't get invited to the right parties."

Mrs. Fox saw Tabitha returning from the bathroom. "Ssh. She's coming," Mrs. Fox whispered. "Just promise me you'll use protection. One of those foam neck braces. I'll buy it for you if you don't have the money—say you have whiplash…"

"Sorry it took me so long. I can't read Elvish. I just closed my eyes and picked a door." As soon as Tabitha sat down, she knew exactly what had transpired. After all, she'd done these dinners for over a hundred years. "Let me guess," she said lightly. "You and Hart have just had a nice little chat about how I'm a psychopath."

"'Psychopath' is such a harsh term," Mrs. Fox said, embarrassed. "I just think you grew up in an extremely repressed household, and have a lively imagination."

"Right, and right," Tabitha said, "but I'm still a vampire. Watch."

Hart knew what Tabitha was planning. "I think you're okay.The smoke-detector's all the way over there by the bar."

Tabitha turned into a mist, and arranged the pinkish curls to say, "Hi there!"

For the second time today, Mrs. Fox was completely surprised. But she also prided herself on her free-thinking. "Tabitha dear, that's quite a trick," she said. "You've convinced me." She signaled their waitress. "I need a drink."

As the evening wore on, the two women got on better and better. Mrs. Fox was fascinated to hear about Tabitha's sex advice column, and insisted she email the link. Hart drank heavily to smooth out moments like that, but the ladies were fine. By the end of the night, a slightly tipsy Tabitha was telling stories about all her earlier boyfriends, and impressing the daylights out of Mrs. Fox. "Hart is definitely weirder than Thelonious Monk was," Tabitha said. "It's no contest."

"Don't look at me," Mrs. Fox said. "I didn't even smoke when I was pregnant." As he listened to the women talk and laugh, Hart felt an uncomfortable feeling, something much more troubling than having to break up a catfight. It was a central fact of life that nobody likes to run up against: the woman who had driven him crazy growing up, and the woman he was crazy about now, weren't all that different.

Mrs. Fox was staying in one of the newer hotels around campus. Its selling point was a big central atrium; from the lobby you could look up and see all the hallways curving around, like the layers of a cake with a hole drilled in the middle. The next morning, Hart and Peter arrived at Mrs. Fox's hotel room just in time to see a television get hurled over the railing.

It hit the floor with a crash, but the desk clerk didn't even look. "Can I help you?" he said.

"Yes," Hart said, only to be interrupted by a scream. Four floors up, a topless woman shrieking with laughter staggered out of her room. She was followed by her pursurer, a flabby man in a towel. Hart glanced at the woman fearing the worst—but it wasn't his mom, thank god.

"Crazy around here," Peter said.

"Every Parents' Weekend," the clerk said with a sigh. "I blame Viagra."

Thirty minutes later, after a brisk walk from the hotel to the Stutts Bowl (it only took fifteen minutes under normal circumstances, but Mrs. Fox had to buy a pennant, and a button, and a knit cap, and a foam finger), the trio got to their seats. "I've never been to a football game before," Mrs. Fox said. She squinted at the players far below. "Are they usually that small?"

"Our players are especially small," Peter said ruefully, adjusting his own foam finger.

"I like yours better," Mrs. Fox said. Peter had made one with the middle finger upraised.

"I'll send you one," Peter said. "I make them."

"All your friends are so creative," Mrs. Fox said to Hart.

"I know," her son replied. "Doesn't it make you sick?"

After getting breakfast—an Eagle-wurst with mustard and kraut—the boys tried to explain the game to Mrs. Fox. They were not successful.

"Where's the ball?" Mrs. Fox asked.

"Across our goal-line," Hart said glumly.

"Ahh, not again," Peter groused. "I thought this was gonna be a good game."

He had every right to expect a closer contest. Since it was Parents' Weekend, the Stutts eleven were actually trying to win, not establish business contacts that would pay off later in life. And the athletic department had even lined up a patsy. Through a (wink-wink) "administrative error," the team opposite Stutts was from Harriet Wrath, a women's college several hours up the road. But even though football was just a club sport at Wrath—meaning their team got no funding, practiced only occasionally, and didn't even have a full compliment of pads—it was more than the Stutts team could handle. "Don't confuse what you're seeing with the actual sport," Peter said.

"Anyway, the real action's up in the stands," Hart said, pointing to a section not far away where everyone was doing a striptease, to the lusty accompaniment of the band.

"What are they throwing?"

"Lunchmeat," Hart said.

"Why?"

"Drink more beer," Peter said. "You'll understand."

Sure enough, two quarters and many beers later, such things made perfect sense. Mrs. Fox was having a heart-to-heart with her son. "Now that your father is out of the picture, at least temporarily," she confided, "I feel like the whole world is opening up. Think about it—I've been married since I was your age. And now I'm free!"

"No, you're not," Hart said, strangely threatened. "You're my mom!"

Mrs. Fox's reply was unequivocal. "Yo! Beerman!" she cried, then turned her attention to the field. "Run, goddamn it! *RUN!*"

"Uh, Mrs. Fox," Peter said, "it's a time-out. Nobody's playing right now."

"I was talking to that streaker!"

Much to the crowd's delight, Chief Constable Ranelli was pursuing a streaker all around the field in his golf cart. Finally, as the streaker passed the Stutts huddle, a lineman blindsided him with a forearm. The streaker was knocked cold.

Mrs. Fox gasped, then began a chant. "ASS...HOLE! ASS...HOLE!" It quickly spread across the stadium.

Hart's mom stayed rowdy after the game, ditching a double feature at the Stutts Subtitle Society with Hart and Tabitha in favor of a party at the CCA house. Well, not exactly a party: the suddenly community-oriented men of Comma Comma Apostrophe were hosting a "Binge-Drinking Demonstration followed by a Q and A."

Hart was dubious. "Mom, I'm serious. It's gross over there. Two guys live in the basement with no toilet."

"Hart, I'm an adult," Mrs. Fox said, "and as far as I know, I have all my shots. I'll say hi to your friend from high school—"

"He's not a friend!" Tabitha and Hart chorused.

"—what's his name, Trot?"

"Close enough," Hart said.

"Have fun sowing those wild oats," Tabitha said.

"Thanks, Tab. It's nice to see everyone isn't painfully inhibited."

Hart hated it when his mother thought he was being overprotective. "Just promise me you'll have your cell-phone, in case you have to call me from jail."

"Hey, who's the parent here?" Mrs Fox said.

"I often ask myself the same thing," Hart said. They kissed, and parted ways.

Mrs. Fox spent a happy hour wandering the central campus, enjoying the weekend bustle, watching the young people. She talked with a bum dressed as Louis Pasteur, and bought him a gyros. Then she went over to the CCA house, where things had been in full swing since 3 pm.

Until around midnight, the party was fairly typical: loud, dark, sweaty, lots of inappropriate touching. Mrs. Fox was the only parent there, and weirdness was felt on both sides; she got over that by teaching the bartender a few drinks.

"A gin and tonic is simple," she said to Beekman. "Gin, and then tonic. Voila!"

"Duh! That makes total sense," Beekman said. "Can I tell you a secret, ma'am?"

"Call me Janelle," Mrs. Fox said.

"Janelle, I have way too much homework to be doing this," Beekman said. "Would you take over for me?"

"Sure," Mrs. Fox said. And so Hart's mother mixed drinks for the better part of an hour, serving prepster girls and their wobbly dates.

Biff walked up to refill his cooler with beers. All night, he had on "roving bar," duty, serving those too plastered to make it to the bar. Biff lugged a cooler filled with bottles and ice; he also wore a neck brace with a bottle-opener mounted on it.

"Where's Beekman?" he demanded, as a passerby jammed a beer into his neck and snapped the cap off.

"You mean the kid who was here before? I gave him the night off," Mrs. Fox said. "He said he had too much work."

"That sucks!" Biff said. "Hey, you look familiar." Biff had been studying the dossiers of all the members of *The Cuckoo*, and amazingly, some information had penetrated.

"Janelle Fox," Mrs. Fox said, extending a hand.

Biff shook it. "You don't happen to be related to Hart Fox?"

"I'm his mother."

"I see," Biff said, becoming sly.

"Do you know Hart?"

"Yes—I mean, no," Biff said. "Why do you ask?"

"Because you asked me if I was related to him. Would you like a drink?" Mrs. Fox asked, trying to be friendly. "It might be kinda dangerous. All I've got left is flat Sprite and grain, and I can't tell which is which."

Biff had gotten hour-by-hour reports from North's operatives since Mrs. Fox had hit town. "Tell me—did you enjoy macing Professor Lemonade?"

"I wish you hadn't brought that up…" Mrs. Fox said, embarrassed. "I feel bad enough as it is." She was unsure of how her actions had been received, and frankly alarmed that they had become so widely known. "I wish you wouldn't say anything."

Biff's eyes grew wide—here was a golden opportunity to strike at *The Cuckoo*! By making the editor's mother have a crappy Parents' Weekend! He turned to the room. "Hey, everybody! The bartender is the lady who kicked Lemonade's ass!"

"Really?" "That's fucking awesome!" The news swept through the crowd, and it was decided by the mob-mind that it would be fun to bring them together again. Before she could escape, Mrs. Fox was swept up and placed on the shoulders of some football players, and the entire population of the party trooped across the Turbid to Lemonade's apartment in Kerouac Towers.

Professor Lemonade sat on his sofa, drinking a glass of milk and watching home-improvement shows. He heard some noise outside; when it didn't go away he decided to investigate. Lemonade went to the sliding glass doors which opened onto his balcony and peeped between the curtains.

When Lemonade saw the mob, he felt a deep sense of satisfaction. Finally, he thought. They'll run me out of town on a rail, and I can go get a real job. He was still embroidering this delightful fantasy of shame when Brother Nipples, the leader of the mob, began to shout.

"This is the old woman" (Mrs. Fox was 45) "that you were coming on to yesterday in class. She thinks you're hot." Brother Nipples turned to Mrs. Fox. "You do, don't you?"

As a rule, Mrs. Fox never contradicted torch-wielding mobs. "Oh, you bet," she said. Somebody offered her another flask; people had been handing her drinks all the way over from the CCA house. She didn't mind. She had a feeling she might need it.

"So we thought," Brother Nipples shouted, "that you two oughta hook up." The crowd began to chant, "Old People! Hook up! Old people! Hook up!"

Though Professor Lemonade had many faults, he was not a monster, and it was clear to him that poor Mrs. Fox was in the middle of a mess he'd created. So even though the quicker route to infamy was surely to deny the mob what it wanted, Lemonade ran downstairs and opened the front door.

Looking at the passel of drunk collegians that surrounded her, Mrs. Fox made a snap decision. Even the apartment of a strange man seemed safer than what was going on out here. A girl's BMW was being rocked, prior to being set on fire. A group of hockey players had ripped a large sycamore out of the ground and was preparing to hurl it into the Turbid. And where had everybody gotten pitchforks? So, as the chant continued, Mrs. Fox walked calmly over to the apartment building and stepped inside.

The crowd cheered.

"Sorry about all this," Professor Lemonade said, as they got into the elevator. It was weird; they both rode in silence up to the fourth floor.

As the doors opened, Mrs. Fox finally spoke. "Listen," she said, "don't get any ideas just because you're famous, I'm tipsy, and there's a mob outside expecting us to have sex."

"Oh, absolutely not," Lemonade said. "You're old enough to be my…"

Mrs. Fox shot him a look.

"…older sister."

"Did she *also* have—what did you call it?—an 'educated cranny'?"

"I just want you to know I felt totally bad about that afterwards," Lemonade said, opening his apartment door. "I'm trying to get fired."

"Why?"

"Long story." He turned on the light—there was a massive cheer from outside. "Would you like to sit down? Just until the mob leaves?"

"Thanks," Mrs. Fox said.

Lemonade peeked through the curtains. "Oh Christ," he said. "It's gotten bigger." Some reporters from the *Spec* had arrived on the scene, and were trying to goose the proceedings into a riot. The crowd refused, and were taking turns lying to reporters. A carnival-like atmosphere reigned; an enterprising townie had even started selling cotton candy.

Lemonade watched the crowd grow. "I am so, so, sorry."

Over on the couch, Mrs. Fox's buzz was wearing off. "Well, it's certainly been a Parents' Weekend to remember."

"I hate to say this, but I think the only way they'll leave is if we—I mean, if they *think* we—"

Mrs. Fox thought for a second. "Okay," she said, "first, turn off the lights."

"Okay." The moment Lemonade did so, there was a cheer from the mob. "So far, so good."

"Where's your bathroom?" Mrs. Fox asked. Lemonade pointed. Mrs. Fox went in, closed the door, and emerged a moment later, bra in hand. "Your trophy."

The pair sat there in the dark. "How long should we wait?" Lemonade asked.

"Depends on how much of a reputation you want," Mrs. Fox joked. This guy wasn't so bad. He had a lot of books, which she always liked. "Get into your bathrobe or something."

"Right. Would you like a glass of wine?" Lemonade yelled from his bedroom. "I was drinking myself to sleep."

"'Fraid I'm already kinda blitzed," Mrs. Fox said.

"Kegstands will do that to you," Lemonade said, walking back into the room. "May I?"

Mrs. Fox handed him the bra. He walked over the sliding glass door, stepped onto the balcony, and waved the bra like a flag. When the crowd saw him do this, they exploded with glee.

"Thanks, people," Lemonade said—then suddenly had a brainstorm. "Now I want you all to go back home, do lots of pointless damage to the campus, and have meaningless, unprotected sex with someone whose name you don't even know." That would get him fired, it had to. But just in case it didn't…"Oh, and one more thing: go drink even more—but only if you're underage. The rest of you should just do some illegal drugs. G'night!"

When his mother showed up at Dacron dining hall the next morning for a quick farewall breakfast, she didn't say a word.

"How was the party?" Hart asked.

"Oh, fine. Nothing much to speak of," Mrs. Fox said, trying to be breezy through her hangover. "Reminded me why I didn't finish college."

Inside Hart, a small alarm bell sounded. "And what does that mean?"

"Nothing, nothing," his mother said. "What did you and Tabitha do besides go to the movie?"

"It was four hours long, and in Danish," Hart said. "We were pretty cashed. When's your train?"

"An hour," Mrs. Fox said, slowly chewing a bagel. "Are these lights always so bright?"

"I wish you had flown," Hart said.

"It's okay," Mrs. Fox said, realizing she wasn't wearing a bra. "I like the train. I've got my sudoku."

"Let me pack you a little something." Hart went to the kitchen and gathered together some food—a few sandwiches, an apple, some potato chips, a yogurt he knew she liked. After he got back, they went to his room, and called a cab. In thirty minutes, she was gone.

At first, Hart couldn't decide whether he was glad she came or not. In a couple of hours, after everybody had woken up, he'd gotten his answer. His voice mail was full of messages. They all started the same way: "Dude! I heard what your mom did last night…" interspersed with the occasional, "Dude! Your mom's in the *Spec* special supplement!"

Hart grabbed the bean-bag chair they'd bought at the bookstore Saturday after the game, and whaled on it until leaked styrofoam pellets. Then he went over to Tab's, and stayed there for the next two weeks, writing an entire *Cuckoo* issue by himself (he even captioned Peter's cartoons). The theme was "Parents: Threat or Menace?"

Hart took an issue—the top one out of the first box, in fact—and stuck it into an envelope, along with a letter asking Quinn Bostwick to come to campus as their guest. Hart had written and rewritten that letter twenty times with no success, but his mom's messy visit had unlocked something inside of him, a who-fucking-cares? bravado. Anger can move mountains, and Hart had reason to be angry: in just one weekend, his mother had turned him into a laughingstock again. He could go to Stutts, and even excel there—but would he ever be able to truly escape where (and who) he'd come from?

So Hart wrote Quinn Bostwick full of hope and need and despair, like someone importuning a god for deliverance. The letter began with the single word: "Help!"

17

Games People Play

Saturday, November 20th, 3:45 pm

On the first Tuesday in November, Sterling Strong, famous actor and Stutts alum, became President-elect of the United States.

It had been a squeaker, a vicious, bloody, nail-biter full of accusations and counter-accusations, but nobody on campus took much notice. The average Stutts student only thought of the outside world as a stage for his/her future exploits. And at the moment there was something much grander at stake than some silly public office. It was time for "Gotterdammerung," the annual football game against Stutts' mortal rival, Keasbey.

The site of the game alternated, to spread out the vandalism. This year "G'rung" was at Keasbey. In such years it was a tradition for Stutts students to pile into U-hauls and make the trek northward in great swerving, bottle-shedding flotillas. With ingenuity and credit cards the students made the trailers quite cozy, and the danger that exhaust from the towing car might seep into the trailer and suffocate them, gave the outing a frisson of danger that most parties just couldn't match.

This year, *The Cuckoo* was going to G'rung in style: when it looked as though the magazine was gone for good, one of the things that Peter had done to cheer himself up was snag an old aluminum Airstream off eBay, with the idea of turning it into a giant football. The resumption of the magazine made this a Herculean task, so Peter called on some of his buddies from the Promethean Society—the club for Stutts' most hot-shot student engineers. They threw themselves into the project, disappearing for the first three weeks of November into a cave-like garage near *The Cuckoo*'s office, emerging only to eat, sleep, and ace the occasional test.

The Saturday of the game, Hart and Guy were allowed to see Peter's masterpiece.

"Appropriate and aerodynamic," Guy said, feeling the pebbled pigskin Peter had glued to the sides of the trailer . "And what was your role in this, Hart?"

"None," Hart said, then added defensively. "I was doing the magazine." Hart was beginning to consider the pint-sized lawyer to be the Yoko Ono of his and Peter's relationship. Hart squatted down to where Peter was working on the undercarriage. "Are you sure the ball will spin like a real ball?"

"At highway speeds, yep. Wind-resistance."

"Cool. Will Reed's car be able to tow this?" Hart asked.

"Yeah," Peter said. "It's superlight. The original body's mostly gone, replaced by molded carbon-fiber."

As always, Hart's mind went to the dark place. "You didn't take out any safety features, did you?"

"Here I am creating art..." Peter grunted as he hefted himself from the creeper to his chair. "...and he wants to know about airbags?"

"Living, dying, we're only here for a brief visit, Hart," Guy said. "The point is to enjoy yourself."

"Guy, part of enjoying myself is not dying in a heap of twisted metal." Peter's mouth opened, but Hart corrected himself before Peter could. "I'm sorry, *molded carbon fiber*."

Hart considered not going, but not because he was afraid of dying. (Well, maybe a little.) "G'rung" signaled the beginning of Stutts' Thanksgiving vacation, and after Parents' Weekend and midterms and doing the last issue himself, Hart was feeling worn down. "Why drive three hours and sit in the cold drinking with a bunch of strangers, when I can do that warm and dry right here?"

He had a point, but then Tabitha dropped a bomb. "I've been thinking about it," she said, "and I want you to come visit my family. They're only forty minutes away from Keasbey. Please."

Hart wriggled, but only for a second—he didn't want to hurt Tabitha's feelings. It would be a learning experience, he thought. That's not dread I'm feeling, that's excitement!

For some time, Hart had simply assumed that vampires didn't have parents. But of course they did, everything does (except perhaps yeast and amoebas and even then there may be tender feelings we don't know about). Speaking of tender feelings, they seemed to be in fairly short supply when it came to Tabitha and her folks. Hart didn't mind this; he found people his age who liked their parents somewhat unnerving.

As far as Hart could divine from her scattered comments, Tabitha had nothing against her parents—nothing except a century-plus to become annoyed at their quirks and frailties. Things that would've been negligable, or even endearing, over a single lifetime became quite annoying over two. And with forever stretching out in front of them all, it was no wonder that Tabitha was a little brittle on the subject. Still, they existed, and it only seemed right to Hart that he meet them. He took it as a compliment that Tabitha wanted him to. "I haven't asked many," Tabitha said. "Not after Charlie Chaplin showed up in his boxer shorts." She sighed. "All my mother said was, 'I can see why you like him, you naughty.'"

Though Ellen had ditched them to spend the day with her Mugwumps pals, no Cuckonians died on the way up to Keasbey—but it was a near thing. A baked ride-moocher (one of Guy's subterranean bohemian friends) kept opening the side window and scorching Tab with sunlight; after the third time Hart was all in favor of heaving Mr. Bong onto the interstate. Luckily Tab was a bit anesthetized. They all were, thanks to the quarter-keg of "C&E Amber" Reed had laid in the night before.

Tabitha couldn't join them in the stands until the beginning of the fourth quarter when it was sufficiently dark, and she hadn't brought a book. The beer helped pass the time, and she was a bit nervous about the big parental powwow. So by the time she joined them, she was a bit tipsy.

"Who's winning?" Tabitha asked, sitting down. "On second thought, I don't give a damn."[44] She picked up some binoculars and started scanning the crowd. "Is that President-Elect Strong? Wow, he's smokin' hot."

"I prefer Sean Connery," Hart sniffed.

"I agree," Reed said. The President-elect's most recent turn as the fictional spy had been filming during his candidacy. He made speeches from the set, brandishing futuristic gadgets from the movie. Instead of a coherent policy on, say, the trade deficit, Strong had a snippet of CGI showing him burning a hole through the Premier of China with his Rolex/laser. 'I think Premier Hu finally saw the light.'"

Nobody knew whether Strong planned to continue as Bond while President, but all signs so far suggested he would. The money was too good, the cross-promo opportunities too fat. "Plus," Strong admitted, "it's a bully pulpit."

Back on the field, the score was still 0-0. Each team's lack of skill was so complete that it could not even take advantage of its equally retarded op-

44 Neither did the teams. Because of the new President's heartthrob status, ESPN had done a piece on this year's Stutts-Keasbey game. The alumni of both schools were up in arms, because the total access showed just how little the two teams tried to win. There were players reading *Daily Money* during practice, making stock trades at halftime, even comparing internships while playing.

"What was JP Morgan/Chase like? I heard the chicks there are bitches."

"They're not so bad, once you get 'em loaded. Ow!"

" Whoops. Didn't mean to get in the way."

"'Salright. Are you going back to Lazard-Freres after graduation?"

"Maybe—shit, I dropped it."

"Sorry. I was distracting you."

As always, any real animosity was reserved for non-athletes at their own schools.

ponent. "They aren't really trying," Reed mused to no one in particular.

"If they are, I despair for our species," Peter said.

Hart jumped up—Stutts had gained a yard, its first of the day. Could this be the breakthrough? Hart urged them on: "Keasbey SUCKS!"

"How about the first team to ten yards, wins?" Peter suggested. Guy was sitting next to him, blinking intently through his thick glasses at a pocket-watch. "Got a train to catch?" Peter asked.

"Don't mind me. Just keep looking at the field," Guy said.

"Do I have to?" Peter said.

Guy began counting down. "Five…four…three…two…one…"

Stutts had started to run the next play, their favorite, "run directly into the ass of the right tackle, stumble, then fall down"—when suddenly both teams stopped.

"What happened, somebody get a stock tip? Who's got the binoculars?" Tabitha asked. "Can anybody tell what's going on?"

"They're all looking at their feet," Hart said, zooming in on the knot of players. "Whoa!" He laughed—some of them had jumped backwards spasmodically. The ballcarrier put down the ball, then started brushing something off his uniform rather violently, almost clawing at it. More and more players followed suit. "I have no idea what's happening."

"Would somebody please take the binoculars from Blindy?" Reed asked.

Tabitha took them. "Things are coming out of the ground. Are they… bugs?"

Down at the end of the wooden bench, Guy gave a little cackle. The students looked at him.

"Seventeen-year cicadas," he said, delighted. "I boobytrapped the whole field, way back when I was at Keasbey Law."

The students were amazed, half at the planning and audacity of the prank, half that such a freak had gone to ultra-stodgy Keasbey Law School.

The whole field began to burst with the bugs, which died immediately, either through the November cold or being stomped on. All around the crowd, confusion was turning to disgust.

Peter was the only one of the group still watching the game. "There's been no whistle," he said. "The play's still going."

A Stutts lineman had the exact same thought. Portly and clumsy, and so superfluous he didn't even make it into the program, the lineman was determined to seize his chance at glory. He scooped up the ball, and began chugging down the sidelines.

Twenty yards later, some Keasbey players realized what was happening. They took off in hot pursuit. With players slipping on cicada carapaces all around him, the lineman plowed forward like an SUV driving through two inches of peanut butter cups. Finally, at the very precipice of the goal, a group of Keasbey players dove at him en masse. They brought him down—but not before he gave one final lunge at the end zone. A cloud of bug guts and shell fragments plumed up as the group hit the ground.

"Did he get in?" Peter asked.

The crowd held its breath (mostly to keep from swallowing any stray bugs). One official unpiled the players, while another got on his hands and knees, trying to scrape away enough insect matter to reveal the goal line. Finally, he raised his arms—it was a touchdown.

The game was immediately called due to grossness, but Stutts had won.

"Does anyone have a cell phone?" Guy asked, cleaning his glasses, something he only did when he was really pleased.

Reed handed his over.

"Thank you. I just won a very large bet with the Chairman of the Keasbey *Outrage* from my year, and would like to gloat. Naturally," Guy said, "dinner's on me."

"Tab and I can't come," Hart said.

"Why not?" Peter said. He was hoping that Hart and Guy would warm to each other.

"I'm going to meet her parents."

"Oh, God," Peter said. He clapped Hart on the back, and spoke in a tone of voice usually reserved for departing kamikazes. "Good luck."

The train ride to Newport was quick. "That's why I didn't go to Keasbey," Tabitha said. "*Oodles* too close to home." As they waited for Tabitha's younger brother Roddy to pick them up from the station, Tabitha seemed sad.

"What's up?" Hart asked. "Anything wrong?"

"Oh, nothing," Tabitha said. "I just remember playing with Roddy here. We used to push each other onto the tracks."

"Jesus!"

"That's nothing. I used to push Roddy off cliffs," Tabitha said. "Then he'd get me back by setting my clothes on fire. Sometimes I wouldn't notice for a block." Tabitha sighed. "Those were good times, back when we first became different. We were still excited by it all. Now…That's the thing about immortality—just because you live forever, that doesn't make life any more interesting."

"Didn't people freak out," Hart asked, "seeing you on fire and not doing anything about it?"

"Nah," Tabitha said. "Only normals, and they were used to seeing stuff like that."

"Why are there so many vampires in Newport?"

Tabitha looked around, making sure that nobody was around.

"I was just making small talk, Tab. If you don't want to—"

"No, no, I was just making sure. Both sides work hard to pretend the other doesn't exist. It's important to be polite," Tabitha said. "This is what my Uncle Whipple told me, so take it with a grain of salt..."

"Is that your 'fairy godfather' Uncle?"[45]

"No, that's a different one. Whipple said that my family used to live in New York. My grandfather Gouverneur was personal physician to a lot of the muckety-mucks. One of them, name of Buckett, built a big cottage—"

"—meaning, 'mansion'—"

"—up here in Newport, and gave granddad a full-time job taking care of his wife. People were a lot more messed-up, health-wise, then they are today, and this one was worse than most. She had diabetes. She had gout. She had TB. She had chilblains—"

"What *are* chilblains?"

"—you name it, this woman had it," Tabitha said. "But she was in good hands. Gouverneur was an excellent doctor. He was also something of a free spirit, and so was always investigating new therapies."

"What does this have to do with vampires?" Hart asked.

"I'm getting to that," Tabitha said. "One day my grandfather came across a pamphlet translated from the *Srebnian Journal of Medicine*. It described some kind of drops you put on your tongue, that could cure any illness, permanently. That sounded pretty good to Gouverneur; just that morning, Mrs. Buckett had started peeing a color he'd never seen before."

"Ick."

"Totally. Not only that, the pamphlet said, but these drops could prevent you from getting any future diseases too. Sounds great, right? The problem was that the translator didn't include anything about side-effects, which were in small print all over the original but not included in the English version."

"Makes sense," Hart said. "My dad did the same thing with No-Preg. Why tell somebody a bunch of stuff that will make them not buy it?"

"I don't know—to stay out of prison, maybe?"

45 Tabitha was fond of this old joke from *The Cuckoo*:
"He: Do you have a fairy godfather?
She: No, but there's an uncle we're not sure about."

"Touché," Hart said. "Continue."

"Gouveneur sends away for these drops, and as soon as they arrive, he gives some to Mrs. Buckett. Bam! One dose, five drops, her scrofula is gone. So he gives her another, and that cures the TB. Another one gets rid of the goiter. Pretty soon, she's a picture of health—a little sun-sensitive, likes her meat a lot rarer than she used to, but on the whole, a new woman. She even has fewer wrinkles than before.

"Naturally she tells her friends," Tabitha said. "Naturally, they all want to try it. Within a week, my grandfather is writing back to Srebnia for as many jugs of the stuff he can get."

"What was it?"

"Vampire spit," Tabitha said. "That's why I'm not such a fan of French kissing."

"Because you don't want to vampire me up."

"Exactly. The risk is minimal, but..."

Hart had a thought. "Does it go both ways? Meaning, can my spit make you human-er?"

"If it does, I'm in trouble," Tabitha said. "Now stop interrupting, I wanna finish before Roddy pulls up. All the rich people in Newport are becoming vampirized, and nobody realizes it, least of all grandpa Gouverneur. Everything's going great—I mean, the social calendar started getting more and more nocturnal, but people hardly even noticed that—because the side-effects don't hit you all at once, and plus, everybody was feeling wonderful. Hart, lemme tell you: back in the old days, everybody was sick *constantly*."

"That must've sucked."

"It did. My grandfather thinks he's discovered the greatest breakthrough in the history of medicine. He's branched out from just treating Mrs. Buckett, and now has a waiting room full of people willing to pay anything he wants to charge. He starts getting rich, but that doesn't feel right. So he approaches his original patron, Mr. Buckett, and says, 'What I would like to do is start a sanatarium, ideally a group of them all across the country, to make this therapy available to everyone."

"So what did Mr. Moneybags say to that?" Hart asked.

"Nothing, at first. Buckett played along until he found out that grandfather was still the only person who knew how to get the medicine. Then he said, 'Let me gather together some of my friends, potential investors who I think might be interested in your plan."

"Gouverneur was over the moon. And later that night, the rich man arrived at Gouveneur's house with a bunch of his friends, just like he said—only it wasn't to talk. While my Grandpa, my Grandma and my little baby father slept, the men set fires all around the house."

Hart was shocked. "Why?"

"They didn't want to share the medicine—it's no fun if everybody has it. The whole fun of being rich is getting special things."

Hart thought about Mr. Darling buying Trip a spot at Stutts. "They never change."

"Not that I can tell," Tabitha said bleakly. "Anyway: Grandpa Gouverneur died in the fire, but my grandmother leaped out of a second-story window with my father in her arms. She survived because she landed right on Buckett. He broke her fall, and she broke his neck."

"Oh, the irony."

"She was able to elude the rest of them just long enough to run to the house of another family that my father had treated, the Twomblys. This was just blind luck on my grandma's part, but Cecil Twombly was one of the few muckety-mucks that hadn't taken part in the mob. They didn't believe my grandma's story, doubting that Buckett and the rest of them—who were all part of their social set—would actually kill anyone. But when the mob burst in, they killed Grandma immediately. One of the Twombly girls grabbed my father and ran up to her room, where she had been keeping her drops instead of taking them for the flu. Vampire spit tastes not-so-good."

"I thought it was just your toothpaste," Hart said.

"She squirted some into my father's mouth and held his nose until he swallowed. Then the mob burst in. They grabbed my dad, and swung him by his feet to break his skull against the wall—but the vampire spit had already gotten into dad's system, and he was already on his way to becoming immortal. When it was obvious that my father couldn't be killed, they left. The Twomblys decided to take Father in and raise him as their own. Father wasn't a full vampire—it was only a tiny bit of medicine. He had to go to Srebnia later to get that done. When he had a family of his own, he made us all 'get bit,' just in case somebody in the mob tried to finish the job."

"Wow," Hart said. "That's one hell of a story."

Tabitha shrugged. "Every family's got 'em, you just have to know who to ask. And when you can't have babies, you take all that energy and focus it on the people who came before. We all go into the past, instead of the future."

"That makes sense," Hart said.

A meticulously restored electric blue Trans-Am lurched uncertainly around the corner. "Oh, look. Here's Roddy."

The boy behind the wheel looked about 13. "Is he old enough to drive?" Hart asked over the blatting of the car's massive engine.

"Don't let him hear you say that," Tabitha said. "He's very sensitive about his appearance."

"Nice wheels," Hart said to Roddy.

"Hello, *Rod*erick," Tabitha said in a fruity, affectionate voice.

"Hello, *Tab*itha." Roddy got a kiss, which he wiped off before they drove away. Roddy was certainly old enough to drive; he was only six years younger than Tabitha, which made him one-hundred thirty-three older than Hart. Yet, because of when he decided to get bit, he was stuck forever in the body of a gangly, half-grown, fuzz-'stached kid.

It was a short ride to the Twombly's. "We all told Roddy to wait," Tabitha said, as they walked inside. "We told him that since he'd be frozen at whatever age he was when he took the treatment, he should wait until his pimples cleared up." Tabitha sighed. "But since Big Sister was doing it…You know how siblings are."

"I don't, actually." Hart was an only child. "Wow, what a house." Tabitha's parents lived in a mansion, the product of buying low and holding forever.

"Hello!" Tabitha yelled as she walked into the front hall.

"We're in the living room," a female voice responded.

Roddy pushed past. "Don't touch my game!" he yelled.

"Roderick," the voice said, "I assure you that I have no interest in playing *Grand Theft Auto*."

Tabitha lead the way through the house. She stopped in the doorway of a room; an older man in a tatty undershirt was watching television in an even tattier recliner. "Sibley, there's someone I'd like you to meet."

The man turned his head slowly, as if every inch were an imposition.

"This is my boyfriend Hart."

"Don't get up," Hart said, trying to be extra polite.

"Wasn't going to," Sibley said. "Another 'farter,' huh?"

"Sibley, you know I don't like that term," Tabitha said, "it's ignorant." (In addition to all its other benefits, the vampiric diet eliminated flatulence.) Tabitha turned to Hart and said, "Sibley's our butler. He's been with us for—how long has it been, Sibley?"

"Ninety-eight years, six months, fourteen days, fifty-three minutes, and a handful of excruciating seconds." Sibley turned back to the television set.

"Um…" Tabitha desperately tried to keep the courtesy from dribbling out of this interaction. "We'll have to have a party for you when you hit one-hundred, won't we?"

Sibley squeezed out a noncommittal grunt and began cycling through the channels without purpose.

"Sibley, it's so dark in here, let me turn on a—"

"I don't want a bloody light!" Sibley said fiercely, then muttered. "Can't a man get some peace?"

"We'll just go," she whispered. They turned and walked down the hall.

"Is he always like that?" Hart said.

"No," Tabitha said. "It's worse when he's drunk."

"Why don't you fire him?"

"Oh, we can't fire him," Tabitha said. "It's our fault he's a vampire. Well, Roddy's actually. Roddy peed in a bottle of his favorite scotch, and Sibley was too drunk to notice."

"Seems like being a vampire's pretty sweet to me," Hart said.

"Anything can be awful if it's mandatory," Tabitha said. "Like being in a family, for example." She gave the tour. "Library, butler's pantry, kitchen, mud room, parlor, Mother's needlepoint room," she said. "And finally, the living room..."

"Wait!" Hart grabbed her arm before they walked in. "Is there anything I should know?"

Tabitha thought for a second. "Don't mention Franklin Roosevelt. Father goes bonkers."

They walked into the living room. Mrs. Twombly sat on the couch clipping coupons from the local circular, and that presumably was Mr. Twombly in the leather recliner reading *Daily Money*.

"Hello, my dears," Mrs. Twombly said, getting to her feet. "How was the trip?"

Tabitha's mom was a gray-blonde version of her daughter—same large, dark eyes, same small, fox-like nose. When the ladies hugged, Hart noted that they were the exact same height; Mrs. Twombly was rather slim where Tabitha had curves, but that might've been age rather than genetics.

"Fine," Tabitha said. Even their voices were similar—though Tab's was a shade smokier. "A surprisingly small proportion of drunks on the train for a G'rung Saturday."

"Nice to meet you, Hart. Tab's told us so many nice things about you."

"Lies, all lies," Hart joked.

Mr. Twombly stood up. He reminded Hart of an actor from "Citizen Kane," not Orson Welles but the other one. "I like your pants," Hart said as they shook hands. Mr. Twombly wore a bright plaid pair.

"Thanks," Mr. Twombly said. "Bit short for you, eh Tab?"

"Oh, Daddy," Tabitha said, then turned to Hart. "Don't mind him, Hart. He's only trying to rile you."

"Just don't believe in meaningless pleasantries," Mr. Twombly said.

Hart began to sweat. Meaningless pleasantries—that was his whole strategy! How would he survive three whole days?

"Like these pants, for example. I know Hart doesn't really like them. He was just saying that to score points."

"No, really—" Hart said, slightly offended at his sincere compliment being called a lie.

Mr. Twombly cut him off. "I've met Tabitha's boyfriends for over one-hundred years, so I know when a young man is—"

Tabitha stepped in. "The game was fun."

"By which you mean 'Stutts won,'" Mr. Twombly grumbled, sitting back down. Seeing Hart's puzzled look, he explained: "I went to Keasbey 'way back when. My daughter went to Stutts just to get back at me."

Tabitha was getting fed up. "Daddy, for the millionth time, Keasbey didn't accept women back then. Stutts did. End of story."

"Excuse me," Mrs. Twombly said, turning to her son. "Roddy, do you think you could mute your abomination for just a bit, while the rest of us are talking?"

"I don't see why you guys can't go in the other room and talk," Roddy said.

"Roddy, don't be a twerp," Tabitha said.

"Get staked, goody-goody," Roddy said.

Hart tried to avoid the bickering by looking around. There was a lot of pheasant-and-Laborador artwork—but a preponderance of light-colored upholstery meant that this was a dog-less family. One wall had a rather large fireplace in it, above which was a portrait of the Twomblys. Although their dress was old-fashioned, their faces were exactly the same. Mrs. Twombly was holding a baby.

"John Singer Sargent, if you're wondering," Mrs. Twombly said

"That can't be Roddy in your arms, can it?" Hart said.

All the air was sucked out of the room. "No," Mrs. Twombly said.

Tabitha jumped in. "That was my brother Grinnell. He died right after that portrait. Measles."

"Whoops," Roddy said, not quite under-his-breath enough.

"Don't be a jerk, Rod," Tabitha said with the savageness reserved only for siblings. "Hart's our guest."

If Hart could've killed himself right then, he would've. But that would've been too easy.

Mr. Twombly leaned back in his recliner. Hart noticed that he was wearing slippers from that catalog his mom always threw away because it was too expensive.

"So," Tabitha's father said psychically, "my daughter tells me you don't have any money."

Tabitha broke off hostilities in one conversation and joined battle in another. *"DADDY!"* she said. "That's an incredibly rude thing to say."

"Maybe," Mr. Twombly said, "but when one has a daughter that must be supported until the sun explodes, a certain amount of scratch is essential." He turned to Hart. "Hart agrees with me—don't you, son?"

Hart felt pulled in two directions at once; he agreed with Tabitha, but didn't want to disagree with Mr. Twombly. He loved Tabitha, but wanted Mr. Twombly to like him. To escape, he grabbed something out of the air. "Uh...can I use your phone?"

"Is it a long-distance call?" Mr. Twombly asked.

"I guess so," Hart said. "I just want to call my mom, to let her know I got here safe."

"Leave a dollar on the front hall table." Mr. Twombly went back to his paper.

"Hart, don't you dare," Tabitha said.

"Phil's such a kidder," Mrs. Twombly said. "Come on, you can use the phone in the kitchen. If you're hungry, we can get Sibley to cook you something. I think he remembers how."

"Mother, *no*," Tabitha said. "Sibley cooks angry." It was true; Sibley had liked to eat, and one of the things that he hated the most about being vampiric was how everything but blood gave him wicked cramps.

"Suit yourselves," Mrs. Twombly said, turning on the lights. "Hunt around, see what you find."

The kitchen was immaculate—Hart would've been shocked to discover that it had ever been used. Some of this could be chalked up to everyone's special diet—meals were probably "slurp 'n' go" affairs—but it was more than that. From the sniping in the other room, he couldn't imagine the Twomblys ever sitting together long enough to share a meal. If the kitchen is the heart of a home, Hart suddenly felt very sad for Tabitha. "There may be some saltines from when we were getting the driveway re-paved," Mrs. Twombly said.

"Thirteen years ago?" Tabitha asked. "Thanks, mother. We can handle it."

"Okay," Mrs. Twombly said. "I'm going upstairs to watch a little television. Nice meeting you, Hart. Glad you're staying with us for Christmas."

"Thanksgiving, mother," Tabitha said.

"Right, right," Mrs. Twombly said, smiling. "After the hundredth year, they all smush together."

Hart tried to kindle the tiny speck of warmth. "Thanks, Mrs. Twombly."

"Certainly, Hart." Mrs. Twombly turned away, then remembered something. "He doesn't sleep in a coffin, does he?"

"Mother, don't tell me there's no bed!" Tabitha said, genuinely angry.

"You've known about this for weeks!"

"It's no problem," Hart said, trying to make peace. "I can just crash on a couch or something."

"See, Tabitha," Mrs. Twombly said. "Hart doesn't mind. Thank you, Hart."

Hart didn't say anything. He'd never seen Tabitha look so angry.

"Oh Tabitha, I almost forgot to tell you—Mrs. Jenkins' daughter Jenny has just had twins."

"What does that bring the total to?" Tabitha fumed. "Thirty?"

"Not for Jenny, no," Mrs. Twombly said, choosing to ignore Tabitha's snipe. "But for grandchildren, yes. Hart, your mother would understand. What I wouldn't give to hear the pitter-patter of little feet around here..."

"You and Dad should've thought of that before you convinced me to get bit, Mother," Tabitha said.

"But there are treatments," Mrs. Twombly said. "Have you looked at any of the things I sent you? Did you try that spermophilic lotion I sent? It was a little tube..."

"I thought that was toothpaste," Tabitha joked.

"Tabitha, be serious," Mrs. Twombly said sternly. "I can't understand why you won't even investigate..."

"Mother, please leave," Tabitha said. "You're giving me a splitting headache."

"All right, all right," Mrs. Twombly said, then left.

After she was out of earshot, Tabitha said, "My god, if I had a stake..."

Hart didn't know what to say. He decided on: "She seemed nice enough."

"You don't have to spend eternity with her."

Hart picked up the phone. "Your dad was kidding, right?"

"I don't care. You're not paying for a phone call."

Uncertain, Hart dialed. "I bet he'll warm up, once he gets to know me."

"This was the worst idea of my entire life," Tabitha said.

"I'm sorry." When anything went wrong, Hart naturally assumed that he was the cause.

"You didn't do anything. They're jerks," Tabitha said. "Call the station and see when the next train to Great Littleton leaves."

"Are you serious? We'll get in ridiculously late."

"I'm serious," Tabitha said. "I'll make it up to you."

Hart knew what that meant: a banquet of carnal delights only a century of practice could perfect. As he dialed the train station with a newfound chipperness, Tabitha continued to grumble. "Like I would subject any children of mine to these monsters...Roddy! Get the car out of the garage! We're going back!"

18
Beekman's Gambit
Wednesday, December 1st, 9:30 AM

Just as Peter had predicted, the stock market had come back stronger than ever, and with a Stuttsie back in the White House, the Stutts Body had calmed down considerably. Rivington, no longer under attack, stopped worrying about *The Cuckoo* and spent his days fine-tuning a plan to issue all students mandatory high-interest credit cards.

For his part, Professor North was occupied fending off yet another mandatory retirement age proposal, mainly by threatening the entire Faculty Senate with blackmail. "I just want to remind the members that I know Photoshop," North had said.

"Professor North, are you threatening us?" Professor Percy Pokington had asked. Pokington was Stutts' famed China scholar and a fellow member of the Pantheon, the school's collection of academic greats.

"No, just stating a fact. It's fascinating software," he said transparently. "You can stick a person in any situation, put their head on any body—and it's completely undetectable. " In fact, North had a particularly salacious bit of fakery showing Pokington giving Mao Tsetung a lapdance. So as usual, North prevailed. But the spook-in-chief's pressing business meant that infiltrating *The Cuckoo* rested solely on the initiative of his young agents, Biff and Beekman.

This task ignited within the two boys vastly different emotions. Beekman went fetal—he spent the entire Thanksgiving break riding out quiet paroxysms of anxiety, and his stomach got so bad that his mother fired their cook. When school started up again, Beekman was straining every mental muscle looking for ways to get out of the job. Biff, on the other hand, was ecstatic—which turned out to be his undoing.

Biff spent all of Thanksgiving Break practicing his infiltration skills. Some days went better than others; infilitrating an empty park near his parents' home was a piece of cake, while infiltrating his father's office downtown was harder. Still, he enjoyed the cat-and-mouse, and after returning to Stutts began infiltrating campus locations with gusto.

Unfortunately, one afternoon Biff decided to infiltrate the girls' showers at Horst Gymnasium. He would've succeeded if he hadn't decided to "gather hum-int"—that is, take pictures. (The flash from his cell-phone camera gave him away.) And he might've gotten off with a reprimand, had the daughter of a prominent donor not been sucking face with her girlfriend in the background of one of the photos. After that hit the internet, Biff had earned himself a one-way trip to The Chamber.

It is tremendously difficult, dear reader, to get into trouble at college, and the more prestigious the college, the more it wants to keep its reputation unsullied by expulsions. On the other hand, keeping big donors happy is an even more powerful force, probably the sole reason such colleges exist. President Rivington aimed for the middle.

"You may come back next September," he said to an appropriately abashed Biff. "From what I have seen of your parents' condo" (it had just made *Architectural Digest*) "your time away shouldn't be too unpleasant."

Biff's mother, who knew exactly how unpleasant it was going to be—for her, at least—piped up. "President Rivington, I know my son has done something wrong, but I find it extremely offensive that Beekman is getting off scot-free. That boy has always been a bad influence on Biff."

"But I was working for Professor North!" Biff yelled from the dock. "Ask Professor North, he'll tell you!"

"North? Never heard of him," Rivington said blandly. (Professor North liked to keep his existence on a 'need-to-know' basis.) "Pack your bags, Biff. We'll see you next September." He brought down the gavel, and that was that.

For Beekman, hearing that gavel come down was like the breaking of a magic spell. Being alone for the first time since age eight gave Beekman time to think. His friendship with Biff had been like a low-pitched buzzing inside his head, keeping him confused, making him do stupid stuff, forcing him to ignore what *he* liked in favor of what Biff did. It wasn't that being with Biff made Beekman unhappy; it was more that being with Biff made him unable to tell. Now that Biff was gone, Beekman had thoughts again.

The only dark cloud in Beekman's personal sky was that he was now responsible for Biff's share of their Gnomery. He simply couldn't handle the amount of homework he was required to do, and a lot of it was the math and science stuff that only Biff had the training in—you can't guess with math, you either knew the answer or you didn't. That was why Beekman didn't like it; math and science couldn't be reasoned with.

Beekman had to do something, and out of his desperation came an idea—a risky, possibly insane idea—but Beekman saw no alternative. So in early December, a week before Finals, he strode into Professor North's office.

North was hard at work faking a photograph on his computer.

"Professor North, I have a proposition for you," Beekman said, brimming with new confidence. For the first time in over a decade, he was doing something he wanted to do, not simply tagging along or enduring the consequences of one of Biff's many idiocies. Beekman pointed to the screen. "Is that Sterling Strong? His head looks weird."

"Everybody always says that!" North said with irritation. He looked at the boy. "Do I know you?"

"I'm Beekman, one of the students you asked to infiltrate *The Cuckoo*."

"The what?"

"The student humor magazine."

"No, I don't want a subscription," North said, and started back to work.

"No, Professor North," Beekman said. "You hired my friend and I to rot it from the inside."

"Oh, sure, I remember now, the two idiots," Professor North said, then tried to cover for his memory. "Forgive me. I'm always running so many operations on campus…"

Idiots? "Spare me how important you are," Beekman said, not really believing his own ears. He almost sounded…tough. Except his voice still cracked, dammit. "I'll do your little errand, but first I need you to do something for me."

"Let me guess: you want me to get you out of Finals." Professor North chuckled at his own feeble joke.

Beekman hated people who did that. "No, I need you to get me out of CCA. I'm a Gnome, and with Biff kicked out, I don't have time to do my own dirty work, much less yours."

Professor North frowned. There were a lot of very powerful, very stupid people connected with CCA. They wouldn't be pleased. "CCA's slavery agreements are awfully hard to break," he said. "The Supreme Court just upheld them again."

"That's not my problem," Beekman said. "Do you, or do you not, want *The Cuckoo* out of business?"

"Maybe you should go see President Rivington," North countered. "He's the one with the grudge."

"Or maybe you should just go into that file cabinet of yours, and see what you can find on a student named Trip Darling," Beekman said. "I'll wait."

Professor North got up, and walked over to the wall of file cabinets. He came back with a folder that was surprisingly thin.

"Not much for someone so prominent, is there?" Beekman said. "After all, he's a Darling."

"Beekman, these files are used for blackmail. If someone is not ashamed of anything—if everybody already knows that a person is a drunk, a liar, or an ass, then they are almost impossible to blackmail."

"Let me see," Beekman said. He was pretending like he was in a movie. It seemed to help. Beekman riffled through the file. "You're right. This is all shit." He dropped the file onto the desk. Then, he took a manila envelope out of the front pouch of his now ridiculously oversized hoodie. "Take a look. I got these last May, at CCA's year-end picnic."[46]

"I don't understand," Professor North said. The photos showed Trip doing things that, pre-Vonnegut, were standard operating procedure. In one, he was sprawled across a bathroom floor, snoozing in his own upchuck. In another, he was naked save for a CCA sock dangling off his manhood, and heaving a beer bottle into the Turbid River. In the third, he had crashed a College Conversation and was grabbing the breast of Queen Eugenie of the Netherlands. "From his file, this is typical behavior."

"Not anymore," Beekman said. "Trip Darling is a changed man. Crunchy. *The Cuckoo* people dosed him with a drug, I forget the name… 'Salinger'?"

"Could it have been 'Vonnegut'?" North said.

"Yeah, that was it."

"They stole that from me years and years ago," North said. "It's lost its potency by now."

"Apparently not," Beekman said. "Anyway, my point is, the frat-rat Trip couldn't be blackmailed, but the hippie Trip can be."

"How?" North asked. This Beekman kid really wasn't as stupid as he looked. He should really hang out with a better class of friend.

"It's simple," Beekman said. He pointed at the comatose shot: "The light's on—wasting energy." He pointed at the naked one: "Littering. What if everybody threw their trash in the Turbid?"

"Everybody does," Professor North said.

"Not Trip Darling, not anymore," Beekman said. Finally, he pointed to the breast-grabbing one. "And in this one—"

"Trip's afraid of causing an international incident?"

"As if. Look closer. Use the lupe."

North studied the photo. "I give up."

"Trip's wearing synthetic fibers. Total no-no." Beekman got up. "Call the frat and tell Trip what you've got on him. Five minutes after you make the call, my membership in CCA will be torn up, I promise you that. Any

46 Knowing they themselves would be drunk unto amnesia, the CCA brothers had made Biff and Beekman stay sober and record the event.

one of these would embarrass the new Trip enough to make him transfer. All three, and he might kill himself—if he could find an environmentally friendly way, obviously."

North looked at the photos again. "These are impressive. Ever consider a career in—"

"Spare me." Beekman slipped his coat back on, and wound his Sand College scarf around his neck. "Consider them my gift to you. When I'm no longer a Gnome, I'll infiltrate *The Cuckoo*. Deal?"

North saw no alternative. If *The Cuckoo* was monkeying around with Vonnegut, it really had to be destroyed. The drug had probably stabilized into water by now, but that wasn't a chance that North could take. "Deal."

Six hours later, and as brutally as possible, Beekman was supervising a group of CCA brothers as they moved his stuff into his new room. "I don't like the dresser there. Move it back."

"Oh, come on!" Brother Nipples said. "We've moved it five times!" Brother Rectal Itch began to cry.

"No backtalk or I'll tell Professor North," Beekman said. "You! Quit crying."

After they had left, Beekman pondered the day's events sitting in an easy chair, by the only working fireplace in Sand College. Professor North really does run this university, he thought, as his hated cloche hat burned. So if somebody could figure out a way to run Professor North…

19
A Very Mugwumps Christmas
Wednesday, December 15th, 11:42 pm

With the exception of Finals, which hung over everything like a bad smell, Christmas at Stutts was Hart's favorite time of year. So much so that Tabitha questioned his parentage.

"Are you sure your father wasn't Santa?" She poked Hart's belly, to check for signs of jiggitude.

"Stop," Hart said, definitely non-jolly. He was sensitive about his abs, so much so that he'd subscribed to *Your Abs & Her G-Spot*, a magazine for men. "Anything's possible, you've met my mother. Maybe she ran out of cookies."

Tabitha laughed, then saw something over Hart's shoulder. "Oh, no," she said, "It's snowing again." She didn't like snow, because it weighed down her mist form and gave her pulled muscles. "Even sleet is better than this."

Most of the time Great Littleton agreed with her. Nowhere else on Earth could it be ten degrees below freezing and still sleeting; nowhere else had sleet ever fallen from a clear blue sky. Some blamed the town's proximity to the ocean, others an ancient Indian curse, but Great Littleton was unquestionably the freezing rain capital of the globe (so much so that "a sleetfoot" was Stutts slang for a past or present student).

But this year was once in-a-decade, exuberantly cold and snowy. The frost-rimed, snow-capped campus looked gorgeous, and President Rivington had heightened the effect by the use of strategic floodlights. "A pretty campus gets used in movies," he said.

This year's unusual frigidity was an opportunity for the Promethean Society to try a project they'd been threatening for years.[47] Using ice mixed with woodchips for strength, they created a mammoth ice slide that stretched across most of the campus. Gliding on a tray stolen from the dining hall, a

47 Naturally, Peter was a prime-mover in the P.S.—following in Ellen's able footsteps. She had "pinched" Peter herself, but then had to leave the Prometheans when she got into the Mugwumps. The Mugwumps were like that, jealous of their members; Ellen had to petition the Mugwumps alumni to remain on *The Cuckoo*. Even so, many of her fellow Wumpspeople wanted her to leave the magazine; divided loyalties were a dangerous thing. So far, she had outwitted them.

student would start their belly flop at the top of the Shot Tower. Then they would slide across the Turbid, over the Law School, down Locust Street, and—just when they had made peace with the possibility of their own death—finally be dumped into a massive snow drift in the middle of the Old Quad. It was particularly fun at night, when every curve felt like you were about to slide over the edge into the darkness and Eternity.

Hart did it once, and felt himself age five years. For thrill-seekers like Peter, however, it was addictive. "I was the first to try it," Peter said. "Being a Promethean has its perks."

"Some perk," Hart said, clambering out of the snowdrift. He'd screamed so hard, he'd split his lip. "You're insane, you know that?"

Peter inhaled the cold night air. "Ahh! This is a winter wonderland!"

Hart jumped up and down. "Yeah, well, I just got some wonderland down my pants."

Their tastes in recreation aside, there could be no disagreement between Peter and Hart over *The Cuckoo*'s Xmas number. It was a huge success, the most sought-after issue in the modern history of the magazine (rivaled only by 1867's infamous "Robert E. Lee is Gay Number"). Whether it was a good thing, however, would be debated for years.

As the semester progressed, it seemed that while going underground had some benefits—editorial freedom, not getting expelled—increased readership wasn't one of them. The thrill of reading something unofficial was balanced by the fact that many students were afraid to be seen with a copy of the outlawed periodical, lest this transgression be noted in their Permanent File and forwarded to future employers. If more people were reading *The Cuckoo*, there certainly wasn't any evidence for it.

This rankled the staff, Hart especially. He complained to Guy, who counseled patience—difficult advice to stomach when you measured a career in just four years. "It's not going to happen overnight," Guy assured them. "Nothing worthwhile ever does."

For once, Peter sided with Hart. "We need something to kick the magazine in the ass," Peter said. "Has Quinn Bostwick written you back?"

"No," Hart admitted glumly. He'd really poured his heart out to that guy, and every day that passed without a response made him feel more idiotic.

They had pretty much resolved to take the rest of the semester off and start fresh in January. So it was surprising when somebody appeared at the final Wednesday post-meeting meeting (as usual held in the back room of the C&E), asking to join.

"*Cuckoo*? Never heard of it," Peter said, plucking his darts from the board.

"Doesn't exist," Hart said tersely, draining his "pi" of beer (other pubs had yards, but the C&E offered glasses 3.14 feet high). This kid could be anyone—he could even be working for the University. Peter thought the University employed spies; everybody else thought he was paranoid, but there was no harm in being cautious. By doing *The Cuckoo* they were defying a ruling of The Chamber. Any public admission could get them booted.

The kid just stood there, so Reed continued with the standard brush-off: "*The Cuckoo* has been disbanded upon the order of Stutts University. As a Stutts student I am forbidden to have any contact with said organization. Were I to learn of its existence, I would be obliged to report immediately to the appropriate authorities, so they could destroy it with all due speed."

"Well, before you do that"—the kid drew out a thick envelope from under his coat—"you might want to look at these." He tossed the envelope onto the heavily carved-up table, and knocked over Hart's pi.

"Hey!"

"Sorry," the kid said.

"Forget it," Hart said; anger never stayed long with him. "Wasn't much left. Reed, close the door." After Reed did so, Hart opened the envelope.

The envelope contained something that had been rumored to exist for centuries: in 1874, a group of four students had broken into the Mugwumps Pyramid, and taken pictures of all the rooms inside. Then, adding insult to injury, they published the photos in the *Spec*. This may not seem like a big deal, but within the world of Stutts, it was utter heresy. It was like using a splinter of the True Cross as a toothpick.

The pictures were a sensation, and established the then-fledgling *Spec* as the college's permanent tabloid. But this was not the only negative effect: Within six weeks of their transgression, all of the interlopers had been expelled. It was said that each later died under mysterious circumstances. Then, as a warning to others, The Mugwumps took their vengeance to the fourth degree—everybody from parents and siblings to second cousins once removed mysteriously lost jobs, had bank accounts closed, lost money in the stock market. They even found their houses infested with exotic, ravenous termites hitherto unknown on this continent.

"Wow," Peter said, spreading them out with his hand. "Are these what I think they are?" he asked the kid.

"Yep," the kid said.

None of *The Cuckoo*'s staffers knew the gory details, and the only person who might have told them, the Stutts history buff Ellen, was at a Mugwumps Christmas party.

"I'm glad Ellen isn't here," Reed said quietly. "She'd totally have to put a bag on her head..."

"If not kill us all," Peter said.

Hart was totally lost. "What are you guys talking about? I don't..."

"Look at that wall, Hart," Peter said, tapping a photo. "See how it's slants? And that one, too?"

"All of the walls are slanting," Reed hinted. "Almost as if they were in a..."

Things finally clicked. "I get it!" Hart said. "This is the inside of the—"

Reed shushed him. "Not so loud..." He turned to the kid. "My dad said there were just old photos. Some of these look new."

The kid shrugged. "Old intelligence is useless."

"What's your name?" Peter asked.

"Beekman Schuyler DeBoers Grimby."

"Well, Beekman whatever-whatever, these are either genuine, or an incredibly good forgery," Peter said. "Look at how some rooms are Victorian, while others are definitely Seventies. The shag carpet, the vacu-formed chairs..."

"What does that prove?" Reed asked.

"First, you can't get furniture that ugly anymore. And second, according to alt.conspiracy.mugwumps, the 'Wumps renovated the Pyramid in 1972."

"Victorian, Victorian, Victorian," Hart said, pointing at rooms, "then, bam! You're on the set of 'A Clockwork Orange.'"

"Where did you get these?" Peter asked.

"I'd rather not say," Beekman said, "but my sources are rock-solid, let's leave it at that." He sat down. "If you let me join, I'll let you print these in your next issue."

Hart paused. "They're not strictly *funny*, Beekman..."

"Everybody would read it," Beekman said,

"Why do you want to join so bad?" Reed asked skeptically. "Assuming that there *is* a magazine, which I'm not saying there is."

"Do we really want the Mugwumps pissed at us?" Hart asked.

Peter thunked his darts into the table. "Are you guys kidding?" he exclaimed. "We gotta run 'em!" He focused on Hart. "I know it's your call, Mr. Nice Guy, but we gotta do this. If you want to be a big-shot—it'll be a collector's item! We'll be gods!"

It was risky—people might get mad—they didn't have time—he still had a final—but Hart knew Peter was right. They couldn't let this opportunity go. "Okay, but you get to tell Ellen," Hart said. "Reed, go to the bar and buy as much coffee as Dennis has left. Then let's hit the office and see what we can throw together. There have got to be plenty of Mugwumps-related pieces we can reprint from old issues," Hart said. "It'll be easy."

"So am I on?" Beekman asked.

"Yes, you're on," Peter said.

Hart called Tabitha, saying that he'd be home late (if at all), so she came over to the office and helped. Snug in their underground lair, the Cuckonians went to work.

Creating the "Wishing You a Very Mugwumps Christmas Number" wasn't as easy as Hart had hoped; 99% of the old stuff was incomprehensible to the modern Stuttsie. But somehow, joke by joke, pages were filled. While Hart worked on a new editorial for the first page, Reed scoured the back issues in boxes from the Lytton Hall office. Peter drew some cartoons, and Tabitha helped "the new guy" fish some appropriate drawings and verse from the centuries of bound volumes. As the ceiling grew orangey-pink (the Great Littleton streetlamps always did that to the dawn), Reed pulled out a bottle of champagne.

"I bought this with the coffee, just in case we made it." They all shared a toast, then Hart hit the key that sent the issue to the *Spec*'s printer.

"I love doing that," he said.

Once the bundles arrived on campus later that morning, the Mugwumps acted predictably, seizing as many copies as they could. But this only made the copies they didn't catch even more valuable. By noon, people were hunting all over campus, grabbing *Spec*s and shaking them, to see if a *Cuckoo* would fall out. By dinnertime, issues were already fetching $500 a pop on eBay.

Since *The Cuckoo* stayed mum, news outlets started interviewing the students who were making thousands of dollars selling back issues. "All I have to say is, 'Thank you, *Cuckoo*!"

Thanks to their mysterious new staffer, they were rebels doing it their way and winning, unabashed campus stars...But second semester, *The Cuckoo* would discover how fickle their fans could be.

20

A Quick Call From Dress Rehearsal

Tuesday, December 27th, 5:19 pm

Being back home was so boring, Hart was seriously considering starting a blog. It's not that things were quiet, exactly—between his mother's new Golden Retriever and the ongoing antics of his cousin Lulu,[48] things were as crazy as ever. A few days after Christmas, Hart had sent out a distress call; a few days after that, Peter was sitting in his living room.

The dog was licking Peter's feet. "What's the dog's name again?"

"Nothing," Hart said.

"How Zen."

"My mother feels that it's speciesist to impose one on him," Hart said. "She's kinda out of control these days."

"I wish my parents would go a little out of control," Peter said.

Nothing was giving Peter's bare feet the licking of their lives. As his broad, pink tongue plumbed the spaces between Peter's toes, Hart got queasy. "Nothing! *Stop!*"

The dog looked up, wearing the expression of puzzled regret that comes so naturally to Labs. "Come on," Peter said, "that's the most action I've gotten since high school."

Whatever had or hadn't happened last summer with Ellen, Peter's inability to find a steady girlfriend was a regular topic of conversation. Everybody blamed Peter's disability—"I want to get a sign made, 'Yes, I can have sex'," Peter joked—but Hart was beginning to think Peter's temper had something to do with it, too. There was always a thin line between funny and angry, and the events of the first semester had, in Hart's opinion, given Peter a shove in the wrong direction.

Peter was flipping through the channels. "Asshole." New channel.

48 Well, "antics" seems the wrong word for something that usually involved plastique. Lulu was nine, and on break from the Grade School of the Americas, where she was drilled in all sorts of mayhem: assassinations, sabotage, cursive. Lulu's parents were out in the woods somewhere preparing for The Rapture. They said they'd come for Lulu when things were ready, but it had been three years. Mrs. Fox simply considered the arrangement permanent, and she and Lulu got along very well. Hart and Lulu were another story, however.

"Liar." New channel. "Crook." New channel. "Pedophile." He stopped on a right-wing talk-show host who had very vocally slammed "the campus hooligans responsible for infringing on the privacy rights of the Mugwumps…"

"Oh, good," Peter said. "Let's hear what the low-normals are supposed to think. This joker's totally a Wumpsman."

"You really think this guy's in the group?" Hart asked.

"Those shifty eyes? That inbred look?" Peter joked. "He's practically a recruiting poster."

"But he denied it."

"Of course he denied it," Peter said, shooting his friend a "how dumb can you be" look. "Wumpsmen are encouraged to lie—just not to each other. Lying to everybody else—to 'the Others'—is considered a virtue."

"According to the listserv, right?" As usual, Hart didn't know what to believe on this topic. Peter seemed to be off the deep end when it came to the Mugwumps. Ellen's getting in had only stoked his paranoia; everything she wouldn't talk about encouraged Peter to think the worst. And Guy wasn't helping, either; God knew what weird conspiratorial cosmologies he spouted. (Hart was always skeptical of people who chose to cut their own hair.)

The phone rang. It was closer to Peter. "Should I get it?"

"Nah," Hart said. All afternoon, they'd been getting crankcalled by disgruntled Mugwumps alumni. Lulu picked it up.

"Fart!" she called upstairs. That was Lulu's little nickname for her surrogate brother, whom she didn't much like. "It's your giiiirlfriend!" Lulu stretched out the first syllable and varied its pitch, then made kissy noises.

"Welcome back to the playground," he said, as Peter handed him the phone. Hart turned it on. "Hi, cutie! What a nice surprise!"

"Oh thank God you're there," Tabitha said. "My parents have gone 'round the bend."

"No! Imagine that!"

"My mother is insane with grandchild-lust," Tab continued. "Every conversation sooner or later turns to reproduction. I can't take it!"

"So let her stew," Hart said. "Eventually she'll get it through her head you can't get pregnant."

"You don't understand," Tabitha said. "These manias of hers—they last decades. And Hart—you'll never believe this—she's started putting stuff into my food, Chinese herbs or something. Everything I eat tastes like cilantro." Tabitha was pacing her bedroom as she talked. *"I hate cilantro!"*

Hart didn't know what to say. "That sucks, Tab. I'm sorry."

"Thanks," she said. "I'm just calling to hear your voice so I don't go insane. And to say that I'm going back to school, so don't try to reach me here."

"Okay," Hart said. "Peter's here for a visit."
"For how long? Are you two having fun?"
"For a week. I think so." He covered the phone. "Are you having fun?"
"Yeah," Peter said. "Say hi."
"Yeah," Hart resumed. "He says hi."
"Great...Hart?" Tabitha said.
"Yeah?"
"I need to ask you a favor," Tabitha said. "It's a big one."
"Whatever you want."
"I want to write that sex column for the *Spec.*"
"Oh, no," Hart said.
"Why is it okay for you to try to write for them, and not me?"
Hart sighed. "Tab, I thought we talked about this."
"We did," Tabitha said. "But then I got home, and had to live with these awful people, and—I have to break away from them, Hart."
"What does a sex column have to do with your parents?" Hart asked.
"They would hate it," Tabitha said. "My mother would be mortified. All the women at her club would find out—they find out about everything. They're like the goddamn CIA."
"So," Hart said. "Because you want to say 'fuck you' to your parents, I have to become known as your gigolo."
"There are worse fates," Tabitha said. "It's not just about my parents. I think I can make something out of it. I think I can actually earn some money."
"Since when do you need money?"
"Since I've wanted to stop taking it from my parents!" Tabitha yelled.
This was something she almost never did, and Hart, a good boyfriend, noticed. He made a quick calculation: his annoyance at being known as Tab's boy-toy was less than Tab's need to do this. "Okay, Tabitha. If you need to do it, do it."
"Thank you," Tabitha said. "I was going to do it anyway."
"I know that," Hart said with a chuckle. "I'm your boyfriend, remember?"
"Yepperoo. And aren't you a lucky one? Love you."
Peter couldn't hear what Tab had said, but Hart got embarrassed anyway. "Me, too..."
"Aren't you going to say it?"
It was such an adult word. "Tabitha, Peter's right here. I should go."
Tabitha made a growl of frustration. "Why, why, why must I always date little boys? I'll call you tomorrow."
Somewhat deflated, Hart put down the phone. "Women," he said in a

weary, man-of-the-world way.

"Let me guess: she's doing the sex column."

"How did you know?"

"I knew you wouldn't win that one, pardner."

The phone rang again; Hart checked the caller ID, thinking it might be Tabitha calling back. "New York City number."

"Bet it's another Mugwump," Peter said. "Should we just rip it out of the wall?"

On a whim, Hart clicked it on.

"May I speak to Hart Fox?" a rapid, urbane voice said.

"Listen," Hart said belligerently, "you and all your Mugwump buddies should stop calling and get a life!" Just before Hart hung up, he heard the voice laugh and say, "This is Quinn Bostwick."

It took a moment for Hart to process the words. As soon as he did, all available oxygen disappeared. "Really?" he whispered.

"Uh-huh. I can't chat, 'cause we're in the middle of dress, but I wanted to tell you: one, quit calling my office; and two, I've been watching this Mugwumps thing and loving every minute."

"Really?" Hart said, even quieter. He was running out of air.

"Why do you keep saying that?" Peter asked. "Who is it?"

Hart covered the mouthpiece and croaked, "Quinn Bostwick." Would he be able to finish this conversation before blacking out? Unclear.

"More powder on the nose," Bostwick said, back in New York. "You still there, cowboy?"

"Gimme the phone," Peter said impatiently. Hart did so. "Hi, Mr. Bostwick," Peter said. "This is Peter Armbruster. I'm Hart's co-editor."

"What is this, a convention? How come nobody invited me? I'm an Old Bird, you know."

"We know," Peter said. "We beat up anybody who says your show is smarmy."

"Glad to hear it," Bostwick said. "That's what I like about being on television—you get your own private army. The trick is keeping the pro-you forces bigger than the anti-ones. As you'll discover, if you haven't already."

Peter laughed.

"I gotta run, but good job on the issue."

"Thanks, Mr. Bostwick, I was the one that pushed for it."

Hart felt a knife in his heart. It was true, but was Peter trying to steal his idol? He got up and walked over; squatting down and putting his ear near the phone, he could just make out the conversation.

"Good for you," Bostwick said. "I assumed it was the Editor in Chief."

"We also kidnapped the Fed Chairman."

Bostwick chuckled. "My writing staff thanks you," he said. "Don't they hold classes anymore in Great Littleton? Okay—that's my call—"

Hart grabbed the phone. "Wait! Did you get the letter I sent?"

"Yeah," Bostwick said. "I can't come. But I'll be at graduation. Maybe I'll see you then."

"Are they giving you a degree?" Hart asked.

"Uh-huh...Tell you what—reserve a room at Der Rathskeller, and I'll take the staff to lunch afterwards. If you all don't get kicked out first."

"We won't!" Hart said excitedly. "Goodbye! Thanks for calling!" He hung up and gave a whoop—he was so happy that even Peter's credit-taking receded into the dim past.

They made so much noise Mrs. Fox called upstairs. "Everything all right?"

That broke the spell. "Yes!" Hart called back. He turned to Peter. "I don't get it. I only called him once to make sure he got—"

Peter's silence told the story.

"Don't tell me you've been calling the show every day and leaving my name."

"Okay," Peter said, "I won't tell you."

Pillows flew, and profanity, too.

21
Peter's Mojito
Friday, December 31st, 7:32 pm

The old saw comparing guests and fish—namely, that guests contain high levels of mercury and can cause severe brain damage—NO! that both guests and fish start to stink after three days—definitely held true in the case of Peter's visit. As Peter's time in frigid, stultifying Sandy Dunes drew to a close, the boys began to snap at each other, and do more things separately. It was either that, or violence. Hart had formed the opinion that no two adults could stand each other more than 72 hours without the soothing emollient of frequent sexual intercourse. And that wasn't happening, so the boys were forced to tough it out.

Still, Peter's last night was New Year's Eve. This not only enforced a certain institutional kind of joviality, it also offered things to do other than watch movies and mentally catalogue the other person's faults. That's exactly what they were doing when Hart turned to Peter and asked, "Do you want to go to that party I told you about?" Hart didn't want Peter to realize how tough these last few days had been, so he tried to offer the option as nonchalantly as possible.

Peter was under no such compunction; he leapt at the chance. "God yes!"

"Okay," Hart said, "but I have to warn you: it's full of people I knew from high school."

"Friends?"

"I had no friends in high school," Hart said. "Just co-workers."

"Then you won't mind if I make fun of them. Especially the trendy ones." Trendiness had become a bête noire for Peter. His opinion was, "Trendiness just means that you don't have enough taste to resist what's popular." Or maybe that was Guy's opinion; all during the visit, Peter had been listening to Guy's radio shows on his iPod.

"I don't think you have to worry," Hart said. "Doreen isn't trendy. She's unchanging, eternal…like a great and powerful evil." The party was being thrown by Doreen Brieth, his former high school nemesis that now went to Keasbey. "If it sucks, we'll just leave." They bundled up and went out to the car Peter had driven from Connecticut.

Doreen lived in the rich part of town, with all the other families whose parents worked important jobs in Chicago. Peter had to park down the street, not because his car was shabby, but because Doreen was still popular enough to pack a party. Hart, a non-entity before he got into Stutts, noted this with a twinge of envy.

The sidewalk was only partially shoveled; it had been a snowy year here, too. "Thank god your chair's got snow tires," Hart said.

"And four-wheel drive," Peter said, hitting a switch. After he'd done a doughnut on someone's lawn, he scooted back and asked, "So what's the lowdown on this chick who's throwing the shindig?"

Hart sketched in the details. Main competition since second grade... cute, but arctic...Doreen-bot...Kissable Conch lipstick...

Peter was intrigued. "We may have to turn this Doreen-bot to the dark side," he said as they walked to the door.

"No man alive is up to that job," Hart said.

"I have a special mojo with girls like that," Peter bragged. Hart was about to express his profound skepticism when the door opened. "Hi, guys! Come on in!"

"You're not wearing a shirt," Peter said.

"Body paint!" Doreen said. "Isn't it great?"

Peter glanced at Hart, who was too dumbfounded to speak. The former ice queen was engaged in a full-on fashion rebellion. In addition to the body paint, her hair had blue tips (it was growing out from an aquamarine buzz-cut) and instead of a skirt, she had her old pink argyle sweater pulled down to her waist, with the arms tied like a belt. And the heavy workman's boots, of course. "Waitaminute," Hart said. "*You're* the girl who blew snot on me at the mall!"[49]

Doreen shrugged. "Let me make it up to you with a beer." They walked through to the kitchen, passing the usual clutches of twos and threes (and forlorn, wandering ones) that make up a party.

"You have a nice house," Peter said.

"Thanks. I hate it," Doreen shouted over the music.

Hart could see why—it was too perfect, full of stuff arranged just so,

49 A group of punks liked to lurk on the top floor of DunesPlace and do "Farmer's hankies" on the shoppers below. Hart had gotten a snot-rocket square in the forehead while Christmas shopping with his high school friend Weird Abigail. Or, as Hart thought of her, "Formerly-Weird-Now-Quite-Hot Abigail." She had told him he should visit her at college this semester. "It's not far," she said. "There are tons of parties. Bring your friends, especially boys—our parties never have enough of those.

"I feel objectified somehow," Hart had said. "Relegated to an item on a list: ice, corkscrew, boys...How is it going to a girl's school?" Then, as if the Universe were rebuking him for being sexist, a moist, sticky loogie hit Hart from a great height.

"Women's college," Abigail said, handing him a tissue. "Let's get under cover."

stuff you could break. A lot of attention had been paid. A lot of monitoring had gone on. When they got to the kitchen, Hart met the monitor: Doreen's mother.

"Hi, Mrs. Breith," Hart said.

"Hi, Hart," Mrs. Breith said, looking up from a stack of thank-you cards. As usual, she had written them before Christmas, then filled in the gifts afterwards; it was important her cards arrived sooner than anybody else's. "Stay a second. Let's chat."

Grateful to have her basilisk-like mom's attention elsewhere, Doreen abandoned Hart to his fate and took Peter on to the backyard.

"So how are you liking Stutts? Is it all it's cracked up to be?"

"I guess," Hart said, then realized Mrs. Breith might still be pissed about Doreen's rejection. She had not taken it well—their mothers had even had a catfight in the grocery store the summer before everybody left for college. "It's a lot like every other school, I'm sure."

"I have to say, the more I see of Keasbey, the more I prefer it," Mrs. Breith said. "It's prettier. Great Littleton's a slum. The food is better at Keasbey, too."

"I sure hope so, for Doreen's sake!" Hart laughed, thankful for the opportunity to keep things light.

"And I think the students are just as smart," Mrs. Breith said. "Only a lot less neurotic." She paused, to see if Hart would take the bait; it would be wonderful to have a spat, kick him out, and tell everyone he'd been drunk and disorderly. But he remained calm. "No offense," she said glumly.

"None taken," Hart lied.

"Were you at G'rung this year?" Mrs. Breith said. "Doreen didn't want to go, so I took a few of her roommates instead."

"Crazy game," Hart said noncommittally.

"I'm sure you agree it was totally unfair to us," Mrs. Breith said. "They should've replayed it."

Hart didn't think it wise to tell Mrs. Breith about Guy's role in the shenanigans. "I'm sure you'll get us back next year," he said lamely. Plus, what was all this 'you' and 'us' stuff? He hated people who talked like that at school, and now he was doing it.

"Easy for you to say," Mrs. Breith said, "you won." Sipping something copper-colored, Mrs. Brieth was as tight as a bowstring and angry as hell; not about the game, which even she must surely see was stupid and meaningless, but about bigger things—what, exactly, Hart didn't know. Or care. He wanted out of this psychodrama.

"I can't say I was surprised you stole it. That kind of thing always happens to Doreen and I," Mrs. Breith said. "We've always had it harder than other people. We've always had to struggle, especially after her shit of a father took off. Anyway, It doesn't really matter where you go to school, it's what you do afterwards that counts."

"Right, right."

"She has an advantage over people like you, because she knows how to cope with adversity. Nothing's been *given* to Doreen and I."

Hart felt his blood-pressure spike. Luckily, he was used to how—back home at least—people only saw the name-brand school, not the person. "Doreen's always been really smart…" he said lamely.

"Remind me: didn't she do *slightly* better on the SATs than you did?"

"Uh, maybe? I don't remember…" Hart wanted to end this conversation before Mrs. Breith took a swing at him. He was trying to craft something appropriately pleasant when he heard his name being called from the backyard.

Hart glanced out the window; It was Bill Lombardi from the high school lacrosse team. "Hart! " Bill shouted. "Come out here, paesan!"

"Would you excuse me, Mrs. Breith?" Hart scampered out the back door, deeply grateful.

The sight that greeted him was pretty amazing. Doreen had obviously been planning this party forever; she'd somehow gotten the whole street's worth of snow dumped in their backyard, and used it to make a huge igloo. Now, light and music pulsed from inside the structure. Occasionally someone would hose the igloo down, to keep a crust of ice holding it all together.

Bill was standing next to one of the heaters placed along the path to the igloo, holding a beer. "Hey, *pal!"* he said, rather more warmly than Hart expected (or indeed had ever felt toward Bill). "How's my favorite brainiac?"

"Fine, Bill," Hart said. "Who made all this? I mean, look at this wall." The path to the igloo had been lined on both sides with blocks of ice five feet tall. Ever couple of feet, a light shone through the blocks from the other side. "This must've taken days."

"Three, to be exact," Bill said. Apparently Doreen had pulled a "Tom Sawyer," and had conned all the guys she'd dated in high school to "come over and help." Hart made a note: nobody works harder than a bunch of drones all trying to court the same queen bee.

"Who planned it all out, though?" Hart said. "Who knew how to build that huge igloo?"

"I did," Bill said. "I'm going to be an architecture major."

"Really?" Hart said. In high school, Bill's favorite subject had been beer.

"Yeah. I quit my frat," Bill said intensely, as if it meant something to him for Hart to hear that fact.

"Why? What for? I mean, you were practically in one in high school."

"That's why. I kinda did it all before," Bill said. "Then, one of my fellow pledges lost his nose, and all the sudden I was like 'Fuck this. Who needs it?'" Bill took a swig. "Hey listen—sorry about my dad's little 'counseling session' last year."

Hart smiled, remembering Mr. Lombardi cornering him during Bill's annual summer bash. "Ahh, Bill, don't worry about it. Parents are crazy."

"Well, I always felt bad," Bill said. "The old man's a nightmare. He just started AA."

Hart didn't know what to say. "That's gotta be good, right?"

"Yeah, except he walks around apologizing for what an asshole he used to be. I'm like 'Okay, fine, but how about you stop being an asshole now?'" Bill took another swig—of Coke, Hart noted. "Hey, how's Trip? He stopped emailing me after I ditched Sigma."

"Give him another try," Hart said. "He's a totally different guy these days. I drove past his house yesterday and he was picketing his own dad."

"Stutts really changes you that much, huh?"

"Sort of..." Hart said. He thought of Vonnegut, which led to Peter. Some people, at least. "Hey, have you seen my friend? Guy in a freaky wheelchair?"

"Yeah. I saw him out here for a little bit, then I saw him and Doreen go back inside."

"Okay," Hart said. "Nice catching up, Bill. Email me any cool buildings you design."

"Sure," Bill said, smiling.

Hart walked away feeling really good. Bill Lombardi, the last person he'd ever expect, seemed to be manufacturing his own Vonnegut. It was slower, but some people discovered their truest, best selves without the crutch of a drug. He walked back into the kitchen, and immediately heard hollering from the front room. "I cannot believe you!" Mrs. Breith screamed. "Are you drunk? You're the hostess of this party, you need to make sure nobody steals anything!"

"My friends don't steal," Doreen replied.

"Maybe not your old friends, but this new crowd...And go put on a shirt!"

"Nobody can see anything, Mom!" Doreen said, near tears. "You promised you wouldn't ruin my party!"

"Oh, you've taken care of that, my little angel!" Mrs. Brieth was breathing fire. "Look at you, your makeup all smeared like a whore—"

Whoa—Mrs. Breith calling her daughter the "w" word. Hart suddenly felt very, very sorry for his old rival. He was shaken from this transfixing moment in the Breith family drama by Peter tugging his sleeve.

"We need to leave," he said.

Hart couldn't look away—Doreen had just swept some expensive-looking items off the mantel. "Why?"

"Come on, Hart! I'll explain in the car."

Hart started towards the front door.

"No! Not towards the fight"—now both sides were crying and screaming—"out the back way."

"I cannot believe this," Hart said a minute later as they walked down the block. "You bagged Doreen Breith?"

"In all honesty, she bagged me," Peter said. "I hardly had time to drink a beer before she pulled me into a walk-in closet off the front hall. Now do you believe in my mojo?"

"Well…" Hart said. "Maybe a little one. A *mojito*." This gave Hart a suspicion. "You didn't slip her any Vonnegut, did you?"

"All I slipped her was—look, I didn't know her in high school, but that girl needs no chemical assistance of any kind." They got into Peter's car. "And fuck you, by the way, for thinking I need to roofie somebody to get laid."

"I didn't mean that," Hart said, realizing how insulting his question was.

Peter turned on the radio. "Crap radio stations out here."

The car was silent. Hart, uncomfortable, asked a question. "So how did her mom find out?"

"She was walking around upstairs and heard funny noises," Peter said. "Through the floor, brother. That's how good I am."

"Were the noises coming from Doreen?" Hart asked.

"Assume so," Peter said. "I wasn't paying attention, I was too busy trying to hit my spots. And the chair was on 'Magic Fingers,' which is loud."

"Wow," Hart said. "You are a stallion."

"Not quite," Peter laughed. "When Mrs. Breith walked in, I was so surprised, I came!"

22

Zombo-American Night

Tuesday, February 2nd, 6:41 pm

The rest of Winter Break was uneventful. Hart tried to rest, but as was always the case, found himself cataloguing worries instead. His friends seemed to be changing, making the friendships between them unstable. Peter hooking up with Doreen—what did it mean? Was it random, or a relationship? He and Hart had been growing apart all year—did Peter feel it as much as Hart did? The Xmas issue had made Ellen miserable—she'd called Reed in tears. Was she still on their side, or had she shifted to the Mugwumps? What did Tabitha care about more, him or her new sex column? Hart returned to the slush-coated spires with a head full of questions.

He took solace in routine, picking classes, planning the next issue. But even in the midst of the familiar, he was unsure, wary. Hart considered going to University Health Services and getting a prescription for anti-anxiety meds, but decided against it. He'd heard they made you less funny.

After all, Hart consoled himself, I have good reason to be anxious. Being underground was stressful, especially when what you were being underground from was as big and rich and imperious as Stutts University. Now, thanks to the Xmas issue, they were openly despised by the Mugwumps, too; if one-tenth of the rumors on Peter's newsgroup were true, *The Cuckoo* was toast. And just in case Hart didn't have enough to fret over, his girlfriend was going to discuss their sex life in public. Oh, god, god, god.

But that wasn't all: When Hart got back, there had been a note in his box from *The Daily Spectacle*, calling their bluff. They were hiring bodyguards for speakers, the note said, and refused to print or distribute anymore issues of *The Cuckoo*. Then, the following day Professor Lemonade had called, and told Hart that "you and your magazine can fuck off." So they didn't have a faculty advisor anymore either.[50]

50 The Xmas issue had enraged Glenbard North, who looked to strike at *The Cuckoo* any way he could. He was busily faking photos showing each staff member in a compromising situation with a vegetable when an agent informed him that a certain visiting lecturer by the name of Lemonade was the magazine's faculty advisor.

North called Lemonade: "Professor, if you have any connection whatsoever with *The Cuckoo*, I will personally make sure you are fired!"

"Cool," Lemonade said, turning on his PDA. "When are their meetings?"

"What?"

On the plus side, however, there was Quinn Bostwick; he thought they were doing good work. The great man had even promised to hang out with them after graduation. Hart couldn't believe his luck—this, surely, was how "it" happened, the first step on the golden road to fame and fortune and the reverence of all. Quinn Bostwick's visit shimmered like El Dorado, and its brightness was more than enough to chase away the dark mists swirling around Hart's life. Or even the gloom of a Great Littleton February.

It was a typical February night at Stutts—chilly and raw, with a petulant sleet and the prospect of a long semester ahead—but the staff of *The Cuckoo* was in a good mood. The Dacron dining hall, though ugly, was warm and dry, and there was plenty of sugary coffee at hand to kindle their spirits. Which, in Peter's case, meant bitching.

"I don't care if you eat it, but why do I have to?" he complained. It was Zombo-American night, which meant all the Stutts dining halls were serving zombie food: sweetbreads, organ meats, steak tartare, *etc.*

"It's good, healthy…fooood," Miles Monaghan said in a sort of moaning monotone. A new convert to zombiedom, Miles was the driving force behind the University's recent recognition of 'Z-Americans' as a campus minority.[51] "Looooook at me."

"That's just it, Miles," Hart said. "You're all pale, your clothes are tattered, and you smell like six feet of scab. You look like crap."

"Double standard," Miles said. "Undead prejoooodice!"

"You'll fire me, but only if I help *The Cuckoo*, right?"

North's synapses struggled to keep up. "Right…"

"So when are their meetings?" Lemonade said. "Would I get fired quicker if I brought some beer?"

This wasn't having the effect North expected. "You want to get fired?"

"Desperately," Lemonade admitted.

"Well, then," North said. "If you continue to be *The Cuckoo*'s faculty advisor, I swear to you I will do all in my power to keep you employed here at Stutts until the day you die. Understood?"

"Understood," Lemonade said. Five minutes later, he was leaving a message on Hart's phone.

51 Over winter break, Miles had seen an ad on a videogaming website promising 'An End to Sleep FOREVER!' After his run-in with Professor North, his grades were shockingly low for a Stutts student; he'd have to pull straight-As for the rest of his Stutts career just to equal everybody else's GPA. Adding to this his determination to succeed Gwen Talbot as EIC of the *Spec*, and sleep was clearly not an option. Miles sent away for the pills, which, when swallowed, irradiated one's innards in much the same way the comet did in *Night of the Living Dead*. Being a zombie wasn't easy—girls tended to dislike the rotting—but his grades were improving, and people at the *Spec* thought he was a god.

"Not true!" Peter said. "We like Tab. Tab doesn't smell like the refrigerator is broken."

"She'll be happy to hear you said that," Ellen said. Tab was absent, spending her "morning" pounding out her column.

"You guys are asshoooooles," Miles moaned, but the rain of comments didn't stop. People were learning never to engage *The Cuckoo* staff as a group. They were like piranha of snark.

"Tabitha doesn't make everybody drink blood, just so she can feel better about vampirism," Reed said.

"Yeah," Peter said, "Why does your self-esteem mean I have to eat a handful of guts?"

"Guys, wait," Hart said. "Miles, I'll make a deal with you: If I eat all the brains on my plate, will you cancel Tab's column?"

"Don't you dare!" Peter said. "I love reading about Hart's sex life!"

Miles paid no attention. "Tonight is simply a waaaay…we remember the contributions of Zombo-Americaaaans throughout history…"

"What contributions?" Peter said. "Name one."

Miles paused.

"See?" Peter said. "*That's* what happens when you eat all the witnesses."

Beaten, Miles shuffled away stiffly.

"Since when did Chuckles become a zombie?" Reed asked.

"Over the break, I heard," Hart said.

"You know what they say," Ellen said, "'There's no zealot like a convert.'"

"It's ludicrous," Peter carped. "'Zombania' isn't even a country."

"Oh, it doesn't hurt anybody, sourpuss. It's a useful construct, like Kwanzaa," Ellen said.

"Subject change," Peter declared. "They've made an impotence ray in a lab in Science Hole.[52] Comments?"

Reed moved the tripe around his plate listlessly. "Peter, you're just mad you didn't get to it first," he said.

"I do pranks, not weapons," Peter said.

"Tell that to the guy who's being made to wet himself from space," Hart said. "Or have you scrapped that prototype?"

"The Urinator is not a weapon," Peter said. "It's a party gag."

"In geosynchronous orbit," Hart countered.

Peter changed tack. "So you think that Stutts *should* be lending its

52 "Science Hole" was student slang for the valley near central campus where all the science buildings were clustered.

brains out to make weapons?"

"There's a whole building called 'Not-a-Secret-Government-Lab Lab," Beekman said.

"Yeah," Hart said. "I don't know what else you expect."

Peter was implacable. "We gotta do something on this in the next issue," he said. "Reed and I were talking about it—"

Ellen broke in. "Funny you should mention the next issue, Peter," she said. "I have to say I had a real problem with the last one."

"I'm sure you did," Peter said. "Blame Beekman here."

Beekman's deep commitment to pacifism came to the fore. "Anybody want more coffee?" he said, then walked away double-quick.

"Sorry we made fun of your little club, Ellen," Peter said.

"You're not really sorry," Ellen said.

"No, I'm not," Peter said. "The issue was a huge hit—or didn't you notice?"

"Oh, I noticed it, all right," Ellen said. "I couldn't help but notice. Everybody thinks I was the one who leaked the photos."

"So tell 'em you weren't," Reed said. "You can't lie to each other, so if you say you didn't, everybody will obviously believe you."

Ellen rolled her eyes, as if to say, "Don't be retarded." Then she hammered the message home: "Don't be retarded."

Hart tried to spread oil on the waters. "I can see where Ellen's coming from, Pete. Maybe we went too far."

"Spoken like a true coward," Peter said. "I want *The Cuckoo* to stand for something."

"How about making people laugh?" Ellen said. "I remember an agreement, way back in August…"

"Is making people laugh enough, in this day and age?" Peter asked. He looked at Reed. "Back me up here."

"Why do I get the impression that we're dividing into those who have taken nips from the Vonnegut jar, and those who haven't?" Hart asked.

"And why do I get the feeling that we're dividing into those who are Wumpsmen or want to be, and those who aren't, or don't?" Peter retorted.

Ellen's face was bright red, a sure signal of her being really mad. "Peter, just because somebody joins a group, that doesn't make them a non-person. They have rights."

"Rights?" Peter said. "Like the right to look down on other people? Or the right to give jobs and stuff to your pals, whether they deserve them or not?"

"You could say that about *The Cuckoo* just as easily!" Ellen's voice grew louder. "What's the difference?"

"*The Cuckoo*, were it still in business, which it is not"—Peter looked around—"would be open to everyone, and it would produce something the whole campus could enjoy. The Mugwumps are closed, and don't."

Hart couldn't resist. "But Peter, couldn't you say the same thing about Stutts?"

Peter rounded on his roommate, a rather savage look on his face. "That's totally different!"

"Bullshit!" Ellen said. "But who cares—you'll be happy to know that they've asked me to choose between them and you guys."

"Those jerks," Reed said. "I hope you told them to eat shit."

"No," Ellen said, "I told them I'd quit *The Cuckoo*."

Reed exploded. "You did what?"

Beekman had just returned to the table, and was just about to sit down when Reed yelled. He promptly turned around. "Cream," he mumbled.

Reed continued, at only slightly fewer decibels. "Ellen, I can't believe this! You and I kept this magazine alive for two years! There wouldn't even *be* a *Cuckoo* without you."

"You guys don't need me anymore," Ellen said.

"And the Mugwumps do?" Hart said.

"Just so you know, Ellen, I don't like the Mugwumps, but I'm fine with you," Peter said. "You're the only one who gets my science jokes."

"I should *hope* you're fine with me!" Ellen grumbled. She'd made her mind up. "It's your guys' magazine now, not mine. Plus, I've gone as far as *The Cuckoo* can take me. I want to go new places now." She looked at Reed. "I'll always have a soft spot for the magazine."

"Like an rotten apple," Reed muttered.

"Well, if you're going to be like that..." Ellen said, standing up with her tray. "Miles was right—you guys are assholes." She left, and avoided their glance on her way out the door.

"Well," Hart said after she had left, "that sure sucked."

"Had to happen sooner or later," Peter shrugged, to hide his remorse.

Reed objected. "That's a little harsh, don't you think?"

Peter didn't answer. "I think we'll be fine," he said in a chipper voice. "No problem. She hadn't been pulling her weight all year. We've got the website, and the magazine, and there are always funny things happening around campus—take this impotence ray, for example...What could we do with that?"

Nobody said anything. Reed poked at the mass of innards on his plate. Beekman drank his coffee silently, trying to divine a pattern in the wood-grain of the table.

Hart took a bite of sweetbreads, then chewed cartoonishly. "Do I detect the distinctive tang of mad cow disease? Yes—yes, I do," he said, trying to lighten the mood a bit. Nobody laughed. He decided to leap into the breach. "Ellen has a point, Peter—ever since you started hanging out with Guy, you've been getting a little serious."

"You oughta listen to him," Peter said.

"Pete, he's obsessed with blimps!" Hart said. "Face it: he's a weirdo."

"Yeah! Just like you! And me, and all of us!" Peter said. "Stop trying so hard to have everybody like you. Everybody here is always so worried about fitting into the outside world, when the fact is, they wouldn't be at Stutts if they did!" Peter said. "We should all just be true to ourselves and let the rest of the world deal with it! I say we rent a cropduster and spray the whole campus with Vonnegut!"

"Have you finished analyzing it?" Reed asked.

"Ellen was in charge of that, actually," Peter said. "She was using the equipment in her advisor's lab."

Hart changed the subject. "Guys, I really think we ought to be figuring out how to distribute the magazine—"

"Not that there is a magazine," the rest of them said loudly, in case anyone was listening.

"—now that the *Spec* won't do it."

"We go on the web, obviously," Reed said.

"And do pranks to drive traffic to the site," Peter said.

"Oh, God," Hart said. "Not another prank. The last one practically caused another Great Depression."

"No, it didn't,"Peter said. "And it gave one person a chance to live the life he should've been living from the beginning."

"Mr. Hang-Ten, you mean?" Beekman interjected.

"Yeah," Peter said. "Now: what would people go to a website for?"

Reed remembered Tabitha's last column. "How about a treasure map?"[53]

"You mean, we bury something valuable somewhere, then post cryptic directions on how to find it?" Hart asked. Reed nodded.

"Oh, me likey," Peter said. "How much money should we bury? How much is enough to really drive people bonkers?"

Beekman got an evil idea; if things worked out, this could force *The Cuckoo* under for good. "Not money," he said. "Lots of Stuttsies have plenty of that. We need to offer something they can't live without: coffee."

53 Tabitha's column had been all about the "treasure trail," that line some women have from their belly-buttons to their nether regions.

° ° °

The staff ended that evening in the back room of the C&E, toasting their new idea. Everything would go off in a week, the night of the Art Students' Costume Ball. The ASCB was the closest thing to Mardi Gras possible at a place as deeply Protestant as Stutts, and while it was a pale comparison to the real thing, it made for great "cover."

The plan was simple: while their fellow students stood shivering on Locust Street, shouting "Show us your tits!"to everybody in the parade, *The Cuckoo* would swipe all the coffee, tea, and cola syrup out of every dining hall on campus. Then they would cart it off to a secret location, and post cryptic directions to that place on their website.

Peter preferred his pranks to be more than just straight heists, but he made an exception in this case. He and Guy believed it would slow down the worst aspects of the campus—the relentless rat-race, the weapons research. The others liked it because it seemed harmless, and it was always a kick to make everybody dance on *The Cuckoo*'s string.

"Shame you won't be joining us," Hart told Beekman the night of the prank.

"This cold totally has me knocked out," Beekman lied, then gave a fake cough for good measure.

Why would Beekman fake-cough? Peter wondered. "Well, wish us luck. I'll call you tomorrow morning to let you know how it went."

"I have a feeling I'll already know," Beekman said.

Beekman wasn't really missed; by now, the Cuckonians were prank ninja-commandoes, and the op itself went off without a hitch. Tabitha mistified her way through keyholes, opening doors from the other side. Once in, it took less than a minute for Reed, Peter and Hart to remove the caffeinated goodies. Then, they loaded it all into the back of the football trailer; which Peter drove then to a vacant lot in East Littleton.

"What if nobody figures out the puzzle?" Reed asked, as they relaxed in the office afterwards. "It's kinda hard."

"Are you suggesting giving them the answer?" Peter said. "Never!"

"Let's not push our luck," Hart said. His gut told there was something dangerous about all this. "I'm worried."

"Hart, that's like me saying, 'I'm breathing,'" Peter said. "Tab, why don't you cheer Hart up with another installment of Horrible Pranks of the Past?"

"Please don't, Tab," Hart said. "I guess I'm just not the pranking type. I always think about what could go wrong."

"Nothing's going to go wrong," Peter said. "As long as you and Tabitha keep your clothes on."

"Jerk!" Tabitha threw a plastic cup at him.

Hart wasn't convinced. "I just keep thinking of what my mom is like in the morning if we've run out of coffee. She's a monster. She once told me that when I was born, I looked deformed."

"That nice lady said *that?*" Tabitha said. "Wow."

"Ahh, don't think of her," Reed said, "think of the coffee lady." He always got his coffee from a weathered old bird who cranked out lattes from a cart on the corner of Locust and Ant. "We're about to make her a millionaire."

"See, Hart?" Peter said. "We're just doing this to help an old lady. We're better than a bunch of Boy Scouts!"

Reed raised his glass. "To the Boy Scouts."

Hart had his doubts, but clinked his glass anyway.

Meanwhile, across campus in Sand College, a perfectly healthy Beekman was placing a call to Miles Monaghan at the *Spec.*

"No," he said to the flunkie who answered the phone, "I need to speak to Miles personally." Miles eventually picked up.

"Monnnaghan."

"I can't tell you how I know this," Beekman whispered, "but *The Cuckoo* has done another prank."

"I coooould give a shit," Miles snapped.

"Your readers will. *The Cuckoo* has stolen all the caffeine on campus."

"Buuuuullshit," Miles moaned. "Whoooo is this?"

"Can't say," Beekman said. "You'll see tomorrow morning."

23

An Amazonian Athens

Wednesday, February 17th, 6:29 pm

Hart was laying in his bed, weighing the sweetness of staying under the covers against the throbbing of his full bladder, when he heard a blood-curdling howl.

Suddenly, fists were pounding on Hart and Peter's dorm room door. "Wake up, you bastards!"

"We know you switched the coffee!" a higher voice yelled.

Peter thought he recognized the voice. "Is that Jennifer from upstairs?" Peter yelled back. "'Teddy Bear' Jen?"

"Goddamn right it is!" the normally meek girl bellowed. "I need some motherfucking caffeine!"

The first, deeper voice chimed in. "Tell us where the real stuff is, or we'll set the building on fire!"

"I have no idea what you're talking about!" Peter bluffed, pulling on a shirt. He rolled through the common room and stuck his head into Hart's room. "Judging by the amount of noise outside, the entire College wants to kill us."

"Why am I your friend?" Hart complained. *"Why?"*

"We can discuss that at length after we survive."

"No promises," Hart said glumly, scrambling into clothes of his own. "How did they find out?"

Peter shrugged. "I hope you weren't using this." With a knot of blood-thirsty maniacs between him and the bathroom, Peter took his morning pee into Hart's Class mug.

"Dude, my mom bought me that."

"Too bad, can't stop now…I don't know, but we're not giving in for at least 24 hours. We have our pride."

"Are you kidding? We've got to give in! What else can we do?"

"First, this." Peter walked over to the front door, which was quivering with the pounding and shouting. He leaned over and poured the urine under the crack.

"Look out!" The pounding stopped, and the shouting changed. "Gross! It's pee!"

"It got on my shoe," 'Teddy Bear' Jen whined.

"Gross! A puddle!" another voice said.

"That'll buy us a little time…Come with me," Peter said, and rolled into his bedroom. He opened a closet. "Move that trunk for me, would you?"

Peter was maddeningly calm. Hart said grumpily, "Did you know this was going to happen, shit-bag?"

"It was a possibility," Peter said.

"After this is over, we are going to talk," Hart said, then hauled the steamer trunk out of the closet. He looked it over. "Both of us can't fit inside of this."

The pounding was back, and louder than before. "Tap the floor with your toe."

Hart did so, and nothing happened. "Pete—" Somebody smashed a window—it was Miles, who was reaching in blindly and moaning.

"Do it like you mean it, sissy!"

Hart gave the floor another jab, stronger this time, and the section of floor popped open, to reveal a small platform.

"Move." Peter rolled his chair over onto the platform; when his wheels found some grooves, there was a clicking sound. He began sinking downwards, slowly.

Hart heard the window in his room break. "They're coming in through the fire escape!" Peter's unconcerned reply was masked by the sounds of rending wood—the front door was going to give way at any moment. "Pete! We gotta tell 'em where the coffee is!"

"Eff that! Just lock the bedroom door." Peter said, head at floor level.

Hart had given Peter a lot of shit for installing a heavy-duty lock on his bedroom door, but now the "beat-off lock" was his dearest friend.

"Then slide the trunk against it, just to slow them down a bit…As soon as I'm clear, jump!"

That wait was the longest five seconds of Hart's life. Through the door he heard their common room being ransacked by addicts. "There's a lock on this door," the deep voice said. "Anybody got a gun?"

"I do," 'Teddy Bear' Jen said. "Mom gave it to me for protection."

"Go get it!" somebody said.

"Shit!" Hart said—they were prying away the hinges. He was watching the last one pull away, mesmerized by his own imminent death, when Peter grabbed him by the ankle and yanked.

Hart fell through the secret passage, landing on a mattress in the subbasement of the building.

"Sorry," Peter said. "You were spacing out." He closed the hatch just as his room was overrun. The pounding now began on the hatch. But unlike the rest of the temporary dorm, it was sturdy (Peter had made sure of that). Once locked, it wasn't about to give way. They listened to the crowd scramble from room-to-room, swearing and breaking things.

"Don't worry, I insured everything," Peter whispered. "We'll buy new."

Jen returned. "I've got my gun! Where are they? Where…the fuck…are they?" she yelled, squeezing off a few rounds.

Peter chuckled. "I could listen to this for hours."

"C'mon, let's go," Hart said.

Hart and Peter walked a bit, until they were in the Catacombs again. "Do you know if Reed got away?" Hart asked.

"He and I talked about what to do if somebody found out," Peter said. "He's down here, somewhere, too. I hope."

"Tabitha's fine, I'm sure," Hart said, "but what about the new guy? Beekman?"

"I wouldn't worry about him," Peter said. "Nobody knows he's joined."

They got to *The Cuckoo* offices; Reed opened the door. "Well, that sucked." Reed was in his pajamas, and was sporting a palm-sized black eye.

"I can't understand how they knew it was us," Peter mused.

"Peter, of course everybody knew it was us," Hart said.

"Not necessarily," Reed said. "The Meistersingers do the occasional prank. And the Mugwumps have a tradition of stealing stuff—not to mention all the Wump-wannabe groups."

Peter kept following the thread. "I wonder: did Beekman tip somebody off?"

"Why would he do that?" Hart said.

"Maybe he's an agent provocateur," Peter said. "Think about it—he gave us the Mugwump photos, knowing there was no way I could resist running them; as a result, Ellen leaves. He suggests this prank, we execute it without him; everybody nearly lynches us. It makes a certain sense."

"But he had nothing to do with the Freshman Assembly prank," Hart said. "I think you're being paranoid."

"Calling Peter paranoid is like calling soup wet," Reed said, "but that doesn't change the fact that the entire campus is pissed off at us. What are we going to do?"

"We're not giving them the coffee," Peter said.

"Pete, come on," Hart said.

"No!" Peter's expression showed that arguing this point would be futile. "We're stopping that impotence ray, if only for a few days. No caffeine, no bench work. No bench work, no evil inventions. People will thank us later."

"Doubt that." Reed took some ice out of the fridge and put it on his eye. "Oh, I need a vacation," he griped. "I just got back from vacation and I need a vacation."

"That's a great idea," Hart said. "Let's leave and come back when the caffeine levels are back to normal."

"I wonder if there'll be an airlift?" Peter said, imagining parachuted pallets of coffee slamming to the ground in the middle of Old Quad. "I'd love to see that."

"Look at Reed's eye—this place is dangerous," Hart said. "I vote we melt into the vast, pulsing mass of Manhattan."

"I vote for someplace else," Reed said. "I went there over break, and maxed out every freakin' credit card I own."

"The longer we wait, the harder its going to be to escape," Peter said. "Let's go to the train station and get on the next train out. We can always switch later."

Leaving *tout suite* was wise; their train was the last one out before the station was overwhelmed. As the train pulled out, it passed within twenty feet of a newly arrived mob. "Hart, Reed, look!" Peter said. "Fans!" The boys scrunched down in their seats.

After they'd handed over their tickets, everybody took out their cell phones. Reed called his dad, and told him to watch the news. Peter called Guy and started discussing what technicalities they could get off on, if it came to that. Hart called Tabitha.

As usual, the vampiress was sleeping the day away in her coffin/futon. "Tab, it's me," he said into her fusty, creaking answering machine. "Somebody snitched on us so there's an angry mob trying to kill everybody on *The Cuckoo*. I'm telling you this so, one, maybe put off buying art supplies for a few days, and two, Peter, Reed, and I wanna get out of town until—"

"'lo, Sugar," Tabitha mumbled in an exquisitely cute sleepy voice. "Hortense! No! *Never* on the carpet, *always* in the litter box! Honestly…" Hart heard rustling, walking, cleaning up. "Did you say something about a mob?"

"There's one after us. For hiding all the caffeine."

"Mobs are so tacky," Tabitha said. "What is it about this place and mobs, all of the sudden?"

"I don't know," Hart said, "but we'd like to consider the question from a distance. We got on the first train we could. Ever been to any of these?" Hart read the schedule. "West Littleton, Badford, Cragton, Hope, Mad Indian, Massacre Bluff, New Hope, Humidity—"

Reed abruptly covered the phone. "Let's go there," he said. "My sister goes to school at Harriet Wrath."

"So does an old girlfriend of mine," Hart said, covering the phone. His high school friend Weird Abigail wasn't really an old girlfriend, but his male pride couldn't resist stretching the truth. He resumed listening to Tabitha.

She was thinking the same thing. "...Wrath College. I'll meet you there."

"Great," Hart said. "So we'll meet at the Humidity train station in about"—he checked his watch—"two hours. Is that enough time?"

"If the wind isn't totally ridic," Tabitha said. (Mistifying had its flaws.)

"Don't worry, I'll wait," Hart said. "We can hang out with Reed's sis. Or a high school friend of mine, I told you about her: Weird Abigail. She'd love to see us."

"Hart, saying that and actually finding you on her doorstep are two totally different things."

"Fair enough, but I don't think she'll actually *kill* us, and from where I'm standing, that's an improvement."

Nestled in the bend of a lazy river, among gently rolling hills, Harriet Wrath College seemed an unlikely cradle for revolution. Yet for over a century, the college had produced a frothing torrent of alumnae, each more ass-kicking than the next. For over a century, Wrath was the place that the WASP aristocracy sent their most headstrong and difficult daughters. Once there, they fed off each other to create an educational environment that was utterly unique, inspiring, and occasionally terrifying.

Equal parts Athens and Amazonia, Wrath produced the famous "Drag Division," a group of bloody-minded debutantes who posed as men during World War I, simply for the privilege of kicking hell out of the Kaiser. After that war, the ladies of Wrath pushed for voting rights in a distinctly Wrathian way: in other countries, suffragettes threw themselves under horses to attract the sympathy of the country's leaders. Wrath alumnae preferred throwing the leaders.

After 1945, Wrath opened up, and admitting firebrands of all races, creeds and colors amped things to an almost frightening degree. Certainly it was frightening for John F. Kennedy, who made a brief campaign stop on campus in 1960. The students sussed out his womanizing ways, and literally ran him out of town. "They were gonna cut off my weinah!" Jack the Zipper said later. This comment got back to the women of Wrath and thoroughly delighted them.

Wrath's town, Humidity,[54] was a mellow ideal of old New England.

54 The town's original name was much more Old Protestant: "Humility." But in the early 1700s, the town fathers became concerned that the Almighty might consider the name ironic—even then, the town had nothing to be humble about. So rather than bring down God's anger, they opted to trumpet one of its few flaws, a pervasive stickiness from May to September.

In all respects, from the good soil to the rampant religious tolerance, gentle, clean Humidity had been as favored as hard, sooty Great Littleton had been cursed. Whereas both Great Littleton and Stutts were likely to slip into the language of cancer when describing one another, Humidity did not host Harriet Wrath as much as hug it to her breast. Alumnae had a habit of staying after graduation, and so the culture of the town and that of the college were the same.

When the Stutts students arrived, Humidity was unashamedly sunny; here, February could be bright, if not yet warm. Dressed in a full-body, burkah-like garment which protected her sensitive skin, Tabitha inhaled lustily.

"Ahhh—smell the estrogen!" she joked. "Whenever I'm up here, I think, 'This is where I should've gone to college.' 'Course, it was just starting out then." She frowned with old pain. "Father dear didn't think it would last."

Peter's mood always lightened whenever he left Stutts, and Humidity intensified his glee; as they rolled down Mill Street, he was almost giggly. He scanned the quaint, pocket-sized main drag for flaws. There were few chain stores; it was clean; everybody was friendly, even the one or two homeless people. "Remind me again why we'd ever go back?" he asked.

Hart nodded—he had to think of something quickly, before he dropped out of Stutts and ended up like that guy over there in the fleece, playing guitar and flirting with women all day. He saw Tabitha writing something in her mini notebook. (It was pink, and had penguins on it.) "Found something for the column?"[55]

"Yepperoo," Tabitha said. She had stopped in front of a store called "A Room of Her Own," which was a combination authentic English tea-and-scone shop and sex toy emporium.

As Tabitha wrote, a middle-aged woman came up to her. She tugged at Tabitha's sleeve. "Sister, you don't have to wear that here."

"What? Oh, thanks," Tabitha replied, "but I really do."

"No, you don't," the woman said forcefully. She had a short haircut, and wore sensible shoes. "You're in a protected space."

Tabitha laughed. "You wouldn't want to see what I look like after five minutes in the sun. I'm like, raisin-y."

"Sister," the woman said, "a lifetime of repression has poisoned your mind. Your body is beautiful, whatever its size or shape."

55 Before wafting up from Great Littleton, Tabitha arranged a stunt with the sex columnist for Wrath's student newspaper, the *Wrath Wraith*: each of them would survey the dating scene at the other's school. "I think you're getting the better of that deal," Hart said when he heard the details. "No doubt," Tabitha agreed. "Wrathies are *bonkers*."

"Oh, for God's sake." Rather than explain, Tabitha mistified.

Suddenly the woman was standing there alone. "Where did…?" She saw the boys. "Did any of you see…Middle-eastern girl, wearing a…"

The boys played dumb. The woman looked around a bit, then gave up and walked into a CD shop. After she was gone, Tabitha re-congealed and finished taking her note.

"This is my kind of town," Reed said, pointing to a handwritten sign in the sex-shop's window: "Ladiez: kitten *and* dolphin strap-ons are SOLD OUT."

Hart noticed that the O's on the sign were hearts. "Must've been a big rush for Valentine's Day," he said.

Reed's sister had enough room for Reed and Peter, but that left Hart and Tabitha bedless. Bravado aside, Hart was far from sure that Weird Abigail would be happy to see them, much less able to put anybody up for the night.

As usual, Tab rose to the occasion. "They've got room for us at Sophia." Sophia was a D.A.R.-like sorority that she belonged to. "It won't be deluxe, but it will do."

Abigail was happy to see Hart and meet his friends. "Listen, Hart," she said the first time they had a moment alone, "I want to apologize to you."

"For what?" Hart said, looking forward to whatever it was. He always enjoyed a good apology.

"For being such a freak in high school," Abigail said. "I kinda stalked you."

"No apologies necessary," Hart said. "Are you kidding? It made me feel good."

Abigail continued. "After I got here, I realized that my 'crush' on you was an awkward, artificial attempt to express myself in an antiquated hetero-sexual-dominant dual-gender-normative milieu," she said. "That's ridiculous for anybody interested in evolving as a person."

"Okay," Hart said, hoping she would stop.

She didn't. "I picked a passive, unthreatening male, knowing that way I could exist within the repressive genderizing of our high school, with no risk of finding myself in a coerced and fraudulent physical situation. Like, say, kissing you," Abigail said. "Or worse."

"Thank God we avoided that," Hart said, a little miffed.

"No kidding," Abigail said, with a lot more relief than Hart's male ego appreciated. "All I wanted to say was, looking back on it, I just really appreciate how understanding you were. I mean, you must've figured out what I was going through. It explains why you never made a move."

"You bet," Hart said, about to black out from mortification. He turned and saw Tabitha standing with the guys a short distance away. "Tabitha—" What Hart wanted to say was, "Would you reaffirm my basic masculinity?" What he said instead was, "Shouldn't we be heading over to Sophia to stake our claim?"

"Good call," Tab said. "I wouldn't want us to get bumped to a couch."

Sleeping arrangements were always a big issue when visiting Wrath. Guests bunked wherever they could. The ideal solution was, of course, to make a new friend. And as luck would have it, one of the year's bigger dances was scheduled for that night. Thus Wrath had switched from "study mode" to "party mode."

However, a century of importing strange men for social occasions had imbued "party mode" with a peculiar mix of hospitality and survelliance.

"I feel like I'm being watched," Peter whispered to Abigail as they bussed their trays after dinner.

"You are," Abigail said bluntly. "Act appropriately, and there'll be no problem."

"O…kay," Peter said.

"When we get back to my room, you should look over our 'Male Visitors' Code of Conduct,'" Abigail said. "Don't worry, it's mostly common sense. I've only seen one guy get beaten up. Well, two. Maybe three…"

Wrath women had the reputation for being capricious, chilly, and—let's just come out and say it—lesbians. Hart sensed that last characterization was a Neanderthal smear. Only a better-than-average chance of hooking up would bring so many males to a theme dance celebrating "Pride and Prejudice."

"Hart, I have to tell you, I'm very impressed with your girlfriend," Abigail confided as they walked from her dorm to the dance. Reed, Peter, and Tabitha all lagged behind, studying the 'Code'—Tabitha for purposes of the column, the boys to find out how to avoid being tasered, stuffed into the trunk of a car, and dumped somewhere in the still-frosty Berkshires. "She's a firecracker," Abigail said. "I pegged you for a man-on-top, ten-quick-thrusts-with-the-lights-off kind of guy."

"Oh, you'd be amazed," Hart said, feeling a little better about his masculinity. "Sometimes I even make it to fifteen." It was nice to see Abigail again; she seemed to genuinely fit in here, something that neither of them could say in high school. "You think it's just a coincidence that they ran out of dolphin strap-ons the week I hit town?"

Abigail laughed. "I saw that sign, too!"

They arrived at the hall where the dance was being held. "Let me get it." Hart grabbed the door and opened it. An alarm went off.

"Whoops," Hart said, letting go. "Must be a fire exit."

"No, that happens whenever a guy does it."

Everybody with a Y chromosome had to sign in, and every door was staffed by a student or two checking IDs. There was no going upstairs to the dorm rooms without a Wrath student to take you, and once upstairs, no going down without an escort, either. The building was in lockdown.

After he had to show ID for the third time, Peter started to make a crack, but Hart interrupted him. "I'd rather have to go through this then have somebody get date-raped."

"Uh, I don't think it's the guys you have to worry about," Peter said, raising an eyebrow.

Hart turned around.

"Guys," Abigail said, "I'd like to introduce you to my date, Casey."

Casey, like roughly half of the party's attendees, was playing Mr. Darcy to the other half's Elizabeth Bennet. She, like Abigail, had gone to the trouble to put together a costume, but the gender switch had caused her to go to more effort. The fitted velvet trousers Casey was sporting showed that, where Nature might've underdressed her for the occasion, she had compensated exuberantly.

Hart didn't notice this. He was too busy wondering whether Abigail was a lesbian, bisexual, or something yet to be determined and what, if anything, that revealed about him. He shook Casey's hand wearing a rather fixed smile, and watched the two trot off to the dance floor.

"I want a dolphin strap-on," Reed said quietly. All three boys stood there, silently contemplating their puny groins.

As a dating environment, a Wrath dance was double-diamond, highest difficulty. Who liked boys? Who liked girls? Who liked boys and girls? Who was a boy and who was a girl? Confronted with this brave new world of gender roles, the Stutts boys declared defeat and held up the wall.

Tabitha, on the other hand, couldn't write things down fast enough. When she decided to explore rumors of a secret Sappho-rama taking place in the black-lit basement, Hart, Reed, and Peter all begged her not to go.

"I'm scared!" Peter said.

"Don't leave us!" Hart begged.

"Don't be ridiculous," Tabitha said. "Have some punch and chill out."

Even in the best of circumstances, dances were difficult for Peter to participate in, for obvious reasons. He'd go for a spin on a rare occasion, but he was usually much too shy. Hart was similarly chickenshit, but told himself that he was refusing out of loyalty to Tabitha. Reed employed the classic Stutts rationale of being a senior.

"I have no idea where I'm going to be next year," he said. "I don't want to lead anybody on," he said.

"That's so goddamn ridiculous," Peter said, as they sat on a couch, watching other people have fun. "You just don't wanna get shot down." It was true—the room outside the dance floor was a meat-market the equal of the fiercest gay bar. Anybody walking in and out singly was thoroughly and obviously appraised by a gauntlet of ladies lounging in chairs and sofas nearby.

"All the sudden, I realize how desperately I need a haircut," Hart said.

Peter leaned over and said quietly, "Reed, have you ever asked your sister how to tell who's interested in what?"

"Unfortunately, no."

"Dating is hard," Hart said. "I mean, Stutts is treacherous, but *this*..."

"Several orders of magnitude more, yeah," Reed said. Having spent the most time at Wrath, Reed was by far the most comfortable; but even he had his "company manners" on. "Stutts' gender thing is more muted. People keep it to themselves, for career reasons, of course." Reed took a drink from a frosted plastic cup. "For example, few people know that Ellen is gay."

Peter stifled a laugh. "Sorry—punch went down the wrong tube."

"Ellen's *gay?*" Hart asked. "I just thought she was...picky."

"So did I," Reed said. Hart sensed there was a story behind that comment.

"Are you sure she's not bi?" Peter said. Hart sensed a story behind that comment, too, and thought the intersection of the two stories might be unfortunate. So he changed the subject.

"I'm empty," Hart said, crunching an ice cube. "Anybody want anything?" The others shook their heads "no." Hart fought his way through the waves of sweaty Darcy's and flushed Bennets to the bar. On his way back to the safety of the sofa, Abigail cruised out of the crowd and snagged Hart.

"Hart," Abigail said, "I want to introduce you to someone." She led him into another, quieter room, where a pleasant-looking girl with curly hair and freckles was lounging on a sofa. "Wanda Huxtable, this is Hart Fox."

"Hi, Wanda."

"Hello."

"Hart and I went to high school together," Abigail said. "Wanda used to go to Stutts." A few rooms away, the recorded music stopped abruptly. "Oh, the band's starting up again," Abigail said. "Casey will be looking for me—wouldn't want to get spanked." She raised her skirts and scampered off. "Let me through! I gotta dance!"

"Too much information," Hart said.

"Too much booze," Wanda corrected.

Hart looked around. "You know, if I had the vodka and cranberry juice concession for this town, I'd be a rich man."

"Aren't you?" Wanda asked.

"No. What makes you ask that?" Hart said, amazed that, for once, he looked prosperous instead of preposterous.

"You go to Stutts. I just assumed."

"Well, thanks for the compliment," Hart said.

"Was it one?"

"Right." The conversation ground to a halt. Hart wondered why she had transferred; she didn't seem like a psycho or a burnout. "Hey, did I sit next to you at the Freshman Assembly last year?"

"Maybe," Wanda shrugged. "How's Great Littleton?"

"Decaying rapidly," Hart said, "but everyone remains hopeful."

Wanda laughed. "It's funny," she said, "but Great Littleton was my favorite part of Stutts. It's real, you know?"

"That's one word for it," Hart said.

"I mean, all of Stutts is about creating this fantasy of being something it's not, this medieval castle tucked away somewhere, filled with princes and princesses. Great Littleton shows how bogus that is—I love that about it."

"How do you like Humidity?"

"How do you like it?" Wanda didn't like to answer questions the first time around.

"I like it a lot. I think it would be really cool to go to school here," Hart said. "I like how there's a couple of big college buildings in the middle of campus, but then all the dorms and stuff have just moved into old houses and stuff." Hart used the word "stuff" a lot when he was nervous.

"Humidity is plastic," Wanda said. "Do you mind if I smink?"

"Smink?"

"I guess this hasn't made it down to you guys yet," Wanda said, pulling a can of something out of her purse. "It's an energy drink, but it's got nicotine in it."

Ick, Hart thought, but smiled. "I guess other people's campuses always look better, 'cause you don't have to work there," he said. "Though you gotta admit: Humidity has a lot less gunfire."

"And fewer sirens," Wanda added.

"So can I ask why you transferred?"

"I couldn't stand the people. Just awful. No offense."

Hart tried to conceal the annoyance that rushed up. He must've done a terrible job, because Wanda immediately added, "I mean, they were fine. Everybody was really accomplished and interesting. I'm sure they'll all be in

The New York Times someday. They just weren't my type."

Aha! She couldn't hack it, Hart thought to himself. "The workload—nothing to like about that."

"No, that was fine. I got straight As," Wanda said. "A couple of my professors tried to convince me to stay."

Shit, Hart thought. The only professor who even knew his name was Lemonade who, a) was just a lecturer, b) was a complete psychotic, and c) had probably boned his mom. "Wow," Hart said. "So obviously you wanted to go someplace where you could have a better social life?"

"I went to tons of parties at Stutts. I even got invited to a bunch of secret ones off-campus."

"Crazy." Goddamn it! Since when are there secret parties off-campus? And why am I not getting invited to them? I will never make the grade, Hart thought glumly.

"I just didn't like the people there," Wanda said. "They were all so full of themselves...I'm sure you're not like that," Wanda added, trying to be nice.

"I run *The Cuckoo*. Do you remember that?"

"Vaguely..." Wanda said. "Everybody was plotting how they were going to be President one day."

"How idiotic," Hart said. I could be President, he thought, if I *really* tried. It just doesn't interest me.

Wanda continued. "I don't want to be President. I just want a happy, interesting life." She finished whatever was in her plastic cup and stood. "Time for another." She waved. "Nice to meet you, Hunt. Give Great Littleton a kiss for me."

"Can it be an air-kiss?" Hart said, not bothering to correct her.

Wanda smiled. As she walked away, melting into the Bennets, Darcys, and imported guys in blue blazers, Hart's certainty crumbled. He began to ponder every choice he'd made since pottytraining. Was all this—Stutts, *The Cuckoo*—leading him to a happy, interesting life? Should he ease off? Could he? In third grade, he had stabbed himself in the hand with a pencil, just because he couldn't figure out the cursive Q. All the people at this dance seemed happy—was he? Should he drop out of Stutts and play guitar on the beach for the rest of his life? Which beach? And what if guitar was too hard?

"There you are," Tabitha said, eyes bright. Her notebook was full, and she was having a lovely time. "Help me find the others. There's a party over at Soph—you look a little freaked, honey. Too many strap-ons for one night?"

"I think I just had my first 'Stutts moment,'" Hart said. "I need a hug."

24
Trying to Kill Your Editor Is A Cuckoo Tradition
Monday, February 21st, 3:45 pm

After a day of turmoil featuring fistfights at Starbucks and a lively black market in old teabags, an emergency convoy arrived. By the time Hart, Peter, Reed, and Tabitha returned to Great Littleton, Stutts was back in harness, and the rat-race was back to full speed. People had gone to *The Cuckoo*'s website, but only to leave long tirades and threats of violence. Whereas before they considered the magazine to be a harmless if disreputable waste of time, public opinion now placed it somewhere between forced celibacy and cancer.

Hart hated every moment; no matter how he looked at it, he just didn't enjoy infamy. His mom told him it would pass, but being liked was the whole reason he was doing *The Cuckoo*. Who knew that shutting off Stutts' caffeine put you up there with Hitler? That's what the Political Union was arguing next week: "Is *The Cuckoo* Worse Than Hitler?"

Hart didn't like their chances.

For safety, he spent a lot of time on the minibus. These were a fleet of screeching, crapped-out old hulks that trundled around Great Littleton picking up and dropping off students. The drivers paid little attention to traffic laws—the buses were already so decrepit that one more dent was meaningless, and besides, an accident made the day go faster. But for Hart at least, the minibus was the safest place on campus. The drivers considered themselves to be the modern equivalent of ship's captains, and would brook no violence—as long as they liked Hart. Hart made sure they did.

"Thanks for the Snickers," Rico said to Hart. "Skipped lunch. Speaking of lunch, I just saw President Whitbread on the Commons stealing bread from the pigeons."

Rico was Hart's favorite driver—Hart liked to hear stories about his three exuberantly godless children, currently terrorizing a parochial school near campus. "President Whitbread was a good man. He was going to buy us a whole new fleet"—Rico took an icy corner and clipped a Volvo—"but this new guy, he says the buses 'aren't essential'..."

Hart made a sympathetic noise.

"I'll tell you what's not essential," Rico said. "That yacht of his."

"Actually, that belongs to the *Spec.*"

"What's that?" Like most inhabitants of the town, Rico tried to stay oblivious to what went on inside Stutts. He assumed—rightly—that it would piss him off.

"School newspaper."

Rico was about to swear, then stopped himself. "You're on that, right?"

"God, no," Hart said, emphasizing the difference. "I'm on the humor magazine."

"You think things are funny around here?" Rico asked, giving Hart a pointed glance in the rear-view. "You got a weird sense of humor, kid."

Four students got on, each one giving Hart a dirty look as they passed. Everybody was still wildly pissed. The staff of *The Cuckoo* was learning that nobody carries a grudge like an addict.

Hart felt heat vision on the back of his neck. Luckily, Beekman got on at the next stop. If things deteriorated, as least they'd have a fighting chance.

"Hey, Beek."

"Hey, Hart." He slid next to Hart.

"Where are you coming from?"

"Just seeing a professor." Beekman had just had his weekly meeting with Professor North. North had spent it at full volume, telling the boy that he wasn't making enough progress destroying *The Cuckoo*.[56]

"I can throw you right back into CCA, Mr.... Whatever-your-name-is!" North had threatened. "I don't want excuses, I want results! *The Cuckoo* is a threat to the university! You must help me keep Stutts safe!"

"Everybody hates them now," Beekman had pointed out.

"I don't want them hated, I want them gone!" North had yelled. "You get it done, or I'll let everybody know you wet the bed until you were 14!"

Mom talked, Beekman thought grimly. "Okay, I—"

"Shut up and get out!"

Back on the bus, the boys were bombarded with hate-rays. They huddled together for protection. "This sucks," Hart said quietly.

"Ahh, I'm used to it," Beekman said. "I was a Gnome for CCA."

"What's that?"

56 North had tried the old reduce-the-grades bit with *The Cuckoo* staffers' marks, but Ellen and Peter had hacked into the system last summer, locking everybody's GPA at 3.5 or above. Then North had spent a week painstakingly creating a vast photocollage featuring *The Cuckoo* staff engaged in a homosexual orgy—not realizing that in the current campus culture, this would actually insulate them from criticism. In fact, one of the magazine's few defenders during the post-coffee-heist period were the officers of the CaberGAY.

"Like a permanent pledge, one that does everybody's homework."

"Why the hell did you ever sign up for that?"

"I didn't," Beekman said. "My friend Biff signed us both up."

Something clicked in Hart's mind. "Beek, did you and Biff ever drag me around with a car? I was wearing a squid costume."

"I was wondering when you'd ask," Beekman said. "It was nothing personal. Mr. Darling—"

"*Governor* Darling," Hart said. "He'd correct you himself if he were here." They slung around another corner, bumping over a curb.

"Get out of the road!" Rico yelled at the President's secretary Judy, who was now sticking out of a bush.

"Governor Darling said that if we killed you, we would get into Mugwumps. I'm really sorry," Beekman said. "It wasn't my idea."

"Whatever," Hart said.

"So you're not going to kick me off the magazine?"

"Trying to kill your editor is a *Cuckoo* tradition. Ever had a piece edited?" Hart said with a smile. "Once on, always on, Slim."

"Why'd you call me that?"

"It just fits," Hart said.

"All right." Beekman smiled. He'd never had a nickname before. A paper wad bounced off his forehead.

Rico saw it. "Yo, dillweed! Knock it off!"

"Mugwumps drives everybody so freaking crazy," Beekman said. "It makes people do things they would never do otherwise. Or it gives them an excuse to do the things they would be embarrassed to do."

"Yeah—an excuse that everybody admires," Hart said. "When you talked about killing me, I thought, 'Maybe I would've done it, too.' I'm ambitious. I'd love to see what goes on inside the Pyramid. Plus, there's the money…do you believe the rumor?"

"A million dollars at graduation? Nah," Beekman said. "Too perfect. I think the university would be better off without 'em. Somebody ought to put the Mugwumps out of business."

"Impossible," Hart said, the traditionalist in him coming to the fore. "Even if you could, something else would just take its place."

"Okay, Guy."

"Don't even joke," Hart said. "I don't mind that the Wumps exist, I just think they need to be held in check. Knocked down a peg every once in a while."

"If you can dream it, you can do it," Beekman said. "My dad always says that."

"Damn," Hart smiled, "do dads have like, a manual or something?"

"I think it's hormonal," Beekman said, smiling back. The more he hung out with Hart—with all the Cuckonians—the happier he felt. Even if the rest of the campus hated them. "By the way, I always tell people I did the coffee prank, too."

"You don't have to," Hart said.

"No, I want to. It was my idea. I should've helped." Beekman stared out of the scratched-up window, then wrote "HELP!" backwards in the condensation. Hart saw it.

"An oldie but a goodie." He countered with "wash me".

Beekman smiled—and in that moment, felt something new. Beekman realized that he didn't want to rot the magazine from the inside, he wanted to preserve it. But Professor North…All Professor North did was yell at him. North wasn't a good guy, working to keep the University safe. He was a mean old codger trying to crush his enemies. Well, *The Cuckoo* guys aren't my enemies, Beekman thought. They're my friends. "There's only one thing I know that the Mugwumps would be scared of," Beekman said.

"An itty-bitty nuclear warhead."

"No. Worse," Beekman whispered. "This is my stop. I'll tell you Wednesday. At the meeting."

When Hart arrived, the meeting was already going full-tilt. "This just in," Hart said, closing the door, "everybody still hates us."

"Tell me about it," Reed said. He pointed at a large, painful-looking welt under his unblackened eye.

"*Another* one?" Hart asked. "You better graduate, before you die."

Reed gave a smile that was partially a grimace. "Travel mugs are fucking heavy."

"They may hate us," Peter said from behind a copy of the Spec, "but they love Tabitha."

"Really?" Whenever Hart thought of Tabitha's column, he was half-proud, 35% terrified, and 15% jealous. Writers are like that.

"Oh yeah," Peter said. "Your girlfriend has found her calling. Listen to this: 'When men talk about having an outsized trouser-pal, they mean length. But when a lady gets doe-eyed, it's more likely to be girth.' Very Tab, don't you think? Peppy and pithy."

"It pithes me off," Hart cracked, then smacked the bird-head gavel on the table. "Meeting in session."

"Where *is* our star, anyway?" Reed asked.

"On deadline. She's coming later."

"Wait," Peter said, "aren't you going to do your thing?"

"What? You mean this?" Hart tipped his chair back on to the rear two legs, then slung his feet onto the table.

"Much better," Peter said. "I don't feel right unless you do it."

"No problem," Hart said. "Beekman here says he has a way to bring down the Mugwumps."

"Finally!" Peter said. "I was wondering when you'd see the light. It's only a matter of time before they retaliate for the Xmas issue. We ought to beat them to the punch."

"Funny you should mention them," Reed said, "because I just got some news from Ellen."

Peter looked surprised. "You guys are talking again?"

"Barely," Reed said. "She's still pretty pissed at you, Pete. She called you a..."

"Leave that," Hart said. "What did she say about the Mugwumps?"

"She said that before our issue, the current group was fighting with the alumni, and it looked like the whole thing was on its way to collapsing."

"For good?" Beekman asked.

"Yeah. But then our issue came out," Reed said. "It brought everybody together—common enemy, all that. The alumni were so embarrassed that they've started pouring money into the group."

"Uh-oh," Beekman said.

"Like how much?" Hart said. "Did she say?"

"Like, total gut renovation," Reed said. "Like, a whole bunch of scholarships and fellowships and prizes. Like, an undisclosed sum to every member that graduates in good standing."

"'Undisclosed' meaning a shitload," Hart said.

"Presumably."

"*Now* I believe the million dollar thing, Hart," Beekman said.

"And you believe her?" Peter asked.

"Yes," Reed said.

"You all know they can lie to 'the Others,'" Peter said.

"Yes, Peter, you've told us all a hundred times," Hart said wearily.

"People are really going to get serious about it now," Beekman said.

"More serious than trying to kill other people?" Hart said. "By the way, everybody: Beekman tried to kill me last year, but I'm cool with it. Remember when I got dragged around in the squid costume?"

"That was you?" Peter asked. "Where's your buddy, the asshole?"

"Long story," Beekman said.

Hart continued. "Beek here is ready to atone for his past misdeeds, by telling us how to get the Mugwumps by the short-and-curlies," Hart said. He pointed the gavel at Beekman. "Spill. I command thee."

"You guys know Professor North, right? The CIA guy?"

"Yeah," Hart said. "He was the lead judge in the Chamber."

"He hired me to infiltrate your group and break it up," Beekman said.

Peter felt the Stutts version of an orgasm. "I was RIGHT!" he whooped.

"You know how I said my dad would pay for the paper for the next issue?" Beekman said. "That was Professor North. He wanted to print it on magnesium-impregnated stock."

"Flash paper." Everybody looked at Reed. "I was into magic as a kid, so?"

"Each issue would burn itself up," Peter said. "I like this guy. He's sneaky, like me."

"Me, or Professor North?" Beekman asked.

"Both," Peter said. "Him, for suggesting it, and you for considering pulling it off—but then telling us about it."

"This is all very interesting listening to you unburden yourself, Beekman, but what does it have to do with the Mugwumps?" Hart said.

"Not just with the Mugwumps, with everybody," Beekman said. "Professor North has files. Dossiers. Tons of them, built up over decades. One for every person here—every professor, every suit, every student. He controls the entire university, because everybody's afraid of what's in those files. But he's getting old; his memory isn't what it used to be..."

Peter sprang. "So we should steal the files."

"Essentially, yeah," Beekman said.

Reed said, "You really think North's got something on the Mugwumps?"

"Are you kidding?" Beekman said. "The group's hundreds of years old. There's gotta be enough dirt in those files to bring them down."

"Which we may or may not decide to do," Hart said, trying to head off Peter's bloodlust.

"Says the Mugwump-lover," Peter said. "Hart, it would make us impossible to shut down."

"We're underground," Hart said. "We're already impossible to shut down."

"*If* nothing happens to us personally," Reed said. "Now that we know this guy North is gunning for us, I don't think we have any choice. We have to hit him before he hits us."

"Now that I've switched sides, he'll bring out the big guns," Beekman said. "He's already pretty pissed off."

"This seems like a big step," Hart said.

"It's a simple transfer of power," Peter said, "from the bad guys to the good guys."

Hart was unsure. Was this what they should be doing? It wouldn't get him any closer to fame, fortune, Quinn Bostwick, or anything else he really wanted. And look at how the coffee prank turned out—that had been Beekman's idea, too.

Reed was thinking along the same lines. "Beekman, how do we know you're not baiting us into doing this, as part of North's plan? If we got caught stealing those files, we'd all be expelled, for sure."

"I can't think of any way to prove it to you," Beekman said. "You'll just have to trust that I'm on your side now."

Hart thought for a bit. "Seems pretty far afield for a humor magazine," he said.

Peter made a big push. "Hart, we'd be doing everybody a huge favor. For the first time since God farted, nobody would have to worry about Professor North digging up some mistake they made, or something they said, or who they slept with," Peter said. "This North dude will come after us harder and harder. Sooner or later, he'll find something that works. If you're looking for a way to protect the magazine—and make the campus love us again—this is it."

"Being loved is nice," Hart said. "Reed?"

"I think it's the right thing to do," he said. "My dad hates this North dude, so he would probably forgive me if I get expelled for trying to steal his files. Three months before graduation, I might add."

Hart closed his eyes and held his breath. He sat there, balanced on two chair legs, trying to figure out what to do. Hart was a reluctant gambler, but if there was one thing he hated more than risk, it was bullies. This guy North was a bully. The Mugwumps—as much as part of him wanted to be picked—they were kinda bullies, too. Smug. Stealing those files would be fighting for the little guy, for the individual. When Guy said stuff like this, it sounded cheesy, because Guy didn't comb his freakin' hair. But deep down, Hart agreed; fighting for the underdog was fighting for himself.

But what if I get kicked out? Hart thought about the possibility, and found it mattered less and less. Things had been crazy from the moment he arrived on campus; he probably wouldn't last all four years. He might as well put the pedal to the metal...

"I think he's dead," Peter said.

Hart opened his eyes. "Let's do it," he said, "'Refreshment Time.'" They broke out some snacks and started to plan. Peter always said that sugar, salt, and partially hydrogenated soybean oil was the lifeblood of every prank. Going up against the most powerful man at Stutts—they needed all the help they could get.

25

Black Ops and Black Elvis

Friday, March 11th, 10:08 pm

Every day that went by, Hart's always-perverse fancy presented another terrible thing Professor North could do to him. Hart couldn't know this, but it was the very imagination of Stutts students that made them so easy to control. North didn't have to pay someone to garrote Mr. Fox in his prison cell; he just needed Hart to realize it was possible.

Though time was of the essence, they did not rush planning the assault on North's files. They'd only have one chance, and if they were caught, it would be impossible to explain away as harmless hijinx; everybody knew what was in those files.

Peter's first idea, which involved tear gas and a busload of Great Littleton schoolchildren, was discarded as too complex. Another was too risky—"no zip-wires, no crampons, no rappelling," Hart said, and he wouldn't budge. Finally, Peter aimed for the middle, and came up with something that *might* work. After over two weeks of refining, and another procuring supplies, the Cuckonians set things into motion.

Hart, Tabitha, Reed, and Beekman all showed up at Professor North's office, dressed in matching coveralls. Peter was in the parking lot below, behind the wheel of the mighty *Cuckoo*-mobile, a 1927 hearse he'd customized to make amphibious, among other things.

"Peter sure loves that car," Reed said. (He'd walked in on him cooing to it.)

"I wonder what he's added lately," Hart replied. "Machine guns? Oil-slick-shooters?"

"He demonstrated the rotating license plates on the way over," Tabitha said. She put her fingers an inch apart. "Peter is this close to being nutso."

"And that's why we love him," Reed said.

"This is it," Beekman said.

"'Electrical Closet,' eh?" Reed tapped the sign. "Sneaky bastard."

"Hold on, Tab." Hart ran to the end of the corridor. "Okay, it's clear."

Tabitha turned into a mist, and seeped under the door. She quickly seeped back out. "He's in there," she said. "He's sitting at his desk."

"At ten o'clock on a Friday? Doesn't he have a wife?" Reed said.

"Who would marry that weasel?" Beekman said. "'C'mere, dear, and let me blackmail you into a blow-job.' Go back in, Tab."

"Why?"

"I have a hunch," Beekman said. "Go tickle his nose."

Tabitha re-wafted under the door. Thirty seconds later, they heard it unlock.

"Mannequin," she said. "How did you—?"

"I am also a sneaky bastard," Beekman said.

"Am I the only one on this magazine who isn't sneaky?" Hart asked.

"Excuse me," Reed said, pushing past to jimmy the lock on the closet where the flash paper was kept.

When they rolled the cart with the reams of paper into North's office, Beekman said, "Don't touch anything. This place is full of stuff that looks normal but isn't."

"Good to know," Tabitha said. "May I sit on the couch?"

"I wouldn't," Beekman said. He pointed to a chair. "Sit there. I tested it the last time I was here."

Just to expand the frontiers of knowledge, Hart picked up a heavy book and threw it on the couch. As soon as he touched it, the book had begun to tick; lucky for them, the moment the book hit the leather chesterfield, the center cushion sprang forward, launching the book through the window.

"Explosive book. Ejector couch," Beekman said matter-of-factly, as the book detonated harmlessly in the sky outside.

"What the hell was that?" Peter asked on the comlink.

"Tell you later," Hart said. "Keep the engine running, in case we have to abort." He and Reed had taken the door off its hinges, and put it inside the office. "Let's not lean it against anything," Hart said.

Now came the dangerous part—Hart and Reed began ripping the door-jamb out with crowbars. It was noisy, and if they were discovered, there was no easy excuse, even though they were wearing official-looking jumpsuits that read, "Ace Contracting."

Finally the noisy work was over, and Hart grabbed a broom from a janitor's closet next door. He swept all the plaster bits and dust into North's office.

"Sorry, guys," he said to Tabitha and Beekman, who were waiting patiently inside. "Gotta cover our tracks."

The boys had just begun fitting a frame of two-by-fours into the space, Reed fastening it with bursts from a drill, when he was hit in the back with a doorknob.

"Scabs!" a man yelled from the end of the hallway. He was wearing a jumpsuit, too, only this one was covered in rhinestones arranged in a vaguely Amer-Indian motif. "Taking good jobs away from the community!" he snarled, eyes hidden behind big sunglasses. The man reached into his box, pulled out another knob, and cocked his arm to hurl it.

"Black Elvis!"[57] Reed shouted, still feeling the sting of the first knob.

"Rodger! We're not scabs!" Hart said. "We're students!"

Rodger, who the students called "Black Elvis" for obvious reasons—he walked around dressed like Elvis, but was African-American—paused. "If you're students, why are you dressed like that?"

Hart wanted to say, "If you work for Buildings and Grounds, why are you dressed like that?" but held his tongue. Instead he said, "We're students doing a prank. My name is Hart Fox. I know your brother Rico."

"It's 11:00 on a Friday night," Rodger said. (He even sounded a little like Elvis.) "Shouldn't y'all be busy conceiving the next generation of irritating white folks?"

"Shouldn't you be plotting a coup with your union buddies?" Reed replied. Relations between Stutts and its unions were always just this side of open warfare. Rodger was high up in the union, and bitterly resented President Rivington's latest cost-cutting measure, farming contracting and upkeep to prisoners from a nearby supermax prison.

"I hate all the people who work in this building," Black Elvis said, "so I wanna install these doorknobs while everybody's gone. Sorry I hit you with that knob. Can I have it back?"

"Sure," Reed said, picking it up. "Here."

"Thanks," Black Elvis said. Introductions were made. "So what are you guys up to?" He waved to Tabitha and Beekman inside Professor North's office. They waved back.

Hart decided to spare him the full story. "This professor's a dickhole," Hart said, "so we're sealing up his office. When he walks in on Monday morning, they'll be nothing here but blank wall."

Black Elvis laughed. Then he said, "You boys know about the watchman who walks 'round here?"

Reed spoke for the group. "Oh, shit," he said.

"Lucky for you, I'm the fastest drywaller in the world," Black Elvis said. "Me and Rico have to do his basement every six months or so, 'cause his kids put holes in the walls with a hammer."

57 Black Elvis, whose given name was Rodger, had as a younger man an unfortunate knack for finding student suicides. These were not common at Stutts, but they happened, and Rodger seemed to discover them all. It was awful, and got so Chief Constable Renalli would call him whenever a student went missing. These repeated traumas had driven him further and further into a fantasy world. Finally, he quit reality completely and became Black Elvis.

"Are Rico's kids as crazy as he makes 'em out to be?" Hart asked.

"Crazier," Black Elvis said. "Hand me that drill, and stand back." Then, between bursts he barked, "Go get your supplies."

Hart and Reed ran down the hall, and came back with the drywall. Then they got a box with spackle, trowels, a hair-dryer, and some paint in it.

The frame was done. "Time to come out," Black Elvis said to Tabitha and Beekman.

"We're staying in," Tabitha said cheerily.

"But—" Black Elvis looked at Hart.

"You don't want to know," Hart said. "Trust me, Rodger."

Reed waved. "Bye! Good luck!" The drywall went up, and Tabitha and Beekman sprang into action.

"I'll open the window," Tabitha said, "just in case it's booby-trapped." Sure enough, a guillotine-style blade slid down, chopping off both Tabitha's hands, which immediately grew back.

Beekman watched the bloody stumps become wreathed in smoke, then re-form, as if from a waxy clay. "Does it…hurt?"

"Nope," Tabitha said, as the shapes hardened into flesh. "Watch, I'll do it again."

"Please don't," Beekman said weakly.

"Suit yourself. Come and help me." Beekman wobbled over and they removed the blade. "What kind of person thinks of something like that?" she wondered aloud, as they put the razor-sharp hunk of metal over by the trophy case. Beekman glanced inside.

"Che Guevara's shrunken head," he said.

"No dawdling, Beekman," Tabitha said. "Got the garbage bags?"

"Yeah." Beekman pulled them out of his voluminous CCA hoodie.

"Now stand back." Tabitha opened the first drawer of the filing cabinet. Nothing happened. She handed the first stack to Beekman, who turned on Professor North's copy machine, loaded in the flash paper, and began to copy the files.

They got into a rhythm; Tabitha removed a bulging folder, and handed it to Beekman. Beekman took the file, loaded it into Professor North's copier (which was state-of-the-art fast, a mark of his top-dog status), and handed Tabitha back a previous folder, re-filled in perfect order. It was a cunning plan: North would never know his files had been copied; they'd take North's originals, and leave a flash-paper version in its place.

A hair dryer started up on the other side of the fake door, as Black Elvis and the boys dried the spackle. "Not much longer now," Tabitha said. "Just a coat of paint, and we'll be free to take as long as we like." She was pleasantly alert and excited; as much as she'd hate to admit this to Peter, these "black ops" were beginning to grow on her.

Beekman cinched the first plastic bag full of originals closed, making sure it wasn't packed too tight and still had some air in it. Then, he walked over to the window, and tossed it out; it landed on the roof deck of *The Cuckoo*mobile with a thud.

Tabitha systematically cleaned out the files, from "A.A., members of" to "Zoophiles, compulsive." Beekman copied them, then decanted them loosely into garbage bags. Whenever she got a particularly nasty paper cut, Tabitha helped Beekman with the bags until it healed.

Beekman paused to look down. "Wow, it's really filling up."

"You should be happy," Tabitha said. "You don't want a broken leg."

There was a knock from Hart and Reed—the wall was finished. Tabitha looked at the filing cabinets, and called out an estimate. "Thirty minutes!"

Hart, Reed, and Peter waited downstairs in the car, listening to the bags hit the open roof deck with a clunk. "Think Slim'll break his leg?" Hart mused.

"Nah," Peter said. "Beek's pretty light."

After the last bag had been tossed and the last file replaced, Tabitha and Beekman paused to enjoy a moment of devious accomplishment. "Amazing," Beekman said, his face streaked with toner. "Who knew college could be so much fun?"

"Stick around for a century or two," Tabitha said. She closed the last cabinet. "I'm looking forward to reading up on all my old boyfriends."

Beekman laughed. "Can I interest you in a Xerox of your face?"

"Not possible," Tabitha said. "But you go ahead."

Beekman smushed his mug against the glass platen and pushed "copy". Mid-chug, the copier began an insistent beeping. "Oh, shit," he said. "Paper jam."

Tabitha heard a noise from the hall outside.

"Hello?" The night watchman had heard Beekman's voice.

Beekman jabbed at various buttons. He opened the copier doors, and reached inside. He could *just* reach the sheet of paper; Beekman grabbed and pulled. A shred came off in his hand. It showed his collar and part of his shirt, but a picture of his face was still in the guts of the machine.

"Anybody in there?" the night watchman said, much closer now. If he noticed the paint on that one swath of wall was wet, or leaned up against the spackled wallboard, and it gave way…

"I can get it," Beekman whispered. "Just give me one minute."

"No time," Tabitha said. She walked over, gathered him into her arms, and leaped out of the window. Halfway down, she mistified. Beekman landed, air whooshing out of the half-filled bags. He was bruised but okay.

Tabitha coalesced in the back seat next to Hart. "Hit it!" she commanded, and Peter did so.

"There's nothing I love more than a clean getaway," Hart said when they arrived back at the offices.

"Uh, not totally clean," Beekman said. With a sheepish look, he told everyone that, deep in the guts of that beeping photocopier nestled a picture of his face. "Maybe I crumpled the rest."

That put a damper on the celebration, and after unloading the files into *The Cuckoo* offices, everybody just went home. As he and Tabitha bedded down for the night, Hart said, "I can't decide whether Beekman is the best thing that ever happened to the magazine, or the worst."

"Who cares?" Tabitha said, turning off the light. "Come over here and help me research my next column."

26
Who's NOT Crazy?
Monday, March 14th, 9:11 AM

Professor North whistled as he walked to work. For once, the sleet had lifted and the sun was meekly shining. Even better, over the weekend a friend at Interpol had given him the name of Mr. Fox's prison guard.

The more North read his files, the more he became convinced that if you neutralized Hart Fox, you neutralized *The Cuckoo*. North was sure that, thirty seconds after Hart's father's body was found, that ridiculous, useless magazine would cease to exist. Now it was just a question of finding some leverage on the guard—bribery, blackmail, religion, everyone was susceptible to something. Ever detail-oriented, North started composing the obituary he'd feed to the wire services. "Depressed by business failures and his recent incarceration, Fox was found hanging in his cell, an apparent suicide..."

Every morning Professor North varied the route he took to his office, in order to avoid detection. That Monday, however, he was shocked to discover that two could play at that game.

"Where the hell is my office?" he yelled forlornly in the hall. "Does anybody know where my office went?" Silence. "What are you looking at?"

Black Elvis had been waiting for this moment all morning. "Nothin'."

"Go do some work," North snapped, then added as B.E. sauntered away, "Don't think I can't get you fired. Your precious union means less than nothing to me."

At first, North thought he'd merely taken a wrong turn, and so retraced his steps. He did this again and again. Three hours later, he trudged home angry, and with a hammering headache. Tuesday proved equally fruitless, though it had been invigorated by an ugly scene with the professor next door.

North's neighbor was a Literature prof named Finks. Finks had a full beard, and North considered that much facial hair untrustworthy—people didn't cover their faces unless they had something to hide. When North confronted him, Finks confirmed North's suspicions completely.

"All right, Finks. What did you do with my office?"

"It was like that when I got in," Finks said.

"You better be ready to prove that, Dr. Seuss." (According to North's files, Finks was writing a children's book.) Referencing the criminal trial that was surely to come, North turned coldly forensic. "Do you agree that my office was here"—North pounded a blank patch of wall—"right next door to yours?"

"Yes. Yes, it was…Much to my regret."

"No editorializing, please," North said. "Well, where did it go? Do you think offices simply disappear?"

"Listen, North, I've got a 10:30—"

"Do you hear that beeping?" The jammed copier was complaining louder than ever.

"No," Finks lied sadistically. "At your age, one's hearing begins to…"[58]

Enraged, North ran over to Finks and kicked him in the shin.

"Ow! Shit! All right, grandpa. Visiting time is over," Finks growled. He grabbed North by the back of the jacket and steered him towards the door.

"How dare you! I—" North grabbed at things as he hurtled past, as if his office could be hiding under a stack of papers or potted plant. Finks tossed him into the hall and slammed the door.

"You'll be sorry, you commie! I'll tell everyone you believe in fairies!"[59]

Finks opened his door just wide enough to fling a stapler. It hit North on the forehead. After a bit more pounding and shouting, North relented. Being separated from his files affected him like Kryptonite.

The stapler left a mark, but the real pain came on Wednesday, which North spent in the downstairs lounge, hunched over a map he'd liberated from Buildings and Grounds. "It's right *there*," he complained to anybody within earshot. "This map mocks me!"

North had ruled by fear for too long to get any sympathy; everyone was secretly thrilled to see the old blackmailer getting his comeuppance. Still, North had enough clout left to keep everybody at bay while he took a whack at the third-floor wall with a fire-ax.

"Ah-HA!" North bellowed, as the sheetrock splintered and plaster plumed. "Y'see? I was RIGHT!" He hacked at the wall *Shining*-style, then

58 North's age had been the subject of a small riot during the autumn meeting of the Faculty Senate. The ruthless coot had kept his job by pulling a last-ditch Joe McCarthy; grabbing an empty folder, North shouted: "Back off! This folder contains naked pictures of everyone in this room!" But rather than being intimidated, this time the perverts were curious. North had to climb out a window to avoid having his bluff called. People of loose morals were impossible to blackmail, he thought with disgust.

59 This was the highlight of Fink's file. For years, North had been in the habit of reviewing the files of people he was likely to meet that day, over breakfast. Though he couldn't resume this practice until he found his office, North had read Fink's file so many times, even senility could not dislodge every fact.

grabbed a passing grad student. "WHO'S CRAZY NOW?"

"Um? Not you?"

"Damn right! NOT me." North released her. "Go tell the world!"

Once he'd hacked out a hole big enough to crawl through, North was possessed by only two questions: who did this? And how can they be punished? Hard?[60] Even before unjamming the copier, he began scouring the room for clues.

The History professor from down the hall stuck her head in the hole. "Could you please find whatever is beeping? It's giving me a migraine."

North didn't even look at her. "I'm not crazy, I'm not crazy," he said, giggling to himself.

After an hour (and several injuries, thanks to mementos he'd forgotten were booby-trapped), North had found nothing but a pink barette with a whale on it. Finally, he approached the photocopier. "Jammed, eh?" Clearing the mechanism, he found a grainy, distorted picture of Beekman's face. "Gotcha."

North fairly sprinted over to his files—but there was nothing there on the boy. (He'd guessed on the bedwetting, and had since forgotten about it.) The lack of info wasn't surprising; the kid was incredibly unimportant, that's why he'd picked him to infiltrate *The Cuckoo*. *The Cuckoo*...Beekman...the disappearing office...it all clicked into place.

North picked up the red phone. He didn't wait for Rivington to speak. "Beekman's flipped."

"What?" President Rivington said.

"Turned. Switched sides," North said. "Didn't you read that glossary I sent you?"

"Glenbard, if you had any idea how much stuff crosses my desk...What did you think of that memo about installing pay toilets?"

"Don't bother me with trifles, nitwit," North barked. "Beekman—the student I had infiltrating *The Cuckoo*, he's gone over to the enemy."

"What, Keasbey?" Rivington said.

North remembered the barette. "I think he's a crossdresser—although given the so-called morality here, that's probably a good thing."

"*Cuckoo, Cuckoo*." President Rivington tried to place it. "Oh, right. The student magazine."

"Yes!" Professor North said exasperatedly. "You asked me to put them out of business, remember?"

60 Okay, two questions and an intensifier. Call it two-and-a-half.

"I think so," President Rivington said. "To be honest, other things have come up. I really think this toilet thing could be great. Did you know that people, on average use the toilet seven times a day? At a quarter a pop, that's—"

"Shut up! Shut up! Shut up!" North screeched, his voice cracking. My God, he thought, what would these people do without me to fend off their enemies? "Do you still want them liquidated?"

"The whatsit? I guess. I mean, why not? I must've had a good reason."

"Do I have your permission to do whatever is necessary?"

"Listen, Glenbard, is it true you lost your off—"

Professor North hung up, then dialed another number. It was time for another approach—the one that always worked.

27
Falling Straight Down, Rising Straight Up
Wednesday, March 30th, 4:19 pm

"So *The Cuckoo* building fell straight down," Hart said. "So what?" He and Peter were walking across New Quad. For once it wasn't raining, it was only misting.

"That seems natural to you?"

"First, I'm not an engineer, so what do I know?" Hart said, counting the reasons off on his fingers. "Second, it was 1969, unnatural things were happening all the time. Guys walking on the moon, people admiring Richard Nixon, the Beatles breaking up..."

Peter didn't buy it; he had no feel for history. "It wasn't metal fatigue, or cheap concrete, or whatever else the university says it was," he said sourly. "The photos show a controlled demolition. dropping straight down into its own footprint—and Trip's dad, your pal Burlington Darling, pushed the button. Look at these photos..."

Hart looked at the ridiculously blurry blow-up Peter had just extracted from Professor North's stolen files, now cool and cozy in a spare room next to *The Cuckoo*'s underground lair. Since there were flash-paper copies in North's office, nobody was the wiser.

The files were perfect loam for Peter's ever-sprouting paranoia. "It's from the *Spec*, June 14, 1969...Note the date," he said professorially. "Classes have ended, only seniors are still around. Two words: fewer witnesses."

"Two words:" Hart said, "Get meds."

"Fine," Peter said, "answer me this: those guys in the picture are all Mugwumps. Why are they still on campus? Why aren't they partying their asses off on their private island, like they do every *other* Graduation Week?"

Hart was very tired of conversations like this. "Pete, can we just talk about TV or something? You're full of it."

"No, I'm a realist, and you're Head Bird, Hart. This is a precedent," Peter said. "Until everybody knows we have the files, we're still in danger. If not from North, then certainly the Mugwumps."

Hart sighed. Peter's battle never ended. "I find it hard to believe the

Mugwumps would blow up the building, then cover it up successfully for decades," Hart said. "Why hasn't anybody talked?"

"Somebody has," Peter said.

"Somebody *besides* Guy! The university wouldn't allow what you're suggesting, not for a minute."

"Hart, you're living in a fantasy world. The administration says whatever's necessary to keep the money flowing. They're corrupt."

"Harsh, " Hart said. "I don't think they're that bad."

"For God's sake, they were going to sell your spot to Trip Darling!"

"But they *didn't.*"

Hart could talk cynical, but in his innermost heart he was a believer. Things were the way they were because sensible people, acting responsibly, had made them so. If that wasn't the case...oh god, the mere *possibility* stressed him out. Hart didn't want to think of life as a Thunderdome full of heavily armed crooks and liars, so despite mounting evidence, he clung to the alternative. "Stutts is not run by goofballs."

"Our magazine is," Peter said. "Why should Stutts be any different?"

"Because it makes me into just another schmo," Hart said. "The more screwed-up they are, the less special I am for getting in."

"We couldn't have that," Peter chuckled, "all us precious Stuttsies being just like everybody else. We might have to be judged on what we did and said, instead of hiding behind that beautiful brand name."

"Go away, and let me have more space behind the brand name." To Hart, it was clear that Peter's distrust of authority stemmed from his feelings about his parents. And his accident, of course. In Peter's world, people said they could protect you, but then it turned out they couldn't. Bad things happened—in an instant, every instant—and after that instant, all you could do was hose down the smoking wreckage and try to salvage something. Trapped in his chair, Peter felt that betrayal every day. Hart could never say all this; Peter was too proud to appreciate five-cent psychoanalysis. Better to change the subject before it slipped out.

"Hey," Hart asked, "heard anything from that summer internship you wanted? The French place?"

"L'institut Pour des Expériences Dangereuses," Peter said. "Not *un peep*, but I think the mailmen have been on strike. How about you? Got a plan?"

"No," Hart admitted. He thought a lot about his future, but when it came to actually doing anything, he always turned chicken. "I'm hoping to ask Bostwick if he needs an intern when he takes us out to lunch at graduation."

"I totally forgot about that," Peter said. "We should do something really great at the ceremony, to impress him. And send Reed and Ellen off properly."

Two guys in expensive trenchcoats were walking in the other direction. Hart whispered so they wouldn't hear. "When you say 'do something,' you mean a pra—"

One slammed into Hart's shoulder, knocking him off-balance. The other caught Hart and steadied him before he slipped on the slate. "Sorry."

"Watch where you're going, asshole!" Peter said combatively.

Hart felt something new in his jacket pocket. "Hey, that guy just slipped this to me."

"It's a love note," Peter said.

Hart opened the envelope. "'Don't be friends with Peter,'" he pretended to read. "'He's a blowhole.'"

"Really?" (Like most self-anointed "realists," Peter could be surprisingly gullible.)

"No, not really," Hart said. "Wow. This is awesome! 'The Society of St. Caesar's invites you to their annual retreat—"

"—and circle jerk."

"Your name is on it, too, smart guy," Hart said. He was excited; St. Caesar's was like an adult version of the Mugwumps, more secret, and even more exclusive. And now he, Hart Nobody, had been invited! This was just the kind of thing he'd hoped would happen when he got accepted to Stutts. Wait—what if he didn't know what to do? Well, Peter would help him figure it out, he was rich.

"Let's go!" Hart said. "I've read all about these guys. It's a huge honor to be invited—everybody's totally famous." Who needed a summer internship if you had a PDA full of St. Caesar's types? I'll jump right on the fast track, Hart thought. I'll catch Quinn Bostwick, then vault right past him. I'll win a fistful of Pulitzers and maybe a Nobel Prize, just to make my mother proud, then I'll devote the rest of my life to doing good...

"Ehh," Peter said, unimpressed.

"Come on, Pete! Can't you quit the act, just once?" Hart couldn't go alone since Peter was on the invitation, too. "Do it for the experience. You could make fun of everybody. Wouldn't that be fun?"

"I've got better things to do with my Spring Break."

"Like what?" Hart asked.

"Like, talk to people with vaginas. St. Caesar's is stag, noob."

"That's bizarre," Hart noted, then continued the hard-sell. "So you won't get lucky. But it would be an awesome career move. Even you might need connections someday, Pete."

"It's out in the woods," Peter griped. "I'm an indoor-toilet kind of hombre."

Hart wasn't ready to give up. Getting slipped an invitation secretly—

how cool was that? Had he turned into a campus bigwig without knowing it? "Captains of Industry have sisters and daughters, y'know."

"So do Captains of Assholery."

"Fine, fine," Hart said, temporarily beaten. "Forget I mentioned it. Be closed off to new experiences." Maybe he'd try later—Peter had an ego, he'd let elitism work its magic. "But if I ever find out it was really cool, I *will* punch you," Hart said. "And you will fall straight down."

Two nights later, Hart was sitting with Tabitha in her crypt. It was a working evening; at Stutts, the couple that studied together, stayed together. Hart was reading a "scratch 'n' sniff" textbook for his Smells of History class. Tabitha was sketching him as he did so.

Hart yawned. "Time for bed," he said, tossing the book aside and stretching.

"Don't—damn, Hart!" Tabitha said. "I wasn't finished."

"Perhaps you could sketch me in another position..." Hart leaned towards her. In his hands, any sentence could be a come-on. Unfortunately he knocked a pile of stuff off her lobster-trap coffee-table.

To a vampiress as deeply tidy as Tabitha, this broke the mood. "You do that constantly," she said, irritated, "and you never pick it up afterwards."

"What's your problem?" Hart said. "I was just being affectionate."

"Well, I don't feel like it," Tabitha said. "I wanted to finish that drawing tonight. As it is I'll have to spend all Spring Break on my portfolio. Now, I have to start over"—she ripped out the page and balled it up—"preferably with something that doesn't move."

"I hate fighting with you," Hart said. "Can we not? Please?"

Tabitha repelled him again. "Get off!"

"It's that sex column," Hart grumbled. "I'm just a lab-rat to you."

"'Tough titty.'"

"You're not funny. I'm still bruised from those damn nipple clamps."

"Admit it, Hart—you're just jealous," Tabitha said. "It burns you up that everybody likes my column but hates *The Cuckoo*."

Hart forced a laugh. "I'm not jealous. And you're on *The Cuckoo*, too," he chided her. "Or have you become a *Spec*ster now?"

"I'm just using them—like you tried to."

"Whatever. I'm going to bed," Hart said, miffed.

"Not here, you're not," Tabitha said. "I have to stay up and work." She tossed him his coat. "Call me tomorrow," Tabitha said.

"Maybe," Hart said. "By the way, fuck you for saying I'm jealous."

"Fuck you for being jealous."

"I'm not jealous!" Hart said, then walked out.

He was totally jealous. Hart, like every writer, considered reading a zero-sum game, and any attention paid to another writer cut him to the quick. All the little twinges of jealousy that had taken root inside him since the appearance of Tab's column suddenly congealed into a spiky knot nestled right under his heart.

He and Tabitha never fought, which made it especially irritating when they did. Why couldn't they just have sex all the time, like they used to? Relationships *sucked*, Hart thought as he stalked over the graves.

The boy grabbed the wrought-iron fence and started to climb. Well, what if we broke up? I don't want to, but it might happen. Hart vaulted over, and landed on the sidewalk. If it does, I'd better be the breaker, not the breakee. Tabitha was sweet, sure, but under that she was tough as nails.

Abigail was right, Hart thought: I'm passive. I rely on Tab too much. She's always saving my ass one way or another. I'm not going to get rich and famous by being passive. Maybe Tabitha doesn't respect me. Even worse, maybe she had passed him—she had this great column everybody read, and he had nothing…or at least it felt that way.

Hart Fox, he said to himself, you have to grab your future by the balls. You have to do something, or else you'll fall farther and farther behind. If that happened, everything would crumble. Tabitha would probably leave him; she was dating a rising star, not Hart Nobody. Suddenly, everything he had—and everything he wanted—depended on making a move.

Five minutes later, he walked into his and Peter's suite. (The door was still kinda busted from the coffee mob.) Peter immediately pretended to be masturbating, as he did whenever he heard Hart's key in the lock. "Ooh! Aah! Ooh!"

"Throw some undies in a backpack, Onan," Hart said, brooking no disagreement. "We're spending the weekend with St. Caesar's."

28
Inside Elysium
Friday, April 1st, 8:07 pm

That Friday at noon, President Rivington set off the ceremonial cannon, inaugurating Stutts' week-long Spring Break. By then, Hart and Peter were already a long way from campus, in a chartered bus firing toward St. Caesar's secret mountain redoubt.

Hart cleared his throat, trying to remove the distinctive tang of chemical toilet from his mouth. He and Peter were sitting in the back of the touring coach with all the other newbies. The boys had originally staked out some choice spots near the driver, but were shooed to the rear by Fanton Mandrake, Hart's old boss from the University Museum.

"Members up front, guests in back, and everyone arranged by income," Mandrake said merrily, then repeated it less nicely when Peter protested.

"I'm handicapped," Peter said.

" St. Caesar's does not recognize the Americans with Disabilities Act," Mandrake said, his smile even chillier. "Roll to the rear."

"I hate these people already," Peter had growled, but his mood improved when the hautboy brought back some champagne.

"This is more like it," he said, sipping greedily. Hart agreed.

Mandrake then handed out pills. "Anybody here allergic to sedatives?"

Hart caught his attention. "Professor, why do we need a sedative?"

"For security reasons, Hart. The location of our camp must remain secret," he said, pressing a large, yellow-and-black capsule into Hart's not-exactly-willing hand. "Take it. Otherwise we'll have to put a bag over your head."

Feeling like a hostage, Hart took the pill. Soon, everything melted into a soporific mush.

After hours of troubled dreams, Hart bobbed unsteadily back to consciousness. He scanned the scene through slitted eyelids; they were skimming along a two-lane road somewhere out in the boonies. Even though Hart had to pee, he stayed in his seat, just in case awakeness was still verboten.

Peter saw him move. "Are you awake?" he whispered ventriloquist-style.

"Yes," Hart said.

"Any idea where we are?"

"No," Hart said. "You?"

The boys saw Mandrake get up and start back.

"Oh, shit," Hart hissed. Both boys pretended to be asleep.

Mandrake squatted down between them in the aisle. "It's all right, fellas. Just don't wake anybody else up." Then he continued on to the bathroom.[61]

Hart and Peter looked around quietly. Since the bus had been sorted by income, the rows closest to them were filled with St. Caesar's Stutts contingent: professors and administrators, even a union leader or two. Ahead of them were the leaders of Great Littleton, people who didn't have the cultural cache of an affiliation with Stutts, but scads of money. The front of the bus was occupied by a few really big fish, local superrich too miserly to pony up for a jet or helicopter. As if to compensate for a form of transport that touched the ground, the big fish got entire rows to themselves.

"That's Ham Barker," Peter said with a subtle gesture. "I just read about him in *Daily Money*. He runs a multinational that makes money off disasters."

"Are those the people who fly in with supplies, and charge fifty bucks for a drink of water?" Hart asked.

"Try $500. I should go talk to him," Peter said. "I've never met somebody who's definitely going to Hell."

"Peter, don't. We'll get kicked out." Hart looked out the window; where the heck were they? He tried to remember what the article had said. St. Caesar's secrecy meant that everyone who cared knew something about it, they just didn't know all the details. This sharpened the pleasure immeasurably for the people who did. "Do you have any idea where we are?"

"Maine? Vermont?" Peter looked at his watch. "We could be in Canada if they don't recognize speed-limits, either."

The bus slowed, then took a dog-leg. Trees brushed the top of the bus, and there was the sound of gravel under the wheels. After they'd jounced along for about a minute, Mandrake said, "Welcome back to Elysium, everybody." The rest of the newbies awoke to the sound of polite cheering.

The bus stopped at the front gate. The driver pressed ID against the side window, and the guard waved them through.

"Private property—no trespassing," Peter read aloud. "Armed response."

"Just in case you didn't see the Uzi," Hart added mordantly, but the thought of unauthorized heads being blown off didn't seem to dampen anyone else's spirits. The bus was thrumming with excitement. They pulled up to a large half-timbered building. As the people up front filed out, Man-

61 Mandrake had always been kind to Hart, out of gratitude. The Day of Stink really loused up the life of Mandrake's rival Mr. Charivari at Harriman Library, and while Hart wasn't responsible for that, Mandrake thought he had been. Hart didn't correct this impression; he needed all the friends he could get.

drake stood. "Newbies, follow me into the receiving center."

Three minutes later, the boys stood outside in the dust, clutching their backpacks. Hart looked up at the sky. It was dusk, and he felt somewhat helpless. "I really wish I knew where we were."

"Wherever it is, it just got a lot less cool," Peter said as Miles Monaghan stumbled out of the bus. Stutts most prominent Zombo-American was fresh from his anointing as the *Spec*'s new Editor-in-Chief; years of assiduous Talbott-nosing, as well as his new ability to work 24 hours a day, had made him the obvious choice. This didn't mean it had gone smoothly; every campus group writhed around like a snake shedding its skin when the time came to transfer power. At the *Spec*, elections were particularly brutal. Sporadic gunfire was common.

"Hi, Peter. Hi, Haaaart," Miles said in his now-familiar moany monotone.

Mandrake came up behind Miles and clapped him on the back, causing a moth to flutter upward. "Already friends? That's good. Let's get you processed, so we can all sit down to dinner. We're having panda," Mandrake said, rubbing his hands together gleefully. "They're endangered!"

Hart and Peter were still investigating their bags of swag (an iPod, a bottle of Dom '52, a box of pre-embargo Cubans, some limited edition caviar-flavored Jelly Bellies) when the man with the folder spoke.

"St. Caesar's retreats are attended by some of the most important people in the world," he said. "Though we are all equal in the eyes of the club, it is important to respect those members who must bear the burden of power, wealth, and celebrity. Discretion is essential. Is that understood?"

"Yes," everyone said in the tone of voice peculiar to browbeaten crowds.

"Good." The man began handing out sheets of paper from the folder, which was marked SECRET. "This is a confidentiality agreement. It's necessary that you agree not to reveal *any* details of this weekend's activities."

An older person spoke up. "My wife thinks this is just an excuse for an orgy." The rest of the crowd gave a mumble of hope. "Can I tell her it isn't?"

"You can tell anyone anything," the man continued, "as long as it isn't the truth."

"We find that lurid rumors tend to increase the glamour of the group," Mandrake chimed in from the back.

The man continued. "Signing this document will give St. Caesar's the right to take certain punitive measures if you reveal any factual information."

This worked on Peter like a red cape on a bull. "It says 'this agreement is governed under the laws of the Duchy of Providencia,'" he said in a not-very-nice tone of voice. "Where the hell is Providencia? It sounds fake."

"It's a small island in the Caribbean, ruled by a member," the man said. "He's structured it so the penalties for any St. Caesar's-related crime are rather…excessive."

"Somebody got their tongue pulled out," a tweedy guy in the crowd said. "It was on pay-per-view."

"One of our few above-ground ventures," the man said. "So please: for your own sakes, think wisely before you sign."

Most people didn't think at all, judging by the amount of scribble-sounds that shot around the room. This convinced Hart, who signed. Would Peter?

The intake specialist with the folder noticed a few people hesitating. "Those who choose not to sign will be escorted back to the bus, given another pill, and driven home. They will get to keep the swag."

Peter hesitated. "C'mon," Hart whispered to him. "Don't make me spend the weekend with Miles."

Just when Hart was sure Peter would tear up the document, throw the pieces into Mandrake's face, and roll out, Peter brought pen to paper. It was a great, John Hancock-style scrawl.

After the sheets were collected, cabin keys were handed out. Hart and Peter were, unfortunately, rooming with Miles. As they walked to their cabin, Hart spoke. "I never thought you'd sign."

"I almost didn't," Peter said, smiling. "Then I remembered how my dad has always wanted to go on one of these. St. Caesar's has never invited him. If I said I'd gone, he'd never believe me unless I spilled all the gory details."

"So you agreed not to reveal the group's secrets, just so you could reveal the group's secrets?"

"Yeah," Peter said. "Plus, I knew you'd never tell me."

"You're right," Hart said, "I wouldn't've."

"So Midwestern," Peter said. "Anyway, I'm not worried. I signed your name."

Hart lunged, but Peter's chair had surprising pickup.

° ° °

That first night—the portion Hart could remember at least—was very strange. It started with a "down-home, old-fashioned cowboy cookout" with wine, and waiters, continued with Henry Kissinger making s'mores, and ended with a boozy canoe excursion across the pond.

"Say what you want about Hank Kissinger," Hart said the next morning, stumbling back to bed post-pee, "but he makes a goddamn good s'more."

"The secret ingredient is honey," Peter said. "I saw him add it." He and Miles were playing a video game. They'd been at it for hours; Peter slept less than anybody Hart knew, and Miles no longer slept at all.

Hart turned over, then discovered something. "Why do I have a pair of tighty-whities in my bed?"

"The Vice-President led a midnight raid on Camp Opportunity across the lake."

"Oh, that's not right," Hart said, flopping back on to the bed. "Those kids are poor. We shouldn't've stolen their underwear."

"That's what I said. But you insisted on 'having the St. Caesar's experience,'" Peter said, shooting a zombie. Miles was playing that side. "Miles, your reflexes are for shit."

"I wish I had your braaaaain..." Miles moaned softly.

Hart was wracked with guilt. "Did we plan to give the underwear back?"

"Unclear," Peter said. "I wasn't part of the flotilla. Wheelchairs and deep water don't mix."

Hart got up and took a shower, determined to put things right. After an absurdly bountiful breakfast, Hart walked to the main gate and left the underwear with the guard. On his way back, he passed Bill Clinton. "Good morning, Mr. President."

"Well if it isn't Mr. Underpants Pirate."

Embarrassed by what he had apparently done last night, Hart spent the morning with Peter, walking around the camp as inconspicuously as possible. It was a beautiful place; they took a fantastic amount of care with the grounds, painstakingly weeding out any vegetation not approved by the Executive Committee. And while accommodations for newbies were perfectly nice, the "cottages" for members were nothing short of mind-blowing.

Loitering outside of a particularly nice one, the boys noticed a man idly bouncing a badminton shuttlecock on a racquet. The man wasn't much older than they were, so Hart introduced himself.

"Hi! I'm Hart, and this is Peter. We're newbies."

"You don't look it," he lied, instantly winning Hart over. "Aristotle. You can call me 'Ari.'"[62]

They started peppering Ari with questions: he was from New York; he'd been a St. Caesar's member for three years; he hadn't gone to college, instead becoming a blogger right out of high school.

"You're not the guy who does 'Starfarker,' are you?" Peter asked. "I read

62 Last names were not used at St. Caesar's out of respect for the members that were too famous to use them (Sting, Bono, *etc*).

that every day, and Hart here makes fun of me for it."

Ari laughed. "I just fell into it. A lot of people I went to high school with got famous." Ari named an actress, two stand-ups, and a sleazy heiress. "Some Hollywood guy wants to pay me a buttload for the movie rights, but it's just something to pay the bills while I write my novel."

"I'd buy it," Peter said. "What's it about?"

"A guy who writes a blog about all his famous friends from high school."

Hart saw the possibility of a connection. "Pete and I do the humor magazine at Stutts."

"Must be pretty damn funny to get you invited here..." Bounce, bounce went the shuttlecock.

"Same goes for your blog," Hart said, spreading the love.

"Nah," Ari said. "Dad's been in St. Caesar's forever. He always wanted me to join. I finally gave in, but I told him: 'I won't be in your Coterie.'"

"What's a Coterie?" Hart asked.

Ari explained that St. Caesar's was actually broken up into many smaller groups of members, each of which competed with all the others. "People of the same temperament and worldview are in the same Coterie. Membership is done that way, too." He grabbed the shuttlecock out of the air and stuffed it into his pocket. "You guys know who invited you?"

Hart shrugged. "No idea," he said.

"The only Stutts Coterie I know is pretty straight-laced. Government types, spooks. Everybody's on the golf team...It's kinda creepy, actually. No offense."

"None taken," Hart said. He was getting better about that.

"There must be others, though," Ari said. "Most of the people in my boarding school ended up in Great Littleton."

"Where's you go to school?" Hart asked.

"Switzerland," Ari said.

A group of even more handsome, even more immaculately turned-out young men trooped out of the door behind Ari. They didn't acknowledge Hart or Peter in any way.

"Gotta run," Ari said. "I'll look for you guys at dinner."

As Peter and Hart watched Ari and his pals walk away, both boys felt a tiny flicker of envy. For Peter it was for the carefree life he might've had, if he'd been born without a soul. For Hart, it was seeing what he aspired to, the immaculate ease-of-being that people of wealth and glamour seemed to exude.

Peter was the first to shake loose. "I hereby challenge you to a game of 'horse,'" he said.

"You're on," Hart said. "I bet they have a solid gold backboard." They strolled over to the courts, where Peter beat Hart soundly three times.

"Too much arm, not enough wrist," Peter said.

Freshly beaten, Hart was in no mood for tips. "My right wrist isn't as strong as yours." He stripped off his t-shirt, knowing that Peter had a bit of a belly and wouldn't do the same. "Feel that sun," he said.

"Bet they paid a bundle for it," Peter joked. A game was starting up on the court next door, a ferocious contest between club Democrats and Republicans. It was hard to keep the teams straight, so they went to lunch.

Lunch was a feast, overseen by a member who was a famous chef/entrepreneur. The afternoon that followed, however, was more like summer camp. Some people played touch football; others made little clay pots; there was a nature walk; the more dissolute indulged in soft drugs.

Hart's drug of choice was a nap, but Miles made that impossible. Just as he'd decided to give up, Peter came in, holding a Gods-eye he'd made out of yarn and popsicle sticks.

"Let's take a walk," Hart said, springing out of bed.

"But I just drove the entire length of the camp. I wanna—"

"Then show me what you discovered," Hart said, spinning Peter's chair around on its large back wheels. "Observant guy like you must've seen lots of neat stuff. Tell me, are the Jimmy Carter nude-sunbathing rumors true?"

When they got outside, Peter asked, "Why the hell did you do that? I wanted to take a nap."

"Impossible. I tried," Hart said. Then he lowered his voice. "Somebody is r-o-t-t-i-n-g..."

"Oh, *man*," Peter said.

"Drink heavily tonight—it's the only way we'll get any sleep." They stopped at a magnetic board showing the day's events. "Wanna go hear a talk?" Hart asked. "We just missed 'Ten Things to Fear in the Coming Year,' but then your pal from the bus is doing 'How to Make Money From Earthquakes.'"

"It's like PBS for the superrich," Peter said. On the way, they passed the main meeting hall and heard crying. Camp Opportunity had sent over some of the older kids to try to win the release of its underpants, and several diplomat-heavy Coteries were taking it out on them.

The boys could only watch for about fifteen seconds. "That's kinda assholish," Hart said.

Peter shrugged. "As Guy says, 'If you squeeze oranges, don't be surprised if you end up with orange juice.'"

"What the hell is that supposed to mean?"

"Nice guys finish last, and losers don't get into St. Caesar's."

◦ ◦ ◦

Their friend Ari seemed like an exception. At dinner, Hart and Peter sat with his Coterie. "We're throwing a private party tonight, you guys should come." Ari glanced around, then whispered, "We're gonna smuggle in girls!"

"Great!" Hart said, flattered by Ari's offer.

Are these dopes eleven? Peter wondered, but held his tongue. He picked up the evening's menu and began to browse. It took both hands to lift it.

"They can make any of 2,500 dishes, your choice," Ari said, then asked thc waiter for a martini. "You guys ought to have one. They're legendary."

Hart followed his advice, but Peter said, "I'm a scotch man." Peter named the oldest, rarest scotch he knew—then tried to conceal his delight when the waiter brought a decanter full of it.

Ari noticed the boys gulping their drinks. "Take it slow—I think you'll want to remember this evening."

"Our tolerances are ten times those of normal men, we're college students," Hart quipped. The fumes off his martini made his eyes water.

Peter went to the men's room. When he was out of earshot, Ari leaned over and said, "Hart, I want to tell you something."

"Okay," Hart said, chalking up the suddenly funny vibe to the powerful gin now attacking his nervous system.

"I think you could be a member of this group. In fact, I'm sure of it."

"Wow," Hart said, amazed to hear somebody else answer the question he'd been pondering since the moment he'd been invited. "Really?"

"You'd need to be sponsored, but I'd be happy to do that for you. I've got a lot of pull in my Coterie at the moment. I just paid to have our cottage feng shui'd."

Hart didn't know what to say. "Ari, that's really nice of you. I think Pete and I—"

"Whoa, whoa, whoa—who said anything about Peter?"

"What? Sorry, I just assumed..."

Ari gave a small sigh. "Hart, Peter seems like a nice guy and everything, but he doesn't seem like St. Caesar's material."

"Excuse me?" Hart said, flabbergasted. To his middle-class Midwestern eyes, one rich boy from Connecticut was as good as any other. "Why? I mean, if you're allowed to tell me."

"I don't know," Ari said, tossing back the last of his drink, "he just seems like a bad fit. I don't think he'd respect our traditions.

"St. Caesar's isn't about being rich or well-connected, Hart. St. Caesar's is about high-quality individuals—the very best our culture has to offer—forming a bond with like-minded people. This bond lasts a lifetime. It's a very special, almost sacred thing, and I'm not sure Peter would treat it that way."

Peter emerged from the men's room. He stopped a waiter and snagged a canapé from a tray, eating it on the way back to their table. Did Peter always chew with his mouth open? Hart wondered.

"I'd appreciate if you didn't mention any of this to him," Ari said.

"Of course not," Hart said.

"Here's my email address," Ari said, writing it down on a napkin. "Think about it."

"You shits!" Peter said in mock-outrage. "I leave for a pee and you guys start passing notes?"

Hart was a bad liar, but Ari had more practice. "I was just giving Hart the number of my editor at the *Times*," he said.

There was a stirring at the far end of the room. The men at the table closest to the ornately carved double doors stood up, opened the doors, and trooped outside. They were followed by the next closest table, then the next.

"What's happening?" Peter asked. "Aren't we going to eat?

Ari didn't answer. "Leave your drink, you'll need your hands free," he said as they joined the line.

Outside it was clear, but slightly chilly. Hart shivered as he and Peter followed Ari along a winding, wooded path to a large clearing ringed with propane torches. The clearing wasn't flat ground, but a U-shaped hollow that surrounded an immense statue of a duck.

"AFLAC!" Peter whispered. Hart gave him a non-committal smile.

The group was clumping around the skinny kerosene heaters that stood every fifteen feet. "Spread out, please, spread out," people temporarily in charge commanded, and the membres shuffled into a more-or-less even ring. Hart heard them complain about the cold and express gratitude for the stiff drinks they'd just consumed.

Hart looked around; for the first time since they arrived, he got a good look at the entire group. Every third face or so he recognized from somewhere. The group was mostly white, but not totally, which made him feel better about being there. Of course, it was still all male...But the martini in his bloodstream bludgeoned his conscience nicely.

When everybody was in position, people temporarily in charge hauled out boxes from the forest's edge. They began handing something small Hart couldn't identify. "Pass it down, pass it down..."

When it got to him, Hart saw that the item was a small wad of dollar bills, folded then pierced through by a sharpened stick. The money had been doused with something strong-smelling and slightly oily.

After everyone had gotten their own wad of bills, someone took out a lighter and lit one. (When Hart saw the currency's fate, he peeled off the top few bills and stuck them into his pocket; he was, after all, a college kid.) The flame was passed wad-to-wad until all the wads were lit.

The entire clearing flickered with several hundred hand-held fires. Ari turned to Hart and Peter. "This burning money symbolizes our group's disdain for the things of this world."

"Then why are they small bills?" Peter joked.

Ari put a finger to his lips. As if following Ari's instructions, the crowd went quiet in anticipation. The heaters were turned down, so that the only light came from the wads of currency, which had been coated in something to make them burn longer. A high, thin creaking sound, and the regular snapping of underbrush could be heard. At regular intervals, this was punctuated by loud cracks.

A man in a loose yellow tunic walked out of the darkness. He was pulling a wooden cart, the type used in movies to transport witches and doomed royals. Sure enough, a large woman—the only one on the premises—stood inside a cage on the cart. She wore rags, and had a wild, feral look.

"The man in the tunic represents 'Talent,'" Ari whispered. "Every year, one man in our group is given the role of 'Talent.' It's like 'Man of the Year.'" Ari wanted it, Hart could see that. "The yellow color represents the gold which he is due."

The cart was followed by a figure in a toga. This much older man cracked the whip every ten seconds or so, in the general direction of the caged woman. "Why's that one in black?" Hart asked.

"Not black, purple," Ari said. "That's 'the Ruler.' He and Talent have conquered the woman, who is 'Fortuna.' Subduing Fortuna requires the strength and courage of Talent, plus the vigilance and ruthlessness of the Ruler."

"This is *so* hokey," Peter mumbled.

Ari didn't hear him, or chose not to. "This ritual has been enacted for over a thousand years," Ari said. "We believe that if it is not performed every Spring, the group will disband."

To cover Peter's snicker, Hart asked, "Who's 'Fortuna'?"

"Just some actress," Ari said. "Nobody important—she's probably not even getting paid. The Ruler is played by whoever has given the most money to the club over the last year. This year it's my Uncle Ham."

"Must've been a good year for disasters," Peter said.

"Is that a—" Hart thought he saw a wolf at the edge of the forest, but convinced himself that it was just his bad eyesight, and the guttering of the money.

Talent put down the harness and bowed to the crowd. The Ruler followed suit, and the crowd broke its silence with a great cheer. The cheering echoed around the hollow. Emboldened by their praise, Ari's Uncle Ham reared back and gave Fortuna a mighty crack. He did it again, and again, with each stroke coming closer to flinching Fortuna.

Just as everyone's money began to go out, the caged female could take no more; With one mighty blow, Fortuna broke the slats of the cart. Ignoring the shouts of Talent and the Ruler's cruel whip, she leaped to the ground.

"Is this supposed to happen?" Hart asked. Ari didn't respond.

The crowd closest to Fortuna shrank back as she raged and lashed out like a wild animal. Talent ran up and tried to restrain her; she tossed him aside like a doll. She turned towards the Ruler and sprang. As the last bits of money went out, she clapped her hands around Breeding's throat. They could hear his gurgles as she strangled him.

"I love this part," Ari whispered. Suddenly floodlights hidden in the trees came on; the hollow was bright again. Fortuna was gone.

Tunic streaked with mud and blood, Talent helped the Ruler to his feet. The crowd was absolutely silent. "Fortuna has escaped," the Ruler said, his very white hair and very pink skin bright in the floodlamps. "The first member who locates her and brings her back as his prize will take my place as first among equals. Those of you with courage, grab your torches and go!"

The lamp-tenders handed out flashlights.

"What do you think?" Ari said. "Wanna go hunting?"

"Sure," Hart said, swept up in the strangeness of it all. What would Tabitha think of all this? Too bad he couldn't tell her.

"Okay. Stay here," Ari said, "I'll get us some lights."

"This is incredibly infantile," Peter murmured. "I can't believe my dad actually wanted to do this."

"I don't know," Hart said. "I think it's kinda cool."

"You *would*," Peter said.

Five minutes later, the two Cuckonians and Ari were dashing through the forest. It had been criss-crossed with paths—local laborers worked all year clearing away the underbrush, all for this endeavor, which was "sacred" to the group. "...that's why we can't have any women around," Art said. "We might mistake one for Fortuna."

The reasoning seemed pretty weak to Hart, but then again, the Supreme Court had just upheld it. "How old is the group, Ari?"

"Lemme put it to you this way," Ari said, "the original name was just 'Caesar's.' Julius was our first patron."

"Like a hardware store sponsoring a Little League team," Peter said.

Ari didn't answer. "When everything became Christian, Constantine added the 'St.'"

Peter blew a raspberry. "You actually believe that?" he said. "My guess is, a bunch of crypto-queer optometrists started getting together every Thursday night to play cards."

"Peter, I don't really care who founded it or how," Ari said. "I just know St. Caesar's was formed to recall an earlier, simpler time, before all the complications of modern life."

"Like unions, or feminism, or uppity wogs—"

The argument was cut short by shouts coming from their immediate left. "I've foooound her! I've fooooound her!"

"Is that *Miles?*" Imagining Miles sitting on the board of directors, Hart said, "Ari, your group is in trouble."

Miles, smeared with mud and smelling worse than ever, was standing over someone. He continued to shout, not knowing that Peter had enveloped them all in a cone of silence. (There was an anti-noise generator on his wheelchair.)[63]

Tabitha stood up, brushing the leaves off her pink hoodie. Miles grabbed at her.

"Hands off, dork," she said, slapping his hand away so hard Miles lost a finger. "Thanks for tripping me."

"This isn't the woman in the cage, you weed," Hart said angrily. "It's Tabitha Twombly! From school!"

"Er..." Miles had a Stutts student's innate horror of admitting a mistake. So he said, "Girls aren't allowed! Noooot allooowed!"

"Hey, Ari, what happens to women who—" Ari was gone.

"Uh-oh," Peter said.

Hart turned to Tabitha. "Tab, why the hell—"

"The column," she said. "Checking out the orgy rumors."

Hart rounded on Miles. "For *your* newspaper, Douche of the Dead!" Hart was about to take a swing, but Peter got between them.

"Hart! There's no time—people are coming!" All around them were the sounds of St. Caesar's men closing in, hoping that Fortuna had gotten away

63 This nifty little device cancelled out noise by analyzing its wave-pattern, then broadcasting the exact opposite wave. Peter used it to drown out people he found annoying.

from her original captor and would run into their arms. "You can settle this later. We gotta get Tab out of here." Peter noticed that Ari was gone. "Mr. Bloggeriffic is bringing his Uncle. We gotta leave!"

"You mean, before the weekend is over?" Hart asked.

Tabitha slugged him, half-hard.

"Ow! I was just kidding," Hart lied.

Peter was, as usual, the voice of reason. "Tab, you've got to hide."

"Why? Because you want to join?" Tabitha said. "Tell me why I shouldn't kick the ass of every male here? I'll *show* them not inviting girls…"

"They'll kick you out of school. You'll probably lose all your degrees. You might even go to vampire jail!"

A flashlight beam pierced the little clearing. "Tab, mistify!" Hart said. "Peter, take a deep breath!"

It was Donald Trump, accompanied by two flunkies. "Did you see a girl?"

Hart and Peter, lungs full of Tabitha, shook their heads.

"Well, if you do, dibs," Trump said, then stumbled off into the woods. "Since when are we admitting mutes…?" they heard him say.

Hart and Peter, still holding their breath, took off away from the voices. After about thirty seconds of hard running, they exhaled, and Tabitha stood beside them.

"Great," she said, sniffing. "Which of you ate onions?"

"Ready? One, two—" The boys inhaled the vampire again, and began to trot. Wherever they heard voices, they went in the opposite direction. After about a half-hour, there were no more voices, and they exhaled Tabitha for good.

"I'm just glad I don't smoke," Peter said.

"Me, too," Tabitha said.

Hart said, "We must be getting close to the road."

"Hold for a second," Tabitha said. She mistified, floating upwards until she got a bird's-eye view. Then she drifted back down. "Brrr," she said. "Cold up there. We're about a hundred feet away."

"Did you see the guard post?" Hart asked. "I don't wanna get shot."

"I wouldn't mind somebody trying," Tabitha said. "I feel like taking my evening out on someone."

Fifteen minutes later, they came crunching out of the underbrush. "I'll say it again: thank God for four-wheel drive," Peter said.

Tabitha assumed hitchhiking position; her good looks attracted a trucker in no time.

29
Free the Great Littleton Three!
Tuesday, April 12th, 10:21 AM

"You've been out here all morning?"

The petite junior brushed her bangs back and spoke forcefully into the microphone. "Yes, in support of our sister, Tabitha Twombly, who has been unfairly and…un-…unjustly accused of vandalism, which she probably didn't do, when the real issue, and everybody knows this, is that she, as a woman, went someplace she was not allowed!" The junior was an ex-spelling bee champ, and having a microphone in her face caused a reflex. "That's wrong, W-R-O-N-G!"

The crowd behind her, about twenty-five strong, shouted its raucous assent. Some wore Wymyn's Cyntyr t-shirts, others ones that said, "Free the Great Littleton Three."

"So you don't think Ms. Twombly should have to pay the $30 million in damages that St. Caesar's is demanding?" the newsman asked.

"No, we don't. We think it's highly unlikely that Tabitha had anything to do with the fire."

"How can you tell? Do you know Ms. Twombly?"

"No, but this isn't about her," the junior said. "This is about the oppression of *all* women."[64]

"But what about the pictures of the damage? What about the photo of Ms. Twombly topless, in the act of lighting the fire, while the other two hold up signs displaying their names and Social Security numbers?"

The tiny girl was unyielding. "Have you ever used a computer? Then you know how to fake a photograph," she said. "F-A-K-E, fake. Plain and simple. Her head is, like, way huge."

"Ah, a *conspiracy*," the newsman said with a knowing smile; he was desperately trying to keep the zany hijinx feeling alive, but it was difficult in the face of the student's Emma Goldman-like intensity. "How about the other members of the 'Great Littleton Three,' the boys? What should hap-

64 And, of course, the girl's parents. In its purest form, politics at Stutts was simply a continuation of the fights people had with their folks.

pen to them? Should they be expelled?"

"Oh, we don't care about them," the tiny student said, brushing back her bangs again. "They probably did it."

Before the newsman could ask another question, there was a great ragged cheer as the Great Littleton Three—better known as Hart, Peter, and Tabitha—emerged. It was a sunny Spring day, and Tabitha was wearing her burkah and sunglasses. She looked rather Garbo-like, glamorous, and some of the Wymyn's Cyntyr delegation screamed her name. "Tabitha!" "We love you, Tab!"

"Hey! What about us?" Hart yelled.

"Screw you!" the tiny girl yelled back.

Things didn't have time to get nasty. Reed was waiting in the Cuckoo-mobile; in thirty seconds, the Three were in the back seat and driving away.

"Why do you think Ms. Twombly was dressed like that?" the newsman asked. "Was it a political statement?"

"Tabitha obviously feels that her current position is just like that of the women of the Middle East," the tiny junior said, "victims of male domination in the service of an outmoded system." She pumped her fist. "Fight the power, sister!"

The newsman turned to face the camera. "So there you have it, Jim and Tracy. Stutts students at play."

"Thanks, Steve, " Jim said. "Thirty million, huh? I remember when a prank was putting plastic wrap over the toilet. Did you ever do that, Tracy?"

Tracy chuckled. "No, Jim. I couldn't afford it!" Ha-ha. Ha-ha-ha.

Nobody was chuckling on campus, least of all our heroes. Even though a trip to the St. Caesar's compound would've shown that the whole case was bogus—nothing had been burned, desecrated, or defaced by anyone[65]—that was exactly why St. Caesar's refused such an inspection.

"Privacy is one of the signal virtues of our group," they said through a spokesman. "This very incident shows what happens when strangers are allowed inside our compound." St. Caesar's hated Hart, Peter and especially Tabitha, because the Cuckonians had seen everything, and realized it wasn't all that. Without its mystique, St. Caesar's was nothing.

Glenbard North hated the three of them for a different reason. He had gone to a lot of trouble to buy Hart off, and the boy had refused it. He'd

65 Well, Hank Kissinger left the ping pong table out in the rain, and it got warped, but that was an accident.

turned it into another opportunity for campus turmoil. This Fox kid was arrogant, ungrateful, anarchic—a "taker," just like his file said. And "takers" didn't belong at Stutts.

As crafted by St. Caesar's (with pictures by Professor North), the story had everything: it was simple, famous people were involved, and there were pictures of a young girl's breasts. Who cared if it wasn't true?

Things looked very bad for Hart, Tabitha and Peter. Even before they had returned to Great Littleton, St. Caesar's spinmeisters (Professor North foremost among them) had distributed talking points to their friends in the media: two Stutts students with a history of antisocial behavior had forged invitations to the group's exclusive spring retreat. Once inside, they had disrupted the usual discussions of charity work and moral uplift, forced everyone to get drunk, then led a devastating raid on Camp Opportunity, a nearby camp serving underprivileged youth. Hopped up on methamphetamines (which they had made from stealing people's hayfever medication), these students had decided to sow yet more mischief by smuggling in a third student who was, horror of horrors, female. After everyone had gone to sleep at 9:30 Saturday night, the three kicks-crazed nihilists set the group's Heritage Room ablaze, destroying many heirlooms and irreplaceable artifacts, "including Sitting Bull's pancreas." The press release included photos supposedly taken by hidden security cameras; one showed Hart taking a squirty dump into a corner pocket of a pool table.

Simple, tawdry, and fact-free, the story naturally exploded. Everyone came back after break into a maelstrom of press interest not seen at Stutts since December, when a misguided high school senior had included a homemade "suitcase nuke" with his application. The student body immediately polarized into defenders (few) and detractors (many); Hart, Peter and Tabitha were not merely "those fuckers who switched the coffee," they were the "Great Littleton Three."

Guy counseled escape, which might've made sense except that he insisted they do it via blimp or hot-air balloon. "Lighter-than-air flight has a magic all its own," Guy said. "Your enemies will be incapacitated by wonderment." Once it was clear that the Three would stay and fight, Guy became their legal counsel, much to their chagrin. As usual, Peter took Guy's side: "We're screwed anyway. He's old, let him have this last fling."

Tabitha was immediately fired from the *Spec*; Miles, naturally, parroted the St. Caesar's line exactly, even adding distasteful details like overhearing Peter and Hart discussing what foods might make their diarrhea more explosive. "At the time I thought nothing of it, chalking it up to idle chatter of the most sophomoric sort. Little did I know these two intended to 'write' their names into the Book of Infamy." His series of editorials in the *Spec*—part breathless "I met the monsters" reportage and part thumbsucking "What's wrong with students today?"—were speedily optioned by a producer, who was talking TV movie.

Miles' masterstroke, however, was to turn it from a minor scandal into something that hit every Stuttsie where they lived. "These students haven't simply shamed themselves," Miles wrote, "but they've made it harder for future Stutts students to be invited to St. Caesar's. Sabotaging your own career is your choice," Miles fulminated. "Sabotaging everyone else's is unforgivable. And lest we forget, there's a pattern here: how many letter-grades were lost on that unforgettable morning without caffeine? Face it, my fellow students: *The Cuckoo* is bad for your career!"

You didn't get between a Stutts student and worldly success; effigies of Tabitha, Peter, and Hart appeared all over campus. Often, they were on fire.

"I think the crucifixion is a little over-the-top," Hart said to Reed as they walked through Old Quad to the library under a row of burning dummies. "And that one doesn't even look like me."

Given the ugly mood of the campus, the Great Littleton Three would've had to finish the semester under armed guard if President Rivington hadn't come out on their side. This surprised most, but in a certain way it made sense: you make more money if there are *two* sides to sell t-shirts to.

President Rivington fanned the controversy, all the while trying to nudge things closer to 50/50 on campus. "Let's wait until all the facts are in," he told the *Spec*. "We must support our students," he said to the Faculty Senate. "Give the system time to work," he said to the *USA Today*.

To eke the maximum amount of merchandise out of the imbroglio, Rivington turned their one day in court into two. The first session in the Chamber was designed to collect the facts. The second was to find them guilty, and confer upon them a sentence.

The first day had gone quickly, and completely according to plan. The proceedings devolved into Hart, Tabitha and Peter's protestations of innocence, versus gorgeous, sharp, full-color photos.

"My clients' heads are not that big!" Guy had said angrily.

North snorted. "Your honors, all Stutts' students are big-headed."

Guy had tried to introduce doubt by explaining how the Moon landings had been faked by NASA, but after the second hour of his slideshow, it was clear that this gambit hurt more than it helped. Also, Peter hadn't done very well under cross-examination.

"Mr. Armbruster," Professor North began, "do you realize that, by telling us what happened, you are breaking the oath you signed when you arrived at the property?"

"That's not actually true," Peter said. "I signed Hart's name."

"That doesn't sound like someone who wanted to join the group."

"I didn't. I thought it was gay."

"'Gay,' as in homosexual?" North asked.

"No," Peter said. "'Gay,' as in lame."

"'Lame,' as in crippled?

"No," Peter said, "'lame,' as in 'retarded.'"

"Retarded,' as in—"

"You know, tired. Busted."

North's eyes flashed as he said to Rivington, Chief Constable Renalli, and the Mayor of Great Littleton, "Let the record show that this student has shown his utter contempt first for homosexuals, then for the disabled, then for the developmentally disabled—and finally for the simply fatigued and/or cash-poor."

"This is absurd," Guy said. "Professor North's line of reasoning is completely asinine."

Renalli thought he'd heard a profanity. "Watch your mouth, chump."

They didn't have a chance.

° ° °

"I don't know about you all," Peter said, as they drove away from the Chamber that first morning, "but Keasbey, here I come."

"If they'll have us," Hart said. He glanced at Tabitha. She seemed to be taking it really hard. "You doing okay, Tab? How's your skin?"

"Fine," Tabitha said. "Just a little flash-burn." (Paparazzi were hard on vampires.)

"Too bad you won't show up," Hart said. (Vampires were also hard on paparazzi.)

Tabitha looked out the window at the drab and squalid town rolling past. They were heading for an off-campus parking lot that had an entrance to the Catacombs. "It didn't used to be like this," she said to no one in particular.

"What didn't used to be like what?" Hart asked.

"The town used to be nice." Tabitha's voice was slightly muffled by her burkah. "And the school used to treat you like a grown-up. You used to be able to give your word and have it mean something."

"More fool them," Peter said. "I'm a Ritalin-scorched, immature punk. And proud of it."

"Me, too," Beekman said from the front seat. They high-fived.

"Now that the trust-funders have been heard from..." Reed muttered from behind the wheel.

"I don't *want* to be treated like an adult," Hart admitted.

"So you want the University to assume you're lying when you're not?" Tabitha said. "They tell us we're the leaders of tomorrow, then they show us what they really think: that we're 'Girls Gone Wild' with wealthier parents. I'm sick of it." Tabitha blew her nose. Was Tab, the iron butterfly, crying?

Everybody was shocked. A prep to the bone, Tabitha never showed much emotion—happy to annoyed was her gamut—and certainly not in semi-public.

"Stutts used to be an island. It used to be better than the rest of the world," Tabitha said. "Now it's a more concentrated version of it." She adjusted her head scarf. "If I can't live in a cloister, I might as well leave. I'll go after money and power just like everyone else."

"I don't understand, Tab," Peter said. "What are you saying?"

"I'm saying this is it for me. I'm graduating with you and Hart."

Hart tried to console her. "Oh, Nipper," he said, using her secret nickname, "you always say that vampires aren't at their best in the early morning. I'm sure you'll feel better after you get some sleep."

"Don't patronize me," Tabitha snapped. "People like North and Rivington have let all the world's poisons in—and then call it 'progress'...Oh, how I'd *love* to break all their necks—and I could do it too, faster than you could sneeze! None of you have ever seen me riled up. You know that bad knee Renalli's always mentioning for sympathy? That creep tried to date-rape me back in '69, so I gave him a flick with my little finger!"

As all the humans in the car drew back a little, Tabitha gave a mirthless snort. "If I hadn't done that, maybe he would've gone pro, or gotten killed in Vietnam instead of hanging around campus making everyone's life hell. Anyway," she said, "I've made my decision, and now I've run out of tissue."

Nobody knew what to say next. Finally Peter asked Guy, "What can we do in the week before the sentencing?"

"Besides hire a hot-air balloon?"

"Forget the freakin' balloon!" Hart said. "We're stayin.'"

"Then we must get public opinion on our side," Guy said briskly. "Get those pro- shirts outselling the con- ones. Unveil our secret weapon. Reed, did I just hear the radio say it was going to be 82 degrees today?"

"Yep."

Guy smiled. "Then our counterattack has already begun."

30
Eagle's Flight
Tuesday, April 12th, 2:21 pm

Professor North was depressed. He had a problem, one so old, and so common, that people in his line of work called it "the Spy's Lament": his boss wasn't acting sensibly. Why wasn't Rivington running those students out of town on a rail? First, he asked North to get rid of *The Cuckoo*. Then he didn't seem to care. And now—now it was like Rivington was on *their* side! This is why so many spies drink, North thought. The old professor stewed all through lunch. Then, he tried to take a nap, but couldn't. Finally, he was so agitated he called a radio show for some advice.

For 23 hours out of the day, a shortwave radio station off the coast of Cuba broadcast groups of numbers—mysterious codes between spies. But from one to two in the afternoon, the station had a call-in show where espionage workers could unburden themselves. North was a regular listener, and had even given money during the pledge drive, but had never called before.

"We hear this problem all the time," said the host, a man known only as "Dr. X." "Wishy-washy politicians giving you an assignment, then doing a 180 when the situation changes. Or getting cold feet when things get messy. Has it gotten messy?"

"No," North said. "Some forgery. A little arson."

"But no wetwork. Good. Let me ask you, 'Eagle,'"—that was North's call-in name—"is there any chance of you getting stuck holding the bag?"

"I don't think so," North said. "I have files." Then he cried a little.

"That's all right," Dr. X said. "Let it out. You said you had some files? On your boss?"

There was a pause, then, "Yeah." North sniffed. Crying sounded weird through the scrambler.

"See, listeners? This is a smart man—it's like I'm always telling you, 'Get some dirt on your boss.' If things ever get sticky, you'll be glad you did," Dr. X said. "Eagle, don't worry about it. You're going to be just fine."

"Really?" North said.

"Really. You're in control of this situation, hear me?"

"Yes," North said quietly.

"As long as you have those files, you've got nothing to worry about. Okay?"

"Okay," North said.

"Thanks, Eagle. We've all been where you are. Call me back and let me know how things went," Dr. X said. "Next caller is Dimitri, and he wants to talk about selling an ex-Soviet nuke on eBay..."

Feeling better, North hung up. He had so much dirt on Rivington, he could get him ousted tomorrow if necessary. North looked at his beloved filing cabinets, and smiled. The old spy was actually comforted enough to take another run at that nap. It got so warm in here on Spring afternoons...

Seventeen minutes later, North awoke. He blinked; there was light pouring from the filing cabinet under the window. It was so bright that it hurt his eyes to look at it. Was he dreaming? Were his filing cabinet a portal to another dimension? He jumped up and dashed over to the lighted cabinet. Fumbling with the key around his neck, North put his hand on the metal top.

"Ow! Son of a—" The cabinet was extremely hot; the wire in-basket that sat on top of it was glowing, as red as a briquet on a grill. North ran to the door. "Help!" he cried. North stuck his head in Finks' office. "Finks! You gotta help me! My filing cabinet is a portal to another dimension!"

"Gee, that's too bad," Finks said, and went back to work, trying not to smile. Nobody did anything.

North rushed back in to see the next cabinet catch—then the next, and the next as the flash paper inside immolated. North watched, amazed, as the light spread from cabinet to cabinet. It reached the final one, and—North didn't know what happened after that.

"Sir," the paramedic said, "please do not throw crab apples at the injured man."

Chief Constable Renalli's first response when he saw the man in the tree was to make fun of him. Then, when the firemen in the cherry picker brought the body down and Renalli saw that it was Professor North, the impulse was impossible to resist.

"What happened to Spookybritches?" Renalli asked the Fire Chief, as North was loaded into an ambulance. The crowd of academics and support staff that had been evacuated from the building broke into applause as their nemesis went by.

"There was an explosion," the fireman said, and went back to directing his men.

Indeed there had been, and not just one, but several. North had absentmindedly rested his briefcase against one of the filing cabinets; when the flash-paper in that cabinet went up, it set off the briefcase, which concealed a small thermite bomb. The thermite, in turn, had detonated the fake explosive logs in North's ornamental fireplace. The force of the blast from the logs propelled him into the branches of the suffering oak outside his window.

Some students below began estimating his flight, like a home run. "Twenty feet." "You're high! Thirty-five at least!" Then, they ran for cover, as more of North's keepsakes and mementoes spontaneously detonated. People found debris on the Old Quad for days.[66]

The fire was quickly contained, but needless to say, Professor North's office was utterly destroyed. The files, so painstakingly copied onto flash paper by Beekman, burned so completely it was if they'd disappeared.

But they hadn't. The next day, there was a full-page ad in *The Daily Spectacle*.

PEOPLE OF STUTTS!

For decades, this campus has functioned under a shroud of fear. Fear that something personal and embarrassing might become public. Fear that any mistake—no matter how distant or regretted —might be brought to light. Fear of losing one's job, or spouse, or simply one's dignity.

This fear allowed a certain professor, Glenbard North, to rule this university.

Ever wonder why Stutts doesn't serve chocolate ice-cream? Professor North didn't like it. Or why Dacron was last on the list of Colleges to be renovated? Dacron's Master once called North 'fatty-fatty-two-by-four.' Or why the golf team has a luxurious training facility in Dubai, while lowly women's soccer has to share socks? Or why they don't offer the class 'Bard for 'tards' anymore? Or why the book you're looking for at the University Library is never in? Six billion volumes and they *never have your book!* Professor North was behind all of this, and more.

A place consecrated to free inquiry and freedom of thought cannot thrive under the threat of blackmail. Professor North's secret files were the source of his power, and we have destroyed those files. The university is now free.

We sincerely regret that Professor North was injured in yesterday's fire. And we will gladly pay for any damage suffered by adjacent facilities (we're talking to you, Profes-

66 Professor Lemonade found North's tiny Mauser rifle. Miraculously, it had come through all the fire and explosions unscathed, save for a small crack in the scope. It gave Lemonade an idea, so he picked it up.

sor Finks). Had there been any other way to remove, to cut this poisonous collection of information from the body of our fair school, we would've preferred it to the explosions that occurred yesterday afternoon. But those detonations were due to Professor North's extensive collection of lethal knickknacks, not any oversight on our part.

Ever since February's coffee prank, we have been widely disliked on campus. In fact, 'loathed' and 'despised' both spring to mind as accurate, if a mite overpositive, ways to describe people's feelings towards us. However, we assure you that our reasons for the coffee switcheroo—as with the immolation of Professor North's files—came out of a genuine desire to make this campus a better place. Now free from the possibility of blackmail, we hope that you will now call it even.—*The Cuckoo*

P.S. Free the Great Littleton Three already. *Sheesh.*"

Peter finished reading Hart's draft. "Perfect," he said, "except for one thing." Peter wrote a postscript below:

P.P.S—We saved one file from the flames; it was just too interesting to destroy. Wanna find out what's inside? Tune into Wise Guy's Radio Hour at 8 pm this evening. Spin the dial until you hear the sound of the theremin.

By 8:47 that night, when Guy's outro music was over, Glenbard North was finished at Stutts. Powerless against his compulsion, the old spook had even compiled a file full of damaging facts about *himself.*

31
Rivington's Decision
Tuesday, April 19th, 10:04 AM

The atmosphere that surrounded the Three's second day in the Chamber was vastly different than the one they'd endured a week before. The affair with North's files had kindled a tremendous affection for the magazine on behalf of most of the faculty and a great number of the alumni as well. And though President Rivington might not have approved of *The Cuckoo*'s methods, he certainly appreciated the defusing of that loose cannon, North.

Stable, but still gravely injured, Professor North had insisted on participating in the session via intercom. His doctors had advised against it, saying that any shock might have grave consequences, but North was adamant; his fight against *The Cuckoo* had turned personal a long time ago.

"President Rivington," North said weakly, "last week this body heard irrefutable testimony, and saw indisputable evidence, that these students not only acted contrary to the laws of our esteemed neighbor the United States,[67] but also endangered our relations with a group for which many in the Stutts community, myself included, have exceedingly warm feelings: The Society of St. Caesar's." The beeping of North's various life-support machines could be heard through the speaker, and added an eerie counterpoint to his statements.

"Therefore," the voluble North continued, "I recommend that these three students be expelled immediately, and by their expulsion be made subject to United States law, so that they may be then tried in a court of law for the damages which St. Caesar's is demanding—and our investigations last week show that they are clearly owed."

As North fell into a coughing jag, President Rivington was blasé.

"That's what I thought you were going to say." Rivington turned to Guy. "Do you have anything to say in your clients' defense?"

Guy stood up. "Just read the t-shirts." Ninety percent of the shirts in the room read "Free the Three." The only ones still wearing "Fry the Three" were Chief Constable Renalli, and a visiting professor who could not read

67 As mentioned earlier, Great Littleton was nominally part of the United Kingdom. However, still smarting from the lessons of 1776, that country refused to have anything to do with Great Littleton's affairs. So, for all intents and purposes, Stutts sat in the middle of a free city-state—quite appropriate for an institution as medieval as a university.

English. "The Stutts community—your constituency— do not want to see my clients expelled.

"Furthermore," Guy continued, "I submit that these students did not do the damage that they are accused of. While it is true that one of them entered the St. Caesar's compound without authorization, she did so as an investigative reporter for *The Daily Spectacle*, fulfilling the essential watchdog function of the Press..."

Miles, who was in the gallery covering the trial for the paper, moaned. "Oh no, don't blame us!" He turned to President Rivington. "Please don't punish us! We'll be good—we won't find anything out ever again, we promise!"

"Relax, Miles," President Rivington said. "Go home and take a shower, I can smell you from here." There was scattered clapping throughout the gallery from fellow sufferers. "Okay, Guy, I think we've—"

Guy barreled ahead. "Furthermore, by harmlessly subverting the activities of a powerful, undemocratic, needlessly secretive group, students Fox, Armbruster and Twombly were fulfilling the mandate of another Stutts institution, *The Cuckoo*..."

"Guy..."

"You may not think this is important, Mr. President. But it is. Humor can educate as well as enlighten. It can contain kernels of truth within the laughter. That is why for centuries, *The Cuckoo* has been protected, as an organ the press. And what is a university that does not protect freedom of the press?" Guy continued. "That freedom to investigate, to discover, to reveal things simply for the common good—"

"That's enough, Guy," President Rivington said.

Guy wasn't listening to anyone but himself. "The common good. I say it again: 'The. Common. Good." It may seem an old-fashioned phrase in this day and age, but I believe that there is a place for dissent, for the one honest man, for jesters to—"

Hart poured a glass of water, and threw it in Guy's face.

"Thanks," Guy said. "Sorry, your honor."

"Pretty words, but totally irrelevant," North grumbled. "These students are not Woodward and Bernstein. They're not even the Marx brothers. They are trespassers and vandals!" His words were bracketed by coughs, and the beeps from the speaker grew louder and more rapid. "Photos do not lie, gentlemen!"

"That's ridic," Peter said. "The heads are freakin' *huge*!"

Rivington banged his gavel.

Guy rebutted. "Not one reputable witness put any of these students at the scene of the crime, and that the two who did, had a material benefit for doing so: Miles Monaghan and Ari Barker."

"Are you saying that they are lying?" Professor North said.

"They are not on trial," Guy said, "these three students are. Given what's at stake, Barker and Monaghan's testimony alone is not enough."

"Sophistry," North sputtered. "I say again: the visual evidence!"

"As I said at our last session"—Guy pulled out a sheaf of photos from his valise.

"Please, Mr. Guillaume. No more photos from the moon landing."

"*Supposed* moon landing, Mr. President," Guy said. "Anyway, these are from my self-published book, *Hey! I've Figured Out The JFK Assassination*."

North shouted so loudly that his speaker began cutting out. "I was nowhere near Dallas—I was never charged—you have NO proof!"

President Rivington leapt in. "Professor North, we don't have time—"

"...As I told the Warren Commission, I was merely visiting a sick aunt," North said, the beeps still fast, "who I mistakenly believed was recuperating on the roof of the Dal-Tex building. I had purchased the half-sized Mauser rifle because my aunt, a gun enthusiast and recreational hunter—"

President Rivington opened and closed his right hand, giving the "blah-blah-blah" sign. He turned down North's speaker. "Okay, moving on. Hart Fox, do you have anything to say before I sentence you?"

"Yes, your honor," Hart said. "I'm sorry for this whole thing. The St. Caesar's people seemed really nice—well, some of them—well, one of them—and I really appreciated being invited to their secret camping trip. I hope it's okay, because a lot of people seem to like it."

"We will convey your apology—"

Guy corrected him, "Not apology, President R. That would imply my client did something wrong. It was merely a expression of existential regret."

"Okay," President Rivington said, wearily. North had talked himself out, so he turned the volume back up on the squawk-box. "Hart Fox, by the power vested in me by this court and the semi-autonomous state of Great Littleton, I sentence you to twenty-five sit ups."

There was a shriek from the intercom. "Pat, you can't be serious!" North said. "This kid is a *taker!* He's got to pay!"

"Okay, okay," President Rivington said. "And, you owe us five bucks. Down on the floor, young man. Give me those sit-ups." He turned to Tabitha. "It's jumping jacks for you, Ms. Twombly."

"But...!" The beeps grew faster.

"Peter, you can hold your breath for a minute," Rivington said. "If that's too long, just do it as long as you can."

The gallery was clapping and laughing; only Miles' moans of anger sounded a discordant note. By this time, North had foregone words for choking sounds; the beeping grew loud and faster and louder and faster, until it became a single continuous tone.

"Professor North has to go now," A pleasant voice said. Then, a different one barked, "Nurse, the paddles! Clear! Cle—"

"That's not good," Renalli said to Rivington.

"We'll send flowers." President Rivington switched the box off. "Case dismissed," he said, bringing down his gavel.

32

The Placebo Effect

Friday, May 13th, 10:04 AM

Graduation at Stutts was almost as complicated as D-Day, and—in the minds of the participants—*at least* as important. Grass was trimmed; trash was collected; bunting was hung. All the lampposts downtown had banners hung showing famous Stutts grads: Wilma Rudolph, Teddy Roosevelt, Vlad the Impaler. This was the signal for all of Great Littleton not affiliated with Stutts to withdraw, avert its eyes, and try not to get too nauseated.

The university spared no expense; where everyone else saw the culmination of four years of hard work, they saw something much more special: the transformation of a wriggling, beer-sodden mass of student caterpillars into beautiful, donating butterflies. And what better way to expunge all those memories of badly heated rooms, lousy food, and general chintziness than with a big blow-out designed to make the departing seniors feel special? As President Rivington always said, "Ritual is free."

First, all the seniors—and however many grad students had survived *that* hellish ordeal—gathered in the Great Littleton Common. In the distant past, this was an opportunity for the inhabitants of the town to get in a few final insults, if not a well-aimed kick or two. Nowdays, friends and relations lined the route too thickly for any unpleasantness to take place. That having been said, Chief Constable Renalli was not above letting a townie or two toss a battery or a bottle (for the right price, of course).

Assuming that things hadn't descended into melee, the cap-and-gowned students walked through their cordon across campus to the New Quad, where they were joined by the faculty. Seated, sweltering,[68] everyone listened to the senior speeches. These came in three flavors: boring, nervous, and pompous. After several of each type, and occasionally one that hit the trifecta, everyone got up and fairly ran to the bucolic, traditional, much cooler

68 Constructed in the Seventies, New Quad was designed solely for ease of cleaning in case of student uprising. The white concrete buildings were blinding, and the dark-green asphalt radiated heat. It was designed to be a central gathering place where no one would ever want to gather; Stutts remembered the student demonstrations of the Sixties, and wanted to make future ones uncomfortable. In the years since, many had proposed tearing it down, but the cost estimates grew with every year. Now, with Rivington in charge, it would *never* happen.

Old Quad. Here, surrounded by the Colleges in all their High Colonic serenity, they were joined by Rivington and the rest of the administration for the final ceremony.

"Ah, memories," Tabitha said. She and Hart were back in the cupola of Truax Assembly Hall.

"Like the corners of my mind…" Hart sang loudly. "Misty watercolored memories, of the way we were…" He was happy—he'd survived another year, almost.

"Here they come!" Tabitha said. After all these years, graduation was still exciting. "Can you see Reed and Ellen?"

"I can't see 'em." Peering through binoculars, Hart watched the mass in black tromp through Saints' Gate—the only time it was opened all year. "I'm glad she and Peter made up." (They'd done so as only two science geeks could've, by sneaking into Ernst Yttrium's lab and analyzing the chemical structure of Vonnegut.)

"Look near the back, near Rivington," Tabitha said. "With the honorands." Reed and Ellen were both receiving prizes—Ellen for most outstanding science student, and Reed for most improved. It was amazing how quickly your grades shot up, once you weren't putting out a magazine.

Hart scanned the back of the crowd, which was much more colorful than the seniors. The grad students, faculty and administrators wore bright satin sashes noting the school that had conferred their highest degree. "I never knew my Smells of History prof went to Keasbey," Hart said, noting her green sash. "Figures." (He'd gotten a B.)

"I see them! I see them!" Tabitha pointed. "There they are!"

Hart focused in with the binocs, then laughed. "Reed just scratched his ass." They were sitting on the stage. "Look, there's Quinn Bostwick."

"Lemme see," Tabitha said. "I can't wait until our lunch, can you?"

"Are you kidding?" Hart said. "I'm so nervous it's like *I'm* graduating."

This final ceremony was always somewhat entertaining, thanks to the honorary degrees. These, like the Class speeches, hewed to a definite pattern: one went to a big donor for excellence in making money; another went to the first woman to do something; another—the only one the students paid attention to—went to somebody really famous, in this case Quinn Bostwick; one went to an (thoroughly unthreatening) activist of some sort; and the final one went to a retiring member of the faculty (Glenbard North, who simply refused to die). This year, however, had extra oomph: an honorary J.D. was being given to President Sterling Strong.

This changed the tenor of the day from mellow/medieval to armed police state. The Secret Service was everywhere, glaring, refusing, ordering.

There were metal-detectors at every entrance to the Old Quad, and black-clad snipers peering over every roof.

Irritated at having *their* day hijacked by something as paltry as a visit from the President of the United States, many seniors protested. But they did so in a way that was pure Stutts: they went naked under their gowns. This made frisking a delicate proposition for the agents, who spent the entire afternoon getting yelled at by parents. "I don't care who you work for, nobody touches my daughter there before the third date! Right, honey?" More shy Stuttsies simply taped snide remarks to the tops of their mortar-boards, "I voted for the other guy" being the least profane.

Spec-fed rumors had been buzzing for days that President Strong was going to make a major policy announcement, something defining and epochal like Kennedy had at Georgetown, or Churchill at Fulton. It made perfect sense—what better place to bust out the grandeur than at one's alma mater?—except that Strong wasn't the kind of President to make important speeches about anything.

Nevertheless, as he stood at the podium, the Old Quad was so silent you could hear a pin drop—and the whop-whop-whop of several helicopter gunships circling overhead. Tilting his chiseled profile to emphasize his best side, President Strong began to speak:

"As I look out on this sea of faces, full of pride and eagerness to wade into the future, I have one thing to say: You spent *what?* Don't you realize you could make a fake diploma in about five minutes? What a bunch of idiots!"

Initial confusion solidified into disgust. The crowd began to boo, tentatively at first, but then quite strongly. President Strong cut through the tumult by braying into the microphone.

"Didn't expect to hear that, did you? Well, tough shit," Strong said. "I'm President. You know what you are? Next month's unemployment figures!"

Peter was standing in the back of the crowd, with Beekman. "Did the President just swear?" he asked.

"Sure as fuck seemed like it," Beekman said.

But Strong had more to say—a lot more. "I'm rich and famous, and get to bang a *ton* of chicks, and nobody cares where I went to school. Nobody cares where you went, either, starting right now! Sure, go ahead and boo! You're just jealous!" President Strong somehow managed to swagger without moving a muscle. "My Stutts education has never once helped me in my career, and that's a fact. Oh," Strong said, "I take that back. When I was young, I used to go to the Stutts Club and score free drinks off the rich broads."

This last word had a galvanizing effect on the tiny senior from the Wymyn's Center, who got so mad, she threw her glasses at President Strong. They hit Reed, who was sitting behind Strong, next to Ellen.

"You throw like a girl…Ahh, go ahead and boo, none of you voted for me anyway. You wanted somebody smart…" For thirty seconds, President Strong stood behind the podium with a big smile on his face, giving the "bring it on" gesture with both hands. "Come on…get it all out, you spoiled brats…When you give ten million bucks to my campaign, then I'll give a shit."

Two minutes later, after at least ten students had booed so hard they suffered small strokes, Strong continued, "Okay, that's enough. I don't want to spend any longer in this crappy town than I absolutely have to."

"Me either!" the Mayor of Great Littleton shouted from behind. "Take me with you!" He wanted to leave the town desperately, but everybody kept re-electing him out of spite.

President Strong gave a Secret Service agent a meaningful look, and within seconds the Mayor had been grabbed by the elbows and taken to an undisclosed location.

"Socrates," Strong continued, "another, less successful Stutts alum, famously said, "The unexamined life is not worth living."

"What a douche!" a graduating member of CCA yelled.

"Who do you mean, him or me?" President Strong said, with a smile. It was this kind of common touch—plus being a movie star, plus the backing of a collection of super-rich people who were convinced they could really call the shots while Strong caroused his way through the corridors of power—that had gotten Strong elected.

"Both of you!" the kid yelled, just before two more Secret Service agents whisked him away. The other students looked on in horror as their classmate was dragged off.

"Thanks, guys…Where was I? Oh, right, Socrates. That guy was right—no, keep taking him—Socrates was a douche. I hated jokers like Socrates when I was a student; people who went around thinking all the time, asking questions and ruining it for all the rest of us. Me and my buddies always used to put 'luudes in their beer, then write 'FAG!' on their foreheads when they were passed out."

Professor Strong now stretched his acting abilities to the limit, mimicking a nasal, wimpy voice. 'You guys are such dicks!' 'Why do you have to be such dicks?' 'Why don't you get a life?' Well, guess what Socrates? We've got a life—we're running the entire goddamn country! We win! You—all the nerds—you LOSE!"

The outraged students began a heartfelt chant. Quiet at first, it rolled across the crowd, building momentum. "Coup d'etat…Coup d'etat…Coup d'etat…"

Meanwhile, from a dorm room across the Old Quad, Professor Lemonade was about to oblige. He had North's half-sized Mauser with the broken sight, and was going to shoot President Rivington. That *had* to get him fired, right? Giddy, the cursed novelist squeezed the trigger.

Lemonade had never fired a gun before, so the recoil took him by surprise. The rifle bucked, knocking him off his feet, and the shot flew wide. It ricocheted off a statue and struck Miles Monaghan harmlessly in the chest.

"Ooow," Miles said, fingering the hole.

The Secret Service sprang into action, but with no idea where the shot came from, pounced on Miles, as if he'd been responsible.

"I guess that guy went off half-cocked," the President said in his Bond persona. This got a smattering of cheers.

"Jeez, graduation is great," Beekman said to Peter, who was programming his cell phone. "Nobody told me they did all this."

Lemonade leaned out of the window. "Did I get him?"

"What?" the crowd yelled.

"Did I shoot Rivington?"

"Noo-oo," the crowd yelled.

"DAMN IT!" Lemonade threw a tremendous tantrum. Then he saw the Secret Service agents streaming towards him. "Uh-oh!" he yelled, and disappeared from the window, the crowd laughing.

The Secret Service went into action, but President Strong called them off. "I know him—he's harmless." (They'd met at the St. Caesar's after-party at last year's MTV Music Awards.)

"But sir," the lead agent said, "nobody's allowed to fire guns around POTUS."

"Wrong, bucko! Go read a little thing I like to call 'the Second Amendment,'" Strong said. "'Course, if you're as lethal as I am, you don't need a gun." President Strong emerged from behind the podium to strike a few karate poses from his latest movie. "Take that, smart kids!" He slashed the air with his hands. "Think you're so special, but can you do…this?" he said, dropping to the stage, rolling a bit, then springing to his feet not-very-agilely. Clapping and whooing, he jabbed both index fingers in the air. "I'm number one! I'm number one! Wooooo!"

The students began throwing things at the stage. Being naked underneath their robes, all they had were their hats.

"Bring it on!" Strong bellowed.

After the first wave caused President Strong to duck, the Secret Service men made a show of reaching for their guns, and the hail of headgear ceased. But the flying mortarboards excited something deep in the feral President Whitbread, who had been hiding in an anti-imperialism shanty erected on the Old Quad. He dashed towards the stage, then after his path was blocked by Secret Service, began running madly through the crowd.

"Look, it's President Whitbread!" Reed said. "Go Preston! It's your birthday!"

His chant was picked up by the rest of the crowd, which enjoyed watching Renalli and the campus cops try to apprehend the elusive ex-Prexy.

After things had calmed down again, President Strong continued. "But I did not come here to gloat. Well, I did, but I would also like to make an announcement, something that will doubtless cement my place in history."

"Here it comes," Hart said from the cupola.

"You'll tell your grandkids you were here," Tabitha said.

"I, Sterling Strong, hereby declare my eligibility for the NBA draft." Booing and scattered calls of "You suck!" did not deter the most powerful man in the world. "Some people will ask me why? Are you good at basketball? No. Do you even like to play basketball? Again the answer is no. The reason I am doing this is, after all my movies, and now the Presidency, I am still not famous enough. So I have decided to become a professional athlete—and if the teams know what's good for them, they'd better draft me! Or else the IRS will be so far up their asses, they'll cough up calculators."

Some graduates decided that they'd heard enough, and started for the exits. They, and their parents, were blocked by burly Secret Service agents determined to keep the area secure. "Nobody leaves before POTUS does," they said.

Ellen saw the scuffles clearly from the stage. "Suddenly, I see the appeal of a state school."

Reed laughed, then something caught his eye. A bright yellow, oddly shaped object was in the sky directly above them. First it was dime-sized, then quarter-sized, then lunchbox-sized. "It's the guys," Reed said. "It's the It's gotta be!"

"Our big send-off," Ellen said proudly.

Indeed, send-offs didn't get much better than this: a hot air balloon shaped like an enormous cuckoobird was descending from the heavens. Written across the bird's breast was "Congratulations Reed and Ellen!"

Students and parents were starting to notice, pointing and laughing. The Secret Service was not so jolly. One snatched a bullhorn from Chief

Constable Renalli.

"You better not get your spit in that," Renalli warned.

The Secret Service man paid no attention. "Balloon pilot!" he yelled. "This is a restricted area. Please leave immediately!"

The balloon continued to descend, ever so slowly, like a twirling leaf—or an approaching doom. Soon, they could make out a figure standing in the gondola.

"It's…Santa Claus," Rivington said to President Strong.

"Balloon pilot!" the agent said again. "Helicopters are in position. If you approach any closer we will be forced to open fire."

Santa had been Hart's touch—he had been a full partner in this prank. Though he still preferred doing issues, and worried about unintended consequences, he agreed that *The Cuckoo* needed to do something special for Reed and Ellen—and Quinn Bostwick. Anyway, what was the worst that could happen? Everybody was leaving campus in an hour anyway.

Hart sat in the window of the cupola, piloting the balloon via remote control. He pulled a toggle back and forth, making the Santa Claus wave. Tabitha, giggling, crouched next to him in the shade of the room.

"They couldn't shoot Santa, could they?" Tabitha said.

On the stage, an agent asked Strong for permission to do that very thing. "What the hell, he's not an American citizen, " Strong said. "Take 'im down."

Several helicopters opened fire; the sound of their nose-mounted gatling guns—or perhaps the sight of Santa vanishing in an explosion of plaster dust—turned the whole affair from puzzling-yet-festive to genuinely alarming. As students and their parents hit the dirt, the balloon continued to descend; by shooting it, the Secret Service had ensured that it would land directly atop the crowd.

Up in the cupola, Hart took out his cell phone. "I hope I can remember the code Peter told me," he said nervously, punching in a series of numbers. He held it to his ear. Nothing happened. "Oh, shit," he said, "I knew I should've written it down."

"Gimme," Tabitha said. "I think I remember." She dialed some numbers. Simultaneously, every other cell phone in the Old Quad rang. Even phones that were off sprang to life.

She handed the phone back to Hart. "You do the honors."

"Uh…hi," Hart said. His voice, reproduced a thousand times, whispered around the Quad "I just wanted to let everybody know that the balloon these idiots have just shot wasn't filled with hot air. It's leaking the aerosol form of a drug called Vonnegut." There was a commotion in the crowd as everybody heard the word "drug." Some yelled "cool!"; others, mainly parents and high government officials, were less enthusiastic.

"Now, don't freak out," Hart said. "It's non-addictive, and completely harmless—in fact, it's better than harmless. Vonnegut is actually beneficial. Once it's in your system, you're powerless to prevent yourself from expressing your true self. Vonnegut dissolves all those stupid things that make us miserable and hold us all back, stuff like fears, or shyness, or worrying what other people think...Obviously, being your true self out here in public might be a little scary. But since you've already taken it, you might as well enjoy it."

Tabitha gestured for the phone, and Hart handed it over. "It's a gift from us at *The Cuckoo* to all of you," she said. "It's a perfect excuse to kiss your wife, or your co-worker, or that boy you've been lusting after since freshman year," she said. "Here's your chance to let your hair down and have a great time—you can always blame it on the drug afterwards. And if by chance you *don't* enjoy yourself, address your complaints to the people who made Vonnegut in the first place: the United States government. Bye!"

Hart grabbed the phone. "Bye!" He hung up.

Two seconds later, the crippled balloon slumped to the ground about ten feet away from the stage. For a moment, everybody stared at each other, wondering what was going to happen next. Then the first kiss happened. This was followed by another, and another. It was too surreal to take seriously—people began laughing and smiling; parents felt their worries wither and blow away; within the graduates, bitter rivals exchanged congratulations, and apologies. Others did not act so nicely, their true selves being less than pleasant. Rivington, for example, truly was a conniving buttkisser; he began fawning over President Strong so intensely that a Secret Service agent had to step in. North sat alone, despising the chaos that had erupted around him. Renalli took out the cash from a wallet someone had dropped.

Down below, Peter and Beekman picked their way through the kissing, cooing crowd. "It was just water, y'know," Peter admitted.

"You're kidding," Beekman said.

"Nope," Peter said. "Ellen and I analyzed it twice, just to be sure. That bottle of Vonnegut had lost all its potency years ago. What you're seeing is purely placebo effect."

A girl in a cap and gown stopped Beekman, then planted a big smooch on him. "I've always wanted to do that," she said, then pressed something into his hand. "I'll be in New York all summer. Call me." Then she left.

Beekman stood there, rubbing his cheek and looking at the phone number, the first one he'd ever received. "Wow," he said. "I *like* the placebo effect."

Peter and Beekman finally got to the stage. Quinn Bostwick sat there, by himself, picking microscopic lint from his suit. Beekman noticed he was just as handsome in person, all wavy hair and cleft chin.

"Hey, Mr. Bostwick!" Beekman said. "I love your show!"

Bostwick didn't say anything, appraising.

"We're from *The Cuckoo*," Peter said. "We reserved a room at Der Ratheskellar like you asked us to. Are you ready to go?"

"Go where?" Bostwick said.

"To lunch," Peter said.

"With *you?*"

"Not just me," Peter said. "With the staff of *The Cuckoo*."

"How do you like the prank?" Beekman said. "We did it in your honor—well, partially."

Bostwick seemed not to hear that. "Oh, I can't stay," he said. "I'm having lunch with President Rivington, then I have to go back to New York. Sorry." He got up and walked away.

Peter calmly picked up his phone, and dialed The Rat. "Hi, are room deposits refundable?...Not even in the case of a real asshole?...Sorry, sorry. I'm part of the Rivington party, and I have some food allergies. May I speak to the kitchen? Thanks...Hi, Jorge, this is Peter Armbruster. I'll give a thousand dollars to anybody who puts dishsoap in Quinn Bostwick's lunch."

The staff decided to go to Der Ratheskellar anyway, so that the deposit wasn't wasted. They invited Reed and Ellen's families, who were very appreciative, and excellent company. And when Hart and Peter went to take a pee, they heard the famous Mr. Bostwick in the end stall, groaning. "Don't mess with the bird," Peter said, banging on the stall as they walked out.

They toasted Reed and Ellen's making it through, and Peter's summer internship in France, and Beekman's being made a full editor, Hart's "future," whatever that turned out to be. Two hours later, well and truly buzzed, Hart and Tabitha left. As the glow of the prank and the nice lunch faded, Hart couldn't help thinking about the lunch that he'd thought would happen, and regretting that Quinn Bostwick, whoever he was, hadn't turned out to be the person Hart wanted him to be.

"What a jerk," Hart said. "I'm never working for that guy, not even if he called me up and offered me an internship right now."

"I don't believe that for a second," Tabitha said. "You? Mr. Ambitious?"

"No, no," Hart said, the sincerity of inebriation in his voice. "Wouldn't do it." Then his spirits fell. "I don't know...I expected him to be nice. On the show, he seems cool. And *he* was the one that suggested lunch."

"Being famous doesn't make you a decent human being," Tabitha said. "When I was younger, I used to look for famous boyfriends, but after the tenth creep, I decided I would switch to pre-famous people instead."

Tabitha wasn't acting very happy, Hart thought, then his emotions took control again. They were shifting unpredictably and strongly. "Those jerks!" he said. "I wish I knew you then, Tab. I would've told all of those famous guys exactly what I thought of them. Nobody should treat you like that!"

"Thanks, Hart," Tabitha said quietly.

Hart didn't notice. "Custer: a-hole! Picasso: a-hole! Bostwick: a-hole!" he said passionately. "So what if they're all talented! There are more important things in life than having everybody know your name. If being famous turns you into the type of guy Quinn Bostwick is, I don't want it."

"You're really drunk," Tabitha said.

"No! Well, maybe I am, but I'm serious, Tabitha!" Hart said. "And if I ever change my mind and get famous, and you see me being an asshole, you tell me. Why? Because I wanna be a good guy. I wanna do the right thing. My dad always said it's important to do the right thing, and that what I'm gonna do. That's the kind of person I'm—" Hart paused.

Tabitha had a look on her face that he'd never seen before.

"What's wrong?"

"Hart," she said, her voice soft and a little hoarse, "I'm pregnant."

Acknowledgments

I'd like to thank the braintrust—Kate, Jon and Edward—for helping me see this book through. "Yes, it's good, Mike. Yes, people will like it. Yes, you should publish it. *Now quit asking us!*"

I'd also like to apologize if the book has a lot of spelling mistakes and stuff. The St. Louis Cardinals won the World Series the night I finished copyediting it, and around page 225, we broke out the champagne.

Here's a tip for all you young copyeditors out there: never proofread durnk.

CPSIA information can be obtained at www.ICGtesting.com
Printed in the USA
LVOW090747111211

258833LV00002B/64/A

9 781890 470036